GREAT ACCLAIM
FOR MICHAEL CONNELLY'S
THE LINCOLN LAWYER

"The author's new tactics are what makes this book a success. Mr. Connelly hurtles into the realm of the legal thriller with excitingly renewed energy and a full bag of tricks. Entertaining as it is during the investigation phase, this book goes up a notch when the courtroom conniving takes over."
—*New York Times*

"Connelly has stepped up to the plate in the overflowing ballpark of legal thrillers and blasted a grand slam his first time at bat."
—*Chicago Tribune*

"Has it all — sharply drawn, engaging characters, snappy dialogue, and a plot that moves like a shot of Red Bull." —*San Francisco Chronicle*

"Brisk pacing, clever twists, artful writing, and an atmosphere of complete authority. Another terrific book from a terrific writer."
—Scott Turow

"[This] intricate, fast-moving tale barrels along . . . Beware of picking up THE LINCOLN LAWYER. You won't want to put it down until you've navigated its rapids to the end." —*Los Angeles Times*

"Fascinating . . . a compelling mystery that has more sudden turns than Mulholland Drive." —*Entertainment Weekly*

"Unexpected twists . . . fast-moving . . . all that Connelly readers have come to expect." —*Denver Post*

"Smokes with intrigue." —*New York Daily News*

"An intricately plotted courthouse thriller . . . The tricks of Haller's trade will fascinate readers new to the genre, and the sophisticated storytelling will dazzle even judicial-thriller junkies." —*People*

more...

"A steamroller plot . . . Mickey is a terrific character."
— *Seattle Times*

"A rollicking read . . . testament to Connelly's talent for story-telling . . . Connelly scores big in his first attempt at a legal thriller."
— *Montreal Gazette*

"A new ride for Connelly . . . His writing is superb, his dialogue vivid. His depictions of deceptions small and large, to oneself and others, are part of what makes this new work so compelling."
— *Pittsburgh Post-Gazette*

"Michael Connelly, who first captured legions of readers a decade ago when he launched the Harry Bosch series, has done the impossible — created a character who is just as flawed, tortured, and beguiling . . . THE LINCOLN LAWYER moves at a mesmerizing pace, culminating in a solution that would have made Machiavelli proud."
— *Orlando Sentinel*

"The same sort of authenticity that marks the Harry Bosch novels can be found in THE LINCOLN LAWYER . . . His narrative is crisp, with the types of details that outsiders wouldn't know and insiders will appreciate . . . Connelly is as good as it gets in the realm of crime stories."
— *Columbus Dispatch*

"Great entertainment from a true master."
— *Mirror* (UK)

"In THE LINCOLN LAWYER, Connelly has built a plot which ticks like a Swiss watch, written some of the best courtroom scenes in crime fiction, and created a cast of wholly believable characters."
— *Birmingham Post*

"Cunning . . . well thought-out . . . a must-read."
— *Chattanooga Times Free Press*

"Is Michael Connelly one of the best mystery writers around? This guy just produces winner after winner, and the latest, THE LINCOLN LAWYER, is no different."
— *Ottawa Sun*

THE
LINCOLN
LAWYER

MICHAEL
CONNELLY

GRAND CENTRAL
PUBLISHING

NEW YORK   BOSTON

Copyright © 2005 by Hieronymus, Inc.
Preview of *Wrong Side of Goodbye* copyright © 2016 by Hieronymus, Inc.

The author wishes to acknowledge the following, whose lyrics are quoted in this book: "To Live And Die In L.A." Words and music by Quincy Jones III, Val Young, and Tupac Shakur copyright © 1996 by Deep Technology Music, Music of Windswept and Songs of Universal, Inc., and Val Young Publishing. All rights for Deep Technology Music administered by Music of Windswept. All rights reserved. Used by permission; "To Live and Die in L.A." by Tupac Amaru Shakur, Quincy Delight Jones III, Val Young © 1996 by Music Corporation of America/Joshua's Dream Music. All rights administered by Songs of Universal, Inc./BMI. Used by permission. All rights reserved.

Grand Central Publishing
Hachette Book Group
1290 Avenue of the Americas
New York, NY 10104
grandcentralpublishing.com
twitter.com/grandcentralpub

Originally published in hardcover and ebook by Little, Brown and Company.
First trade paperback edition: September 2008
Trade paperback reissue edition: June 2016

Grand Central Publishing is a division of Hachette Book Group, Inc.
The Grand Central Publishing name and logo are trademarks of Hachette Book Group, Inc.

The publisher is not responsible for websites (or their content) that are not owned by the publisher.

The Hachette Speakers Bureau provides a wide range of authors for speaking events. To find out more, go to www.hachettespeakersbureau.com or call (866) 376-6591.

Library of Congress Cataloging-in-Publication Data
Connelly, Michael.
  The Lincoln lawyer : a novel / by Michael Connelly—1st ed.
    p. cm.
  ISBN 0-316-73493-4
  1. Attorney and client—Fiction. I. Title.
PS3553.O51165L56 2005
813'.54—dc22   2005012863

ISBN 978-1-4555-3648-1 (pbk.) / 978-0-7595-1471-3 (ebook)

Printed in the United States of America

RRD-C

10 9 8 7 6 5 4 3 2 1

THIS IS FOR DANIEL F. DALY
AND ROGER O. MILLS

There is no client as scary as an innocent man.

— J. MICHAEL HALLER, CRIMINAL DEFENSE ATTORNEY,
LOS ANGELES, 1962

PART ONE
— Pretrial Intervention

T he morning air off the Mojave in late winter is as clean and crisp as you'll ever breathe in Los Angeles County. It carries the taste of promise on it. When it starts blowing in like that I like to keep a window open in my office. There are a few people who know this routine of mine, people like Fernando Valenzuela. The bondsman, not the baseball pitcher. He called me as I was coming into Lancaster for a nine o'clock calendar call. He must have heard the wind whistling in my cell phone.

"Mick," he said, "you up north this morning?"

"At the moment," I said as I put the window up to hear him better. "You got something?"

"Yeah, I got something. I think I got a franchise player here. But his first appearance is at eleven. Can you make it back down in time?"

Valenzuela has a storefront office on Van Nuys Boulevard a block from the civic center, which includes two courthouses and the Van Nuys jail. He calls his business Liberty Bail Bonds. His phone number, in red neon on the roof of his establishment, can be seen from the high-power wing on the third floor of the jail. His number is scratched into the paint on the wall next to every pay phone on every other ward in the jail.

You could say his name is also permanently scratched onto my Christmas list. At the end of the year I give a can of salted nuts to everybody on it. Planters holiday mix. Each can has a ribbon and bow on it. But no nuts inside. Just cash. I have a lot of bail bondsmen on my Christmas list. I eat holiday mix out of Tupperware well into spring. Since my last divorce, it is sometimes all I get for dinner.

Before answering Valenzuela's question I thought about the calendar call I was headed to. My client was named Harold Casey. If the docket was handled alphabetically I could make an eleven o'clock hearing down in Van Nuys, no problem. But Judge Orton Powell was in his last term on the bench. He was retiring. That meant he no longer faced reelection pressures, like those from the private bar. To demonstrate his freedom — and possibly as a form of payback to those he had been politically beholden to for twelve years — he liked to mix things up in his courtroom. Sometimes the calendar went alphabetical, sometimes reverse alphabetical, sometimes by filing date. You never knew how the call would go until you got there. Often lawyers cooled their heels for better than an hour in Powell's courtroom. The judge liked that.

"I think I can make eleven," I said, without knowing for sure. "What's the case?"

"Guy's gotta be big money. Beverly Hills address, family lawyer waltzing in here first thing. This is the real thing, Mick. They booked him on a half mil and his mother's lawyer came in here today ready to sign over property in Malibu to secure it. Didn't even ask about getting it lowered first. I guess they aren't too worried about him running."

"Booked for what?" I asked.

I kept my voice even. The scent of money in the water often leads to a feeding frenzy but I had taken care of Valenzuela on enough Christmases to know I had him on the hook exclusively. I could play it cool.

"The cops booked him for ag-assault, GBI and attempted rape for starters," the bondsman answered. "The DA hasn't filed yet as far as I know."

The police usually overbooked the charges. What mattered was what the prosecutors finally filed and took to court. I always say cases go in like a lion and come out like a lamb. A case going in as attempted rape and aggravated assault with great bodily injury could easily come out as simple battery. It wouldn't surprise me and it wouldn't make for much of a franchise case. Still, if I could get to the client and make a fee agreement based on the announced charges, I could look good when the DA later knocked them down.

"You got any of the details?" I asked.

"He was booked last night. It sounds like a bar pickup gone bad. The family lawyer said the woman's in it for the money. You know, the civil suit to follow the criminal case. But I'm not so sure. She got beat up pretty good from what I heard."

"What's the family lawyer's name?"

"Hold on a sec. I've got his card here somewhere."

I looked out the window while waiting for Valenzuela to find the business card. I was two minutes from the Lancaster courthouse and twelve minutes from calendar call. I needed at least three of those minutes in between to confer with my client and give him the bad news.

"Okay, here it is," Valenzuela said. "Guy's name is Cecil C. Dobbs, Esquire. Out of Century City. See, I told you. Money."

Valenzuela was right. But it wasn't the lawyer's Century City address that said money. It was the name. I knew of C. C. Dobbs by reputation and guessed that there wouldn't be more than one or two names on his entire client list that didn't have a Bel-Air or Holmby Hills address. His kind of client went home to the places where the stars seemed to reach down at night to touch the anointed.

"Give me the client's name," I said.

"That would be Louis Ross Roulet."

He spelled it and I wrote it down on a legal pad.

"Almost like the spinning wheel but you pronounce it Roo-*lay*," he said. "You going to be here, Mick?"

Before responding I wrote the name C. C. Dobbs on the pad. I then answered Valenzuela with a question.

"Why me?" I asked. "Was I asked for? Or did you suggest me?"

I had to be careful with this. I had to assume Dobbs was the kind of lawyer who would go to the California bar in a heartbeat if he came across a criminal defense attorney paying off bondsmen for client referrals. In fact, I started wondering if the whole thing might be a bar sting operation that Valenzuela hadn't picked up on. I wasn't one of the bar's favorite sons. They had come at me before. More than once.

"I asked Roulet if he had a lawyer, you know? A criminal defense lawyer, and he said no. I told him about you. I didn't push it. I just said you were good. Soft sell, you know?"

"Was this before or after Dobbs came into it?"

"No, before. Roulet called me this morning from the jail. They got him up on high power and he saw the sign, I guess. Dobbs showed up after that. I told him you were in, gave him your pedigree, and he was cool with it. He'll be there at eleven. You'll see how he is."

I didn't speak for a long moment. I wondered how truthful Valenzuela was being with me. A guy like Dobbs would have had his own man. If it wasn't his own forte, then he'd have had a criminal specialist in the firm or, at least, on standby. But Valenzuela's story seemed to contradict this. Roulet came to him empty-handed. It told me that there was more to this case I didn't know than what I did.

"Hey, Mick, you there?" Valenzuela prompted.

I made a decision. It was a decision that would eventually lead me back to Jesus Menendez and that I would in many ways come to regret. But at the moment it was made, it was just another choice made of necessity and routine.

"I'll be there," I said into the phone. "I'll see you at eleven."

I was about to close the phone when I heard Valenzuela's voice come back at me.

"And you'll take care of me for this, right, Mick? I mean, you know, if this is the franchise."

It was the first time Valenzuela had ever sought assurance of a payback from me. It played further into my paranoia and I carefully constructed an answer that would satisfy him and the bar — if it was listening.

"Don't worry, Val. You're on my Christmas list."

I closed the phone before he could say anything else and told my driver to drop me off at the employee entrance to the courthouse. The line at the metal detector would be shorter and quicker there and the security men usually didn't mind the lawyers — the regulars — sneaking through so they could make court on time.

As I thought about Louis Ross Roulet and the case and the possible riches and dangers that waited for me, I put the window back down so I could enjoy the morning's last minute of clean, fresh air. It still carried the taste of promise.

TWO

The courtroom in Department 2A was crowded with lawyers negotiating and socializing on both sides of the bar when I got there. I could tell the session was going to start on time because I saw the bailiff seated at his desk. This meant the judge was close to taking the bench.

In Los Angeles County the bailiffs are actually sworn deputy sheriffs who are assigned to the jail division. I approached the bailiff, whose desk was right next to the bar railing so citizens could come up to ask questions without having to violate the space assigned to the lawyers, defendants and courtroom personnel. I saw the calendar on the clipboard in front of him. I checked the nameplate on his uniform — R. Rodriguez — before speaking.

"Roberto, you got my guy on there? Harold Casey?"

The bailiff used his finger to start down the list on the call sheet but stopped quickly. This meant I was in luck.

"Yeah, Casey. He's second up."

"Alphabetical today, good. Do I have time to go back and see him?"

"No, they're bringing the first group in now. I just called. The judge is coming out. You'll probably have a couple minutes to see your guy in the pen."

"Thank you."

I started to walk toward the gate when he called after me.

"And it's Reynaldo, not Roberto."

"Right, right. I'm sorry about that, Reynaldo."

"Us bailiffs, we all look alike, right?"

I didn't know if that was an attempt at humor or just a dig at me. I didn't answer. I just smiled and went through the gate. I nodded at a couple lawyers I didn't know and a couple that I did. One stopped me to ask how long I was going to be up in front of the judge because he wanted to gauge when to come back for his own client's appearance. I told him I was going to be quick.

During a calendar call incarcerated defendants are brought to the courtroom in groups of four and held in a wood-and-glass enclosure known as the pen. This allows the defendants to confer with their attorneys in the moments before their case is called for whatever matter is before the court.

I got to the side of the pen just as the door from the interior holding cell was opened by a deputy, and the first four defendants on the docket were marched out. The last of the four to step into the pen was Harold Casey, my client. I took a position near the side wall so that we would have privacy on at least one side and signaled him over.

Casey was big and tall, as they tend to recruit them in the Road Saints motorcycle gang — or club, as the membership prefers to be known. While being held in the Lancaster jail he had cut his hair and shaved, as I had requested, and he looked reasonably presentable, except for the tattoos that wrapped both arms and poked up above his collar. But there is only so much you can do. I don't know much about the effect of tattoos on a jury but I suspect it's not overly positive, especially when grinning skulls are involved. I *do* know that jurors in general don't care for ponytails — on either the defendants or the lawyers who represent them.

Casey, or Hard Case, as he was known in the club, was charged with cultivation, possession and sale of marijuana as well as other drug and weapons charges. In a predawn raid on the ranch where he lived and worked, sheriff's deputies found a barn and Quonset hut complex that had been turned into an indoor growing facility. More than two thousand fully mature plants were seized along with sixty-three pounds of harvested marijuana packaged in various weights in plastic bags. Additionally, twelve ounces of crystal meth which the packagers sprinkled on the harvested crop to give it an extra kick were seized, along with a small arsenal of weapons, many of them later determined to be stolen.

It would appear that Hard Case was fucked. The state had him cold. He was actually found asleep on a couch in the barn, five feet from the packaging table. Added to this, he had twice previously been convicted of drug offenses and was currently still on parole for the most recent. In the state of California the third time is the charm. Realistically, Casey was facing at least a decade in prison, even with good time.

But what was unusual about Casey was that he was a defendant who was looking forward to trial and even to the likelihood of conviction. He had refused to waive his right to a speedy trial and now, less than three months after his arrest, eagerly wanted to bring it on. He was eager because it was likely that his only hope lay in an appeal of that likely conviction. Thanks to his attorney, Casey saw a glimmer of hope — that small, twinkling light that only a good attorney can bring to the darkness of a case like this. From this glimmer a case strategy was born that might ultimately work to free Casey. It was daring and would cost Casey time as he waited out the appeal, but he knew as well as I did that it was the only real shot he had.

The crack in the state's case was not in its assumption that Casey was a marijuana grower, packager and seller. The state was absolutely correct in these assumptions and the evidence more than proved it. It was in how the state came to that evidence that the case tottered on an unsteady foundation. It was my job to probe that crack in trial, exploit it, put it on record and then convince an appellate court of what I had not been able to convince Judge Orton Powell of during a pretrial motion to suppress the evidence in the case.

The seed of the prosecution of Harold Casey was planted on a

Tuesday in mid-December when Casey walked into a Home Depot in Lancaster and made a number of mundane purchases that included three lightbulbs of the variety used in hydroponic farming. The man behind him in the checkout line happened to be an off-duty sheriff's deputy about to purchase outdoor Christmas lights. The deputy recognized some of the artwork on Casey's arms — most notably the skull with halo tattoo that is the emblematic signature of the Road Saints — and put two and two together. The off-duty man then dutifully followed Casey's Harley as he rode to the ranch in nearby Pearblossom. This information was passed to the sheriff's drug squad, which arranged for an unmarked helicopter to fly over the ranch with a thermal imaging camera. The subsequent photographs, detailing rich red heat blooms from the barn and Quonset hut, along with the statement of the deputy who saw Casey purchase hydroponic lights, were submitted in an affidavit to a judge. The next morning Casey was rousted from sleep on the couch by deputies with a signed search warrant.

In an earlier hearing I argued that all evidence against Casey should be excluded because the probable cause for the search constituted an invasion of Casey's right to privacy. Using an individual's commonplace purchases at a hardware store as a springboard to conduct a further invasion of privacy through surveillance on the ground and in the air and by thermal imaging would surely be viewed as excessive by the framers of the Constitution.

Judge Powell rejected my argument and the case moved toward trial or disposition by plea agreement. In the meantime new information came to light that would bolster Casey's appeal of a conviction. Analysis of the photographs taken during the flyover of Casey's house and the focal specifications of the thermal camera used by the deputies indicated the helicopter was flying no more than two hundred feet off the ground when the photographs were taken. The U.S. Supreme Court has held that a law enforcement observation flight over a suspect's property does not violate an individual's right to privacy so long as the aircraft is in public airspace. I had Raul Levin, my investigator, check with the Federal Aviation Administration.

Casey's ranch was located beneath no airport flight pattern. The floor for public airspace above the ranch was a thousand feet. The deputies had clearly invaded Casey's privacy while gathering the probable cause to raid the ranch.

My job now was to take the case to trial and elicit testimony from the deputies and pilot as to the altitude they were flying when they went over the ranch. If they told the truth, I had them. If they lied, I had them. I don't relish the idea of embarrassing law enforcement officers in open court, but my hope was that they would lie. If a jury sees a cop lie on the witness stand, then the case might as well end right there. You don't have to appeal a not-guilty verdict. The state has no comebacks from a not-guilty verdict.

Either way, I was confident I had a winner. We just had to get to trial and there was only one thing holding us back. That was what I needed to talk to Casey about before the judge took the bench and called the case.

My client sauntered over to the corner of the pen and didn't offer a hello. I didn't, either. He knew what I wanted. We'd had this conversation before.

"Harold, this is calendar call," I said. "This is when I tell the judge if we're ready to go to trial. I already know the state's ready. So today's about us."

"So?"

"So, there's a problem. Last time we were here you told me I'd be getting some money. But here we are, Harold, and no money."

"Don't worry. I have your money."

"That's why I am worried. *You* have my money. I don't have my money."

"It's coming. I talked to my boys yesterday. It's coming."

"You said that last time, too. I don't work for free, Harold. The expert I had go over the photos doesn't work for free, either. Your retainer is long gone. I want some more money or you're going to have to get yourself a new lawyer. A public defender."

"No PD, man. I want you."

"Well, I got expenses and I gotta eat. You know what my nut is each week just to pay for the yellow pages? Take a guess."

Casey said nothing.

"A grand. Averages out a grand a week just to keep my ad in there and that's before I eat or pay the mortgage or the child support or put gas in the Lincoln. I'm not doing this on a promise, Harold. I work on green inspiration."

Casey seemed unimpressed.

"I checked around," he said. "You can't just quit on me. Not now. The judge won't let you."

A hush fell over the courtroom as the judge stepped out of the door to his chambers and took the two steps up to the bench. The bailiff called the courtroom to order. It was showtime. I just looked at Casey for a long moment and stepped away. He had an amateur, jailhouse knowledge of the law and how it worked. He knew more than most. But he was still in for a surprise.

I took a seat against the rail behind the defendant's table. The first case called was a bail reconsideration that was handled quickly. Then the clerk called the case of *California v. Casey* and I stepped up to the table.

"Michael Haller for the defense," I said.

The prosecutor announced his presence as well. He was a young guy named Victor DeVries. He had no idea what was going to hit him when we got to trial. Judge Orton Powell made the usual inquiries about whether a last-minute disposition in the case was possible. Every judge had an overflowing calendar and an overriding mandate to clear cases through disposition. The last thing any judge wanted to hear was that there was no hope of agreement and that a trial was inevitable.

But Powell took the bad news from DeVries and me in stride and asked if we were ready to schedule the trial for later in the week. DeVries said yes. I said no.

"Your Honor," I said, "I would like to carry this over until next week, if possible."

"What is the cause of your delay, Mr. Haller?" the judge asked impatiently. "The prosecution is ready and I want to dispose of this case."

"I want to dispose of it as well, Your Honor. But the defense is having trouble locating a witness who will be necessary to our case. An indispensable witness, Your Honor. I think a one-week carryover should be sufficient. By next week we should be ready to go forward."

As expected, DeVries objected to the delay.

"Your Honor, this is the first the state has heard about a missing witness. Mr. Haller has had almost three months to locate his witnesses. He's the one who wanted the speedy trial and now he wants to wait. I think this is just a delay tactic because he's facing a case that —"

"You can hold on to the rest of that for the jury, Mr. DeVries," the judge said. "Mr. Haller, you think one week will solve your problem?"

"Yes, Your Honor."

"Okay, we'll see you and Mr. Casey next Monday and you will be ready to go. Is that understood?"

"Yes, Your Honor. Thank you."

The clerk called the next case and I stepped away from the defense table. I watched a deputy lead my client out of the pen. Casey glanced back at me, a look on his face that seemed to be equal parts anger and confusion. I went over to Reynaldo Rodriguez and asked if I could be allowed back into the holding area to further confer with my client. It was a professional courtesy allowed to most of the regulars. Rodriguez got up, unlocked a door behind his desk and ushered me through. I made sure to thank him by his correct name.

Casey was in a holding cell with one other defendant, the man whose case had been called ahead of his in the courtroom. The cell was large and had benches running along three sides. The bad thing about getting your case called early in the courtroom is that after the hearing you have to sit in this cage until it fills with enough people to run a full bus back to the county jail. Casey came right up to the bars to speak to me.

"What witness were you talking about in there?" he demanded.

"Mr. Green," I said. "Mr. Green is all we need for this case to go forward."

Casey's face contorted in anger. I tried to cut him off at the pass.

"Look, Harold, I know you want to move this along and get to the trial and then the appeal. But you've got to pay the freight along the way. I know from long, hard experience that it does me no good to chase people for money after the horse is out of the barn. You want to play now, then you pay now."

I nodded and was about to turn back to the door that led to freedom. But then I spoke to him again.

"And don't think the judge in there didn't know what was going on," I said. "You got a young prosecutor who's wet behind the ears and doesn't have to worry about where his next paycheck's coming from. But Orton Powell spent a lot of years in the defense bar before he got to the bench. He knows about chasing indispensable witnesses like Mr. Green and he probably won't look too kindly upon a defendant who doesn't pay his lawyer. I gave him the wink, Harold. If I want off the case, I'll get off. But what I'd rather do is come in here next Monday and stand up out there and tell him we found our witness and we are ready to go. You understand?"

Casey didn't say anything at first. He walked to the far side of the cell and sat down on the bench. He didn't look at me when he finally spoke.

"As soon as I get to a phone," he said.

"Sounds good, Harold. I'll tell one of the deputies you have to make a call. Make the call, then sit tight and I'll see you next week. We'll get this thing going."

I headed back to the door, my steps quick. I hate being inside a jail. I'm not sure why. I guess it's because sometimes the line seems so thin. The line between being a criminal attorney and a *criminal* attorney. Sometimes I'm not sure which side of the bars I am on. To me it's always a dead-bang miracle that I get to walk out the way I walked in.

THREE

I n the hallway outside the courtroom I turned my cell phone back on and called my driver to tell him I was coming out. I then checked voicemail and found messages from Lorna Taylor and Fernando Valenzuela. I decided to wait until I was in the car to make the callbacks.

Earl Briggs, my driver, had the Lincoln right out front. Earl didn't get out and open the door or anything. His deal was just to drive me while he worked off the fee he owed me for getting him probation on a cocaine sales conviction. I paid him twenty bucks an hour to drive me but then held half of it back to go against the fee. It wasn't quite what he was making dealing crack in the projects but it was safer, legal and something that could go on a résumé. Earl said he wanted to go straight in life and I believed him.

I could hear the sound of hip-hop pulsing behind the closed windows of the Town Car as I approached. But Earl killed the music as soon as I reached for the door handle. I slid into the back and told him to head toward Van Nuys.

"Who was that you were listening to?" I asked him.

"Um, that was Three Six Mafia."

"Dirty south?"

"That's right."

Over the years, I had become knowledgeable in the subtle distinctions, regional and otherwise, in rap and hip-hop. Across the board, most of my clients listened to it, many of them developing their life strategies from it.

I reached over and picked up the shoebox full of cassette tapes from the Boyleston case and chose one at random. I noted the tape number and the time in the little logbook I kept in the shoebox. I handed the tape over the seat to Earl and he slid it into the dashboard stereo. I didn't have to tell him to play it at a volume so low that it would amount to little more than background noise. Earl had been with me for three months. He knew what to do.

Roger Boyleston was one of my few court-appointed clients. He was facing a variety of federal drug-trafficking charges. DEA wiretaps on Boyleston's phones had led to his arrest and the seizure of six kilos of cocaine that he had planned to distribute through a network of dealers. There were numerous tapes — more than fifty hours of recorded phone conversations. Boyleston talked to many people about what was coming and when to expect it. The case was a slam dunk for the government. Boyleston was going to go away for a long time and there was almost nothing I could do but negotiate a deal, trading Boyleston's cooperation for a lower sentence. That didn't matter, though. What mattered to me were the tapes. I took the case because of the tapes. The federal government would pay me to listen to the tapes in preparation for defending my client. That meant I would get a minimum of fifty billable hours out of Boyleston and the government before it was all settled. So I made sure the tapes were in heavy rotation whenever I was riding in the Lincoln. I wanted to make sure that if I ever had to put my hand on the book and swear to tell the truth, I could say in good conscience that I played every one of those tapes I billed Uncle Sugar for.

I called Lorna Taylor back first. Lorna is my case manager. The phone number that runs on my half-page ad in the yellow pages and on thirty-six bus benches scattered through high-crime areas in the south and east county goes directly to the office/second bedroom of her Kings Road condo in West Hollywood. The address the California bar and all the clerks of the courts have for me is the condo as well.

Lorna is the first buffer. To get to me you start with her. My cell number is given out to only a few and Lorna is the gatekeeper. She is tough, smart, professional and beautiful. Lately, though, I only get to verify this last attribute once a month or so when I take her to lunch and sign checks — she's my bookkeeper, too.

"Law office," she said when I called in.

"Sorry, I was still in court," I said, explaining why I didn't get her call. "What's up?"

"You talked to Val, right?"

"Yeah. I'm heading down to Van Nuys now. I got that at eleven."

"He called here to make sure. He sounds nervous."

"He thinks this guy is the golden goose, wants to make sure he's along for the ride. I'll call him back to reassure him."

"I did some preliminary checking on the name Louis Ross Roulet. Credit check is excellent. The name in the *Times* archive comes up with a few hits. All real estate transactions. Looks like he works for a real estate firm in Beverly Hills. It's called Windsor Residential Estates. Looks like they handle all exclusive pocket listings — not the sort of properties where they put a sign out front."

"That's good. Anything else?"

"Not on that. And just the usual so far on the phone."

Which meant that she had fielded the usual number of calls drawn by the bus benches and the yellow pages, all from people who wanted a lawyer. Before the callers hit my radar they had to convince Lorna that they could pay for what they wanted. She was sort of like the nurse behind the desk in the emergency room. You have to convince her you have valid insurance before she sends you back to see the doc. Next to Lorna's phone she keeps a rate schedule that starts with a $5,000 flat fee to handle a DUI and ranges to the hourly fees I charge for felony trials. She makes sure every potential client is a paying client and knows the costs of the crime they have been charged with. There's that saying, Don't do the crime if you can't do the time. Lorna likes to say that with me, it's Don't do the crime if you can't pay for my time. She accepts MasterCard and Visa and will get purchase approval before a client ever gets to me.

"Nobody we know?" I asked.

"Gloria Dayton called from Twin Towers."

I groaned. The Twin Towers was the county's main lockup in downtown. It housed women in one tower and men in the other. Gloria Dayton was a high-priced prostitute who needed my legal services from time to time. The first time I represented her was at least ten years earlier, when she was young and drug-free and still had life in her eyes. Now she was a pro bono client. I never charged her. I just tried to convince her to quit the life.

"When did she get popped?"

"Last night. Or rather, this morning. Her first appearance is after lunch."

"I don't know if I can make that with this Van Nuys thing."

"There's also a complication. Cocaine possession as well as the usual."

I knew that Gloria worked exclusively through contacts made on the Internet, where she billed herself on a variety of websites as Glory Days. She was no streetwalker or barroom troller. When she got popped, it was usually after an undercover vice officer was able to penetrate her check system and set up a date. The fact that she had cocaine on her person when they met sounded like an unusual lapse on her part or a plant from the cop.

"All right, if she calls back tell her I will try to be there and if I'm not there I will have somebody take it. Will you call the court and firm up the hearing?"

"I'm on it. But, Mickey, when are you going to tell her this is the last time?"

"I don't know. Maybe today. What else?"

"Isn't that enough for one day?"

"It'll do, I guess."

We talked a little more about my schedule for the rest of the week and I opened my laptop on the fold-down table so I could check my calendar against hers. I had a couple hearings set for each morning and a one-day trial on Thursday. It was all South side drug stuff. My meat and potatoes. At the end of the conversation I told her that I would call her after the Van Nuys hearing to let her know if and how the Roulet case would impact things.

"One last thing," I said. "You said the place Roulet works handles pretty exclusive real estate deals, right?"

"Yeah. Every deal his name was attached to in the archives was in seven figures. A couple got up into the eights. Holmby Hills, Bel-Air, places like that."

I nodded, thinking that Roulet's status might make him a person of interest to the media.

"Then why don't you tip Sticks to it," I said.

"You sure?"

"Yeah, we might be able to work something there."

"Will do."

"Talk to you later."

By the time I closed the phone, Earl had us back on the Antelope Valley Freeway heading south. We were making good time and getting to Van Nuys for Roulet's first appearance wasn't going to be a problem. I called Fernando Valenzuela to tell him.

"That's real good," the bondsman said. "I'll be waiting."

As he spoke I watched two motorcycles glide by my window. Each rider wore a black leather vest with the skull and halo patch sewn on the back.

"Anything else?" I asked.

"Yeah, one other thing I should probably tell you," Valenzuela said. "I was double-checking with the court on when his first appearance was going to be and I found out the case was assigned to Maggie McFierce. I don't know if that's going to be a problem for you or not."

Maggie McFierce as in Margaret McPherson, who happened to be one of the toughest and, yes, fiercest deputy district attorneys assigned to the Van Nuys courthouse. She also happened to be my first ex-wife.

"It won't be a problem for me," I said without hesitation. "She's the one who'll have the problem."

The defendant has the right to his choice of counsel. If there is a conflict of interest between the defense lawyer and the prosecutor, then it is the prosecutor who must bow out. I knew Maggie would hold me personally responsible for her losing the reins on what might be a big case but I couldn't help that. It had happened before. In my laptop I still had a motion to disqualify from the last case in which we had crossed paths. If necessary, I would just have to change the name of the defendant and print it out. I'd be good to go and she'd be as good as gone.

The two motorcycles had now moved in front of us. I turned and looked out the back window. There were three more Harleys behind us.

"You know what that means, though," I said.

"No, what?"

"She'll go for no bail. She always does with crimes against women."

"Shit, can she get it? I'm looking at a nice chunk of change on this, man."

"I don't know. You said the guy's got family and C. C. Dobbs. I can make something out of that. We'll see."

"Shit."

Valenzuela was seeing his major payday disappear.

"I'll see you there, Val."

I closed the phone and looked over the seat at Earl.

"How long have we had the escort?" I asked.

"Just came up on us," Earl said. "You want me to do something?"

"Let's see what they —"

I didn't have to wait until the end of my sentence. One of the riders from the rear came up alongside the Lincoln and signaled us toward the upcoming exit for the Vasquez Rocks County Park. I recognized him as Teddy Vogel, a former client and the highest-ranked Road Saint not incarcerated. He might have been the largest

Saint as well. He went at least 350 pounds and he gave the impression of a fat kid riding his little brother's bike.

"Pull off, Earl," I said. "Let's see what he's got."

We pulled into the parking lot next to the jagged rock formation named after an outlaw who had hid in them a century before. I saw two people sitting and having a picnic on the edge of one of the highest ledges. I didn't think I would feel comfortable eating a sandwich in such a dangerous spot and position.

I lowered my window as Teddy Vogel approached on foot. The other four Saints had killed their engines but remained on their bikes. Vogel leaned down to the window and put one of his giant forearms on the sill. I could feel the car tilt down a few inches.

"Counselor, how's it hanging?" he said.

"Just fine, Ted," I said, not wanting to call him by his obvious gang sobriquet of Teddy Bear. "What's up with you?"

"What happened to the ponytail?"

"Some people objected to it, so I cut it off."

"A jury, huh? Must've been a collection of stiffs from up this way."

"What's up, Ted?"

"I got a call from Hard Case over there in the Lancaster pen. He said I might catch you heading south. Said you were stalling his case till you got some green. That right, Counselor?"

It was said as routine conversation. No threat in his voice or words. And I didn't feel threatened. Two years ago I got an abduction and aggravated assault case against Vogel knocked down to a disturbing the peace. He ran a Saints-owned strip club on Sepulveda in Van Nuys. His arrest came after he learned that one of his most productive dancers had quit and crossed the street to work at a competing club. Vogel had crossed the street after her, grabbed her off the stage and carried her back to his club. She was naked. A passing motorist called the police. Knocking the case down was one of my better plays and Vogel knew this. He had a soft spot for me.

"He's pretty much got it right," I said. "I work for a living. If he wants me to work for him he's gotta pay me."

"We gave you five grand in December," Vogel said.

"That's long gone, Ted. More than half went to the expert who is going to blow the case up. The rest went to me and I already worked off those hours. If I'm going to take it to trial, then I need to refill the tank."

"You want another five?"

"No, I need ten and I told Hard Case that last week. It's a three-day trial and I'll need to bring my expert in from Kodak in New York. I've got his fee to cover and he wants first class in the air and the Chateau Marmont on the ground. Thinks he's going to be drinking at the bar with movie stars or something. That place is four hundred a night just for the cheap rooms."

"You're killing me, Counselor. Whatever happened to that slogan you had in the yellow pages? 'Reasonable doubt for a reasonable fee.' You call ten grand reasonable?"

"I liked that slogan. It brought in a lot of clients. But the California bar wasn't so pleased with it, made me get rid of it. Ten is the price and it is reasonable, Ted. If you can't or don't want to pay it, I'll file the paperwork today. I'll drop out and he can go with a PD. I'll turn everything I have over. But the PD probably won't have the budget to fly in the photo expert."

Vogel shifted his position on the window sill and the car shuddered under the weight.

"No, no, we want you. Hard Case is important to us, you know what I mean? I want him out and back to work."

I watched him reach inside his vest with a hand that was so fleshy that the knuckles were indented. It came out with a thick envelope that he passed into the car to me.

"Is this cash?" I asked.

"That's right. What's wrong with cash?"

"Nothing. But I have to give you a receipt. It's an IRS reporting requirement. This is the whole ten?"

"It's all there."

I took the top off of a cardboard file box I keep on the seat next to me. My receipt book was behind the current case files. I started writing out the receipt. Most lawyers who get disbarred go down because of financial violations. The mishandling or misappropriation of client fees. I kept meticulous records and receipts. I would never let the bar get to me that way.

"So you had it all along," I said as I wrote. "What if I had backed down to five? What would you have done then?"

Vogel smiled. He was missing one of his front teeth on the bottom. Had to have been a fight at the club. He patted the other side of his vest.

"I got another envelope with five in it right here, Counselor," he said. "I was ready for you."

"Damn, now I feel bad, leaving you with money in your pocket."

I tore out his copy of the receipt and handed it out the window.

"I receipted it to Casey. He's the client."

"Fine with me."

He took the receipt and dropped his arm off the window sill as he stood up straight. The car returned to a normal level. I wanted to ask him where the money came from, which of the Saints' criminal enterprises had earned it, whether a hundred girls had danced a hundred hours for him to pay me, but that was a question I was better off not knowing the answer to. I watched Vogel saunter back to his Harley and struggle to swing a trash can–thick leg over the seat. For the first time I noticed the double shocks on the back wheel. I told Earl to get back on the freeway and get going to Van Nuys, where I now needed to make a stop at the bank before hitting the courthouse to meet my new client.

As we drove I opened the envelope and counted out the money, twenties, fifties and hundred-dollar bills. It was all there. The tank was refilled and I was good to go with Harold Casey. I would go to trial and teach his young prosecutor a lesson. I would win, if not in trial, then certainly on appeal. Casey would return to the family and work of the Road Saints. His guilt in the crime he was charged with was not something I even considered as I filled out a deposit slip for my client fees account.

"Mr. Haller?" Earl said after a while.

"What, Earl?"

"That man you told him was coming in from New York to be the expert? Will I be picking him up at the airport?"

I shook my head.

"There is no expert coming in from New York, Earl. The best camera and photo experts in the world are right here in Hollywood."

Now Earl nodded and his eyes held mine for a moment in the rearview mirror. Then he looked back at the road ahead.

"I see," he said, nodding again.

And I nodded to myself. No hesitation in what I had done or said. That was my job. That was how it worked. After fifteen years of practicing law I had come to think of it in very simple terms. The law was a large, rusting machine that sucked up people and lives and money. I was just a mechanic. I had become expert at going into the machine and fixing things and extracting what I needed from it in return.

There was nothing about the law that I cherished anymore. The law school notions about the virtue of the adversarial system, of the system's checks and balances, of the search for truth, had long since eroded like the faces of statues from other civilizations. The law was not about truth. It was about negotiation, amelioration, manipulation. I didn't deal in guilt and innocence, because everybody was guilty. Of something. But it didn't matter, because every case I took on was a house built on a foundation poured by overworked and underpaid laborers. They cut corners. They made mistakes. And then they painted over the mistakes with lies. My job was to peel away the paint and find the cracks. To work my fingers and tools into those cracks and widen them. To make them so big that either the house fell down or, failing that, my client slipped through.

Much of society thought of me as the devil but they were wrong. I was a greasy angel. I was the true road saint. I was needed and wanted. By both sides. I was the oil in the machine. I allowed the gears to crank and turn. I helped keep the engine of the system running.

But all of that would change with the Roulet case. For me. For him. And certainly for Jesus Menendez.

FOUR

Louis Ross Roulet was in a holding tank with seven other men who had made the half-block bus ride from the Van Nuys jail to the Van Nuys courthouse. There were only two white men in the cell and they sat next to each other on a bench while the six black men took the other side of the cell. It was a form of Darwinian segregation. They were all strangers but there was strength in numbers.

Since Roulet supposedly came from Beverly Hills money, I looked at the two white men and it was easy to choose between them. One was rail thin with the desperate wet eyes of a hype who was long past fix time. The other looked like the proverbial deer in the headlights. I chose him.

"Mr. Roulet?" I said, pronouncing the name the way Valenzuela had told me to.

The deer nodded. I signaled him over to the bars so I could talk quietly.

"My name is Michael Haller. People call me Mickey. I will be representing you during your first appearance today."

We were in the holding area behind the arraignment court, where attorneys are routinely allowed access to confer with clients before court begins. There is a blue line painted on the floor outside the cells. The three-foot line. I had to keep that distance from my client.

Roulet grasped the bars in front of me. Like the others in the cage, he had on ankle, wrist and belly chains. They wouldn't come off until he was taken into the courtroom. He was in his early thirties and, though at least six feet tall and 180 pounds, he seemed slight. Jail will do that to you. His eyes were pale blue and it was rare for me to see the kind of panic that was so clearly set in them. Most of the time my clients have been in lockup before and they have the stone-cold look of the predator. It's how they get by in jail.

But Roulet was different. He looked like prey. He was scared and he didn't care who saw it and knew it.

"This is a setup," he said urgently and loudly. "You have to get me out of here. I made a mistake with that woman, that's all. She's trying to set me up and —"

I put my hands up to stop him.

"Be careful what you say in here," I said in a low voice. "In fact, be careful what you say until we get you out of here and can talk in private."

He looked around, seemingly not understanding.

"You never know who is listening," I said. "And you never know who will say he heard you say something, even if you didn't say anything. Best thing is to not talk about the case at all. You understand? Best thing is not to talk to anyone about anything, period."

He nodded and I signaled him down to the bench next to the bars. There was a bench against the opposite wall and I sat down.

"I am really here just to meet you and tell you who I am," I said. "We'll talk about the case after we get you out. I already spoke to your family lawyer, Mr. Dobbs, out there and we will tell the judge that we are prepared to post bail. Do I have all of that right?"

I opened a leather Mont Blanc folder and prepared to take notes on a legal pad. Roulet nodded. He was learning.

"Good," I said. "Tell me about yourself. How old you are, whether you're married, what ties you have to the community."

"Um, I'm thirty-two. I've lived here my whole life — even went to school here. UCLA. Not married. No kids. I work —"

"Divorced?"

"No, never married. I work for my family's business. Windsor Residential Estates. It's named after my mother's second husband. It's real estate. We sell real estate."

I was writing notes. Without looking up at him, I quietly asked, "How much money did you make last year?"

When Roulet didn't answer I looked up at him.

"Why do you need to know that?" he asked.

"Because I am going to get you out of here before the sun goes down today. To do that, I need to know everything about your standing in the community. That includes your financial standing."

"I don't know exactly what I made. A lot of it was shares in the company."

"You didn't file taxes?"

Roulet looked over his shoulder at the others in the cell and then whispered his answer.

"Yes, I did. On that my income was a quarter million."

"But what you're saying is that with the shares you earned in the company you really made more."

"Right."

One of Roulet's cellmates came up to the bars next to him. The other white man. He had an agitated manner, his hands in constant motion, moving from hips to pockets to each other in desperate grasps.

"Hey, man, I need a lawyer, too. You got a card?"

"Not for you, pal. They'll have a lawyer out there for you."

I looked back at Roulet and waited a moment for the hype to move away. He didn't. I looked back at him.

"Look, this is private. Could you leave us alone?"

The hype made some kind of motion with his hands and shuffled back to the corner he had come from. I looked back at Roulet.

"What about charitable organizations?" I asked.

"What do you mean?" Roulet responded.

"Are you involved in any charities? Do you give to any charities?"

"Yeah, the company does. We give to Make a Wish and a runaway shelter in Hollywood. I think it's called My Friend's Place or something like that."

"Okay, good."

"Are you going to get me out?"

"I'm going to try. You've got some heavy charges on you — I checked before coming back here — and I have a feeling the DA is going to request no bail, but this is good stuff. I can work with it."

I indicated my notes.

"No bail?" he said in a loud, panicked voice.

The others in the cell looked in his direction because what he had said was their collective nightmare. No bail.

"Calm down," I said. "I said that is what she is going to go for. I didn't say she would get it. When was the last time you were arrested?"

I always threw that in out of the blue so I could watch their eyes and see if there was going to be a surprise thrown at me in court.

"Never. I've never been arrested. This whole thing is —"

"I know, I know, but we don't want to talk about that here, remember?"

He nodded. I looked at my watch. Court was about to start and I still needed to talk to Maggie McFierce.

"I'm going to go now," I said. "I'll see you out there in a few minutes and we'll see about getting you out of here. When we are out there, don't say anything until you check with me. If the judge asks you how you are doing, you check with me. Okay?"

"Well, don't I say 'not guilty' to the charges?"

"No, they're not going to even ask you that. Today all they do is read you the charges, talk about bail and set a date for an arraignment. That's when we say 'not guilty.' So today you say nothing. No outbursts, nothing. Got that?"

He nodded and frowned.

"Are you going to be all right, Louis?"

He nodded glumly.

"Just so you know," I said. "I charge twenty-five hundred dollars for a first appearance and bail hearing like this. Is that going to be a problem?"

He shook his head no. I liked that he wasn't talking. Most of my clients talk way too much. Usually they talk themselves right into prison.

"Good. We can talk about the rest of it after you are out of here and we can get together in private."

I closed my leather folder, hoping he had noticed it and was impressed, then stood up.

"One last thing," I said. "Why'd you pick me? There's a lot of lawyers out there, why me?"

It was a question that didn't matter to our relationship but I wanted to test Valenzuela's veracity.

Roulet shrugged.

"I don't know," he said. "I remembered your name from something I read in the paper."

"What did you read about me?"

"It was a story about a case where the evidence got thrown out against some guy. I think it was drugs or something. You won the case because they had no evidence after that."

"The Hendricks case?"

It was the only one I could think of that had made the papers in recent months. Hendricks was another Road Saint client and the sheriff's department had put a GPS bug on his Harley to track his deliveries. Doing that on public roads was fine. But when he parked his bike in the kitchen of his home at night, that bug constituted unlawful entry by the cops. The case was tossed by a judge during the preliminary hearing. It made a decent splash in the *Times*.

"I can't remember the name of the client," Roulet said. "I just remembered your name. Your last name, actually. When I called the bail bondsman today I gave him the name Haller and asked him to get you and to call my own attorney. Why?"

"No reason. Just curious. I appreciate the call. I'll see you in the courtroom."

I put the differences between what Roulet had said about my hiring and what Valenzuela had told me into the bank for later consideration and made my way back into the arraignment court. I saw Maggie McFierce sitting at one end of the prosecution table. She was there along with five other prosecutors. The table was large and L-shaped so it could accommodate an endlessly revolving number of lawyers who could sit and still face the bench. A prosecutor assigned to the courtroom handled most of the routine appearances and arraignments that were paraded through each day. But special cases brought the big guns out of the district attorney's office on the second floor of the courthouse next door. TV cameras did that, too.

As I stepped through the bar I saw a man setting up a video camera on a tripod next to the bailiff's desk. There was no network symbol on the camera or the man's clothes. The man was a freelancer who had gotten wind of the case and would shoot the hearing and then try to sell it to one of the local stations whose news director needed a thirty-second story. When I had checked with the bailiff earlier about Roulet's place on the calendar, he told me the judge had already authorized the filming.

I walked up to my ex-wife from behind and bent down to whisper into her ear. She was looking at photographs in a file. She was wearing a navy suit with a thin gray stripe. Her raven-colored hair was tied back with a matching gray ribbon. I loved her hair when it was back like that.

"Are you the one who used to have the Roulet case?"

She looked up, not recognizing the whisper. Her face was involuntarily forming a smile but then it turned into a frown when she saw it was me. She knew exactly what I had meant by using the past tense and she slapped the file closed.

"Don't tell me," she said.

"Sorry. He liked what I did on Hendricks and gave me a call."

"Son of a bitch. I wanted this case, Haller. This is the second time you've done this to me."

"I guess this town ain't big enough for the both of us," I said in a poor Cagney imitation.

She groaned.

"All right," she said in quick surrender. "I'll go peacefully after this hearing. Unless you object to even that."

"I might. You going for a no-bail hold?"

"That's right. But that won't change with the prosecutor. That was a directive from the second floor."

I nodded. That meant a case supervisor must have called for the no-bail hold.

"He's connected in the community. And has never been arrested."

I studied her reaction, not having had the time to make sure Roulet's denial of ever being previously arrested was the truth. It's always amazing how many clients lie about previous engagements with the machine, when it is a lie that has no hope of going the distance.

But Maggie gave no indication that she knew otherwise. Maybe it was true. Maybe I had an honest-to-goodness first-time offender for a client.

"It doesn't matter whether he's done anything before," Maggie said. "What matters is what he did last night."

She opened the file and quickly checked through the photos until she saw the one she liked and snatched it out.

"Here's what your pillar of the community did last night. So I don't really care what he did before. I'm just going to make sure he - doesn't get out to do this again."

The photo was an 8 × 10 close-up of a woman's face. The swelling around the right eye was so extensive that the eye was completely and tightly closed. The nose was broken and pushed off center. Blood-soaked gauze protruded from each nostril. There was a deep gash over the right eyebrow that had been closed with nine butterfly stitches. The lower lip was cut and had a marble-size swelling as well. The worst thing about the photo was the eye that was undamaged. The woman looked at the camera with fear, pain and humiliation undeniably expressed in that one tearful eye.

"If he did it," I said, because that is what I would be expected to say.

"Right," Maggie said. "Sure, if he did it. He was only arrested in her home with her blood on him, but you're right, that's a valid question."

"I like it when you're sarcastic. Do you have the arrest report there? I'd like to get a copy of it."

"You can get it from whoever takes the case over from me. No favors, Haller. Not this time."

I waited, expecting more banter, more indignation, maybe another shot across the bow, but that was all she said. I decided that getting more out of her on the case was a lost cause. I changed the subject.

"So," I said. "How is she?"

"She's scared shitless and hurting like hell. How else would she be?"

She looked up at me and I saw the immediate recognition and then judgment in her eyes.

"You weren't even asking about the victim, were you?"

I didn't answer. I didn't want to lie to her.

"Your daughter is doing fine," she said perfunctorily. "She likes the things you send her but she would rather *you* show up a little more often."

That wasn't a shot across the bow. That was a direct hit and it was deserved. It seemed as though I was always chasing cases, even on weekends. Deep down inside I knew I needed to start chasing my daughter around the backyard more often. The time to do it was going by.

"I will," I said. "Starting right now. What about this weekend?"

"Fine. You want me to tell her tonight?"

"Uh, maybe wait until tomorrow so I know for sure."

She gave me one of those knowing nods. We had been through this before.

"Great. Let me know tomorrow."

This time I didn't enjoy the sarcasm.

"What does she need?" I asked, trying to stumble back to just being even.

"I just told you what she needs. More of you in her life."

"Okay, I promise. I will do that."

She didn't respond.

"I really mean that, Maggie. I'll call you tomorrow."

She looked up at me and was ready to hit me with both barrels.

She had done it before, saying I was all talk and no action when it came to fatherhood. But I was saved by the start of the court session. The judge came out of chambers and bounded up the steps to the bench. The bailiff called the courtroom to order. Without another word to Maggie I left the prosecution table and went back to one of the seats along the bar.

The judge asked his clerk if there was any business to be discussed before the custodies were brought out. There was none, so the judge ordered the first group out. As with the courtroom in Lancaster, there was a large holding area for in-custody defendants. I got up and moved to the opening in the glass. When I saw Roulet come through the door I signaled him over.

"You're going first," I told him. "I asked the judge to take you out of order as a favor. I want to try to get you out of here."

This was not the truth. I hadn't asked the judge anything, and even if I had, the judge would do no such thing for me as a favor. Roulet was going first because of the media presence in the courtroom. It was a general practice to deal with the media cases first. This was a courtesy to the cameramen who supposedly had other assignments to get to. But it also made for less tension in the courtroom when lawyers, defendants and even the judge could operate without a television camera on them.

"Why's that camera here?" Roulet asked in a panicked whisper. "Is that for me?"

"Yes, it's for you. Somebody tipped him to the case. If you don't want to be filmed, try to use me as a shield."

Roulet shifted his position so I was blocking the view of him from the camera across the courtroom. This lowered the chances that the cameraman would be able to sell the story and film to a local news program. That was good. It also meant that if he was able to sell the story, I would be the focal point of the images that went with it. This was also good.

The Roulet case was called, his name mispronounced by the clerk, and Maggie announced her presence for the prosecution and then I announced mine. Maggie had upped the charges, as was her usual MO as Maggie McFierce. Roulet now faced attempted murder along with the attempted rape count. It would make it easier for her to argue for a no-bail hold.

The judge informed Roulet of his constitutional rights and set an arraignment date for March 21. Speaking for Roulet, I asked to address the no-bail hold. This set off a spirited back-and-forth between Maggie and me, all of which was refereed by the judge, who knew we were formerly married because he had attended our wedding. While Maggie listed the atrocities committed upon the victim, I in turn listed Roulet's ties to the community and charitable efforts and pointed to C. C. Dobbs in the gallery and offered to put him on the stand to further discuss Roulet's good standing. Dobbs was my ace in the hole. His stature in the legal community would supersede Roulet's standing and certainly be influential with the judge, who held his position on the bench at the behest of the voters — and campaign contributors.

"The bottom line, Judge, is that the state cannot make a case for this man being a flight risk or a danger to the community," I said in closing. "Mr. Roulet is anchored in this community and intends to do nothing other than vigorously attack the false charges that have been leveled against him."

I used the word *attack* purposely in case the statement got on the air and happened to be watched by the woman who had leveled the charges.

"Your Honor," Maggie responded, "all grandstanding aside, what should not be forgotten is that the victim in this case was brutally —"

"Ms. McPherson," the judge interrupted. "I think we have gone back and forth on this enough. I am aware of the victim's injuries as well as Mr. Roulet's standing. I also have a busy calendar today. I am going to set bail at one million dollars. I am also going to require Mr. Roulet to be supervised by the court with weekly check-ins. If he misses one, he forfeits his freedom."

I quickly glanced out into the gallery, where Dobbs was sitting next to Fernando Valenzuela. Dobbs was a thin man who shaved his

head to hide male-pattern balding. His thinness was exaggerated by
Valenzuela's girth. I waited for a signal as to whether I should take
the judge's bail order or try to argue for a lower amount. Sometimes,
when a judge thinks he is giving you a gift, it can backfire to press for
more — or in this case less.

Dobbs was sitting in the first seat in the first row. He simply got
up and started to walk out of the courtroom, leaving Valenzuela behind. I took that to mean that I should leave well enough alone, that
the Roulet family could handle the million. I turned back to the bench.

"Thank you, Your Honor," I said.

The clerk immediately called the next case. I glanced at Maggie
as she was closing the file on the case she would no longer prosecute.
She then stood up and walked out through the bar and down the center aisle of the courtroom. She spoke to no one and she did not look
back at me.

"Mr. Haller?"

I turned to my client. Behind him I saw a deputy coming to take
him back into holding. He'd be bused the half block back to jail and
then, depending on how fast Dobbs and Valenzuela worked, released later in the day.

"I'll work with Mr. Dobbs and get you out," I said. "Then we'll
sit down and talk about the case."

"Thank you," Roulet said as he was led away. "Thank you for
being here."

"Remember what I said. Don't talk to strangers. Don't talk to
anybody."

"Yes, sir."

After he was gone I walked to the bar. Valenzuela was waiting at
the gate for me with a big smile on his face. Roulet's bail was likely
the highest he had ever secured. That meant his cut would be the
highest he'd ever received. He clapped me on the arm as I came
through the gate.

"What'd I tell you?" he said. "We got ourselves a franchise here,
boss."

"We'll see, Val," I said. "We'll see."

FIVE

Every attorney who works the machine has two fee schedules. There is schedule A, which lists the fees the attorney would like to get for certain services rendered. And there is schedule B, the fees he is willing to take because that is all the client can afford. A franchise client is a defendant who wants to go to trial and has the money to pay his lawyer's schedule A rates. From first appearance to arraignment to preliminary hearing and on to trial and then appeal, the franchise client demands hundreds if not thousands of billable hours. He can keep gas in the tank for two to three years. From where I hunt, they are the rarest and most highly sought beast in the jungle.

And it was beginning to look like Valenzuela had been on the money. Louis Roulet was looking more and more like a franchise client. It had been a dry spell for me. It had been almost two years since I'd had anything even approaching a franchise case or client. I'm talking about a case earning six figures. There were many that started out looking like they might reach that rare plateau but they never went the distance.

C. C. Dobbs was waiting in the hallway outside the arraignment court when I got out. He was standing next to the wall of glass windows that looked down upon the civic center plaza below. I walked up to him quickly. I had a few seconds' lead on Valenzuela coming out of the court and I wanted some private time with Dobbs.

"Sorry," Dobbs said before I could speak. "I didn't want to stay in there another minute. It was so depressing to see the boy caught up in that cattle call."

"The boy?"

"Louis. I've represented the family for twenty-five years. I guess I still think of him as a boy."

"Are you going to be able to get him out?"

"It won't be a problem. I have a call in to Louis's mother to see how she wants to handle it, whether to put up property or go with a bond."

To put up property to cover a million-dollar bail would mean that at least a million dollars in the property's value could not be encumbered by a mortgage. Additionally, the court might require a current appraisal of the property, which could take days and keep Roulet waiting in jail. Conversely, a bond could be purchased through Valenzuela for a ten percent premium. The difference was that the ten percent was never returned. That stayed with Valenzuela for his risks and trouble and was the reason for his broad smile in the courtroom. After paying his insurance premium on the million-dollar bail, he'd end up clearing close to ninety grand. And he was worried about me taking care of *him*.

"Can I make a suggestion?" I asked.

"Please do."

"Louis looked a little frail when I saw him back in the lockup. If I were you I would get him out of there as soon as possible. To do that you should have Valenzuela write a bond. It will cost you a hundred grand but the boy will be out and safe, you know what I mean?"

Dobbs turned to the window and leaned on the railing that ran along the glass. I looked down and saw that the plaza was filling up with people from the government buildings on lunch break. I could see many people with the red-and-white name tags I knew were given to jurors.

"I know what you mean."

"The other thing is that cases like this tend to bring the rats out of the walls."

"What do you mean?"

"I mean other inmates who will say they heard somebody say something. Especially a case that gets on the news or into the newspapers. They'll take that info off the tube and make it sound like our guy was talking."

"That's criminal," Dobbs said indignantly. "That shouldn't be allowed."

"Yeah, I know, but it happens. And the longer he stays in there, the wider the window of opportunity is for one of these guys."

Valenzuela joined us at the railing. He didn't say anything.

"I will suggest we go with the bond," Dobbs said. "I already called and she was in a meeting. As soon as she calls me back we will move on this."

His words prompted something that had bothered me during the hearing.

"She couldn't come out of a meeting to talk about her son in jail? I was wondering why she wasn't in court today if this boy, as you call him, is so clean and upstanding."

Dobbs looked at me like I hadn't used mouthwash in a month.

"Mrs. Windsor is a very busy and powerful woman. I am sure that if I had stated it was an emergency concerning her son, she would have been on the phone immediately."

"Mrs. Windsor?"

"She remarried after she and Louis's father divorced. That was a long time ago."

I nodded, then realized that there was more to talk about with Dobbs but nothing I wanted to discuss in front of Valenzuela.

"Val, why don't you go check on when Louis will be back at Van Nuys jail so you can get him out."

"That's easy," Valenzuela said. "He'll go on the first bus back after lunch."

"Yeah, well, go double-check that while I finish with Mr. Dobbs."

Valenzuela was about to protest that he didn't need to double-check it when he realized what I was telling him.

"Okay," he said. "I'll go do it."

After he was gone I studied Dobbs for a moment before speaking. Dobbs looked to be in his late fifties. He had a deferential presence that probably came from thirty years of taking care of rich people. My guess was that he had become rich in the process himself but it hadn't changed his public demeanor.

"If we're going to be working together, I guess I should ask what you want to be called. Cecil? C.C.? Mr. Dobbs?"

"Cecil will be fine."

"Well, my first question, Cecil, is whether we are going to be working together. Do I have the job?"

"Mr. Roulet made it clear to me he wanted you on the case. To be honest, you would not have been my first choice. You might not have been any choice, because frankly I had never heard of you. But you are Mr. Roulet's first choice, and that is acceptable to me. In fact, I thought you acquitted yourself quite well in the courtroom, especially considering how hostile that prosecutor was toward Mr. Roulet."

I noticed that the boy had become "Mr. Roulet" now. I wondered what had happened to advance him in Dobbs's view.

"Yeah, well, they call her Maggie McFierce. She's pretty dedicated."

"I thought she was a bit overboard. Do you think there is any way to get her removed from the case, maybe get someone a little more . . . grounded?"

"I don't know. Trying to shop prosecutors can be dangerous. But if you think she needs to go, I can get it done."

"That's good to hear. Maybe I should have known about you before today."

"Maybe. Do you want to talk about fees now and get it out of the way?"

"If you would like."

I looked around the hallway to make sure there were no other lawyers hanging around in earshot. I was going to go schedule A all the way on this.

"I get twenty-five hundred for today and Louis already approved that. If you want to go hourly from here, I get three hundred an hour and that gets bumped to five in trial because I can't do anything else. If you'd rather go with a flat rate, I'll want sixty thousand to take it from here through a preliminary hearing. If we end it with a plea, I'll take twelve more on top of that. If we go to trial instead, I need another sixty on the day we decide that and twenty-five more when we start picking a jury. This case doesn't look like more than a week, including jury selection, but if it goes past a week, I get twenty-five-a-week extra. We can talk about an appeal if and when it becomes necessary."

I hesitated a moment to see how Dobbs was reacting. He showed nothing so I pressed on.

"I'll need thirty thousand for a retainer and another ten for an investigator by the end of the day. I don't want to waste time on this. I want to get an investigator out and about on this thing before it hits the media and maybe before the cops talk to some of the people involved."

Dobbs slowly nodded.

"Are those your standard fees?"

"When I can get them. I'm worth it. What are you charging the family, Cecil?"

I was sure he wouldn't walk away from this little episode hungry.

"That's between me and my client. But don't worry. I will include your fees in my discussion with Mrs. Windsor."

"I appreciate it. And remember, I need that investigator to start today."

I gave him a business card I pulled from the right pocket of my suit coat. The cards in the right pocket had my cell number. The cards in my left pocket had the number that went to Lorna Taylor.

"I have another hearing downtown," I said. "When you get him out call me and we'll set up a meeting. Let's make it as soon as possible. I should be available later today and tonight."

"Perfect," Dobbs said, pocketing the card without looking at it. "Should we come to you?"

"No, I'll come to you. I'd like to see how the other half lives in those high-rises in Century City."

Dobbs smiled glibly.

"It is obvious by your suit that you know and practice the adage that a trial lawyer should never dress too well. You want the jury to like you, not to be jealous of you. Well, Michael, a Century City lawyer can't have an office that is nicer than the offices his clients come from. And so I can assure you that our offices are very modest."

I nodded in agreement. But I was insulted just the same. I was wearing my best suit. I always did on Mondays.

"That's good to know," I said.

The courtroom door opened and the videographer walked out, lugging his camera and folded tripod with him. Dobbs saw him and immediately tensed.

"The media," he said. "How can we control this? Mrs. Windsor won't —"

"Hold on a sec."

I called to the cameraman and he walked over. I immediately put my hand out. He had to put his tripod down to take it.

"I'm Michael Haller. I saw you in there filming my client's appearance."

Using my formal name was a code.

"Robert Gillen," the cameraman said. "People call me Sticks."

He gestured to his tripod in explanation. His use of his formal name was a return code. He was letting me know he understood that I had a play working here.

"Are you freelancing or on assignment?" I asked.

"Just freelancing today."

"How'd you hear about this thing?"

He shrugged as though he was reluctant to answer.

"A source. A cop."

I nodded. Gillen was locked in and playing along.

"What do you get for that if you sell it to a news station?"

"Depends. I take seven-fifty for an exclusive and five for a nonexclusive."

Nonexclusive meant that any news director who bought the tape from him knew that he might sell the footage to a competing news station. Gillen had doubled the fees he actually got. It was a good move. He must have been listening to what had been said in the courtroom while he shot it.

"Tell you what," I said. "How about we take it off your hands right now for an exclusive?"

Gillen was perfect. He hesitated like he was unsure of the ethics involved in the proposition.

"In fact, make it a grand," I said.

"Okay," he said. "You got a deal."

While Gillen put the camera on the floor and took the tape out of it, I pulled a wad of cash from my pocket. I had kept twelve hundred from the Saints cash Teddy Vogel had given me on the way down. I turned to Dobbs.

"I can expense this, right?"

"Absolutely," he said. He was beaming.

I exchanged the cash for the tape and thanked Gillen. He pocketed the money and moved toward the elevators a happy man.

"That was brilliant," Dobbs said. "We have to contain this. It could literally destroy the family's business if this — in fact, I think that is one reason Mrs. Windsor was not here today. She didn't want to be recognized."

"Well, we'll have to talk about that if this thing goes the distance. Meantime, I'll do my best to keep it off the radar."

"Thank you."

A cell phone began to play a classical number by Bach or Beethoven or some other dead guy with no copyright and Dobbs reached inside his jacket, retrieved the device and checked the small screen on it.

"This is she," he said.

"Then I'll leave you to it."

As I walked off I heard Dobbs saying, "Mary, everything is

under control. We need now to concentrate on getting him out. We are going to need some money . . ."

While the elevator made its way up to me, I was thinking that I was pretty sure that I was dealing with a client and family for which "some money" meant more than I had ever seen. My mind moved back to the sartorial comment Dobbs had made about me. It still stung. The truth was, I didn't have a suit in my closet that cost less than six hundred dollars and I always felt good and confident in any one of them. I wondered if he had intended to insult me or he had intended something else, maybe trying at this early stage of the game to imprint his control over me and the case. I decided I would need to watch my back with Dobbs. I would keep him close but not that close.

SIX

Traffic heading downtown bottlenecked in the Cahuenga Pass. I spent the time in the car working the phone and trying not to think about the conversation I'd had with Maggie McPherson about my parenting skills. My ex-wife had been right about me, and that's what hurt. For a long time I had put my law practice ahead of my parenting practice. It was something I promised myself to change. I just needed the time and the money to slow down. I thought that maybe Louis Roulet would provide both.

In the back of the Lincoln I first called Raul Levin, my investigator, to put him on alert about the potential meeting with Roulet. I asked him to do a preliminary run on the case to see what he could find out. Levin had retired early from the LAPD and still had contacts and friends who did him favors from time to time. He probably had his own Christmas list. I told him not to spend a lot of time on it until I was sure I had Roulet locked down as a paying client. It didn't matter what C. C. Dobbs had said to me face-to-face in the courthouse hallway. I wouldn't believe I had the case until I got the first payment.

Next I checked on the status of a few cases and then called Lorna Taylor again. I knew the mail was delivered at her place most days right before noon. But she told me nothing of importance had come in. No checks and no correspondence I had to pay immediate attention to from the courts.

"Did you check on Gloria Dayton's arraignment?" I asked her.

"Yes. It looks like they might hold her over until tomorrow on a medical."

I groaned. The state has forty-eight hours to charge an individual after arrest and bring them before a judge. Holding Gloria Dayton's first appearance over until the next day because of medical reasons meant that she was probably drug sick. This would help explain why she had been holding cocaine when she was arrested. I had not seen or spoken to her in at least seven months. Her slide must have been quick and steep. The thin line between controlling the drugs and the drugs controlling her had been crossed.

"Did you find out who filed it?" I asked.

"Leslie Faire," she said.

I groaned again.

"That's just great. Okay, well, I'm going to go down and see what I can do. I've got nothing going until I hear about Roulet."

Leslie Faire was a misnamed prosecutor whose idea of giving a defendant a break or the benefit of the doubt was to offer extended parole supervision on top of prison time.

"Mick, when are you going to learn with this woman?" Lorna said about Gloria Dayton.

"Learn what?" I asked, although I knew exactly what Lorna would say.

"She drags you down every time you have to deal with her. She's never going to get out of the life, and now you can bet she's never going to be anything less than a twofer every time she calls. That would be fine, except you never charge her."

What she meant by *twofer* was that Gloria Dayton's cases would from now on be more complicated and time-consuming because it was likely that drug charges would always accompany solicitation or prostitution charges. What bothered Lorna was that this meant more work for me but no more income in the process.

"Well, the bar requires that all lawyers practice some pro bono work, Lorna. You know —"

"You don't listen to me, Mick," she said dismissively. "That's exactly why we couldn't stay married."

I closed my eyes. What a day. I had managed to get both my ex-wives angry with me.

"What does this woman have on you?" she asked. "Why don't you charge even a basic fee with her?"

"Look, she doesn't have anything on me, okay?" I said. "Can we sort of change the subject now?"

I didn't tell her that years earlier when I had looked through the dusty old account books from my father's law practice, I had found that he'd had a soft spot for the so-called women of the night. He defended many and charged few. Maybe I was just continuing a family tradition.

"Fine," Lorna said. "How did it go with Roulet?"

"You mean, did I get the job? I think so. Val's probably getting him out right now. We'll set up a meeting after that. I already asked Raul to sniff around on it."

"Did you get a check?"

"Not yet."

"Get the check, Mick."

"I'm working on it."

"How's the case look?"

"I've only seen the pictures but it looks bad. I'll know more after I see what Raul comes up with."

"And what about Roulet?"

I knew what she was asking. How was he as a client? Would a jury, if it came to a jury, like him or despise him? Cases could be won or lost based on jurors' impressions of the defendant.

"He looks like a babe in the woods."

"He's a virgin?"

"Never been inside the iron house."

"Well, did he do it?"

She always asked the irrelevant question. It didn't matter in terms of the strategy of the case whether the defendant "did it" or not. What mattered was the evidence against him — the proof — and if and how it could be neutralized. My job was to bury the proof, to color the proof a shade of gray. Gray was the color of reasonable doubt.

But the question of did he or didn't he always seemed to matter to her.

"Who knows, Lorna? That's not the question. The question is whether or not he's a paying customer. The answer is, I think so."

"Well, let me know if you need any — oh, there's one other thing."

"What?"

"Sticks called and said he owes you four hundred dollars next time he sees you."

"Yeah, he does."

"You're doing pretty good today."

"I'm not complaining."

We said our good-byes on a friendly note, the dispute over Gloria Dayton seemingly forgotten for the moment. Probably the security that comes with knowing money is coming in and a high-paying client is on the hook made Lorna feel a bit better about my working some cases for free. I wondered, though, if she'd have minded so much if I was defending a drug dealer for free instead of a prostitute. Lorna and I had shared a short and sweet marriage, with both of us quickly finding out that we had moved too quickly while rebounding from divorces. We ended it, remained friends, and she continued to work with me, not for me. The only time I felt uncomfortable about the arrangement was when she acted like a wife again and second-guessed my choice of client and who and what I charged or didn't charge.

Feeling confident in the way I had handled Lorna, I called the DA's office in Van Nuys next. I asked for Margaret McPherson and caught her eating at her desk.

"I just wanted to say I'm sorry about this morning. I know you wanted the case."

"Well, you probably need it more than me. He must be a paying customer if he's got C. C. Dobbs carrying the roll behind him."

By that she was referring to a roll of toilet paper. High-priced family lawyers were usually seen by prosecutors as nothing more than ass wipers for the rich and famous.

"Yeah, I could use one like him — the paying client, not the wiper. It's been a while since I had a franchise."

"Well, you didn't get as lucky a few minutes ago," she whispered into the phone. "The case was reassigned to Ted Minton."

"Never heard of him."

"He's one of Smithson's young guns. Just brought him in from downtown, where he was filing simple possession cases. He didn't see the inside of a courtroom until he came up here."

John Smithson was the ambitious head deputy in charge of the Van Nuys Division. He was a better politician than a prosecutor and had parlayed that skill into a quick climb over other more experienced deputies to the division chief's post. Maggie McPherson was among those he'd passed by. Once he was in the slot, he started building a staff of young prosecutors who did not feel slighted and were loyal to him for giving them a shot.

"This guy's never been in court?" I asked, not understanding how going up against a trial rookie could be unlucky, as Maggie had indicated.

"He's had a few trials up here but always with a babysitter. Roulet will be his first time flying solo. Smithson thinks he's giving him a slam dunk."

I imagined her sitting in her cubicle, probably not far from where my new opponent was sitting in his.

"I don't get it, Mags. If this guy's green, why wasn't I lucky?"

"Because these guys Smithson picks are all cracked out of the same mold. They're arrogant assholes. They think they can do no wrong and what's more . . ."

She lowered her voice even more.

"They don't play fair. And the word on Minton is that he's a cheater. Watch yourself, Haller. Better yet, watch him."

"Well, thanks for the heads-up."

But she wasn't finished.

"A lot of these new people just don't get it. They don't see it as a calling. To them it's not about justice. It's just a game — a batting average. They like to keep score and to see how far it will get them in the office. In fact, they're all just like junior Smithsons."

A calling. It was her sense of calling that ultimately cost us our marriage. On an intellectual level she could deal with being married to a man who worked the other side of the aisle. But when it came down to the reality of what we did, we were lucky to have lasted the eight years we had managed. *Honey, how was your day? Oh, I got a guy who murdered his roommate with an ice pick a seven-year deal. And you? Oh, I put a guy away for five years because he stole a car stereo to feed his habit . . .* It just didn't work. Four years in, a daughter arrived, but through no fault of her own, she only kept us going another four years.

Still, I didn't regret a thing about it. I cherished my daughter. She was the only thing that was really good about my life, that I could be proud of. I think deep down, the reason I didn't see her enough — that I was chasing cases instead of her — was because I felt unworthy of her. Her mother was a hero. She put bad people in jail. What could I tell her was good and holy about what I did, when I had long ago lost the thread of it myself?

"Hey, Haller, are you there?"

"Yeah, Mags, I'm here. What are you eating today?"

"Just the oriental salad from downstairs. Nothing special. Where are you?"

"Heading downtown. Listen, tell Hayley I'll see her this Saturday. I'll make a plan. We'll do something special."

"You really mean that? I don't want to get her hopes up."

I felt something lift inside me, the idea that my daughter would get her hopes up about seeing me. The one thing Maggie never did was run me down with Hayley. She wasn't the kind that would do that. I always admired that.

"Yes, I'm sure," I said.

"Great, I'll tell her. Let me know when you're coming or if I can drop her off."

"Okay."

I hesitated. I wanted to talk to her longer but there was nothing else to say. I finally said good-bye and closed the phone. In a few minutes we broke free of the bottleneck. I looked out the window and saw no accident. I saw nobody with a flat tire and no highway patrol cruiser parked on the shoulder. I saw nothing that explained what had caused the traffic tie-up. It was often like that. Freeway traffic in Los Angeles was as mysterious as marriage. It moved and flowed, then stalled and stopped for no easily explainable reason.

I am from a family of attorneys. My father, my half brother, a niece and a nephew. My father was a famous lawyer in a time when there was no cable television and no Court TV. He was the dean of criminal law in L.A. for almost three decades. From Mickey Cohen to the Manson girls, his clients always made the headlines. I was just an afterthought in his life, a surprise visitor to his second marriage to a B-level movie actress known for her exotic Latin looks but not her acting skills. The mix gave me my black Irish looks. My father was old when I came, so he was gone before I was old enough to really know him or talk to him about the calling of the law. He only left me his name. Mickey Haller, the legal legend. It still opened doors.

But my older brother — the half brother from the first marriage — told me that my father used to talk to him about the practice of law and criminal defense. He used to say he would defend the devil himself just as long as he could cover the fee. The only big-time case and client he ever turned down was Sirhan Sirhan. He told my brother that he had liked Bobby Kennedy too much to defend his killer, no matter how much he believed in the ideal that the accused deserved the best and most vigorous defense possible.

Growing up I read all the books about my father and his cases. I admired the skill and vigor and strategies he brought to the defense table. He was damn good and it made me proud to carry his name. But the law was different now. It was grayer. Ideals had long been downgraded to notions. Notions were optional.

My cell phone rang and I checked the screen before answering.

"What's up, Val?"

"We're getting him out. They already took him back to the jail and we're processing him out now."

"Dobbs went with the bond?"

"You got it."

I could hear the delight in his voice.

"Don't be so giddy. You sure he's not a runner?"

"I'm never sure. I'm going to make him wear a bracelet. I lose him, I lose my house."

I realized that what I had taken as delight at the windfall that a million-dollar bond would bring to Valenzuela was actually nervous energy. Valenzuela would be taut as a wire until this one was over, one way or the other. Even if the court had not ordered it, Valenzuela was going to put an electronic tracking bracelet on Roulet's ankle. He was taking no chances with this guy.

"Where's Dobbs?"

"Back at my office, waiting. I'll bring Roulet over as soon as he's out. Shouldn't be too much longer."

"Is Maisy over there?"

"Yeah, she's there."

"Okay, I'm going to call over."

I ended the call and hit the speed-dial combo for Liberty Bail Bonds. Valenzuela's receptionist and assistant answered.

"Maisy, it's Mick. Can you put Mr. Dobbs on the line?"

"Sure thing, Mick."

A few seconds later Dobbs got on the line. He seemed put out by something. Just in the way he said, "This is Cecil Dobbs."

"This is Mickey Haller. How is it going over there?"

"Well, if you consider I am letting my duties to other clients slide while I sit here and read year-old magazines, not good."

"You don't carry a cell phone to do business?"

"I do. But that's not the point. My clients aren't cell phone people. They're face-to-face people."

"I see. Well, the good news is, I hear our boy is about to be released."

"Our boy?"

"Mr. Roulet. Valenzuela should have him out inside the hour. I am about to go into a client conference, but as I said before, I am free in the afternoon. Do you want to meet to go over the case with our mutual client or do you want me to take it from here?"

"No, Mrs. Windsor has insisted that I monitor this closely. In fact, she may choose to be there as well."

"I don't mind the meet-and-greet with Mrs. Windsor, but when it comes down to talking about the case, it's just going to be the defense team. That can include you but not the mother. Okay?"

"I understand. Let's say four o'clock at my office. I will have Louis there."

"I'll be there."

"My firm employs a crack investigator. I'll ask him to join us."

"That won't be necessary, Cecil. I have my own and he's already on the job. We'll see you at four."

I ended the call before Dobbs could start a debate about which investigator to use. I had to be careful that Dobbs didn't control the investigation, preparation and strategy of the case. Monitoring was one thing. But I was Louis Roulet's attorney now. Not him.

When I called Raul Levin next, he told me he was already on his way to the LAPD Van Nuys Division to pick up a copy of the arrest report.

"Just like that?" I asked.

"No, not just like that. In a way, you could say it took me twenty years to get this report."

I understood. Levin's connections, procured over time and experience, traded over trust and favors, had come through for him. No wonder he charged five hundred dollars a day when he could get it. I told him about the meeting at four and he said he would be there and would be ready to furnish us with the law enforcement view of the case.

The Lincoln pulled to a stop when I closed the phone. We were in front of the Twin Towers jail facility. It wasn't even ten years old but the smog was beginning to permanently stain its sand-colored walls a dreary gray. It was a sad and forbidding place that I spent too much time in. I opened the car door and got out to go inside once again.

SEVEN

There was an attorney's check-in window that allowed me to bypass the long line of visitors waiting to get in to see loved ones incarcerated in one of the towers. When I told the window deputy whom I wanted to see, he tapped the name into the computer and never said anything about Gloria Dayton being in medical and unavailable. He printed out a visitor's pass which he slid into the plastic frame of a clip-on badge and told me to put it on and wear it at all times in the jail. He then told me to step away from the window and wait for an attorney escort.

"It will be a few minutes," he said.

I knew from prior experience that my cell phone did not get a signal inside the jail and that if I stepped outside to use it, I might miss my escort and then have to go through the whole sign-in process again. So I stayed put and watched the faces of the people who came to visit those being held inside. Most were black and brown. Most had the look of routine on their faces. They all probably knew the ropes here much better than I.

After twenty minutes a large woman in a deputy's uniform came into the waiting area and collected me. I knew that she had not gotten into the sheriff's department with her current dimensions. She was at least a hundred pounds overweight and seemed to struggle just to carry it while walking. But I also knew that once somebody was in, it was hard to get them out. About the best this one could do if there was a jail break was lean up against a door to keep it closed.

"Sorry it took so long," she told me as we waited between the double steel doors of a mantrap in the women's tower. "I had to go find her, make sure we still had her."

She signaled that everything was all right to a camera above the next door and its lock clacked open. She pushed through.

"She was up in medical getting fixed up," she said.

"Fixed up?"

I wasn't aware of the jail having a drug-treatment program that included "fixing up" addicts.

"Yeah, she got hurt," the deputy said. "Got a little banged up in a scuffle. She can tell you."

I let the questions go at that. In a way, I was relieved that the medical delay was not due — not directly, at least — to drug ingestion or addiction.

The deputy led me to the attorney room, which I had been in many times before with many different clients. The vast majority of my clients were men and I didn't discriminate, but the truth was I hated representing women who were incarcerated. From prostitutes to murderers — and I had defended them all — there was something pitiful about a woman in jail. I had found that almost all of the time, their crimes could be traced back to men. Men who took advantage of them, abused them, deserted them, hurt them. This is not to say they were not responsible for their actions or that some of them did not deserve the punishments they received. There were predators among the female ranks that easily rivaled those among the males. But, even still, the women I saw in jail seemed so different from the men in the other tower. The men still lived by wiles and strength. The women had nothing left by the time they locked the door on them.

The visiting area was a row of booths in which an attorney could sit on one side and confer with a client who sat on the other side, separated by an eighteen-inch sheet of clear Plexiglas. A deputy sat in a glassed-in booth at the end of the room and observed but supposedly didn't listen. If paperwork needed to be passed to the client, it was held up for the booth deputy to see and approve.

I was led to a booth and my escort left me. I then waited another ten minutes before the same deputy appeared on the other side of the Plexiglas with Gloria Dayton. Immediately, I saw that my client had a swelling around her left eye and a single butterfly stitch over a small laceration just below her widow's peak. Gloria Dayton had jet-black hair and olive skin. She had once been beautiful. The first time I represented her, seven or eight years before, she was beautiful. The kind of beauty that leaves you stunned at the fact she was selling it, that she had decided that selling herself to strangers was her best or only option. Now she just looked hard to me. The lines of her face were taut. She had visited surgeons who were not the best, and anyway, there was nothing they could do about eyes that had seen too much.

"Mickey Mantle," she said. "You're going to bat for me again?"

She said it in her little girl's voice that I suppose her regular clients enjoyed and responded to. It just sounded strange to me, coming from that tightly drawn mouth and face with eyes that were as hard and had as much life in them as marbles.

She always called me Mickey Mantle, even though she was born after the great slugger had long retired and probably knew little about him or the game he played. It was just a name to her. I guess the alternative would have been to call me Mickey Mouse, and I probably wouldn't have liked it much.

"I'm going to try, Gloria," I told her. "What happened to your face? How'd you get hurt?"

She made a dismissive gesture with her hand.

"There was a little disagreement with some of the girls in my dorm."

"About what?"

"Just girl stuff."

"Are you getting high in there?"

She looked indignant and then she tried putting a pouting look on her face.

"No, I'm not."

I studied her. She seemed straight. Maybe she wasn't getting high and that was not what the fight had been about.

"I don't want to stay in here, Mickey," she said in her real voice.

"I don't blame you. I don't like being in here myself and I get to leave."

I immediately regretted saying the last part and reminding her of her situation. She didn't seem to notice.

"You think maybe you could get me into one of those pretrial whatchamacallits where I can get myself right?"

I thought it was interesting how addicts call both getting high and getting sober the same thing — *getting right*.

"The problem is, Gloria, we got into a pretrial intervention program last time, remember? And it obviously didn't work. So this time I don't know. They only have so many spaces in those things and the judges and prosecutors don't like sending people back when they didn't take advantage of it in the first place."

"What do you mean?" she protested. "I took advantage. I went the whole damn time."

"That's right. That was good. But then after it was over, you went right back to doing what you do and here we are again. They wouldn't call that a success, Gloria. I have to be honest with you. I don't think I can get you into a program this time. I think you have to be ready for them to be tougher this time."

Her eyes drooped.

"I can't do it," she said in a small voice.

"Look, they have programs in the jail. You'll get straight and come out with another chance to start again clean."

She shook her head; she looked lost.

"You've had a long run but it can't go on," I said. "If I were you I'd think about getting out of this place. L.A., I mean. Go somewhere and start again."

She looked up at me with anger in her eyes.

"Start over and do what? Look at me. What am I going to do? Get married, have kids and plant flowers?"

I didn't have an answer and neither did she.

"Let's talk about that when the time comes. For now, let's worry about your case. Tell me what happened."

"What always happens. I screened the guy and it all checked out. He looked legit. But he was a cop and that was that."

"You went to him?"

She nodded.

"The Mondrian. He had a suite — that's another thing. The cops usually don't have suites. They don't have the budget."

"Didn't I tell you how stupid it would be to take coke with you when you work? And if a guy even asks you to bring coke with you, then you know he's a cop."

"I know all of that and he didn't ask me to bring it. I forgot I had it, okay? I got it from a guy I went to see right before him. What was I supposed to do, leave it in the car for the Mondrian valets to take?"

"What guy did you get it from?"

"A guy at the Travelodge on Santa Monica. I did him earlier and he offered it to me, you know, instead of cash. Then after I left I checked my messages and I had the call from the guy at the Mondrian. So I called him back, set it up and went straight there. I forgot I had the stuff in my purse."

Nodding, I leaned forward. I was seeing a glimmer on this one, a possibility.

"This guy in the Travelodge, who was he?"

"I don't know, just some guy who saw my ad on the site."

She arranged her liaisons through a website which carried photos, phone numbers and e-mail addresses of escorts.

"Did he say where he was from?"

"No. He was Mexican or Cuban or something. He was sweaty from using."

"When he gave you the coke, did you see if he had any more?"

"Yeah, he had some. I was hoping for a call back . . . but I don't think I was what he was expecting."

Last time I had checked her ad on LA-Darlings.com to see if she was still in the life, the photos she'd put up were at least five years old and looked ten. I imagined that it could lead to some disappointment when her clients opened their hotel room doors.

"How much did he have?"

"I don't know. I just knew he had to have more because if it was all he had left, he wouldn't have given it to me."

It was a good point. The glimmer was getting brighter.

"Did you screen him?"

"'Course."

"What, his driver's license?"

"No, his passport. He said he didn't have a license."

"What was his name?"

"Hector something."

"Come on, Gloria, Hector what? Try to re—"

"Hector something Moya. It was three names. But I remember 'Moya' because I said 'Hector give me Moya' when he brought out the coke."

"Okay, that's good."

"You think it's something you can use to help me?"

"Maybe, depending on who this guy is. If he's a trade-up."

"I want to get out."

"Okay, listen, Gloria. I'm going to go see the prosecutor and see what she's thinking and see what I can do for you. They've got you in here on twenty-five thousand dollars' bail."

"What?"

"It's higher than usual because of the drugs. You don't have twenty-five hundred for the bond, do you?"

She shook her head. I could see the muscles in her face constricting. I knew what was coming.

"Could you front it to me, Mickey? I promise I'd —"

"I can't do that, Gloria. That's a rule and I could get in trouble if I broke it. You're going to have to be in here overnight and they'll take you over to arraignment in the morning."

"No," she said, more like a moan than a word.

"I know it's going to be tough but you have to nut it out. And you have to be straight in the morning when you come into court or I'll have no shot at lowering your bond and getting you out. So none of that shit they trade in here. You got that?"

She raised her arms over her head, almost as if she was protecting herself from falling debris. She squeezed her hands into tight fists of dread. It would be a long night ahead.

"You've got to get me out tomorrow."

"I'll do my best."

I waved to the deputy in the observation booth. I was ready to go.

"One last thing," I said. "Do you remember what room the guy at the Travelodge was in?"

She thought a moment before answering.

"Yeah, it's an easy one. Three thirty-three."

"Okay, thanks. I'm going to see what I can do."

She stayed sitting when I stood up. Soon the escort deputy came back and told me I would have to wait while she first took Gloria back to her dorm. I checked my watch. It was almost two. I hadn't eaten and was getting a headache. I also had only two hours to get to Leslie Faire in the DA's office to talk about Gloria and then out to Century City for the case meeting with Roulet and Dobbs.

"Isn't there somebody else who can take me out of here?" I said irritably. "I need to get to court."

"Sorry, sir, that's how it works."

"Well, please hurry."

"I always do."

Fifteen minutes later I realized that my complaining to the deputy had only succeeded in her making sure she left me waiting even longer than had I just kept my mouth shut. Like a restaurant customer who gets the cold soup he sent back to the kitchen returned hot with the piquant taste of saliva in it, I should have known better.

On the quick drive over to the Criminal Courts Building I called Raul Levin. He was back at his home office in Glendale, looking through the police reports on the Roulet investigation and arrest. I asked him to put it aside to make some calls. I wanted to see what he could find out about the man in room 333 at the Travelodge on Santa Monica. I told him I needed the information yesterday. I knew he had sources and ways of running the name Hector Moya. I just didn't want to know who or what they were. I was only interested in what he got.

As Earl pulled to a stop in front of the CCB, I told him that while I was inside he should take a run over to Philippe's to get us roast beef sandwiches. I'd eat mine on my way out to Century City. I passed a twenty-dollar bill over the seat to him and got out.

While waiting for an elevator in the always crowded lobby of the CCB, I popped a Tylenol from my briefcase and hoped it would head off the migraine I felt coming on from lack of food. It took me ten minutes to get to the ninth floor and another fifteen waiting for Leslie Faire to grant me an audience. I didn't mind the wait, though, because Raul Levin called back just before I was allowed entrance. If Faire had seen me right away, I wouldn't have gone in with the added ammunition.

Levin had told me that the man in room 333 at the Travelodge had checked in under the name Gilberto Garcia. The motel did not require identification, since he paid cash in advance for a week and put a fifty-dollar deposit on phone charges. Levin had also run a trace on the name I had given him and came up with Hector Arrande Moya, a Colombian wanted on a fugitive warrant issued after he fled San Diego when a federal grand jury handed down an indictment for drug trafficking. It added up to real good stuff and I planned to put it to use with the prosecutor.

Faire was in an office shared with three other prosecutors. Each had a desk in a corner. Two were gone, probably in court, but a man I didn't know sat at the desk in the corner opposite Faire. I had to speak to her with him in earshot. I hated doing this because I found that the prosecutor I was dealing with in these situations would often play to the others in the room, trying to sound tough and shrewd, sometimes at the expense of my client.

I pulled a chair away from one of the empty desks and brought it over to sit down. I skipped the pleasantries because there weren't any and got right to the point because I was hungry and didn't have a lot of time.

"You filed on Gloria Dayton this morning," I said. "She's mine. I want to see what we can do about it."

"Well, we can plead her guilty and she can do one to three years at Frontera."

She said it matter-of-factly with a smile that was more of a smirk.

"I was thinking of PTI."

"I was thinking she already got a bite out of that apple and she spit it out. No way."

"Look, how much coke did she have on her, a couple grams?"

"It's still illegal, no matter how much she had. Gloria Dayton has had numerous opportunities to rehabilitate herself and avoid prison. But she's run out of chances."

She turned to her desk, opened a file and glanced at the top sheet.

"Nine arrests in just the last five years," she said. "This is her third drug charge and she's never spent more than three days in jail. Forget PTI. She's got to learn sometime and this is that time. I'm not open to discussion on this. If she pleads, I'll give her one to three. If she doesn't, I'll go get a verdict and she takes her chances with the judge at sentencing. I will ask for the max on it."

I nodded. It was going about the way I thought it would with Faire. A one-to-three-year sentence would likely result in a nine-month stay in the slam. I knew Gloria Dayton could do it and maybe should do it. But I still had a card to play.

"What if she had something to trade?"

Faire snorted like it was a joke.

"Like what?"

"A hotel room number where a major dealer is doing business."

"Sounds a little vague."

It was vague but I could tell by the change in her voice she was interested. Every prosecutor likes to trade up.

"Call your drug guys. Ask them to run the name Hector Arrande Moya on the box. He's a Colombian. I can wait."

She hesitated. She clearly didn't like being manipulated by a defense attorney, especially when another prosecutor was in earshot. But the hook was already set.

She turned again to her desk and made a call. I listened to one side of the conversation, her telling someone to give her a background check on Moya. She waited awhile and then listened to the response. She thanked whoever it was she had called and hung up. She took her time turning back to me.

"Okay," she said. "What does she want?"

I had it ready.

"She wants a PTI slot. All charges dropped upon successful completion. She doesn't testify against the guy and her name is on no documents. She simply gives the hotel and room number where he's at and your people do the rest."

"They'll need to make a case. She's got to testify. I take it the two grams she had came from this guy. Then she has to tell us about it."

"No, she doesn't. Whoever you just talked to told you there's already a warrant. You can take him down for that."

She worked it over for a few moments, moving her jaw back and forth as if tasting the deal and deciding whether to eat more. I knew what the stumble was. The deal was a trade-up but it was a trade-up to a federal case. That meant that they would bust the guy and the feds would take over. No prosecutorial glory for Leslie Faire — unless she had designs on jumping over to the U.S. Attorney's Office one day.

"The feds will love you for this," I said, trying to wedge into her conscience. "He's a bad guy and he'll probably check out soon and the chance to get him will be lost."

She looked at me like I was a bug.

"Don't try that with me, Haller."

"Sorry."

She went back to her thinking. I tried again.

"Once you have his location, you could always try to set up a buy."

"Would you be quiet, please? I can't think."

I raised my hands in surrender and shut up.

"All right," she finally said. "Let me talk to my boss. Give me your number and I'll call you later. But I'll tell you right now, if we go for it, she'll have to go to a lockdown program. Something at County-USC. We're not going to waste a residency slot on her."

I thought about it and nodded. County-USC was a hospital with a jail wing where injured, sick, and addicted inmates were treated. What she was offering was a program where Gloria Dayton could be treated for her addiction and released upon completion. She would not face any charges or further time in jail or prison.

"Fine with me," I said.

I looked at my watch. I had to get going.

"Our offer is good until first appearance tomorrow," I said. "After that I'll call the DEA and see if they want to deal directly. Then it will be taken out of your hands."

She looked indignantly at me. She knew that if I got a deal with the feds, they would squash her. Head to head, the feds always trumped the state. I stood up to go and put a business card down on her desk.

"Don't try to back-door me, Haller," she said. "If it goes sideways on you, I'll take it out on your client."

I didn't respond. I pushed the chair I had borrowed back to its desk. She then dropped the threat with her next line.

"Anyway, I'm sure we can handle this on a level that makes everybody happy."

I looked back at her as I got to the office door.

"Everybody except for Hector Moya," I said.

EIGHT

The law offices of Dobbs and Delgado were on the twenty-ninth floor of one of the twin towers that created the signature skyline of Century City. I was right on time but everyone was already gathered in a conference room with a long polished wood table and a wall of glass that framed a western exposure stretching across Santa Monica to the Pacific and the charter islands beyond. It was a clear day and I could see Catalina and Anacapa out there at the very edge of the world. Because the sun was going down and seemed to be almost at eye level, a film had been rolled down over the window to cut the glare. It was like the room had sunglasses on.

And so did my client. Louis Roulet sat at the head of the table with a pair of black-framed Ray-Bans on. Out of his gray jail jumpsuit, he now wore a dark brown suit over a pale silk T-shirt. He looked like a confident and cool young real estate executive, not the scared boy I saw in the holding pen in the courthouse.

To Roulet's left sat Cecil Dobbs and next to him was a well-preserved, well-coiffed and bejeweled woman I assumed to be Roulet's mother. I also assumed that Dobbs hadn't told her that the meeting would not include her.

To Roulet's right the first seat was empty and waiting for me. In the seat next to it sat my investigator, Raul Levin, with a closed file in front of him on the table.

Dobbs introduced Mary Alice Windsor to me. She shook my hand with a strong grip. I sat down and Dobbs explained that she would be paying for her son's defense and had agreed to the terms I had outlined earlier. He slid an envelope across the table to me. I looked inside and saw a check for sixty thousand dollars with my name on it. It was the retainer I had asked for, but I had expected only half of it in the initial payment. I had made more in total on cases before but it was still the largest single check I had ever received.

The check was drawn on the account of Mary Alice Windsor. The bank was solid gold — First National of Beverly Hills. I closed the envelope and slid it back across the table.

"I'm going to need that to come from Louis," I said, looking at Mrs. Windsor. "I don't care if you give him the money and then he gives it to me. But I want the check I get to come from Louis. I work for him and that's got to be clear from the start."

I knew this was different from even my practice of that morning — accepting payment from a third party. But it was a control issue. One look across the table at Mary Alice Windsor and C. C. Dobbs and I knew I had to make sure that they knew this was my case to manage, to win or to lose.

I wouldn't have thought it could happen but Mary Windsor's face hardened. For some reason she reminded me of an old grandfather clock, her face flat and square.

"Mother," Roulet said, heading something off before it started. "It's all right. I will write him a check. I should be able to cover it until you give me the money."

She looked from me to her son and then back to me.

"Very well," she said.

"Mrs. Windsor," I said. "Your support for your son is very important. And I don't mean just the financial end of things. If we are not successful in getting these charges dropped and we choose the alternative of trial, it will be very important for you to show your support in public ways."

"Don't be silly," she said. "I will back him come hell or high water. These ridiculous charges must be removed, and that woman . . . she isn't going to get a penny from us."

"Thank you, Mother," Roulet said.

"Yes, thank you," I said. "I will be sure to inform you, probably through Mr. Dobbs, where and when you are needed. It's good to know you will be there for your son."

I said nothing else and waited. It didn't take her long to realize she had been dismissed.

"But you don't want me here right now, is that it?"

"That's right. We need to discuss the case and it is best and most appropriate for Louis to do this only with his defense team. The attorney-client privilege does not cover anyone else. You could be compelled to testify against your son."

"But if I leave, how will Louis get home?"

"I have a driver. I will get him home."

She looked at Dobbs, hoping he might have higher standing and be able to overrule me. Dobbs smiled and stood up so he could pull her chair back. She finally let him and stood up to go.

"Very well," she said. "Louis, I will see you at dinner."

Dobbs walked her through the door of the conference room and I saw them exchange conversation in the hallway. I couldn't hear what was said. Then she left and Dobbs came back, closing the door.

I went through some preliminaries with Roulet, telling him he would have to be arraigned in two weeks and submit a plea. He would have the opportunity at that time to put the state on notice that he was not waiving his right to a speedy trial.

"That's the first choice we have to make," I said. "Whether you want this thing to drag out or you want to move quickly and put the pressure on the state."

"What are the options?" Dobbs asked.

I looked at him and then back at Roulet.

"I'll be very honest with you," I said. "When I have a client who is not incarcerated, my inclination is to drag it out. It's the client's freedom that is on the line — why not get the most of it before the hammer comes down."

"You're talking about a guilty client," Roulet said.

"On the other hand," I said, "if the state's case is weak, then delaying things only gives them time to strengthen their hand. You see, time is our only leverage at this point. If we refuse to waive our right to a speedy trial, it puts a lot of pressure on the prosecutor."

"I didn't do what they are saying I did," Roulet said. "I don't want to waste any time. I want this shit behind me."

"If we refuse to waive, then theoretically they must put you on trial within sixty days of arraignment. The reality is that it gets pushed back when they move to a preliminary hearing. In a prelim a judge hears the evidence and decides if there is enough there to warrant a trial. It's a rubber-stamp process. The judge will hold you over for trial, you will be arraigned again and the clock is reset to sixty days."

"I can't believe this," Roulet said. "This is going to last forever."

"We could always waive the prelim, too. It would really force their hand. The case has been reassigned to a young prosecutor. He's pretty new to felonies. It may be the way to go."

"Wait a minute," Dobbs said. "Isn't a preliminary hearing useful in terms of seeing what the state's evidence is?"

"Not really," I said. "Not anymore. The legislature tried to streamline things a while back and they turned the prelim into a rubber stamp because they relaxed hearsay rules. Now you usually just get the case cop on the stand and he tells the judge what everybody said. The defense usually doesn't get a look at any witnesses other than the cop. If you ask me, the best strategy is to force the prosecution to put up or shut up. Make them go sixty days from first arraignment."

"I like that idea," Roulet said. "I want this over with as soon as possible."

I nodded. He had said it as though a not-guilty verdict was a foregone conclusion.

"Well, maybe it doesn't even get to a trial," Dobbs said. "If these charges don't hold muster —"

"The DA is not going to drop this," I said, cutting him off. "Usually, the cops overcharge and then the DA cuts the charges back. That didn't happen here. Instead, the DA upped the charges. That tells me two things. One is that they believe the case is solid and, two, they upped the charges so that when we start to negotiate they will deal from a higher ground."

"You're talking about a plea bargain?" Roulet asked.

"Yeah, a disposition."

"Forget it, no plea bargain. I'm not going to jail for something I didn't do."

"It might not mean going to jail. You have a clean rec—"

"I don't care if it means I could walk. I'm not going to plead guilty to something I didn't do. If that is going to be a problem for you, then we need to part company right here."

I looked closely at him. Almost all of my clients make protestations of innocence at one point along the way. Especially if it is our first case together. But Roulet's words came with a fervor and directness I hadn't seen in a long time. Liars falter. They look away. Roulet's eyes were holding mine like magnets.

"There is also the civil liability to consider," Dobbs added. "A guilty plea will allow this woman to —"

"I understand all of that," I said, cutting him off again. "I think we're all getting ahead of ourselves here. I only wanted to give Louis a general idea of the way this was going to go. We don't have to make any moves or any hard-and-fast decisions for at least a couple of weeks. We just need to know at the arraignment how we are going to play it."

"Louis took a year of law at UCLA," Dobbs said. "I think he has baseline knowledge of the situation."

Roulet nodded.

"Okay, good," I said. "Then let's just get to it. Louis, let's start with you. Your mother said she expects to see you at dinner. Do you live at home? I mean at her home?"

"I live in the guesthouse. She lives in the main house."

"Anyone else live on the premises?"

"The maid. In the main house."

"No siblings, boyfriends, girlfriends?"

"That's it."

"And you work at your mother's firm?"

"More like I run it. She's not there too much anymore."

"Where were you Saturday night?"

"Satur— you mean last night, don't you?"

"No, I mean Saturday night. Start there."

"Saturday night I didn't do anything. I stayed home and watched television."

"By yourself?"

"That's right."

"What did you watch?"

"A DVD. An old movie called *The Conversation*. Coppola."

"So nobody was with you or saw you. You just watched the movie and then went to bed."

"Basically."

"Basically. Okay. That brings us to Sunday morning. What did you do yesterday during the day?"

"I played golf at Riviera, my usual foursome. Started at ten and finished at four. I came home, showered and changed, had dinner at my mother's house — you want to know what we had?"

"That won't be necessary. But later on I probably will need the names of the guys you played golf with. What happened after dinner?"

"I told my mother I was going to my place but instead I went out."

I noticed that Levin had started taking notes on a small notebook he had taken out of a pocket.

"What kind of car do you drive?"

"I have two, an oh-four Range Rover I use for taking clients around in and an oh-one Carrera I use for myself."

"You used the Porsche last night, then?"

"That's right."

"Where'd you go?"

"I went over the hill and down into the Valley."

He said it as though it was a risky move for a Beverly Hills boy to descend into the working-class neighborhoods of the San Fernando Valley.

"Where did you go?" I asked.

"Ventura Boulevard. I had a drink at Nat's North and then I went down the street a ways to Morgan's and I had a drink there, too."

"Those places are pickup bars, wouldn't you say?"

"Yes. That's why I went to them."

He was matter-of-fact about it and I appreciated his honesty.

"So you were looking for someone. A woman. Anyone in particular, someone you knew?"

"No one in particular. I was looking to get laid, pure and simple."

"What happened at Nat's North?"

"What happened was that it was a slow night, so I left. I didn't even finish my drink."

"You go there often? Do the bartenders know you?"

"Yeah, they know me. A girl named Paula was working last night."

"Okay, so it wasn't working for you there and you left. You drove down to Morgan's. Why Morgan's?"

"It's just another place I go."

"They know you there?"

"They should. I'm a good tipper. Last night Denise and Janice were behind the bar. They know me."

I turned to Levin.

"Raul, what is the victim's name?"

Levin opened his file to pull out a police report but answered before having to look it up.

"Regina Campo. Friends call her Reggie. Twenty-six years old. She told police she's an actress working as a telephone solicitor."

"And hoping to retire soon," Dobbs said.

I ignored him.

"Louis, did you know Reggie Campo before last night?" I asked.

Roulet shrugged.

"Sort of. I'd seen her around the bar scene. But I had never been with her before. I'd never even spoken to her."

"Had you ever tried?"

"No, I never could really get to her. She always seemed to be with someone or more than one person. I don't like to have to penetrate the crowd, you know? My style is to look for the singles."

"What was different last night?"

"Last night she came to me, that was what was different."

"Tell us about it."

"Nothing to tell. I was at the bar at Morgan's, minding my own business, having a look at the possibilities, and she was at the other end and she was with some guy. So she wasn't even on my radar because she looked like she was already taken, you know?"

"Uh-huh, so what happened?"

"Well, after a while the guy she was with gets up to go take a leak or go outside for a smoke, and as soon as he's gone she gets up and slides on down the bar to me and asks if I'm interested. I said I was but what about the guy she's already with? She says don't worry about him, he'll be out the door by ten and then she's free the rest of the night. She wrote her address down for me and said to come by after ten. I told her I'd be there."

"What did she write the address down on?"

"A napkin, but the answer to your next question is no, I don't still have it. I memorized the address and threw out the napkin. I work in real estate. I can remember addresses."

"About what time was this?"

"I don't know."

"Well, she said come by at ten. Did you look at your watch at any point to see how long you would have to wait until then?"

"I think it was between eight and nine. As soon as the guy came back in they left."

"When did you leave the bar?"

"I stayed for a few minutes and then I left. I made one more stop before I went to her place."

"Where was that?"

"Well, she lived in an apartment in Tarzana so I went up to the Lamplighter. It was on the way."

"Why?"

"Well, you know, I wanted to see what the possibilities were. You know, see if there was something better out there, something I didn't have to wait around for or . . ."

"Or what?"

He still didn't finish the thought.

"Take seconds on?"

He nodded.

"Okay, so who'd you talk to at the Lamplighter? Where is that, by the way?"

It was the only place so far I was unfamiliar with.

"It's on Ventura near White Oak. I didn't really talk to anybody. It was crowded but there really wasn't anybody I was interested in there."

"The bartenders know you there?"

"No, not really. I don't go there all that much."

"You usually get lucky before you hit the third option?"

"Nah, I usually just give up after two."

I nodded just to buy a little time to think about what else to ask before we got to what happened at the victim's house.

"How long were you at the Lamplighter?"

"About an hour, I'd say. Maybe a little less."

"At the bar? How many drinks?"

"Yeah, two drinks at the bar."

"How many drinks in all did you have last night before getting to Reggie Campo's apartment?"

"Um, four at the most. Over two, two and a half, hours. I left one drink untouched at Morgan's."

"What were you drinking?"

"Martinis. Gray Goose."

"Did you pay for any of these drinks in any of these places with a credit card?" Levin asked, offering his first question of the interview.

"No," Roulet said. "When I go out, I pay cash."

I looked at Levin and waited to see if he had anything else to ask. He knew more about the case than I did at this moment. I wanted to give him free rein to ask what he wanted. He looked at me and nodded. He was good to go.

"Okay," I said. "What time was it when you got to Reggie's place?"

"It was twelve minutes to ten. I looked at my watch. I wanted to make sure I didn't knock on her door early."

"So what did you do?"

"I waited in the parking lot. She said ten so I waited till ten."

"Did you see the guy she left Morgan's with come out?"

"Yeah, I saw him. He came out and left, then I went up."

"What kind of car was he driving?" Levin asked.

"A yellow Corvette," Roulet said. "It was a nineties version. I don't know the exact year."

Levin nodded. He was finished. I knew he was just trying to get a line on the man who had been in Campo's apartment before Roulet. I took the questioning back.

"So he leaves and you go in. What happens?"

"I go in the building and her place is on the second floor. I go up and knock and she answers and I walk in."

"Hold on a second. I don't want the shorthand. You went up? How? Stairs, elevator, what? Give us the details."

"Elevator."

"Anybody else on it? Anybody see you?"

Roulet shook his head. I signaled him to continue.

"She opened the door a crack, saw it was me and told me to come in. There was a hallway by the front door so it was kind of a tight space. I walked by her so she could close the door. That's how come she was behind me. And so I didn't see it coming. She had something. She hit me with something and I went down. It got black real fast."

I was silent while I thought about this, tried to picture it in my mind.

"So before a single thing happened, she just knocked you out?

She didn't say anything, yell anything, just sort of came up behind and *bang*."

"That's right."

"Okay, then what? What do you remember next?"

"It's still pretty foggy. I remember waking up and these two guys are sitting on me. Holding me down. And then the police came. And the paramedics. I was sitting up against the wall and my hands were cuffed and the paramedic put that ammonia or something under my nose and that's when I really came out of it."

"You were still in the apartment?"

"Yeah."

"Where was Reggie Campo?"

"She was sitting on the couch and another paramedic was working on her face and she was crying and telling the other cop that I had attacked her. All these lies. That I had surprised her at the door and punched her, that I said I was going to rape her and then kill her, all these things I didn't do. And I moved my arms so I could look down at my hands behind my back. I saw they had my hand in like a plastic bag and I could see blood on my hand, and that's when I knew the whole thing was a setup."

"What do you mean by that?"

"She put blood on my hand to make it look like I did it. But it was my left hand. I'm not left-handed. If I was going to punch somebody, I'd use my right hand."

He made a punching gesture with his right hand to illustrate this for me in case I didn't get it. I got up from my spot and paced over to the window. It now seemed like I was higher than the sun. I was looking down at the sunset. I felt uneasy about Roulet's story. It seemed so far-fetched that it might actually be true. And that bothered me. I was always worried that I might not recognize innocence. The possibility of it in my job was so rare that I operated with the fear that I wouldn't be ready for it when it came. That I would miss it.

"Okay, let's talk about this for a second," I said, still facing the sun. "You're saying that she puts blood on your hand to set you up. And she puts it on your left. But if she was going to set you up, wouldn't she put the blood on your right, since the vast majority of people out there are right-handed? Wouldn't she go with the numbers?"

I turned back to the table and got blank stares from everyone.

"You said she opened the door a crack and then let you in," I said. "Could you see her face?"

"Not all of it."

"What could you see?"

"Her eye. Her left eye."

"So did you ever see the right side of her face? Like when you walked in."

"No, she was behind the door."

"That's it!" Levin said excitedly. "She already had the injuries when he got there. She hid it from him, then he steps in and she clocks him. All the injuries were to the right side of her face and that dictated that she put the blood on his left hand."

I nodded as I thought about the logic of this. It seemed to make sense.

"Okay," I said, turning back to the window and continuing to pace. "I think that'll work. Now, Louis, you've told us you had seen this woman around the bar scene before but had never been with her. So, she was a stranger. Why would she do this, Louis? Why would she set you up like you say she did?"

"Money."

But it wasn't Roulet who answered. It had been Dobbs. I turned from the window and looked at him. He knew he had spoken out of turn but didn't seem to care.

"It's obvious," Dobbs said. "She wants money from him, from the family. The civil suit is probably being filed as we speak. The criminal charges are just the prelude to the suit, the demand for money. That's what she's really after."

I sat back down and looked at Levin, exchanging eye contact.

"I saw a picture of this woman in court today," I said. "Half her face was pulped. You are saying that's our defense, that she did that to herself?"

Levin opened his file and took out a piece of paper. It was a black-and-white photocopy of the evidence photograph Maggie McPherson had showed me in court. Reggie Campo's swollen face. Levin's source was good but not good enough to get him actual photos. He slid the photocopy across the table to Dobbs and Roulet.

"We'll get the real photos in discovery," I said. "They look worse, a lot worse, and if we go with your story, then the jury — that is, if this gets to a jury — is going to have to buy that she did that to herself."

I watched Roulet study the photocopy. If it had been he who attacked Reggie Campo, he showed no tell while studying his handiwork. He showed nothing at all.

"You know what?" I said. "I like to think I'm a good lawyer and a good persuader when it comes to juries. But even I'm having trouble believing myself with that story."

NINE

It was now Raul Levin's turn in the conference room. We'd spoken while I had been riding into Century City and eating bites of roast beef sandwich. I had plugged my cell into the car's speaker phone and told my driver to put his earbuds in. I'd bought him an iPod his first week on the job. Levin had given me the basics of the case, just enough to get me through the initial questioning of my client. Now Levin would take command of the room and go through the case, using the police and evidence reports to tear Louis Roulet's version of events to shreds, to show us what the prosecution would have on its side. At least initially I wanted Levin to be the one to do this because if there was going to be a good guy/bad guy aspect to the defense, I wanted to be the one Roulet would like and trust. I wanted to be the good guy.

Levin had his own notes in addition to the copies of the police reports he had gotten through his source. It was all material the defense was certainly entitled to and would receive through the discovery process, but usually it took weeks to get it through court channels instead of the hours it had taken Levin. As he spoke he held his eyes down on these documents.

"At ten-eleven last night the LAPD communications center received a nine-one-one emergency call from Regina Campo of seventeen-sixty White Oak Boulevard, apartment two-eleven. She reported an intruder had entered her home and attacked her. Patrol officers responded and arrived on the premises at ten-seventeen. Slow night, I guess, because that was pretty quick. Better than average response to a hot shot. Anyway, the patrol officers were met in the parking lot by Ms. Campo, who said she had fled the apartment after the attack. She informed the officers that two neighbors named Edward Turner and Ronald Atkins were in her apartment, holding the intruder. Officer Santos proceeded to the apartment, where he found the suspect intruder, later identified as Mr. Roulet, lying on the floor and in the command and control of Turner and Atkins."

"They were the two faggots who were sitting on me," Roulet said.

I looked at Roulet and saw the flash of anger quickly fade.

"The officers took custody of the suspect," Levin continued, as if he had not been interrupted. "Mr. Atkins —"

"Wait a minute," I said. "Where was he found on the floor? What room?"

"Doesn't say."

I looked at Roulet.

"It was the living room. It wasn't far from the front door. I never got that far in."

Levin wrote a note to himself before continuing.

"Mr. Atkins produced a folding knife with the blade open, which he said had been found on the floor next to the intruder. The officers handcuffed the suspect, and paramedics were called to treat both Campo and Roulet, who had a head laceration and slight concussion. Campo was transported to Holy Cross Medical Center for continued treatment and to be photographed by an evidence technician. Roulet was taken into custody and booked into Van Nuys jail. The premises of Ms. Campo's apartment were sealed for crime scene processing and the case was assigned to Detective Martin Booker of Valley Bureau detectives."

Levin spread more photocopies of the police photos of Regina Campo's injuries out on the table. There were front and profile shots of her face and two close-ups of bruising around her neck and a small puncture mark under her jaw. The copy quality was poor and I knew the photocopies weren't worthy of serious study. But I did notice that all the facial injuries were on the right side of Campo's face. Roulet had been correct about that. She had either been repeatedly punched by someone's left hand — or possibly her own right hand.

"These were taken at the hospital, where Ms. Campo also gave a statement to Detective Booker. In summary, she said she came home about eight-thirty Sunday night and was home alone when there was a knock at her door at about ten o'clock. Mr. Roulet represented himself as someone Ms. Campo knew and so she opened the door. Upon opening the door she was immediately struck by the intruder's fist and driven backwards into the apartment. The intruder entered and closed and locked the door. Ms. Campo attempted to defend herself but was struck at least twice more and driven to the floor."

"This is such bullshit!" Roulet yelled.

He slammed his fists down on the table and stood up, his seat rolling backwards and banging loudly into the glass window behind him.

"Hey, easy now!" Dobbs cautioned. "You break the window and it's like a plane. We all get sucked out of here and go down."

No one smiled at his attempt at levity.

"Louis, sit back down," I said calmly. "These are police reports, nothing more or less. They are not supposed to be the truth. They are one person's view of the truth. All we are doing here is getting a first look at the case, seeing what we are up against."

Roulet rolled his chair back to the table and sat down without further protest. I nodded to Levin and he continued. I noted that Roulet had long stopped acting like the meek prey I had seen earlier in the day in lockup.

"Ms. Campo reported that the man who attacked her had his fist wrapped in a white cloth when he punched her."

I looked across the table at Roulet's hands and saw no swelling or bruising on the knuckles or fingers. Wrapping his fist could have allowed him to avoid such telltale injuries.

"Was it taken into evidence?" I asked.

"Yes," Levin said. "In the evidence report it is described as a cloth dinner napkin with blood on it. The blood and the cloth are being analyzed."

I nodded and looked at Roulet.

"Did the police look at or photograph your hands?"

Roulet nodded.

"The detective looked at my hands but nobody took pictures."

I nodded and told Levin to continue.

"The intruder straddled Ms. Campo on the floor and grasped one hand around her neck," he said. "The intruder told Ms. Campo that he was going to rape her and that it didn't matter to him whether she was alive or dead when he did it. She could not respond because the suspect was choking her with his hand. When he released pressure she said she told him that she would cooperate."

Levin slid another photocopy onto the table. It was a photo of a black-handled folding knife that was sharpened to a deadly point. It explained the earlier photo of the wound under the victim's neck.

Roulet slid the photocopy over to look at it more closely. He slowly shook his head.

"This is not my knife," he said.

I didn't respond and Levin continued.

"The suspect and the victim stood up and he told her to lead the way to the bedroom. The suspect maintained a position behind the victim and pressed the point of the knife against the left side of her throat. As Ms. Campo entered a short hallway that led to the apartment's two bedrooms she turned in the confined space and pushed her attacker backwards into a large floor vase. As he stumbled backwards over the vase, she made a break for the front door. Realizing that her attacker would recover and catch her at the front door, she ducked into the kitchen and grabbed a bottle of vodka off the counter. When the intruder passed by the kitchen on his way to the front door to catch her, Ms. Campo stepped out of the blind and struck him on the back of the head, knocking him to the floor. Ms. Campo then stepped over the fallen man and unlocked the front door. She ran out the door and called the police from the first-floor apartment shared by Turner and Atkins. Turner and Atkins returned to the apartment, where they found the intruder unconscious on the floor. They maintained control of him as he started to regain consciousness and remained in the apartment until police arrived."

"This is incredible," Roulet said. "To have to sit here and listen to this. I can't believe what has happened to me. I DID NOT do this. This is like a dream. She is lying! She —"

"If it is all lies, then this will be the easiest case I ever had," I said. "I will tear her apart and throw her entrails into the sea. But we have to know what she has put on the record before we can construct traps and go after her. And if you think this is hard to sit through, wait until we get to trial and it's stretched out over days instead of minutes. You have to control yourself, Louis. You have to remember that you will get your turn. The defense always gets its turn."

Dobbs reached over and patted Roulet on the forearm, a nice fatherly gesture. Roulet pulled his arm away.

"Damn right you are going to go after her," Roulet said, pointing a finger across the table at my chest. "I want you to go after her with everything we've got."

"That's what I am here for, and you have my promise I will. Now, let me ask my associate a few questions before we finish up here."

I waited to see if Roulet had anything else to say. He didn't. He leaned back into his chair and clasped his hands together.

"You finished, Raul?" I asked.

"For now. I'm still working on all the reports. I should have a transcript of the nine-one-one call tomorrow morning and there will be more stuff coming in."

"Good. What about a rape kit?"

"There wasn't one. Booker's report said she declined, since it never got to that."

"What's a rape kit?" Roulet asked.

"It's a hospital procedure where bodily fluids, hair and fibers are collected from the body of a rape victim," Levin said.

"There was no rape!" Roulet exclaimed. "I never touched —"

"We know that," I said. "That's not why I asked. I am looking for cracks in the state's case. The victim said she was not raped but was reporting what was certainly a sex crime. Usually, the police insist on a rape kit, even when a victim claims there was no sexual assault. They do this just in case the victim actually has been raped and is just too humiliated to say so or might be trying to keep the full extent of the crime from a husband or family member. It's standard procedure, and the fact that she was able to talk her way out of it might be significant to us."

"She didn't want the first guy's DNA showing up in her," Dobbs said.

"Maybe," I said. "It might mean any number of things. But it might be a crack. Let's move on. Raul, is there any mention anywhere about this guy who Louis saw her with?"

"No, none. He's not in the file."

"And what did crime scene find?"

"I don't have the report but I am told that no evidence of any significant nature was located during the crime scene evaluation of the apartment."

"That's good. No surprises. What about the knife?"

"Blood and prints on the knife. But nothing back on that yet. Tracing ownership will be unlikely. You can buy those folding knives in any fishing or camping store around."

"I'm telling you, that is not my knife," Roulet interjected.

"We have to assume the fingerprints will be from the man who turned it in," I said.

"Atkins," Levin responded.

"Right, Atkins," I said, turning to Louis. "But it would not surprise me to find prints from you on it as well. There is no telling what occurred while you were unconscious. If she put blood on your hand, then she probably put your prints on the knife."

Roulet nodded his agreement and was about to say something, but I didn't wait for him.

"Is there any statement from her about being at Morgan's earlier in the evening?" I asked Levin.

He shook his head.

"No, the interview with the victim was in the ER and not formal. It was basic and they didn't go back with her to the early part of the evening. She didn't mention the guy and she didn't mention Morgan's. She just said she had been home since eight-thirty. They asked about what happened at ten. They didn't really get into what she had been doing before. I'm sure that will all be covered in the fol-low-up investigation."

"Okay, if and when they go back to her for a formal, I want that transcript."

"I'm on it. It will be a sit-down on video when they do it."

"And if crime scene does a video, I want that, too. I want to see her place."

Levin nodded. He knew I was putting on a show for the client and Dobbs, giving them a sense of my command of the case and all the irons that were going into the fire. The reality was I didn't need to tell Raul Levin any of this. He already knew what to do and what to get for me.

"Okay, what else?" I asked. "Do you have any questions, Cecil?"

Dobbs seemed surprised by the focus suddenly shifting to him. He quickly shook his head.

"No, no, I'm fine. This is all good. We're making good progress."

I had no idea what he meant by "progress," but I let it go by with-out question.

"So what do you think?" Roulet asked.

I looked at him and waited a long moment before answering.

"I think the state has got a strong case against you. They have you in her home, they have a knife and they have her injuries. They also have what I am assuming is her blood on your hands. Added to that, the photos are powerful. And, of course, they will have her testi-mony. Having never seen or spoken to the woman, I don't know how impressive she will be."

I stopped again and milked the silence even longer before con-tinuing.

"But there is a lot they don't have — evidence of break-in, DNA from the suspect, a motive or even a suspect with a past record of this or any sort of crime. There are a lot of reasons — legitimate reasons — for you to have been in that apartment. Plus . . ."

I looked past Roulet and Dobbs and out the window. The sun was dropping behind Anacapa and turning the sky pink and purple. It beat anything I ever saw from the windows of my office.

"Plus what?" Roulet asked, too anxious to wait on me.

"Plus you have me. I got Maggie McFierce off the case. The new prosecutor is good but he's green and he'll have never come up against someone like me before."

"So what's our next step?" Roulet asked.

"The next step is for Raul to keep doing his thing, finding out what he can about this alleged victim and why she lied about being alone. We need to find out who she is and who her mystery man is and to see how that plays into our case."

"And what will you do?"

"I'll be dealing with the prosecutor. I'll set something up with him, try to see where he's going and we'll make our choice on which way to go. I have no doubt that I'll be able to go to the DA and knock all of this down to something you can plea to and get behind you. But it will require a concession. You —"

"I told you. I will not —"

"I know what you said but you have to hear me out. I may be able to get a no-contest plea so that you don't actually ever say the word 'guilty,' but I am not seeing the state completely dropping this. You will have to concede responsibility in some regard. It is possible to avoid jail time but you will likely have to perform community service of some sort. There, I've said it. That is the first recitation. There will be more. I am obligated as your attorney to tell you and make sure you understand your options. I know it's not what you want or are willing to do but it is my duty to educate you on the choices. Okay?"

"Fine. Okay."

"Of course, as you know, any concession on your part will pretty much make any civil action Ms. Campo takes against you a slam dunk. So, as you can guess, disposing of the criminal case quickly will probably end up costing you a lot more than my fee."

Roulet shook his head. The plea bargain was already not an option.

"I understand my choices," he said. "You have fulfilled your duty. But I'm not going to pay her a cent for something I didn't do. I'm not going to plead guilty or no contest to something I didn't do. If we go to trial, can you win?"

I held his gaze for a moment before answering.

"Well, you understand that I don't know what will come up between now and then and that I can't guarantee anything . . . but, yes, based on what I see now, I can win this case. I'm confident of that."

I nodded to Roulet and I think I saw a look of hope enter his eyes. He saw the glimmer.

"There is a third option," Dobbs said.

I looked from Roulet to Dobbs, wondering what wrench he was about to throw into the franchise machine.

"And what's that?" I asked.

"We investigate the hell out of her and this case. Maybe help Mr. Levin out with some of our people. We investigate six ways from Sunday and establish our own credible theory and evidence and present it to the DA. We head this off before it ever gets to trial. We show this greenhorn prosecutor where he will definitely lose the case and get him to drop all charges before he suffers that professional embarrassment. Added to this, I am sure this man works for a man who runs that office and is susceptible, shall we say, to political pressures. We apply it until things turn our way."

I felt like kicking Dobbs under the table. Not only did his plan involve cutting my biggest fee ever by more than half, not only did it see the lion's share of client money going to the investigators, including his own, but it could only have come from a lawyer who had never defended a criminal case in his entire career.

"That's an idea but it is very risky," I said calmly. "If you can blow their case out of the water and you go in before trial to show them how, you are also giving them a blueprint for what to do and what to avoid in trial. I don't like to do that."

Roulet nodded his agreement and Dobbs looked a bit taken

aback. I decided to leave it at that and to address Dobbs further on it when I could do it without the client present.

"What about the media?" Levin asked, thankfully changing the subject.

"That's right," Dobbs said, anxious to change it himself now. "My secretary says I have messages from two newspapers and two television stations."

"I probably do as well," I said.

What I didn't mention was that the messages left with Dobbs were left by Lorna Taylor at my direction. The case had not attracted the media yet, other than the freelance videographer who showed up at the first appearance. But I wanted Dobbs and Roulet and his mother to believe they all could be splashed across the papers at any moment.

"We don't want publicity on this," Dobbs said. "This is the worst kind of publicity to get."

He seemed to be adept at stating the obvious.

"All media should be directed to me," I said. "I will handle the media and the best way to do that is to ignore it."

"But we have to say something to defend him," Dobbs said.

"No, we don't have to say anything. Talking about the case legit-imizes it. If you get into a game of talking to the media, you keep the story alive. Information is oxygen. Without it they die. As far as I am concerned, let 'em die. Or at least wait until there is no avoiding them. If that happens, only one person speaks for Louis. That's me."

Dobbs reluctantly nodded his agreement. I pointed a finger at Roulet.

"Under no circumstances do you talk to a reporter, even to deny the charges. If they contact you, you send them to me. Got it?"

"I got it."

"Good."

I decided that we had said enough for a first meeting. I stood up.

"Louis, I'll take you home now."

But Dobbs wasn't going to release his grasp on his client so quickly.

"Actually, I've been invited to dinner by Louis's mother," he said. "I could take him, since I am going there."

I nodded my approval. The criminal defense attorney never seemed to get invited to dinner.

"Fine," I said. "But we'll meet you there. I want Raul to see his place and Louis needs to give me that check we spoke about earlier."

If they thought I had forgotten about the money, they had a lot to learn about me. Dobbs looked at Roulet and got an approving nod. Dobbs then nodded to me.

"Sounds like a plan," he said. "We'll meet again there."

Fifteen minutes later I was riding in the back of the Lincoln with Levin. We were following a silver Mercedes carrying Dobbs and Roulet. I was checking with Lorna on the phone. The only message of importance had come from Gloria Dayton's prosecutor, Leslie Faire. The message was we had a deal.

"So," Levin said when I closed the phone. "What do you really think?"

"I think there is a lot of money to be made on this case and we're about to go get the first installment. Sorry I'm dragging you over there. I didn't want it to seem like it was all about the check."

Levin nodded but didn't say anything. After a few moments I continued.

"I'm not sure what to think yet," I said. "Whatever happened in that apartment happened quick. That's a break for us. No actual rape, no DNA. That gives us a glimmer of hope."

"It sort of reminds me of Jesus Menendez, only without DNA. Remember him?"

"Yeah, but I don't want to."

I tried not to think about clients who were in prison without appellate hopes or anything else left but years of time in front of them to nut out. I do what I can with each case but sometimes there is nothing that can be done. Jesus Menendez's case was one of those.

"How's your time on this?" I asked, putting us back on course.

"I've got a few things but I can move them around."

"You are going to have to work nights on this. I need you to go into those bars. I want to know everything about him and everything about her. This case looks simple at this point. We knock her down and we knock the case down."

Levin nodded. He had his briefcase on his lap.

"You got your camera in there?"

"Always."

"When we get to the house take some pictures of Roulet. I don't want you showing his mug shot in the bars. It'll taint things. Can you get a picture of the woman without her face being all messed up?"

"I got her driver's license photo. It's recent."

"Good. Run them down. If we find a witness who saw her come over to him at the bar in Morgan's last night, then we're gold."

"That's where I was thinking I'd start. Give me a week or so. I'll come back to you before the arraignment."

I nodded. We drove in silence for a few minutes, thinking about the case. We were moving through the flats of Beverly Hills, heading up into the neighborhoods where the real money was hidden and waiting.

"And you know what else I think?" I said. "Money and everything aside, I think there's a chance he isn't lying. His story is just quirky enough to be true."

Levin whistled softly between his teeth.

"You think you might have found the innocent man?" he said.

"That would be a first," I said. "If I had only known it this morning, I would have charged him the innocent man premium. If you're innocent you pay more because you're a hell of a lot more trouble to defend."

"Ain't that the truth."

I thought about the idea of having an innocent client and the dangers involved.

"You know what my father said about innocent clients?"

"I thought your father died when you were like six years old."

"Five, actually. They didn't even take me to the funeral."

"And he was talking to you about innocent clients when you were five?"

"No, I read it in a book long after he was gone. He said the scari-est client a lawyer will ever have is an innocent client. Because if you fuck up and he goes to prison, it'll scar you for life."

"He said it like that?"

"Words to that effect. He said there is no in-between with an in-nocent client. No negotiation, no plea bargaining, no middle ground. There's only one verdict. You have to put an NG up on the score-board. There's no other verdict but not guilty."

Levin nodded thoughtfully.

"The bottom line was my old man was a damn good lawyer and he didn't like having innocent clients," I said. "I'm not sure I do, either."

TEN

The first ad I ever put in the yellow pages said "Any Case, Anytime, Anywhere" but I changed it after a few years. Not because the bar objected to it, but because *I* objected to it. I got more particular. Los Angeles County is a wrinkled blanket that covers four thousand square miles from the desert to the Pacific. There are more than ten million people fighting for space on the blanket and a considerable number of them engage in criminal activity as a lifestyle choice. The latest crime stats show almost a hundred thousand violent crimes are reported each year in the county. Last year there were 140,000 felony arrests and then another 50,000 high-end misdemeanor arrests for drug and sex offenses. Add in the DUIs and every year you could fill the Rose Bowl twice over with potential clients. The thing to remember is that you don't want clients from the cheap seats. You want the ones sitting on the fifty-yard line. The ones with money in their pockets.

When the criminals get caught they get funneled into a justice system that has more than forty courthouses spread across the county like Burger Kings ready to serve them — as in serve them up on a plate. These stone fortresses are the watering holes where the legal lions come to hunt and to feed. And the smart hunter learns quickly where the most bountiful locations are, where the paying clients graze. The hunt can be deceptive. The client base of each courthouse does not necessarily reflect the socioeconomic structure of the surrounding environs. Courthouses in Compton, Downey and East Los Angeles have produced a steady line of paying clients for me. These clients are usually accused of being drug dealers but their money is just as green as a Beverly Hills stock swindler's.

On the morning of the seventeenth I was in the Compton courthouse representing Darius McGinley at his sentencing. Repeat offenders mean repeat customers and McGinley was both, as many of my clients tend to be. For the sixth time since I had known him, he had been arrested and charged with dealing crack cocaine. This time it was in Nickerson Gardens, a housing project known by most of its residents as Nixon Gardens. No one I ever asked knew whether this was an abbreviation of the true name of the place or a name bestowed in honor of the president who held office when the vast apartment complex and drug market was built. McGinley was arrested after making a direct hand-to-hand sale of a balloon containing a dozen rocks to an undercover narcotics officer. At the time, he had been out on bail after being arrested for the exact same offense two months earlier. He also had four prior convictions for drug sales on his record.

Things didn't look good for McGinley, who was only twenty-three years old. After he'd taken so many previous swings at the system, the system had now run out of patience with him. The hammer was coming down. Though McGinley had been coddled previously with sentences of probation and county jail time, the prosecutor set the bar at the prison level this time. Any negotiation of a plea agreement would begin and end with a prison sentence. Otherwise, no deal. The prosecutor was happy to take the two outstanding cases to trial and go for a conviction and a double-digit prison sentence.

The choice was hard but simple. The state held all of the cards. They had him cold on two hand-to-hand sales with quantity. The reality was that a trial would be an exercise in futility. McGinley knew this. The reality was that his selling of three hundred dollars in rock cocaine to a cop was going to cost him at least three years of his life.

As with many of my young male clients from the south side of the city, prison was an anticipated part of life for McGinley. He grew up knowing he was going. The only questions were when and for how long and whether he would live long enough to make it there. In my many jailhouse meetings with him over the years, I had learned that McGinley carried a personal philosophy inspired by the life and death and rap music of Tupac Shakur, the thug poet whose rhymes carried the hope and hopelessness of the desolate streets McGinley called home. Tupac correctly prophesied his own violent death. South L.A. teemed with young men who carried the exact same vision.

McGinley was one of them. He would recite to me long riffs from Tupac's CDs. He would translate the meanings of the ghetto lyrics for me. It was an education I valued because McGinley was only one of many clients with a shared belief in a final destiny that was "Thug Mansion," the place between heaven and earth where all gangsters ended up. To McGinley, prison was only a rite of passage on the road to that place and he was ready to make the journey.

"I'll lay up, get stronger and smarter, then I'll be back," he said to me.

He told me to go ahead and make a deal. He had five thousand dollars delivered to me in a money order — I didn't ask where it came from — and I went back to the prosecutor, got both pending cases folded into one, and McGinley agreed to plead guilty. The only thing he ever asked me to try to get for him was an assignment to a prison close by so his mother and his three young children wouldn't have to be driven too far or too long to visit him.

When court was called into session, Judge Daniel Flynn came through the door of his chambers in an emerald green robe, which brought false smiles from many of the lawyers and court workers in the room. He was known to wear the green on two occasions each year — St. Patrick's Day and the Friday before the Notre Dame Fighting Irish took on the Southern Cal Trojans on the football field. He was also known among the lawyers who worked the Compton courthouse as "Danny Boy," as in, "Danny Boy sure is an insensitive Irish prick, isn't he?"

The clerk called the case and I stepped up and announced.

McGinley was brought in through a side door and stood next to me in an orange jumpsuit with his wrists locked to a waist chain. He had no one out in the gallery to watch him go down. He was alone except for me.

"Top o' the morning to you, Mr. McGinley," Flynn said in an Irish brogue. "You know what today is?"

I lowered my eyes to the floor. McGinley mumbled his response.

"The day I get my sentence."

"That, too. But I am talking about St. Patrick's Day, Mr. McGinley. A day to revel in Irish heritage."

McGinley turned slightly and looked at me. He was street smart but not life smart. He didn't understand what was happening, whether this was part of the sentencing or just some form of white man disrespect. I wanted to tell him that the judge was being insensitive and probably racist. Instead I leaned over and whispered in his ear, "Just be cool. He's an asshole."

"Do you know the origin of your name, Mr. McGinley?" the judge asked.

"No, sir."

"Do you care?"

"Not really, sir. It's a name from a slaveholder, I 'spect. Why would I care who that motherfucka be?"

"Excuse me, Your Honor," I said quickly.

I leaned over to McGinley again.

"Darius, cool it," I whispered. "And watch your language."

"He's dissing me," he said back, a little louder than a whisper.

"And he hasn't sentenced you yet. You want to blow the deal?"

McGinley stepped back from me and looked up at the judge.

"Sorry about my language, Y'Honor. I come from the street."

"I can tell that," Flynn said. "Well, it is a shame you feel that way about your history. But if you don't care about your name, then I don't either. Let's get on with the sentencing and get you off to prison, shall we?"

He said the last part cheerfully, as if he were taking great delight in sending McGinley off to Disneyland, the happiest place on earth.

The sentencing went by quickly after that. There was nothing in the presentencing investigation report besides what everybody already knew. Darius McGinley had had only one profession since age eleven, drug dealer. He'd had only one true family, a gang. He'd never gotten a driver's license, though he drove a BMW. He'd never gotten married, though he'd fathered three babies. It was the same old story and same old cycle trotted out a dozen times a day in courtrooms across the county. McGinley lived in a society that intersected mainstream America only in the courtrooms. He was just fodder for the machine. The machine needed to eat and McGinley was on the plate. Flynn sentenced him to the agreed-upon three to five years in prison and read all of the standard legal language that came with a plea agreement. For laughs — though only his own courtroom staff complied — he read the boilerplate using his brogue again. And then it was over.

I know McGinley dealt death and destruction in the form of rock cocaine and probably committed untold violence and other offenses he was never charged with, but I still felt bad for him. I felt like he was another one who'd never had a shot at anything but thug life in the first place. He'd never known his father and had dropped out of school in the sixth grade to learn the rock trade. He could accurately count money in a rock house but he had never had a checking account. He had never been to a county beach, let alone outside of Los Angeles. And now his first trip out would be on a bus with bars over the windows.

Before he was led back into the holding cell for processing and transfer to prison I shook his hand, his movement restricted by the waist chain, and wished him good luck. It is something I rarely do with my clients.

"No sweat," he said to me. "I'll be back."

And I didn't doubt it. In a way, Darius McGinley was just as much a franchise client as Louis Roulet. Roulet was most likely a one-shot deal. But over the years, I had a feeling McGinley would be one of what I call my "annuity clients." He would be the gift that would keep on giving — as long as he defied the odds and kept on living.

I put the McGinley file in my briefcase and headed back through the gate while the next case was called. Outside the courtroom Raul Levin was waiting for me in the crowded hallway. We had a scheduled meeting to go over his findings in the Roulet case. He'd had to come to Compton because I had a busy schedule.

"Top o' the morning," Levin said in an exaggerated Irish accent.

"Yeah, you saw that?"

"I stuck my head in. The guy's a bit of a racist, isn't he?"

"And he can get away with it because ever since they unified the courts into one countywide district, his name goes on the ballot everywhere. Even if the people of Compton rose up like a wave to vote him off, the Westsiders could still cancel them out. It's fucked up."

"How'd he get on the bench in the first place?"

"Hey, you get a law degree and make the right contributions to the right people and you could be a judge, too. He was appointed by the governor. The hard part is winning that first retention election. He did. You've never heard the 'In like Flynn' story?"

"Nope."

"You'll love it. About six years ago Flynn gets his appointment from the governor. This is before unification. Back then judges were elected by the voters of the district where they presided. The supervising judge for L.A. County checks out his credentials and pretty quickly realizes that he's got a guy with lots of political connections but no talent or courthouse experience to go with it. Flynn was basically an office lawyer. Probably couldn't find a courthouse, let alone try a case, if you paid him. So the presiding judge dumps him down here in Compton criminal because the rule is you have to run for retention the year after being appointed to the bench. He figures Flynn will fuck up, anger the folks and get voted out. One year and out."

"Headache over."

"Exactly. Only it didn't work that way. In the first hour on the first day of filing for the ballot that year, Fredrica Brown walks into the clerk's office and puts in her papers to run against Flynn. You know Downtown Freddie Brown?"

"Not personally. I know of her."

"So does everybody else around here. Besides being a pretty good defense lawyer, she's black, she's a woman and she's popular in the community. She would have crushed Flynn five to one or better."

"Then how the hell did Flynn keep the seat?"

"That's what I'm getting to. With Freddie on the ballot, nobody else filed to run. Why bother, she was a shoo-in — though it was kind of curious why she'd want to be a judge and take the pay cut. Back then she had to have been well into mid six figures with her practice."

"So what happened?"

"What happened was, a couple months later on the last hour before filing closed, Freddie walks back into the clerk's office and withdraws from the ballot."

Levin nodded.

"So Flynn ends up running unopposed and keeps the seat," he said.

"You got it. Then unification comes in and they'll never be able to get him out of there."

Levin looked outraged.

"That's bullshit. They had some kind of deal and that's gotta be a violation of election laws."

"Only if you could prove there was a deal. Freddie has always maintained that she wasn't paid off or part of some plan Flynn cooked up to stay on the bench. She says she just changed her mind and pulled out because she realized she couldn't sustain her lifestyle on a judge's pay. But I'll tell you one thing, Freddie sure seems to do well whenever she has a case in front of Flynn."

"And they call it a justice system."

"Yeah, they do."

"So what do you think about Blake?"

It had to be brought up. It was all anybody else was talking about. Robert Blake, the movie and television actor, had been acquitted of murdering his wife the day before in Van Nuys Superior Court. The DA and the LAPD had lost another big media case and you couldn't go anywhere without it being the number one topic of discussion. The media and most people who lived and worked outside the machine didn't get it. The question wasn't whether Blake did it, but whether there was enough evidence presented in trial to convict him of doing it. They were two distinctly separate things but the public discourse that had followed the verdict had entwined them.

"What do I think?" I said. "I think I admire the jury for staying focused on the evidence. If it wasn't there, it wasn't there. I hate it when the DA thinks they can ride in a verdict on common sense — 'If it wasn't him, who else could it have been?' Give me a break with that. You want to convict a man and put him in a cage for life, then put up the fucking evidence. Don't hope a jury is going to bail your ass out on it."

"Spoken like a true defense attorney."

"Hey, you make your living off defense attorneys, pal. You should memorize that rap. So forget Blake. I'm jealous and I'm already tired of hearing about it. You said on the phone that you had good news for me."

"I do. Where do you want to go to talk and look at what I've got?"

I looked at my watch. I had a calendar call on a case in the Criminal Courts Building downtown. I had until eleven to be there and I couldn't miss it because I had missed it the day before. After that I was supposed to go up to Van Nuys to meet for the first time with Ted Minton, the prosecutor who had taken the Roulet case over from Maggie McPherson.

"I don't have time to go anywhere," I said. "We can go sit in my car and grab a coffee. You got your stuff with you?"

In answer Levin raised his briefcase and rapped his knuckles on its side.

"But what about your driver?"

"Don't worry about him."

"Then let's do it."

ELEVEN

After we were in the Lincoln I told Earl to drive around and see if he could find a Starbucks. I needed coffee.

"Ain' no Starbuck 'round here," Earl responded.

I knew Earl was from the area but I didn't think it was possible to be more than a mile from a Starbucks at any given point in the county, maybe even the world. But I didn't argue the point. I just wanted coffee.

"Okay, well, drive around and find a place that has coffee. Just don't go too far from the courthouse. We need to get back to drop Raul off after."

"You got it."

"And Earl? Put on your earphones while we talk about a case back here for a while, okay?"

Earl fired up his iPod and plugged in the earbuds. He headed the Lincoln down Acacia in search of java. Soon we could hear the tinny sound of hip-hop coming from the front seat and Levin opened his briefcase on the fold-down table built into the back of the driver's seat.

"Okay, what do you have for me?" I said. "I'm going to see the prosecutor today and I want to have more aces in my hand than he does. We also have the arraignment Monday."

"I think I've got a few aces here," Levin replied.

He sorted through things in his briefcase and then started his presentation.

"Okay," he said, "let's begin with your client and then we'll check in on Reggie Campo. Your guy is pretty squeaky. Other than parking and speeding tickets — which he seems to have a problem avoiding and then a bigger problem paying — I couldn't find squat on him. He's pretty much your standard citizen."

"What's with the tickets?"

"Twice in the last four years he's let parking tickets — a lot of them — and a couple speeding tickets accumulate unpaid. Both times it went to warrant and your colleague C. C. Dobbs stepped in to pay them off and smooth things over."

"I'm glad C.C.'s good for something. By 'paying them off,' I assume you mean the tickets, not the judges."

"Let's hope so. Other than that, only one blip on the radar with Roulet."

"What?"

"At the first meeting when you were giving him the drill about what to expect and so on and so forth, it comes out that he'd had a year at UCLA law and knew the system. Well, I checked on that. See, half of what I do is try to find out who is lying or who is the biggest liar of the bunch. So I check damn near everything. And most of the time it's easy to do because everything's on computer."

"Right, I get it. So what about the law school, was that a lie?"

"Looks like it. I checked the registrar's office and he's never been enrolled in the law school at UCLA."

I thought about this. It was Dobbs who had brought up UCLA law and Roulet had just nodded. It was a strange lie for either one of them to have told because it didn't really get them anything. It made me think about the psychology behind it. Was it something to do with me? Did they want me to think of Roulet as being on the same level as me?

"So if he lied about something like that . . . ," I said, thinking out loud.

"Right," Levin said. "I wanted you to know about it. But I gotta say, that's it on the negative side for Mr. Roulet so far. He might've lied about law school but it looks like he didn't lie about his story — at least the parts I could check out."

"Tell me."

"Well, his track that night checks out. I got wits in here who put him at Nat's North, Morgan's and then the Lamplighter, bing, bing, bing. He did just what he told us he did. Right down to the number of martinis. Four total and at least one of them he left on the bar unfinished."

"They remember him that well? They remember that he didn't even finish his drink?"

I am always suspicious of perfect memory because there is no such thing. And it is my job and my skill to find the faults in the memory of witnesses. Whenever someone remembers too much, I get nervous — especially if the witness is for the defense.

"No, I'm not just relying on a bartender's memory. I've got something here that you are going to love, Mick. And you better love me for it because it cost me a grand."

From the bottom of his briefcase he pulled out a padded case that contained a small DVD player. I had seen people using them on planes before and had been thinking about getting one for the car. The driver could use it while waiting on me in court. And I could probably use it from time to time on cases like this one.

Levin started loading in a DVD. But before he could play it the car pulled to a stop and I looked up. We were in front of a place called The Central Bean.

"Let's get some coffee and then see what you've got there," I said.

I asked Earl if he wanted anything and he declined the offer. Levin and I got out and went in. There was a short line for coffee. Levin spent the waiting time telling me about the DVD we were about to watch in the car.

"I'm in Morgan's and want to talk to this bartender named Janice but she says I have to clear it first with the manager. So I go back to see him in the office and he's asking me what exactly I want to ask

Janice about. There's something off about this guy. I'm wondering why he wants to know so much, you know? Then it comes clear when he makes an offer. He tells me that last year they had a problem behind the bar. Pilferage from the cash register. They have as many as a dozen bartenders working back there in a given week and he couldn't figure out who had sticky fingers."

"He put in a camera."

"You got it. A hidden camera. He caught the thief and fired his ass. But it worked so good he kept the camera in place. The system records on high-density tape from eight till two every night. It's on a timer. He gets four nights on a tape. If there is ever a problem or a shortage he can go back and check it. Because they do a weekly profit-and-loss check, he rotates two tapes so he always has a week's worth of film to look at."

"He had the night in question on tape?"

"Yes, he did."

"And he wanted a thousand dollars for it."

"Right again."

"The cops don't know about it?"

"They haven't even come to the bar yet. They're just going with Reggie's story so far."

I nodded. This wasn't all that unusual. There were too many cases for the cops to investigate thoroughly and completely. They were already loaded for bear, anyway. They had an eyewitness victim, a suspect caught in her apartment, they had the victim's blood on the suspect and even the weapon. To them, there was no reason to go further.

"But we're interested in the bar, not the cash register," I said.

"I know that. And the cash register is against the wall behind the bar. The camera is up above it in a smoke detector on the ceiling. And the back wall is a mirror. I looked at what he had and pretty quickly realized that you can see the whole bar in the mirror. It's just reversed. I had the tape transferred to a disc because we can manipulate the image better. Blow it up and zero in, that sort of thing."

It was our turn in line. I ordered a large coffee with cream and sugar and Levin ordered a bottle of water. We took our refreshments back to the car. I told Earl not to drive until after we'd viewed the DVD. I can read while riding in a car but I thought looking at the small screen of Levin's player while bumping along south county streets might give me a dose of motion sickness.

Levin started the DVD and gave a running commentary to go with the visuals.

On the small screen was a downward view of the rectangular-shaped bar at Morgan's. There were two bartenders on patrol, both women in black jeans and white shirts tied off to show flat stomachs, pierced navels and tattoos creeping up out of their rear belt lines. As Levin had explained, the camera was angled toward the back of the bar area and cash register but the mirror that covered the wall behind the register displayed the line of customers sitting at the bar. I saw Louis Roulet sit down by himself in the dead center of the frame. There was a frame counter in the bottom left corner and a time and date code in the right corner. It said that it was 8:11 P.M. on March 6.

"There's Louis showing up," Levin said. "And over here is Reggie Campo."

He manipulated buttons on the player and froze the image. He then shifted it, bringing the right margin into the center. On the short side of the bar to the right a woman and a man sat next to each other. Levin zoomed in on them.

"Are you sure?" I asked.

I had only seen pictures of the woman with her face badly bruised and swollen.

"Yeah, it's her. And that's our Mr. X."

"Okay."

"Now watch."

He started the film moving again and widened the picture back to full frame. He then started moving it in fast-forward mode.

"Louis drinks his martini, he talks with the bartenders and nothing much happens for almost an hour," Levin said.

He checked a notebook page that had notes attributed to specific frame numbers. He slowed the image to normal speed at the right moment and shifted the frame again so that Reggie Campo and Mr. X were in the center of the screen. I noticed that we had advanced to 8:43 on the time code.

On the screen Mr. X took a pack of cigarettes and a lighter off the bar and slid off his stool. He then walked out of camera range to the right.

"He's heading to the front door," Levin said. "They have a smoking porch in the front."

Reggie Campo appeared to watch Mr. X go and then she slid off her stool and started walking along the front of the bar, just behind the patrons on stools. As she passed by Roulet she appeared to drag the fingers of her left hand across his shoulders, almost in a tickling gesture. This made Roulet turn and watch her as she kept going.

"She just gave him a little flirt there," Levin said. "She's heading to the bathroom."

"That's not how Roulet said it went down," I said. "He claimed she came on to him, gave him her —"

"Just hold your horses," Levin said. "She's got to come back from the can, you know."

I waited and watched Roulet at the bar. I checked my watch. I was doing okay for the time being but I couldn't miss the calendar call at the CCB. I had already pushed the judge's patience to the max by not showing up the day before.

"Here she comes," Levin said.

Leaning closer to the screen I watched as Reggie Campo came back along the bar line. This time when she got to Roulet she squeezed up to the bar between him and a man on the next stool to the right. She had to move into the space sideways and her breasts were clearly pushed against Roulet's right arm. It was a come-on if I had ever seen one. She said something and Roulet bent over closer to her lips to hear. After a few moments he nodded and then I saw her put what looked like a crumpled cocktail napkin into his hand. They had one more verbal exchange and then Reggie Campo kissed Louis

Roulet on the cheek and pulled backwards away from the bar. She headed back to her stool.

"You're beautiful, Mish," I said, using the name I gave him after he told me of his mishmash of Jewish and Mexican descent.

"And you say the cops don't have this?" I added.

"They didn't know about it last week when I got it and I still have the tape. So, no, they don't have it and probably don't know about it yet."

Under the rules of discovery, I would need to turn it over to the prosecution after Roulet was formally arraigned. But there was still some play in that. I didn't technically have to turn over anything until I was sure I planned to use it in trial. That gave me a lot of leeway and time.

I knew that what was on the DVD was important and no doubt would be used in trial. All by itself it could be cause for reasonable doubt. It seemed to show a familiarity between victim and alleged attacker that was not included in the state's case. More important, it also caught the victim in a position in which her behavior could be interpreted as being at least partially responsible for drawing the action that followed. This was not to suggest that what followed was acceptable or not criminal, but juries are always interested in the causal relationships of crime and the individuals involved. What the video did was move a crime that might have been viewed through a black-and-white prism into the gray area. As a defense attorney I lived in the gray areas.

The flip side of that was that the DVD was so good it might be too good. It directly contradicted the victim's statement to police about not knowing the man who attacked her. It impeached her, showed her in a lie. It only took one lie to knock a case down. The tape was what I called "walking proof." It would end the case before it even got to trial. My client would simply walk away.

And with him would go the big franchise payday.

Levin was fast-forwarding the image again.

"Now watch this," he said. "She and Mr. X split at nine. But watch when he gets up."

Levin had shifted the frame to focus on Campo and the unknown man. When the time code hit 8:59 he put the playback in slow motion.

"Okay, they're getting ready to leave," he said. "Watch the guy's hands."

I watched. The man took a final draw on his drink, tilting his head far back and emptying the glass. He then slipped off his stool, helped Campo off hers and they walked out of the camera frame to the right.

"What?" I said. "What did I miss?"

Levin moved the image backwards until he got to the moment the unknown man was finishing his drink. He then froze the image and pointed to the screen. The man had his left hand down flat on the bar for balance as he reared back to drink.

"He drinks with his right hand," he said. "And on his left you can see a watch on his wrist. So it looks like the guy is right-handed, right?"

"Yeah, so? What does that get us? The injuries to the victim came from blows from the left."

"Think about what I've told you."

I did. And after a few moments I got it.

"The mirror. Everything's backwards. He's left-handed."

Levin nodded and made a punching motion with his left fist.

"This could be the whole case right here," I said, not sure that was a good thing.

"Happy Saint Paddy's Day, lad," Levin said in his brogue again, not realizing I might be staring at the end of the gravy train.

I took a long drink of hot coffee and tried to think about a strategy for the video. I didn't see any way to hold it for trial. The cops would eventually get around to the follow-up investigations and they would find out about it. If I held on to it, it could blow up in my face.

"I don't know how I'm going to use it yet," I said. "But I think it's safe to say Mr. Roulet and his mother and Cecil Dobbs are going to be very happy with you."

"Tell them they can always express their thanks financially."

"All right, anything else on the tape?"

Levin started to fast-forward the playback.

"Not really. Roulet reads the napkin and memorizes the address. He then hangs around another twenty minutes and splits, leaving a fresh drink on the bar."

He slowed the image down at the point Roulet was leaving. Roulet took one sip out of his fresh martini and put it down on the bar. He picked up the napkin Reggie Campo had given him, crumpled it in his hand and then dropped it to the floor as he got up. He left the bar, leaving the drink behind.

Levin ejected the DVD and returned it to its plastic sleeve. He then turned off the player and started to put it away.

"That's it on the visuals that I can show you here."

I reached forward and tapped Earl on the shoulder. He had his sound buds in. He pulled out one of the ear plugs and looked back at me.

"Let's head back to the courthouse," I said. "Keep your plugs in."

Earl did as instructed.

"What else?" I said to Levin.

"There's Reggie Campo," he said. "She's not Snow White."

"What did you find out?"

"It's not necessarily what I found out. It's what I think. You saw how she was on the tape. One guy leaves and she's dropping love notes on another guy alone at the bar. Plus, I did some checking. She's an actress but she's not currently working as an actress. Except for private auditions, you could say."

He handed me a professional photo collage that showed Reggie Campo in different poses and characters. It was the kind of photo sheet sent to casting directors all over the city. The largest photo on the sheet was a head shot. It was the first time I had seen her face up close without the ugly bruises and swelling. Reggie Campo was a very attractive woman and something about her face was familiar to me but I could not readily place it. I wondered if I had seen her in a television show or a commercial. I flipped the head shot over and read her credits. They were for shows I never watched and commercials I didn't remember.

"In the police reports she lists her current employer as Topsail Telemarketing. They're over in the Marina. They take the calls for a lot of the crap they sell on late-night TV. Workout machines and stuff like that. Anyway, it's day work. You work when you want. The only thing is, Reggie hasn't worked a day there for five months."

"So what are you telling me, she's been tricking?"

"I've been watching her the last three nights and —"

"You what?"

I turned and looked at him. If a private eye working for a criminal defendant was caught tailing the victim of a violent crime, there could be hell to pay and I would be the one to pay it. All the prosecution would have to do is go see a judge and claim harassment and intimidation and I'd be held in contempt faster than the Santa Ana wind through the Sepulveda Pass. As a crime victim Reggie Campo was sacrosanct until she was on the stand. Only then was she mine.

"Don't worry, don't worry," Levin said. "It was a very loose tail. Very loose. And I'm glad I did it. The bruises and the swelling and all of that have either gone away or she's using a lot of makeup, because this lady has been getting a lot of visitors. All men, all alone, all different times of the night. It looks like she tries to fit at least two into her dance card each night."

"Is she picking them up in the bars?"

"No, she's been staying in. These guys must be regulars or something because they know their way to her door. I got some plate numbers. If necessary I can visit them and try to get some answers. I also shot some infrared video but I haven't transferred it to disc yet."

"No, let's hold off on visiting any of these guys for now. Word could get back to her. We have to be very careful around her. I don't care if she's tricking or not."

I drank some more coffee and tried to decide how to move with this.

"You ran a check on her, right? No criminal record?"

"Right, she's clean. My guess is that she's new to the game. You know, these women who want to be actresses, it's a tough gig. It wears you down. She probably started by taking a little help from these guys here and there, then it became a business. She went from amateur to pro."

"And none of this is in the reports you got before?"

"Nope. Like I told you, there hasn't been a lot of follow-up by the cops. At least so far."

"If she graduated from amateur to pro, she could've graduated to setting a guy like Roulet up. He drives a nice car, wears nice clothes . . . have you seen his watch?"

"Yeah, a Rolex. If it's real, then he's wearing ten grand right there on his wrist. She could have seen that from across the bar. Maybe that's why she picked him out of all the rest."

We were back by the courthouse. I had to start heading toward downtown. I asked Levin where he was parked and he directed Earl to the lot.

"This is all good," I said. "But it means Louis lied about more than UCLA."

"Yeah," Levin agreed. "He knew he was going into a pay-for-play deal with her. He should have told you about it."

"Yeah, and now I'm going to talk to *him* about it."

We pulled up next to the curb outside a pay lot on Acacia. Levin took a file out of his briefcase. It had a rubber band around it that held a piece of paper to the outside cover. He held it out to me and I saw the document was an invoice for almost six thousand dollars for eight days of investigative services and expenses. Based on what I had heard during the last half hour, the price was a bargain.

"That file has everything we just talked about, plus a copy of the video from Morgan's on disc," Levin said.

I hesitantly took the file. By taking it I was moving it into the realm of discovery. Not accepting it and keeping everything with Levin would have given me a buffer, wiggle room if I got into a discovery scrap with the prosecutor.

I tapped the invoice with my finger.

"I'll call this in to Lorna and we'll send out a check," I said.

"How is Lorna? I miss seeing her."

When we were married, Lorna used to ride with me a lot and go into court with me to watch. Sometimes when I was short a driver she would take the wheel. Levin saw her more often back then.

"She's doing great. She's still Lorna."

Levin cracked his door open but didn't get out.

"You want me to stay on Reggie?"

That was the question. If I approved I would lose all deniability if something went wrong. Because now I would know what he was doing. I hesitated but then I nodded.

"Very loose. And don't farm it out. I only trust you on it."

"Don't worry. I'll handle it myself. What else?"

"The left-handed man. We have to figure out who Mr. X is and whether he was part of this thing or just another customer."

Levin nodded and pumped his left-handed fist again.

"I'm on it."

He put on his sunglasses, opened the door and slid out. He reached back in for his briefcase and his unopened bottle of water, then said good-bye and closed the door. I watched him start walking through the lot in search of his car. I should have been ecstatic about all I had just learned. It tilted everything steeply toward my client. But I still felt uneasy about something I couldn't quite put my finger on.

Earl had turned his music off and was awaiting direction.

"Take me downtown, Earl," I said.

"You got it," he replied. "The CCB?"

"Yeah and, hey, who was that you were listening to on the 'Pod? I could sort of hear it."

"That was Snoop. Gotta play him up loud."

I nodded. L.A.'s own. And a former defendant who faced down the machine on a murder charge and walked away. There was no better story of inspiration on the street.

"Earl?" I said. "Take the seven-ten. We're running late."

TWELVE

Sam Scales was a Hollywood con man. He specialized in Internet schemes designed to gather credit card numbers and verification data that he would then turn and sell in the financial underworld. The first time we had worked together he had been arrested for selling six hundred card numbers and their attendant verification information — expiration dates and the addresses, social security numbers and passwords of the rightful owners of the cards — to an undercover sheriff's deputy.

Scales had gotten the numbers and information by sending out an e-mail to five thousand people who were on the customer list of a Delaware-based company that sold a weight-loss product called TrimSlim6 over the Internet. The list had been stolen from the company's computer by a hacker who did freelance work for Scales. Using a rent-by-the-hour computer in a Kinko's and a temporary e-mail address, Scales then sent out a mass mailing to all those on the list. He identified himself as counsel for the federal Food and Drug Administration and told the recipients that their credit cards would be refunded the full amount of their purchases of TrimSlim6 following an FDA recall of the product. He said FDA testing of the product proved it to be ineffective in promoting weight loss. He said the makers of the product had agreed to refund all purchases in an effort to avoid fraud charges. He concluded the e-mail with instructions for confirming the refund. These included providing the credit card number, expiration date and all other pertinent verification data.

Of the five thousand recipients of the message, there were six hundred who bit. Scales then made an Internet contact in the under-world and set up a hand-to-hand sale, six hundred credit card numbers and vitals for ten thousand in cash. It meant that within days the numbers would be stamped on plastic blanks and then put to use. It was a fraud that would reach into the millions of dollars in losses.

But it was stunted in a West Hollywood coffee shop where Scales handed over a printout to his buyer and was given a thick envelope containing cash in return. When he walked out carrying the enve-lope and an iced decaf latte he was met by sheriff's deputies. He had sold his numbers to an undercover.

Scales hired me to get him a deal. He was thirty-three years old at the time and had a clean record, even though there were indications and evidence that he had never held a lawful job. By focusing the prosecutor assigned to the case on the theft of card numbers rather than the potential losses of the fraud, I was able to get Scales a dispo-sition to his liking. He pleaded guilty to one felony count of identity theft and received a one-year suspended sentence, sixty days of CalTrans work and four years of probation.

That was the first time. That was three years ago. Sam Scales did not take the opportunity afforded him by the no-jail sentence. He was now back in custody and I was defending him in a fraud case so reprehensible that it was clear from the start that it was going to be beyond my ability to keep him out of prison.

On December 28 of the previous year Scales used a front com-pany to register a domain name of SunamiHelp.com on the World Wide Web. On the home page of the website he put photographs of the destruction and death left two days earlier when a tsunami in the Indian Ocean devastated parts of Indonesia, Sri Lanka, India and Thailand. The site asked viewers to please help by making a dona-tion to SunamiHelp which would then distribute it among the numerous agencies responding to the disaster. The site also carried the photograph of a handsome white man identified as Reverend Charles, who was engaged in the work of bringing Christianity to Indonesia. A personal note from Reverend Charles was posted on the site and it asked viewers to give from the heart.

Scales was smart but not that smart. He didn't want to steal the donations made to the site. He only wanted to steal the credit card information used to make the donations. The investigation that followed his arrest showed that all contributions made through the site actually were forwarded to the American Red Cross and did go to efforts to help victims of the devastating tsunami.

But the numbers and information from the credit cards used to make those donations were also forwarded to the financial underworld. Scales was arrested when a detective with the LAPD's fraud-by-trick unit named Roy Wunderlich found the website. Knowing that disasters always drew out the con artists in droves, Wunderlich had started typing in possible website names in which the word *tsunami* was misspelled. There were several legitimate tsunami donation sites on the web and he typed in variations of these, always misspelling the word. His thinking was that the con artists would misspell the word when they set up fraud sites in an effort to draw potential victims who were likely to be of a lower education level. SunamiHelp.com was among several questionable sites the detective found. Most of these he forwarded to an FBI task force looking at the problem on a nationwide scale. But when he checked the domain registration of SunamiHelp.com, he found a Los Angeles post office box. That gave Wunderlich jurisdiction. He was in business. He kept SunamiHelp.com for himself.

The PO box turned out to be a dead address but Wunderlich was undeterred. He floated a balloon, meaning he made a controlled purchase, or in this case a controlled donation.

The credit card number the detective provided while making a twenty-dollar donation would be monitored twenty-four hours a day by the Visa fraud unit and he would be informed instantly of any purchase made on the account. Within three days of the donation the credit card was used to purchase an eleven-dollar lunch at the Gumbo Pot restaurant in the Farmers Market at Fairfax and Third. Wunderlich knew that it had simply been a test purchase. Something small and easily coverable with cash if the user of the counterfeit credit card encountered a problem at the point of purchase.

The restaurant purchase was allowed to go through and Wunderlich and four other detectives from the trick unit were dispatched to the Farmers Market, a sprawling blend of old and new shops and restaurants that was always crowded and therefore a perfect place for credit card con artists to operate. The investigators would spread out in the complex and wait while Wunderlich continued to monitor the card's use by phone.

Two hours after the first purchase the control number was used again to purchase a six-hundred-dollar leather jacket at the Nordstrom in the market. The credit card approval was delayed but not stopped. The detectives moved in and arrested a young woman as she was completing the purchase of the jacket. The case then became what is known as a "snitch chain," the police following one suspect to the next as they snitched each other off and the arrests moved up the ladder.

Eventually they came to the man sitting at the top of that ladder, Sam Scales. When the story broke in the press Wunderlich referred to him as the Tsunami Svengali because so many victims of the scam turned out to be women who had wanted to help the handsome minister pictured on the website. The nickname angered Scales, and in my discussions with him he took to referring to the detective who had brought him down as Wunder Boy.

I got to Department 124 on the thirteenth floor of the Criminal Courts Building by 10:45 but the courtroom was empty except for Marianne, the judge's clerk. I went through the bar and approached her station.

"You guys still doing the calendar?" I asked.

"Just waiting on you. I'll call everybody and tell the judge."

"She mad at me?"

Marianne shrugged. She wouldn't answer for the judge.

Especially to a defense attorney. But in a way, she was telling me that the judge wasn't happy.

"Is Scales still back there?"

"Should be. I don't know where Joe went."

I turned and went over to the defense table and sat down and waited. Eventually, the door to the lockup opened and Joe Frey, the bailiff assigned to 124, stepped out.

"You still got my guy back there?"

"Just barely. We thought you were a no-show again. You want to go back?"

He held the steel door open for me and I stepped into a small room with a stairwell going up to the courthouse jail on the fourteenth floor and two doors leading to the smaller holding rooms for 124. One of the doors had a glass panel. It was for attorney-client meetings and I could see Sam Scales sitting by himself at a table behind the glass. He was wearing an orange jumpsuit and had steel cuffs on his wrists. He was being held without bail because his latest arrest violated his probation on the TrimSlim6 conviction. The sweet deal I had gotten him on that was about to go down the tubes.

"Finally," Scales said as I walked in.

"Like you're going anywhere. You ready to do this?"

"If I have no choice."

I sat down across from him.

"Sam, you always have a choice. But let me explain it again. They've got you cold on this, okay? You were caught ripping off people who wanted to help the people caught in one of the worst natural disasters in recorded history. They've got three co-conspirators who took deals to testify against you. They have the list of card numbers found in your possession. What I am saying is that at the end of the day, you are going to get about as much sympathy from the judge and a jury — if it should come to that — as they would give a child raper. Maybe even less."

"I know all of that but I am a useful asset to society. I could educate people. Put me in the schools. Put me in the country clubs. Put me on probation and I'll tell people what to watch out for out there."

"*You* are who they have to watch out for. You blew your chance with the last one and the prosecution said this is the final offer on this one. You don't take it and they're going to go to the wall on this. The one thing I can guarantee you is that there will be no mercy."

So many of my clients are like Sam Scales. They hopelessly believe there is a light behind the door. And I'm the one who has to tell them the door is locked and that the bulb burned out long ago anyway.

"Then I guess I have to do it," Scales said, looking at me with eyes that blamed me for not finding a way out for him.

"It's your choice. You want a trial, we'll go to trial. Your exposure will be ten years plus the one you've got left on the probation. You make 'em real mad and they can also ship you over to the FBI so the feds can take a swing at you on interstate wire fraud if they want."

"Let me ask you something. If we go to trial, could we win?"

I almost laughed but I still had some sympathy left for him.

"No, Sam, we can't win. Haven't you been listening to what I've been telling you for two months? They got you. You can't win. But I'm here to do what you want. Like I said, if you want a trial we'll go to trial. But I gotta tell you that if we go, you'll have to get your mother to pay me again. I'm only good through today."

"How much did she pay you already?"

"Eight thousand."

"Eight grand! That's her fucking retirement account money!"

"I'm surprised she has anything left in the account with you for a son."

He looked at me sharply.

"I'm sorry, Sam. I shouldn't have said that. From what she told me, you're a good son."

"Jesus Christ, I should have gone to fucking law school. You're a con no different from me. You know that, Haller? Only that paper they give you makes you street legal, that's all."

They always blame the lawyer for making a living. As if it's a crime to want to be paid for doing a day's work. What Scales had just said to me would have brought a near violent reaction back when I was maybe a year or two out of law school. But I'd heard the same insult too many times by now to do anything but roll with it.

"What can I say, Sam? We've already had this conversation."

He nodded and didn't say anything. I took it to mean he would take the DA's offer. Four years in the state penal system and a ten-thousand-dollar fine, followed by five years' parole. He'd be out in two and a half but the parole would be a killer for a natural-born con man to make it through unscathed. After a few minutes I got up and left the room. I knocked on the outer door and Deputy Frey let me back into the courtroom.

"He's good to go," I said.

I took my seat at the defense table and soon Frey brought Scales out and sat him next to me. He still had the cuffs on. He said nothing to me. In another few minutes Glenn Bernasconi, the prosecutor who worked 124, came down from his office on the fifteenth floor and I told him we were ready to accept the case disposition.

At 11 A.M. Judge Judith Champagne came out of chambers and onto the bench and Frey called the courtroom to order. The judge was a diminutive, attractive blonde and ex-prosecutor who had been on the bench at least as long as I'd had my ticket. She was old school all the way, fair but tough, running her courtroom as a fiefdom. Sometimes she even brought her dog, a German shepherd named Justice, to work with her. If the judge had had any kind of discretion in the sentence when Sam Scales faced her, he would have gone down hard. That was what I did for Sam Scales, whether he knew it or not. With this deal I had saved him from that.

"Good morning," the judge said. "I am glad you could make it today, Mr. Haller."

"I apologize, Your Honor. I got held up in Judge Flynn's court in Compton."

That was all I had to say. The judge knew about Flynn. Everybody did.

"And on St. Patrick's Day, no less," she said.

"Yes, Your Honor."

"I understand we have a disposition in the Tsunami Svengali matter."

She immediately looked over at her court reporter.

"Michelle, strike that."

She looked back at the lawyers.

"I understand we have a disposition in the Scales case. Is that correct?"

"That is correct," I said. "We're ready to go on that."

"Good."

Bernasconi half read, half repeated from memory the legalese needed to take a plea from the defendant. Scales waived his rights and pleaded guilty to the charges. He said nothing other than the word. The judge accepted the disposition agreement and sentenced him accordingly.

"You're a lucky man, Mr. Scales," she said when it was over. "I believe Mr. Bernasconi was quite generous with you. I would not have been."

"I don't feel so lucky, Judge," Scales said.

Deputy Frey tapped him on the shoulder from behind. Scales stood up and turned to me.

"I guess this is it," he said.

"Good luck, Sam," I said.

He was led off through the steel door and I watched it close behind them. I had not shaken his hand.

THIRTEEN

The Van Nuys Civic Center is a long concrete plaza enclosed by government buildings. Anchoring one end is the Van Nuys Division of the LAPD. Along one side are two courthouses sitting opposite a public library and a city administration building. At the end of the concrete and glass channel is a federal administration building and post office. I waited for Louis Roulet in the plaza on one of the concrete benches near the library. The plaza was largely deserted despite the great weather. Not like the day before, when the place was overrun with cameras and the media and the gadflies, all crowding around Robert Blake and his lawyers as they tried to spin a not-guilty verdict into innocence.

It was a nice, quiet afternoon and I usually liked being outside. Most of my work is done in windowless courtrooms or the backseat of my Town Car, so I take it outside whenever I can. But I wasn't feeling the breeze or noticing the fresh air this time. I was annoyed because Louis Roulet was late and because what Sam Scales had said to me about being a street-legal con was festering like cancer in my mind. When finally I saw Roulet crossing the plaza toward me I got up to meet him.

"Where've you been?" I said abruptly.

"I told you I'd get here as soon as I could. I was in the middle of a showing when you called."

"Let's walk."

I headed toward the federal building because it would give us the longest stretch before we would have to turn around to cross back. I had my meeting with Minton, the new prosecutor assigned to his case, in twenty-five minutes in the older of the two courthouses. I realized that we didn't look like a lawyer and his client discussing a case. Maybe a lawyer and his realtor discussing a land grab. I was in my Hugo Boss and Roulet was in a tan suit over a green turtleneck. He had on loafers with small silver buckles.

"There won't be any showings up in Pelican Bay," I said to him.

"What's that supposed to mean? Where's that?"

"It's a pretty name for a super max prison where they send violent sex offenders. You're going to fit in there pretty good in your turtleneck and loafers."

"Look, what's the matter? What's this about?"

"It's about a lawyer who can't have a client who lies to him. In twenty minutes I'm about to go up to see the guy who wants to send you to Pelican Bay. I need everything I can get my hands on to try to keep you out of there and it doesn't help when I find out you're lying to me."

Roulet stopped and turned to me. He raised his hands out, palms open.

"I haven't lied to you! I did not do this thing. I don't know what that woman wants but I —"

"Let me ask you something, Louis. You and Dobbs said you took a year of law at UCLA, right? Did they teach you anything at all about the lawyer-client bond of trust?"

"I don't know. I don't remember. I wasn't there long enough."

I took a step toward him, invading his space.

"You see? You are a fucking liar. You didn't go to UCLA law school for a year. You didn't even go for a goddamn day."

He brought his hands down and slapped them against his sides.

"Is that what this is all about, Mickey?"

"Yeah, that's right and from now on, don't call me Mickey. My friends call me that. Not my lying clients."

"What does whether or not I went to law school ten years ago have to do with this case? I don't —"

"Because if you lied to me about that, then you'd lie to me about anything, and I can't have that and be able to defend you."

I said it too loud. I saw a couple of women on a nearby bench watching us. They had juror badges on their blouses.

"Come on. This way."

I started walking back the other way, heading toward the police station.

"Look," Roulet said in a weak voice. "I lied because of my mother, okay?"

"No, not okay. Explain it to me."

"Look, my mother and Cecil think I went to law school for a year. I want them to continue to believe that. He brought it up with you and so I just sort of agreed. But it was ten years ago! What is the harm?"

"The harm is in lying to me," I said. "You can lie to your mother, to Dobbs, to your priest and to the police. But when I ask you something directly, do not lie to me. I need to operate from the standpoint of having facts from you. Incontrovertible facts. So when I ask you a question, tell me the truth. All the rest of the time you can say what you want and whatever makes you feel good."

"Okay, okay."

"If you weren't in law school, where were you?"

Roulet shook his head.

"Nowhere. I just didn't do anything for a year. Most of the time I stayed in my apartment near campus and read and thought about what I really wanted to do with my life. The only thing I knew for sure was that I didn't want to be a lawyer. No offense intended."

"None taken. So you sat there for a year and came up with selling real estate to rich people."

"No, that came later."

He laughed in a self-deprecating way.

"I actually decided to become a writer — I had majored in English lit — and I tried to write a novel. It didn't take me long to figure out that I couldn't do it. I eventually went to work for Mother. She wanted me to."

I calmed down. Most of my anger had been a show, anyway. I was trying to soften him up for the more important questioning. I thought he was now ready for it.

"Well, now that you are coming clean and confessing everything, Louis, tell me about Reggie Campo."

"What about her?"

"You were going to pay her for sex, weren't you?"

"What makes you say —"

I shut him up when I stopped again and grabbed him by one of his expensive lapels. He was taller than me and bigger, but I had the power in this conversation. I was pushing him.

"Answer the fucking question."

"All right, yes, I was going to pay. But how did you know that?"

"Because I'm a good goddamn lawyer. Why didn't you tell me this on that first day? Don't you see how that changes the case?"

"My mother. I didn't want my mother to know I . . . you know."

"Louis, let's sit down."

I walked him over to one of the long benches by the police station. There was a lot of space and no one could overhear us. I sat in the middle of the bench and he sat to my right.

"Your mother wasn't even in the room when we were talking about the case. I don't even think she was in there when we talked about law school."

"But Cecil was and he tells her everything."

I nodded and made a mental note to cut Cecil Dobbs completely out of the loop on case matters from now on.

"Okay, I think I understand. But how long were you going to let it go without telling me? Don't you see how this changes everything?"

"I'm not a lawyer."

"Louis, let me tell you a little bit about how this works. You know what I am? I'm a neutralizer. My job is to neutralize the state's case. Take each piece of evidence or proof and find a way to eliminate it from contention. Think of it like one of those street entertainers you see on the Venice boardwalk. You ever gone down there and seen the guy spinning all those plates on those little sticks?"

"I think so. I haven't been down there in a long time."

"Doesn't matter. The guy has these thin little sticks and he puts a plate on each one and starts spinning the plate so it will stay balanced and upright. He gets a lot of them going at once and he moves from plate to plate and stick to stick making sure everything is spinning and balanced and staying up. You with me?"

"Yes. I understand."

"Well, that's the state's case, Louis. A bunch of spinning plates. And every one of those plates is an individual piece of evidence against you. My job is to take each plate, stop it from spinning and knock it to the ground so hard that it shatters and can't be used anymore. If the blue plate contains the victim's blood on your hands, then I need to find a way to knock it down. If the yellow plate has a knife with your bloody fingerprints on it, then once again I need to knock that sucker down. Neutralize it. You follow?"

"Yes, I follow. I —"

"Now, in the middle of this field of plates is a big one. It's a fucking platter, Louis, and if that baby falls over it's going to take everything down with it. Every plate. The whole case goes down. Do you know what that platter is, Louis?"

He shook his head no.

"That big platter is the victim, the chief witness against you. If we can knock that platter over, then the whole act is over and the crowd moves on."

I waited a moment to see if he would react. He said nothing.

"Louis, for almost two weeks you have concealed from me the method by which I could knock the big platter down. It asks the question why. Why would a guy with money at his disposal, a Rolex watch on his wrist, a Porsche out in the parking lot and a Holmby Hills address need to use a knife to get sex from a woman who sells it anyway? When you boil it all down to that question, the case starts to collapse, Louis, because the answer is simple. He wouldn't. Common sense says he wouldn't. And when you come to that conclusion, all the plates stop spinning. You see the setup, you see the trap, and now it's the defendant who starts to look like the victim."

I looked at him. He nodded.

"I'm sorry," he said.

"You should be," I said. "The case would have started coming apart almost two weeks ago and we probably wouldn't be sitting here right now if you had been up-front with me from the start."

In that moment I realized where my anger was truly coming from and it wasn't because Roulet had been late or had lied or because of Sam Scales calling me a street-legal con. It was because I saw the franchise slipping away. There would be no trial in this case, no six-figure fee. I'd be lucky just to keep the retainer I'd gotten at the start. The case was going to end today when I walked into the DA's office and told Ted Minton what I knew and what I had.

"I'm sorry," Roulet said again in a whiny voice. "I didn't mean to mess things up."

I was looking down at the ground between my feet now. Without looking at him I reached over and put my hand on his shoulder.

"I'm sorry I yelled at you before, Louis."

"What do we do now?"

"I have a few more questions to ask you about that night, and then I'm going to go up into that building over there and meet the prosecutor and knock down all his plates. I think that by the time I come out of there this may all be over and you'll be free to go back to showing your mansions to rich people."

"Just like that?"

"Well, formally he may want to go into court and ask a judge to dismiss the case."

Roulet opened his mouth in shock.

"Mr. Haller, I can't begin to tell you how —"

"You can call me Mickey. Sorry about that before."

"No problem. Thank you. What questions do you want to ask?"

I thought for a moment. I really didn't need anything else to go into the meeting with Minton. I was locked and loaded. I had walking proof.

"What did the note say?" I asked.

"What note?"

"The one she gave you at the bar in Morgan's."

"Oh, it said her address and then underneath she wrote 'four hundred dollars' and then under that she wrote 'Come after ten.' "

"Too bad we don't have that. But I think we have enough."

I nodded and looked at my watch. I still had fifteen minutes until the meeting but I was finished with Roulet.

"You can go now, Louis. I'll call you when it's all over."

"You sure? I could wait out here if you want."

"I don't know how long it will take. I'm going to have to lay it all out for him. He'll probably have to take it to his boss. It could be a while."

"All right, well, I guess I'll go then. But you'll call me, right?"

"Yes, I will. We'll probably go in to see the judge Monday or Tuesday, then it will all be over."

He put his hand out and I shook it.

"Thanks, Mick. You're the best. I knew I had the best lawyer when I got you."

I watched him walk back across the plaza and go between the two courthouses toward the public parking garage.

"Yeah, I'm the best," I said to myself.

I felt the presence of someone and turned to see a man sit down on the bench next to me. He turned and looked at me and we recognized each other at the same time. It was Howard Kurlen, a homicide detective from the Van Nuys Division. We had bumped up against each other on a few cases over the years.

"Well, well, well," Kurlen said. "The pride of the California bar. You're not talking to yourself, are you?"

"Maybe."

"That could be bad for a lawyer if that got around."

"I'm not worried. How are you doing, Detective?"

Kurlen was unwrapping a sandwich he had taken out of a brown bag.

"Busy day. Late lunch."

He produced a peanut butter sandwich from the wrap. There was a layer of something else besides peanut butter in it but it wasn't jelly. I couldn't identify it. I looked at my watch. I still had a few minutes before I needed to get in line for the metal detectors at the courthouse entrance but I wasn't sure I wanted to spend them with Kurlen and his horrible-looking sandwich. I thought about bringing up the Blake verdict, sticking it to the LAPD a little bit, but Kurlen stuck one in me first.

"How's my man Jesus doin'?" the detective asked.

Kurlen had been lead detective on the Jesus Menendez case. He had wrapped him up so tightly that Menendez had no choice but to plead and hope for the best. He still got life.

"I don't know," I answered. "I don't talk to Jesus anymore."

"Yeah, I guess once they plead out and go upstate they're not much use to you. No appeal work, no nothing."

I nodded. Every cop had a jaundiced eye when it came to defense lawyers. It was as if they believed their own actions and investigations were beyond questioning or reproach. They didn't believe in a justice system based on checks and balances.

"Just like you, I guess," I said. "On to the next one. I hope your busy day means you're working on getting me a new client."

"I don't look at it that way. But I was wondering, do you sleep well at night?"

"You know what I was wondering? What the hell is in that sandwich?"

He held what was left of the sandwich up on display.

"Peanut butter and sardines. Lots of good protein to get me through another day of chasing scumbags. Talking to them, too. You didn't answer my question."

"I sleep fine, Detective. You know why? Because I play an important part in the system. A needed part — just like your part.

When somebody is accused of a crime, they have the opportunity to test the system. If they want to do that, they come to me. That's all any of this is about. When you understand that, you have no trouble sleeping."

"Good story. When you close your eyes I hope you believe it."

"How about you, Detective? You ever put your head on the pillow and wonder whether you've put innocent people away?"

"Nope," he said quickly, his mouth full of sandwich. "Never happened, never will."

"Must be nice to be so sure."

"A guy told me once that when you get to the end of your road, you have to look at the community woodpile and decide if you added to it while you were here or whether you just took from it. Well, I add to the woodpile, Haller. I sleep good at night. But I wonder about you and your kind. You lawyers are all takers from the woodpile."

"Thanks for the sermon. I'll keep it in mind next time I'm chopping wood."

"You don't like that, then I've got a joke for you. What's the difference between a catfish and a defense attorney?"

"Hmmm, I don't know, Detective."

"One's a bottom-feeding scum sucker and one's a fish."

He laughed uproariously. I stood up. It was time to go.

"I hope you brush your teeth after you eat something like that," I said. "I'd hate to be your partner if you don't."

I walked away, thinking about what he had said about the woodpile and what Sam Scales had said about my being a street-legal con. I was getting it from all sides today.

"Thanks for the tip," Kurlen called after me.

FOURTEEN

Ted Minton had arranged for us to discuss the Roulet case in private by scheduling our conference at a time he knew the deputy district attorney he shared space with had a hearing in court. Minton met me in the waiting area and walked me back. He did not look to me to be older than thirty but he had a self-assured presence. I probably had ten years and a hundred trials on him, yet he showed no sign of deference or respect. He acted as though the meeting was a nuisance he had to put up with. That was fine. That was the usual. And it put more fuel in my tank.

When we got to his small, windowless office, he offered me his office partner's seat and closed the door. We sat down and looked at each other. I let him go first.

"Okay," he said. "First off, I wanted to meet you. I'm sort of new up here in the Valley and haven't met a lot of the members of the defense bar. I know you're one of those guys that covers the whole county but we haven't run across each other before."

"Maybe that's because you haven't worked many felony trials before."

He smiled and nodded like I had scored a point of some kind.

"That might be true," he said. "Anyway, I gotta tell you, when I was in law school at SC I read a book about your father and his cases.

I think it was called *Haller for the Defense*. Something like that. Interesting guy and interesting times."

I nodded back.

"He was gone before I really knew him, but there were a few books about him and I read them all more than a few times. It's probably why I ended up doing this."

"That must have been hard, getting to know your father through books."

I shrugged. I didn't think that Minton and I needed to know each other that well, particularly in light of what I was about to do to him.

"I guess it happens," he said.

"Yeah."

He clapped his hands together once, a let's-get-down-to-business gesture.

"Okay, so we're here to talk about Louis Roulet, aren't we?"

"It's pronounced Roo-*lay*."

"Roooo-*lay*. Got it. So, let's see, I have some things for you here."

He swiveled his seat to turn back to his desk. He picked up a thin file and turned back to hand it to me.

"I want to play fair. That's the up-to-the-minute discovery for you. I know I don't have to give it to you until after the arraignment but, hell, let's be cordial."

My experience is that when prosecutors tell you they are playing fair or better than fair, then you better watch your back. I fanned through the discovery file but didn't really read anything. The file Levin had gathered for me was at least four times as thick. I wasn't thrilled because Minton had so little. I was suspicious that he was holding back on me. Most prosecutors made you work for the discovery by having to demand it repeatedly, to the point of going to court to complain to the judge about it. But Minton had just casually handed at least some of it over. Either he had more to learn than I imagined about felony prosecutions or there was some sort of play here.

"This is everything?" I asked.

"Everything I've gotten."

That was always the way. If the prosecutor didn't have it, then he could stall its release to the defense. I knew for a fact — as in having been married to a prosecutor — that it was not out of the ordinary for a prosecutor to tell the police investigators on a case to take their time getting all the paperwork in. They could then turn around and tell the defense lawyer they wanted to play fair and hand over practically nothing. The rules of discovery were often referred to by defense pros as the rules of dishonesty. This of course went both ways. Discovery was supposed to be a two-way street.

"And you're going to trial with this?"

I waved the file as if to say its thin contents were as thin as the case.

"I'm not worried about it. But if you want to talk about a disposition, I'll listen."

"No, no disposition on this. We're going balls out. We're going to waive the prelim and go right to trial. No delays."

"He won't waive speedy?"

"Nope. You've got sixty days from Monday to put up or shut up."

Minton pursed his lips as though what I had just told him were only a minor inconvenience and surprise. It was a good cover-up. I knew I had landed a solid punch.

"Well, then, I guess we ought to talk about unilateral discovery. What do you have for me?"

He had dropped the pleasant tone.

"I'm still putting it together," I said. "But I'll have it at the arraignment Monday. But most of what I've got is probably already in this file you gave me, don't you think?"

"Most likely."

"You have that the supposed victim is a prostitute who had solicited my client in here, right? And that she has continued that line of work since the alleged incident, right?"

Minton's mouth opened maybe a half inch and then closed, but it was a good tell. I had hit him with another solid shot. But then he recovered quickly.

"As a matter of fact," he said, "I am aware of her occupation. But what surprises me is that you know this already. I hope you aren't sniffing around my victim, Mr. Haller?"

"Call me Mickey. And what I am doing is the least of your problems. You better take a good look at this case, Ted. I know you're new to felony trials and you don't want to come out of the box with a loser like this. Especially after the Blake fiasco. But this one's a dog and it's going to bite you on the ass."

"Really? How so?"

I looked past his shoulder at the computer on his desk.

"Does that thing play DVDs?"

Minton looked back at the computer. It looked ancient.

"It should. What have you got?"

I realized that showing him the surveillance video from the bar at Morgan's would be giving an early reveal of the biggest ace that I held, but I was confident that once he saw it, there would be no arraignment Monday and no case. My job was to neutralize the case and get my client out from under the government's weight. This was the way to do it.

"I don't have all my discovery together but I do have this," I said.

I handed Minton the DVD I had gotten earlier from Levin. The prosecutor put it into his computer.

"This is from the bar at Morgan's," I told him as he tried to get it playing. "Your guys never went there but my guy did. This is the Sunday night of the supposed attack."

"And this could have been doctored."

"It could have been but it wasn't. You can have it checked. My investigator has the original and I will tell him to make it available after the arraignment."

After a short struggle Minton got the DVD to play. He watched silently as I pointed out the time code and all the same details Levin had pointed out to me, including Mr. X and his left-handedness. Minton fast-forwarded as I instructed and then slowed it to watch the moment when Reggie Campo approached my client at the bar.

He had a frown of concentration on his face. When it was over he ejected the disc and held it up.

"Can I keep this until I get the original?"

"Be my guest."

Minton put the disc back in its case and placed it on top of a stack of files on his desk.

"Okay, what else?" he asked.

Now my mouth let some light in.

"What do you mean, what else? Isn't that enough?"

"Enough for what?"

"Look, Ted, why don't we cut the bullshit?"

"Please do."

"What are we talking about here? That disc blows this case out of the water. Let's forget about arraignment and trial and talk about going into court next week with a joint motion to dismiss. I want this shit-canned with prejudice, Ted. No coming back at my guy if some-body in here decides to change their mind."

Minton smiled and shook his head.

"Can't do that, Mickey. This woman was injured quite badly. She was victimized by an animal and I'm not going to dismiss any-thing against —"

"Quite badly? She's been turning tricks again all week. You —"

"How do you know that?"

I shook my head.

"Man, I am trying to help you here, save you some embarrass-ment, and all you're worried about is whether I've crossed some line with the victim. Well, I've got news for you. She ain't the victim. Don't you see what you have here? If this thing gets to a jury and they see that disc, all the plates fall, Ted. Your case is over and you have to come back in here and explain to your boss Smithson why you didn't see it coming. I don't know Smithson all that well, but I do know one thing about him. He doesn't like to lose. And after what happened yesterday, I would say that he feels a little more urgent about that."

"Prostitutes can be victims, too. Even amateurs."

I shook my head. I decided to show my whole hand.

"She set him up," I said. "She knew he had money and she laid a trap. She wants to sue him and cash in. She either hit herself or she had her boyfriend from the bar, the left-handed man, do it. No jury in the world is going to buy what you're selling. Blood on the hand or fingerprints on the knife — it was all staged after he was knocked out."

Minton nodded as if he followed the logic but then came out with something from left field.

"I'm concerned that you may be trying to intimidate my victim by following her and harassing her."

"What?"

"You know the rules of engagement. Leave the victim alone or we'll next talk about it with a judge."

I shook my head and spread my hands wide.

"Are you listening to anything I'm saying here?"

"Yes, I have listened to it all and it doesn't change the course I am taking. I do have an offer for you, though, and it will be good only until Monday's arraignment. After that, all bets are off. Your client takes his chances with a judge and jury. And I'm not intimidated by you or the sixty days. I will be ready and waiting."

I felt like I was underwater and everything that I said was trapped in bubbles that were drifting up and away. No one could hear me correctly. Then I realized that there was something I was missing. Something important. It didn't matter how green Minton was, he wasn't stupid and I had just mistakenly thought he was acting stupid. The L.A. County DA's office got some of the best of the best out of law school. He had already mentioned Southern Cal and I knew that was a law school that turned out top-notch lawyers. It was only a matter of experience. Minton might be short on experience but it didn't mean he was short on legal intelligence. I realized that I should be looking at myself, not Minton, for understanding.

"What am I missing here?" I asked.

"I don't know," Minton said. "You're the one with the high-powered defense. What could you be missing?"

I stared at him for a moment and then knew. There was a glitch in the discovery. There was something in his thin file that was not in the thick one Levin had put together. Something that would get the prosecution past the fact that Reggie Campo was selling it. Minton had so much as told me already. *Prostitutes can be victims, too.*

I wanted to stop everything and look through the state's discovery file to compare it with everything about the case that I knew. But I could not do it now in front of him.

"Okay," I said. "What's your offer? He won't take it but I'll present it."

"Well, he's got to do prison time. That's a given. We're willing to drop it all down to an ADW and attempted sexual battery. We'll go to the middle of the guidelines, which would put him at about seven years."

I nodded. Assault with a deadly weapon and attempted sexual battery. A seven-year sentence would likely mean four years actual. It wasn't a bad offer but only from the standpoint of Roulet having committed the crime. If he was innocent, then no offer was acceptable.

I shrugged.

"I'll take it to him," I said.

"Remember, only until the arraignment. So if he wants it you better call me Monday morning first thing."

"Right."

I closed my briefcase and stood up to go. I was thinking about how Roulet was probably waiting for a phone call from me, telling him the nightmare was over. Instead, I would be calling about a seven-year deal.

Minton and I shook hands and I said I would call him, then I headed out. In the hallway leading to the reception area I ran into Maggie McPherson.

"Hayley had a great time Saturday," she said about our daughter. "She's still talking about it. She said you were going to see her this weekend, too."

"Yeah, if that's okay."

"Are you all right? You look like you're in a daze."

"It's turning into a long week. I'm glad I have an empty calendar tomorrow. Which works better for Hayley, Saturday or Sunday?"

"Either's fine. Were you just meeting Ted on the Roulet thing?"

"Yeah. I got his offer."

I raised my briefcase to show I was taking the prosecution's plea offer with me.

"Now I have to go try to sell it," I added. "That's going to be tough. Guy says he didn't do it."

"I thought they all said that."

"Not like this guy."

"Well, good luck."

"Thanks."

We headed opposite ways in the hallway and then I remembered something and called back to her.

"Hey, Happy St. Patrick's."

"Oh."

She turned and came back toward me.

"Stacey's staying a couple hours late with Hayley and a bunch of us are going over to Four Green Fields after work. You feel like a pint of green beer?"

Four Green Fields was an Irish pub not far from the civic center. It was frequented by lawyers from both sides of the bar. Animosities grew slack under the taste of room-temperature Guinness.

"I don't know," I said. "I think I have to head over the hill to see my client but you never know, I might come back."

"Well, I only have till eight and then I have to go relieve Stacey."

"Okay."

We parted again and I left the courthouse. The bench where I had sat with Roulet and then Kurlen was empty. I sat down, opened my case and pulled out the discovery file Minton had given me. I flipped through reports I already had gotten copies of through Levin. There seemed to be nothing new until I came to a comparative fingerprint analysis report that confirmed what we had thought all along; the bloody fingerprints on the knife belonged to my client, Louis Roulet.

It still wasn't enough to justify Minton's demeanor. I kept looking and then I found it in the weapon analysis report. The report I
had gotten from Levin was completely different, as if from another
case and another weapon. As I quickly read it I felt perspiration pop-
ping in my hair. I had been set up. I had been embarrassed in the
meeting with Minton and worse yet had tipped him early to my hole
card. He had the video from Morgan's and had all the time he would
need to prepare for it in court.

Finally, I slapped the folder closed and pulled out my cell phone.
Levin answered after two rings.

"How'd it go?" he asked. "Bonuses for everybody?"

"Not quite. Do you know where Roulet's office is?"

"Yeah, on Canon in Beverly Hills. I've got the exact address in
the file."

"Meet me there."

"Now?"

"I'll be there in thirty minutes."

I punched the button, ending the call without further discussion,
and then called Earl on speed dial. He must have had his iPod plugs
in his ears because he didn't answer until the seventh ring.

"Come get me," I said. "We're going over the hill."

I closed the phone and got off the bench. Walking toward the
opening between the two courthouses and the place where Earl
would pick me up, I felt angry. At Roulet, at Levin, and most of all at
myself. But I also was aware of the positive side of this. The one thing
that was certain now was that the franchise — and the big payday
that came with it — was back in play. The case was going to go the
distance to trial unless Roulet took the state's offer. And I thought the
chances of that were about the same as the chances for snow in L.A. It
could happen but I wouldn't believe it until I saw it.

FIFTEEN

When the rich in Beverly Hills want to drop small fortunes on clothes and jewelry, they go to Rodeo Drive. When they want to drop larger fortunes on houses and condominiums, they walk a few blocks over to Canon Drive, where the high-line real estate companies roost, photographs of their multimillion-dollar offerings presented in showroom windows on ornate gold easels like Picassos and Van Goghs. This is where I found Windsor Residential Estates and Louis Roulet on Thursday afternoon.

By the time I got there, Raul Levin was already waiting — and I mean waiting. He had been kept in the showroom with a fresh bottle of water while Louis worked the phone in his private office. The receptionist, an overly tanned blonde with a haircut that hung down one side of her face like a scythe, told me it would be just a few minutes more and then we both could go in. I nodded and stepped away from her desk.

"You want to tell me what's going on?" Levin asked.

"Yeah, when we get in there with him."

The showroom was lined on both sides with steel wires that ran from ceiling to floor and on which were attached 8 × 10 frames containing the photos and pedigrees of the estates offered for sale. Acting like I was studying the rows of houses I couldn't hope to afford in a hundred years, I moved toward the back hallway that led to the offices. When I got there I noticed an open door and heard Louis Roulet's voice. It sounded like he was setting up a showing of a Mulholland Drive mansion for a client he told the realtor on the other end of the phone wanted his name kept confidential. I looked back at Levin, who was still near the front of the showroom.

"This is bullshit," I said and signaled him back.

I walked down the hallway and into Roulet's plush office. There was the requisite desk stacked with paperwork and thick multiple-listing catalogs. But Roulet wasn't there. He was in a sitting area to the right of the desk, slouched on a sofa with a cigarette in one hand and the phone in the other. He looked shocked to see me and I thought maybe the receptionist hadn't even told him he had visitors.

Levin came into the office behind me, followed by the receptionist, the hair scythe swinging back and forth as she hurried to catch up. I was worried that the blade might cut off her nose.

"Mr. Roulet, I'm sorry, these men just came back here."

"Lisa, I have to go," Roulet said into the phone. "I'll call you back."

He put the phone down in its cradle on the glass coffee table.

"It's okay, Robin," he said. "You can go now."

He made a dismissive gesture with the back of his hand. Robin looked at me like I was wheat she wanted to cut down with that blond blade and then left the room. I closed the door and looked back at Roulet.

"What happened?" he said. "Is it over?"

"Not by a long shot," I said.

I was carrying the state's discovery file. The weapon report was front and center. I stepped over and dropped it onto the coffee table.

"I only succeeded in embarrassing myself in the DA's office. The case against you still stands and we'll probably be going to trial."

Roulet's face dropped.

"I don't understand," he said. "You said you were going to tear that guy a new asshole."

"Turns out the only asshole in there was me. Because once again you didn't level with me."

Then, turning to look at Levin, I said, "And because you got us set up."

Roulet opened the file. On the top page was a color photograph of a knife with blood on its black handle and the tip of its blade. It was not the same knife that was photocopied in the records Levin got from his police sources and that he had showed us in the meeting in Dobbs's office the first day of the case.

"What the hell is that?" said Levin, looking down at the photo.

"That is a knife. The real one, the one Roulet had with him when he went to Reggie Campo's apartment. The one with her blood and his *initials* on it."

Levin sat down on the couch on the opposite side from Roulet. I stayed standing and they both looked up at me. I started with Levin.

"I went in to see the DA to kick his ass today and he ended up kicking mine with that. Who was your source, Raul? Because he gave you a marked deck."

"Wait a minute, wait a minute. That's not —"

"No, you wait a minute. The report you had on the knife being untraceable was bogus. It was put in there to fuck us up. To trick us and it worked perfectly, because I waltzed in there thinking I couldn't lose today and just gave him the Morgan's bar video. Just trotted it out like it was the hammer. Only it wasn't, goddamn it."

"It was the runner," Levin said.

"What?"

"The runner. The guy who runs the reports between the police station and the DA's office. I tell him which cases I'm interested in and he makes extra copies for me."

"Well, they're onto his ass and they worked it perfectly. You better call him and tell him if he needs a good criminal defense attorney I'm not available."

I realized I was pacing in front of them on the couch but I didn't stop.

"And you," I said to Roulet. "I now get the real weapon report and find out not only is the knife a custom-made job but it is traceable right back to you because it has your fucking initials on it! You lied to me again!"

"I didn't lie," Roulet yelled back. "I tried to tell you. I said it wasn't my knife. I said it twice but nobody listened to me."

"Then you should have clarified what you meant. Just saying it wasn't your knife was like saying you didn't do it. You should have said, 'Hey, Mick, there might be a problem with the knife because I did have a knife but this picture isn't it.' What did you think, that it was just going to go away?"

"Please, can you keep it down," Roulet protested. "There might be customers out there."

"I don't care! Fuck your customers. You're not going to need customers anymore where you're going. Don't you see that this knife trumps everything we've got? You took a murder weapon to a meeting with a prostitute. The knife was no plant. It was yours. And that means we no longer have the setup. How can we claim she set you up when the prosecutor can prove you had that knife with you when you walked through the door?"

He didn't answer but I didn't give him a lot of time to.

"You fucking did this thing and they've got you," I said, pointing at him. "No wonder they didn't bother with any follow-up investigation at the bar. No follow-up needed when they've got *your* knife and *your* fingerprints in blood on it."

"I didn't do it! It's a setup. I'm TELLING YOU! It was —"

"Who's yelling now? Look, I don't care what you're telling me. I can't deal with a client who doesn't level, who doesn't see the percentage in telling his own attorney what is going on. So the DA has made an offer to you and I think you better take it."

Roulet sat up straight and grabbed the pack of cigarettes off the table. He took one out and lit it off the one he already had going.

"I'm not pleading guilty to something I didn't do," he said, his voice suddenly calm after a deep drag off the fresh smoke.

"Seven years. You'll be out in four. You have till court time

Monday and then it disappears. Think about it, then tell me you want to take it."

"I won't take it. I didn't do this thing and if you won't take it to trial, then I will find somebody who will."

Levin was holding the discovery file. I reached down and rudely grabbed it out of his hands so I could read directly from the weapon report.

"You didn't do it?" I said to Roulet. "Okay, if you didn't do it, then would you mind telling me why you went to see this prostitute with a custom-made Black Ninja knife with a five-inch blade, complete with your initials engraved not once, but twice on both sides of the blade?"

Finished reading from the report, I threw it back to Levin. It went through his hands and slapped against his chest.

"Because I always carry it!"

The force of Roulet's response quieted the room. I paced back and forth once, staring at him.

"You always carry it," I said, not a question.

"That's right. I'm a realtor. I drive expensive cars. I wear expensive jewelry. And I often meet strangers alone in empty houses."

Again he gave me pause. As hyped up as I was, I still knew a glimmer when I saw one. Levin leaned forward and looked at Roulet and then at me. He saw it, too.

"What are you talking about?" I said. "You sell homes to rich people."

"How do you know they are rich when they call you up and say they want to see a place?"

I stretched my hands out in confusion.

"You must have some sort of system for checking them out, right?"

"Sure, we can run a credit report and we can ask for references. But it still comes down to what they give us and these kind of people don't like to wait. When they want to see a piece of property, they want to see it. There are a lot of realtors out there. If we don't act quickly, there will be somebody else who will."

I nodded. The glimmer was getting brighter. There might be something here I could work with.

"There have been murders, you know," Roulet said. "Over the years. Every realtor knows the danger exists when you go to some of these places alone. For a while there was somebody out there called the Real Estate Rapist. He attacked and robbed women in empty houses. My mother . . ."

He didn't finish. I waited. Nothing.

"What about your mother?"

Roulet hesitated before answering.

"She was showing a place in Bel-Air once. She was alone and she thought it was safe because it was Bel-Air. The man raped her. He left her tied up. When she didn't come back to the office, I went to the house. I found her."

Roulet's eyes were staring at the memory.

"How long ago was this?" I asked.

"About four years. She stopped selling after it happened. Just stayed in her office and never showed another property again. I did the selling. And that's when and why I got the knife. I've had it for four years and carry it everywhere but on planes. It was in my pocket when I went to that apartment. I didn't think anything about it."

I dropped into the chair across the table from the couch. My mind was working. I was seeing how it could work. It was still a defense that relied on coincidence. Roulet was set up by Campo and the setup was aided coincidentally when she found the knife on him after knocking him out. It could work.

"Did your mother file a police report?" Levin asked. "Was there an investigation?"

Roulet shook his head as he stubbed out his cigarette in the ashtray.

"No, she was too embarrassed. She was afraid it would get into the paper."

"Who else knows about it?" I asked.

"Uh, me . . . and Cecil I'm sure knows. Probably nobody else. You can't use this. She would —"

"I won't use it without her permission," I said. "But it could be important. I'll have to talk to her about it."

"No, I don't want you —"

"Your life and livelihood are on the line here, Louis. You get sent to prison and you're not going to make it. Don't worry about your mother. A mother will do what she has to do to protect her young."

Roulet looked down and shook his head.

"I don't know . . . ," he said.

I exhaled, trying to lose all my tension with the breath. Disaster might have been averted.

"I know one thing," I said. "I'm going to go back to the DA and say pass on the deal. We'll go to trial and take our chances."

SIXTEEN

The hits kept coming. The other shoe didn't drop on the prosecution's case until after I'd dropped Earl off at the commuter lot where he parked his own car every morning and I drove the Lincoln back to Van Nuys and Four Green Fields. It was a shotgun pub on Victory Boulevard — maybe that was why lawyers liked the place — with the bar running down the left side and a row of scarred wooden booths down the right. It was crowded as only an Irish bar can be the night of St. Patrick's Day. My guess was that the crowd was swollen even bigger than in previous years because of the fact that the drinker's holiday fell on a Thursday and many revelers were kicking off a long weekend. I had made sure my own calendar was clear on Friday. I always clear the day after St. Pat's.

As I started to fight my way through the mass in search of Maggie McPherson, the required "Danny Boy" started blaring from a jukebox somewhere in the back. But it was a punk rock version from the early eighties and its driving beat obliterated any chance I had of hearing anything when I saw familiar faces and said hello or asked if they had seen my ex-wife. The small snippets of conversation I overheard as I pushed through seemed to all be about Robert Blake and the stunning verdict handed down the day before.

I ran into Robert Gillen in the crowd. The cameraman reached into his pocket and pulled out four crisp hundred-dollar bills and handed them to me. The bills were probably four of the original ten I had paid him two weeks earlier in the Van Nuys courthouse as I tried to impress Cecil Dobbs with my media manipulation skills. I had already expensed the thousand to Roulet. The four hundred was profit.

"I thought I'd run into you here," he yelled in my ear.

"Thanks, Sticks," I replied. "It'll go toward my bar tab."

He laughed. I looked past him into the crowd for my ex-wife.

"Anytime, my man," he said.

He slapped me on the shoulder as I squeezed by him and pushed on. I finally found Maggie in the last booth in the back. It was full of six women, all prosecutors or secretaries from the Van Nuys office. Most I knew at least in passing but the scene was awkward because I had to stand and yell over the music and the crowd. Plus the fact that they were prosecutors and viewed me as being in league with the devil. They had two pitchers of Guinness on the table and one was full. But my chances of getting through the crowd to the bar to get a glass were negligible. Maggie noticed my plight and offered to share her glass with me.

"It's all right," she yelled. "We've swapped spit before."

I smiled and knew the two pitchers on the table had not been the first two. I took a long drink and it tasted good. Guinness always gave me a solid center.

Maggie was in the middle on the left side of the booth and between two young prosecutors whom I knew she had taken under her wing. In the Van Nuys office, many of the younger females gravitated toward my ex-wife because the man in charge, Smithson, surrounded himself with attorneys like Minton.

Still standing at the side of the booth, I raised the glass in toast to her but she couldn't respond because I had her glass. She reached over and raised the pitcher.

"Cheers!"

She didn't go so far as to drink from the pitcher. She put it down and whispered to the woman on the outside of the booth. She got up to let Maggie out. My ex-wife stood up and kissed me on the cheek and said, "It's always easier for a lady to get a glass in these sorts of situations."

"Especially beautiful ladies," I said.

She gave me one of her looks and turned toward the crowd that was five deep between us and the bar. She whistled shrilly and it caught the attention of one of the pure-bred Irish guys who worked the tap handles and could etch a harp or an angel or a naked lady in the foam at the top of the glass.

"I need a pint glass," she yelled.

The bartender had to read her lips. And like a teenager being passed over the heads of the crowd at a Pearl Jam concert, a clean glass made its way back to us hand to hand. She filled it from the freshest pitcher on the booth's table and then we clicked glasses.

"So," she said. "Are you feeling a little better than when I saw you today?"

I nodded.

"A little."

"Did Minton sandbag you?"

I nodded again.

"Him *and* the cops did, yeah."

"With that guy Corliss? I told them he was full of shit. They all are."

I didn't respond and tried to act like what she had just said was not news to me and that Corliss was a name I already knew. I took a long and slow drink from my glass.

"I guess I shouldn't have said that," she said. "But my opinion doesn't matter. If Minton is dumb enough to use him, then you'll take the guy's head off, I'm sure."

I guessed that she was talking about a witness. But I had seen nothing in my review of the discovery file that mentioned a witness named Corliss. The fact that it was a witness she didn't trust led me further to believe that Corliss was a snitch. Most likely a jailhouse snitch.

"How come you know about him?" I finally asked. "Minton talked to you about him?"

"No, I'm the one who sent him to Minton. Doesn't matter what I think of what he said, it was my duty to send him to the right prosecutor and it was up to Minton to evaluate him."

"I mean, why did he come to you?"

She frowned at me because the answer was so obvious.

"Because I handled the first appearance. He was there in the pen. He thought the case was still mine."

Now I understood. Corliss was a *C*. Roulet was taken out of alphabetical order and called first. Corliss must have been in the group of inmates taken into the courtroom with him. He had seen Maggie and me argue over Roulet's bail. He therefore thought Maggie still had the case. He must have made a snitch call to her.

"When did he call you?" I asked.

"I am telling you too much, Haller. I'm not —"

"Just tell me when he called you. That hearing was on a Monday, so was it later that day?"

The case did not make any notice in the newspapers or on TV. So I was curious as to where Corliss would have gotten the information he was trying to trade to prosecutors. I had to assume it didn't come from Roulet. I was pretty sure I had scared him silent. Without a media information point, Corliss would have been left with the information gleaned in court when the charges were read and Maggie and I argued bail.

It was enough, I realized. Maggie had been specific in detailing Regina Campo's injuries as she was trying to impress the judge to hold Roulet without bail. If Corliss had been in court, he'd have been privy to all the details he would need to make up a jailhouse confession from my client. Add that to his proximity to Roulet and a jailhouse snitch is born.

"Yes, he called me late Monday," Maggie finally answered.

"So why did you think he was full of shit? He's done it before, hasn't he? The guy's a professional snitch, right?"

I was fishing and she knew it. She shook her head.

"I am sure you will find out all you need to know during discovery. Can we just have a friendly pint of Guinness here? I have to leave in about an hour."

I nodded but wanted to know more.

"Tell you what," I said. "You've probably had enough Guinness for one St. Patrick's Day. How about we get out of here and get something to eat?"

"Why, so you can keep asking me about your case?"

"No, so we can talk about our daughter."

Her eyes narrowed.

"Is something wrong?" she asked.

"Not that I know of. But I want to talk to you about her."

"Where are you taking me to dinner?"

I mentioned an expensive Italian restaurant on Ventura in Sherman Oaks and her eyes got warm. It had been a place we had gone to celebrate anniversaries and getting pregnant. Our apartment, which she still had, was a few blocks away on Dickens.

"Think we can eat there in an hour?" she asked.

"If we leave right now and order without looking."

"You're on. Let me just say some quick good-byes."

"I'll drive."

And it was a good thing I drove because she was unsteady on her feet. We had to walk hip to hip to the Lincoln and then I helped her get in.

I took Van Nuys south to Ventura. After a few moments Maggie reached beneath her legs and pulled out a CD case she had been uncomfortably sitting on. It was Earl's. One of the CDs he listened to on the car stereo when I was in court. It saved juice on his iPod. The CD was by a dirty south performer named Ludacris.

"No wonder I was so uncomfortable," she said. "Is this what you're listening to while driving between courthouses?"

"Actually, no. That's Earl's. He's been doing the driving lately.

Ludacris isn't really to my liking. I'm more of an old school guy. Tupac and Dre and people like that."

She laughed because she thought I was kidding. A few minutes later we drove down the narrow alley that led to the door of the restaurant. A valet took the car and we went in. The hostess recognized us and acted like it had only been a couple weeks since the last time we had been in. The truth was, we had probably both been in there recently, but each with other partners.

I asked for a bottle of Singe Shiraz and we ordered pasta dishes without looking at a menu. We skipped salads and appetizers and told the waiter not to delay bringing the food out. After he left I checked my watch and saw we still had forty-five minutes. Plenty of time.

The Guinness was catching up with Maggie. She smiled in a fractured sort of way that told me she was drunk. Beautifully drunk. She never got mean under a buzz. She always got sweeter. It was probably how we'd ended up having a child together.

"You should probably lay off the wine," I told her. "Or you'll have a headache tomorrow."

"Don't worry about me. I'll lay what I want and lay off what I want."

She smiled at me and I smiled back.

"So how you been, Haller? I mean really."

"Fine. You? And I mean really."

"Never better. Are you past Lorna now?"

"Yeah, we're even friends."

"And what are we?"

"I don't know. Sometimes adversaries, I guess."

She shook her head.

"We can't be adversaries if we can't stay on the same case together. Besides, I'm always looking out for you. Like with that dirtbag, Corliss."

"Thanks for trying, but he still did the damage."

"I just have no respect for a prosecutor who would use a jailhouse snitch. Doesn't matter that your client is an even bigger dirtbag."

"He wouldn't tell me exactly what Corliss said my guy said."

"What are you talking about?"

"He just said he had a snitch. He wouldn't reveal what he said."

"That's not fair."

"That's what I said. It's a discovery issue but we don't get a judge assigned until after the arraignment Monday. So there's nobody I can really complain to yet. Minton knows that. It's like you warned me. He doesn't play fair."

Her cheeks flushed. I had pushed the right buttons and she was angry. For Maggie, winning fair was the only way to win. That was why she was a good prosecutor.

We were sitting at the end of the banquette that ran along the back wall of the restaurant. We were on both sides of a corner. Maggie leaned toward me but went too far and we banged heads. She laughed but then tried again. She spoke in a low voice.

"He said that he asked your guy what he was in for and your guy said, 'For giving a bitch exactly what she deserved.' He said your client told him he punched her out as soon as she opened her door."

She leaned back and I could tell she had moved too quickly, bringing on a swoon of vertigo.

"You okay?"

"Yes, but can we change the subject? I don't want to talk about work anymore. There are too many assholes and it's too frustrating."

"Sure."

Just then the waiter brought our wine and our dinners at the same time. The wine was good and the food was like home comfort. We started out eating quietly. Then Maggie hit me with a pitch right out of the blue.

"You didn't know anything about Corliss, did you? Not till I opened my big mouth."

"I knew Minton was hiding something. I thought it was a jail-house —"

"Bullshit. You got me drunk so you could find out what I knew."

"Uh, I think you were already drunk when I hooked up with you tonight."

She was poised with her fork up over her plate, a long string of linguine with pesto sauce hanging off it. She then pointed the fork at me.

"Good point. So what about our daughter?"

I wasn't expecting her to remember that. I shrugged.

"I think what you said last week is right. She needs her father more in her life."

"And?"

"And I want to play a bigger part. I like watching her. Like when I took her to that movie on Saturday. I was sort of sitting sideways so I could watch her watching the movie. Watch her eyes, you know?"

"Welcome to the club."

"So I don't know. I was thinking maybe we should set up a schedule, you know? Like make it a regular thing. She could even stay overnight sometimes — I mean, if she wanted."

"Are you sure about all of that? This is new from you."

"It's new because I didn't know about it before. When she was smaller and I couldn't really communicate with her, I didn't really know what to do with her. I felt awkward. Now I don't. I like talking to her. Being with her. I learn more from her than she does from me, that's for sure."

I suddenly felt her hand on my leg under the table.

"This is great," she said. "I am so happy to hear you say that. But let's move slow. You haven't been around her much for four years and I am not going to let her build up her hopes only to have you pull a disappearing act."

"I understand. We can take it any way you want. I'm just telling you I am going to be there. I promise."

She smiled, wanting to believe. And I made the same promise I just made to her to myself.

"Well, great," she said. "I'm really glad you want to do this. Let's get a calendar and work out some dates and see how it goes."

She took her hand away and we continued eating in silence until we both had almost finished. Then Maggie surprised me once again.

"I don't think I can drive my car tonight," she said.

I nodded.

"I was thinking the same thing."

"You seem all right. You only had half a pint at —"

"No, I mean I was thinking the same thing about you. But don't worry, I'll drive you home."

"Thank you."

Then she reached across the table and put her hand on my wrist.

"And will you take me back to get my car in the morning?"

She smiled sweetly at me. I looked at her, trying to read this woman who had told me to hit the road four years before. The woman I had never been able to get by or get over, whose rejection sent me reeling into a relationship I knew from the beginning couldn't go the distance.

"Sure," I said. "I'll take you."

I n the morning I awoke to find my eight-year-old daughter sleeping between me and my ex-wife. Light was leaking in from a cathedral window high up on the wall. When I had lived here that window had always bothered me because it let in too much light too early in the mornings. Looking up at the pattern it threw on the inclined ceiling, I reviewed what had happened the night before and remembered that I had ended up drinking all but one glass of the bottle of wine at the restaurant. I remembered taking Maggie home to the apartment and coming in to find our daughter had already fallen asleep for the night — in her own bed.

After the babysitter had been released, Maggie opened another bottle of wine. When we finished it she took me by the hand and led me to the bedroom we had shared for four years, but not in four years. What bothered me now was that my memory had absorbed all the wine and I could not remember whether it had been a triumphant return to the bedroom or a failure. I also could not remember what words had been spoken, what promises had possibly been made.

"This is not fair to her."

I turned my head on the pillow. Maggie was awake. She was looking at our sleeping daughter's angelic face.

"What isn't fair?"

"Her waking up and finding you here. She might get her hopes up or just get the wrong idea."

"How'd she get in here?"

"I carried her in. She had a nightmare."

"How often does she have nightmares?"

"Usually, when she sleeps alone. In her room."

"So she sleeps in here all the time?"

Something about my tone bothered her.

"Don't start. You have no idea what it's like to raise a child by yourself."

"I know. I'm not saying anything. So what do you want me to do, leave before she wakes up? I could get dressed and act like I just came by to get you and drive you back to your car."

"I don't know. Get dressed for now. Try not to wake her up."

I slipped out of the bed, grabbed my clothes and went down the hall to the guest bathroom. I was confused by how much Maggie's demeanor toward me had changed overnight. Alcohol, I decided. Or maybe something I did or said after we'd gotten back to the apartment. I quickly got dressed and went back up the hallway to the bedroom and peeked in.

Hayley was still asleep. With her arms spread across two pillows she looked like an angel with wings. Maggie was pulling a long-sleeve T-shirt over an old pair of sweats she'd had since back when we were married. I walked in and stepped over to her.

"I'm going to go and come back," I whispered.

"What?" she said with annoyance. "I thought we were going to get the car."

"But I thought you didn't want her to wake up and see me. So let me go and I'll have some coffee or something and be back in an hour. We can all go together and get your car and then I'll take Hayley to school. I'll even pick her up later if you want. My calendar's clear today."

"Just like that? You're going to start driving her to school?"

"She's my daughter. Don't you remember anything I told you last night?"

She shifted the line of her jaw and I knew from experience that this was when the heavy artillery came out. I was missing something. Maggie had shifted gears.

"Well, yes, but I thought you were just saying that," she said.

"What do you mean?"

"I just thought you were trying to get into my head on your case or just plain get me into bed. I don't know."

I laughed and shook my head. Any fantasies about us that I'd had the night before were vanishing quickly.

"I wasn't the one who led the other up the steps to the bedroom," I said.

"Oh, so it was really about the case. You wanted what I knew about your case."

I just stared at her for a long moment.

"I can't win with you, can I?"

"Not when you're underhanded, when you act like a criminal defense attorney."

She was always the better of the two of us when it came to verbal knife throwing. The truth was, I was thankful we had a built-in conflict of interest and I would never have to face her in trial. Over the years some people — mostly defense pros who suffered at her hands — had gone so far as to say that was the reason I had married her. To avoid her professionally.

"Tell you what," I said. "I'll be back in an hour. If you want a ride to the car that you were too drunk to drive last night, be ready and have her ready."

"It's okay. We'll take a cab."

"I will drive you."

"No, we'll take a cab. And keep your voice down."

I looked over at my daughter, still asleep despite her parents' verbal sparring.

"What about her? Do you want me to take her tomorrow or Sunday?"

"I don't know. Call me tomorrow."

"Fine. Good-bye."

I left her there in the bedroom. Outside the apartment building I walked a block and a half down Dickens before finding the Lincoln parked awkwardly against the curb. There was a ticket on the windshield citing me for parking next to a fire hydrant. I got in the car and threw it into the backseat. I'd deal with it the next time I was riding back there. I wouldn't be like Louis Roulet, letting my tickets go to warrant. There was a county full of cops out there who would love to book me on a warrant.

Fighting always made me hungry and I realized I was starved. I worked my way back to Ventura and headed toward Studio City. It was early, especially for the morning after St. Patrick's Day, and I got to the DuPar's by Laurel Canyon Boulevard before it was crowded. I got a booth in the back and ordered a short stack of pancakes and coffee. I tried to forget about Maggie McFierce by opening up my briefcase and pulling out a legal pad and the Roulet files.

Before diving into the files I made a call to Raul Levin, waking him up at his home in Glendale.

"I've got something for you to do," I said.

"Can't this wait till Monday? I just got home a couple hours ago. I was going to start the weekend today."

"No, it can't wait and you owe me one after yesterday. Besides, you're not even Irish. I need you to background somebody."

"All right, wait a minute."

I heard him put down the phone while he probably grabbed pen and paper to take notes.

"Okay, go ahead."

"There's a guy named Corliss who was arraigned right after Roulet back on the seventh. He was in the first group out and they were in the holding pen at the same time. He's now trying to snitch Roulet off and I want to know everything there is to know about the guy so I can put his dick in the dirt."

"Got a first name?"

"Nope."

"Do you know what he's in there for?"

"No, and I don't even know if he is still in there."

"Thanks for the help. What's he saying Roulet told him?"

"That he beat up some bitch who had it coming. Words to that effect."

"Okay, what else you got?"

"That's it other than I got a tip that he's a repeat snitch. Find out who he's crapped on in the past and there might be something there I can use. Go back as far as you can go with this guy. The DA's people usually don't. They're afraid of what they might find. They'd rather be ignorant."

"Okay, I'll get on it."

"Let me know when you know."

I closed the phone just as my pancakes arrived. I doused them liberally with maple syrup and started eating while looking through the file containing the state's discovery.

The weapon report remained the only surprise. Everything else in the file, except the color photos, I had already seen in Levin's file.

I moved on to that. As expected with a contract investigator, Levin had larded the file with everything found in the net he had cast. He even had copies of the parking tickets and speeding citations Roulet had accumulated and failed to pay in recent years. It annoyed me at first because there was so much to weed through to get to what was going to be germane to Roulet's defense.

I was nearly through it all when the waitress swung by my booth with a coffee pot, looking to refill my mug. She recoiled when she saw the battered face of Reggie Campo in one of the color photos I had put to the side of the files.

"Sorry about that," I said.

I covered the photo with one of the files and signaled her back. The waitress came back hesitantly and poured the coffee.

"It's work," I said in feeble explanation. "I didn't mean to do that to you."

"All I can say is I hope you get the bastard that did that to her."

I nodded. She thought I was a cop. Probably because I hadn't shaved in twenty-four hours.

"I'm working on it," I said.

She went away and I went back to the file. As I slid the photo of Reggie Campo out from underneath it I saw the undamaged side of her face first. The left side. Something struck me and I held the file in position so that I was only looking at the good half of her face. The wave of familiarity came over me again. But again I could not place its origin. I knew this woman looked like another woman I knew or was at least familiar with. But who?

I also knew it was going to bother me until I figured it out. I thought about it for a long time, sipping my coffee and drumming my fingers on the table, and then decided to try something. I took the face shot of Campo and folded it lengthwise down the middle so that one side of the crease showed the damaged right side of her face and the other showed the unblemished left side. I then slipped the folded photo into the inside pocket of my jacket and got up from the booth.

There was no one in the restroom. I quickly went to the sink and took out the folded photo. I leaned over the sink and held the crease of the photo against the mirror with the undamaged side of Reggie Campo's face on display. The mirror reflected the image, creating a full and undamaged face. I stared at it for a long time and then finally realized why the face was familiar.

"Martha Renteria," I said.

The door to the restroom suddenly burst open and two teenagers stormed in, their hands already tugging on their zippers. I quickly pulled the photo back from the mirror and shoved it inside my jacket. I turned and walked toward the door. I heard them burst into laughter as I left. I couldn't imagine what it was they thought I was doing.

Back at the booth I gathered my files and photos and put them all back into my briefcase. I left a more than adequate amount of cash on the table for tab and tip and left the restaurant in a hurry. I felt like I was having a strange food reaction. My face felt flushed and I was hot under the collar. I thought I could hear my heart pounding beneath my shirt.

Fifteen minutes later I was parked in front of my storage warehouse on Oxnard Avenue in North Hollywood. I have a fifteen-hundred-square-foot space behind a double-wide garage door. The place is owned by a man whose son I defended on a possession case, getting him out of jail and into pretrial intervention. In lieu of a fee, the father gave me the warehouse rent-free for a year. But his son the drug addict kept getting into trouble and I kept getting free years of warehouse rent.

I keep the boxes of files from dead cases in the warehouse as well as two other Lincoln Town Cars. Last year when I was flush I bought four Lincolns at once so I could get a fleet rate. The plan was to use each one until it hit sixty thousand on the odometer and then dump it on a limousine service to be used to ferry travelers to and from the airport. The plan was working out so far. I was on the second Lincoln and it would soon be time for the third.

Once I got one of the garage doors up I went to the archival area, where the file boxes were arranged by year on industrial shelving. I found the section of shelves for boxes from two years earlier and ran my finger down the list of client names written on the side of each box until I found the name Jesus Menendez.

I pulled the box off the shelf and squatted down and opened it on the floor. The Menendez case had been short-lived. He took a plea early, before the DA pulled it back off the table. So there were only four files and these mostly contained copies of the documents relating to the police investigation. I paged through the files looking for photographs and finally saw what I was looking for in the third file.

Martha Renteria was the woman Jesus Menendez had pleaded guilty to murdering. She was a twenty-four-year-old dancer who had a dark beauty and a smile of big white teeth. She had been found stabbed to death in her Panorama City apartment. She had been beaten before she was stabbed and her facial injuries were to the left side of her face, the opposite of Reggie Campo. I found the close-up shot of her face contained in the autopsy report. Once more I folded the photo lengthwise, one side of her face damaged, one side untouched.

On the floor I took the two folded photographs, one of Reggie and one of Martha, and fitted them together along the fold lines. Putting aside the fact that one woman was dead and one wasn't, the half faces damn near formed a perfect match. The two women looked so much alike they could have passed for sisters.

EIGHTEEN

Jesus Menendez was serving a life sentence in San Quentin because he had wiped his penis on a bathroom towel. No matter how you looked at it, that is what it really came down to. That towel had been his biggest mistake.

Sitting spread-legged on the concrete floor of my warehouse, the contents of Menendez files fanned out around me, I was reacquainting myself with the facts of the case I had worked two years before. Menendez was convicted of killing Martha Renteria after following her home to Panorama City from a strip club in East Hollywood called The Cobra Room. He raped her and then stabbed her more than fifty times, causing so much blood to leave her body that it seeped through the bed and formed a puddle on the wood floor below it. In another day it seeped through cracks in the floor and formed a drip from the ceiling in the apartment below. That is when the police were called.

The case against Menendez was formidable but circumstantial. He had also hurt himself by admitting to police — before I was on the case — that he had been in her apartment on the night of the murder. But it was the DNA on the fluffy pink towel in the victim's bathroom that ultimately did him in. It couldn't be neutralized. It was a spinning plate that couldn't be knocked down. Defense pros call a piece of evidence like this the iceberg because it is the evidence that sinks the ship.

I had taken on the Menendez murder case as what I would call a "loss leader." Menendez had no money to pay for the kind of time and effort it would take to mount a thorough defense but the case had garnered substantial publicity and I was willing to trade my time and work for the free advertising. Menendez had come to me because just a few months before his arrest I had successfully defended his older brother Fernando in a heroin case. At least in my opinion I had been successful. I had gotten a possession and sales charge knocked down to a simple possession. He got probation instead of prison.

Those good efforts resulted in Fernando calling me on the night Jesus was arrested for the murder of Martha Renteria. Jesus had gone to the Van Nuys Division to voluntarily talk to detectives. A drawing of his face had been shown on every television channel in the city and was getting heavy rotation in particular on the Spanish channels. He had told his family that he would go to the detectives to straighten things out and be back. But he never came back, so his brother called me. I told the brother that the lesson to be learned was never to go to the detectives to straighten things out until after you've consulted an attorney.

I had already seen numerous television news reports on the murder of the exotic dancer, as Renteria had been labeled, when Menendez's brother called me. The reports had included the police artist's drawing of the Latin male believed to have followed her from the club. I knew that the pre-arrest media interest meant the case would likely be carried forward in the public consciousness by the television news and I might be able to get a good ride out of it. I agreed to take the case on the come line. For free. Pro bono. For the good of the system. Besides, murder cases are few and far between. I take them when I can get them. Menendez was the twelfth accused murderer I had defended. The first eleven were still in prison but none of them were on death row. I considered that a good record.

By the time I got to Menendez in a holding cell at Van Nuys

Division, he had already given a statement that implicated him to the police. He had told detectives Howard Kurlen and Don Crafton that he had not followed Renteria home, as suggested by the news reports, but had been an invited guest to her apartment. He explained that earlier in the day he had won eleven hundred dollars on the California lotto and had been willing to trade some of it to Renteria for some of her attention. He said that at her apartment they had engaged in consensual sex — although he did not use those words — and that when he left she was alive and five hundred dollars in cash richer.

The holes Kurlen and Crafton punched in Menendez's story were many. First of all, there had been no state lotto on the day of or day before the murder and the neighborhood mini-market where he said he had cashed his winning ticket had no record of paying out an eleven-hundred-dollar win to Menendez or anyone else. Additionally, no more than eighty dollars in cash was found in the victim's apartment. And lastly, the autopsy report indicated that bruising and other damage to the interior of the victim's vagina precluded what could be considered consensual sexual relations. The medical examiner concluded that she had been brutally raped.

No fingerprints other than the victim's were found in the apartment. The place had been wiped clean. No semen was found in the victim's body, indicating her rapist had used a condom or had not ejaculated during the assault. But in the bathroom off the bedroom where the attack and murder had taken place, a crime scene investigator using a black light found a small amount of semen on a pink towel hanging on a rack near the toilet. The theory that came into play was that after the rape and murder the killer had stepped into the bathroom, removed the condom and flushed it down the toilet. He had then wiped his penis with the nearby towel and then hung the towel back on the rack. When cleaning up after the crime and wiping surfaces he might have touched, he forgot about that towel.

The investigators kept the discovery of the DNA deposit and their attendant theory secret. It never made it into the media. It would become Kurlen and Crafton's hole card.

Based on Menendez's lies and the admission that he had been in the victim's apartment, he was arrested on suspicion of murder and held without bail. Detectives got a search warrant, and oral swabs were collected from Menendez and sent to the lab for DNA typing and comparison to the DNA recovered from the bathroom towel.

That was about when I entered the case. As they say in my profession, by then the *Titanic* had already left the dock. The iceberg was out there waiting. Menendez had badly hurt himself by talking — and lying — to the detectives. Still, unaware of the DNA comparison that was under way, I saw a glimmer of light for Jesus Menendez. There was a case to be made for neutralizing his interview with detectives — which, by the way, became a full-blown confession by the time it got reported by the media. Menendez was Mexican born and had come to this country at age eight. His family spoke only Spanish at home and he had attended a school for Spanish speakers until dropping out at age fourteen. He spoke only rudimentary English, and his cognition level of the language seemed to me to be even lower than his speaking level. Kurlen and Crafton made no effort to bring in a translator and, according to the taped interview, not once asked if Menendez even wanted one.

This was the crack I would work my way into. The interview was the foundation of the case against Menendez. It was the spinning platter. If I could knock it down most of the other plates would come down with it. My plan was to attack the interview as a violation of Menendez's rights because he could not have understood the Miranda warning he had been read by Kurlen or the document listing these rights in English that he had signed at the detective's request.

This is where the case stood until two weeks after Menendez's arrest when the lab results came back matching his DNA to that found on the towel in the victim's bathroom. After that the prosecution didn't need the interview or his admissions. The DNA put Menendez directly on the scene of a brutal rape and murder. I could try an O.J. defense — attack the credibility of the DNA match. But prosecutors and lab techs had learned so much from that debacle and in the years since that I knew I was unlikely of prevailing with a jury.

The DNA was the iceberg and the momentum of the ship made it impossible to steer around it in time.

The district attorney himself revealed the DNA findings at a press conference and announced that his office would seek the death penalty for Menendez. He added that detectives had also located three eyewitnesses who had seen Menendez throw a knife into the Los Angeles River. The DA said the river was searched for the weapon but it was not recovered. Regardless, he characterized the witness accounts as solid — they were Menendez's three roommates.

Based on the prosecution's case coming together and the threat of the death penalty, I decided the O.J. defense would be too risky. Using Fernando Menendez as my translator, I went to the Van Nuys jail and told Jesus that his only hope was for a deal the DA had floated by me. If Menendez would plead guilty to murder I could get him a life sentence with the possibility of parole. I told him he'd be out in fifteen years. I told him it was the only way.

It was a tearful discussion. Both brothers cried and beseeched me to find another way. Jesus insisted that he did not kill Martha Renteria. He said he had lied to the detectives to protect Fernando, who had given him the money after a good month selling tar heroin. Jesus thought that revealing his brother's generosity would lead to another investigation of Fernando and his possible arrest.

The brothers urged me to investigate the case. Jesus told me Renteria had had other suitors that night in The Cobra Room. The reason he had paid her so much money was because she had played him off another bidder for her services.

Lastly, Jesus told me it was true that he had thrown a knife into the river but it was because he was afraid. It wasn't the murder weapon. It was just a knife he used on day jobs he picked up in Pacoima. It looked like the knife they were describing on the Spanish channel and he got rid of it before going to the police to straighten things out.

I listened and then told them that none of their explanations mattered. The only thing that mattered was the DNA. Jesus had a choice. He could take the fifteen years or go to trial and risk getting the death penalty or life *without* the possibility of parole. I reminded

Jesus that he was a young man. He could be out by age forty. He could still have a life.

By the time I left the jailhouse meeting, I had Jesus Menendez's consent to make the deal. I only saw him one more time after that. At his plea-and-sentencing hearing when I stood next to him in front of the judge and coached him through the guilty plea. He was shipped off to Pelican Bay initially and then down to San Quentin after that. I had heard through the courthouse grapevine that his brother had gotten himself popped again — this time for using heroin. But he didn't call me. He went with a different lawyer and I didn't have to wonder why.

On the warehouse floor I opened the report on the autopsy of Martha Renteria. I was looking for two specific things that had probably not been looked at very closely by anyone else before. The case was closed. It was a dead file. Nobody cared anymore.

The first was the part of the report that dealt with the fifty-three stab wounds Renteria suffered during the attack on her bed. Under the heading "Wound Profile" the unknown weapon was described as a blade no longer than five inches and no wider than an inch. Its thickness was placed at one-eighth of an inch. Also noted in the report was the occurrence of jagged skin tears at the top of the victim's wounds, indicating that the top of the blade had an uneven line, to wit, it was designed as a weapon that would inflict damage going in as well as coming out. The shortness of the blade suggested that the weapon might be a folding knife.

There was a crude drawing in the report that depicted the outline of the blade without a handle. It looked familiar to me. I pulled my briefcase across the floor from where I had put it down and opened it up. From the state's discovery file I pulled the photo of the open folding knife with Louis Roulet's initials etched on the blade. I compared the blade to the outline drawn on the page in the autopsy report. It wasn't an exact match but it was damn close.

I then pulled out the recovered weapon analysis report and read the same paragraph I had read during the meeting in Roulet's office the day before. The knife was described as a custom-made Black

Ninja folding knife with a blade measuring five inches long, one inch wide and one-eighth of an inch thick — the same measurements belonging to the unknown knife used to kill Martha Renteria. The knife Jesus Menendez supposedly threw into the L.A. River.

I knew that a five-inch blade wasn't unique. Nothing was conclusive but my instincts told me I was moving toward something. I tried not to let the burn that was building in my chest and throat distract me. I tried to stay on point. I moved on. I needed to check for a specific wound but I didn't want to look at the photos contained in the back of the report, the photos that coldly documented the horribly violated body of Martha Renteria. Instead I went to the page that had two side-by-side generic body profiles, one for the front and one for the back. On these the medical examiner had marked the wounds and numbered them. Only the front profile had been used. Dots and numbers 1 through 53. It looked like a macabre connect-the-dots puzzle and I didn't doubt that Kurlen or some detective looking for anything in the days before Menendez walked in had connected them, hoping the killer had left his initials or some other bizarre clue behind.

I studied the front profile's neck and saw two dots on either side of the neck. They were numbered 1 and 2. I turned the page and looked at the list of individual wound descriptions.

The description for wound number 1 read: *Superficial puncture on the lower right neck with ante-mortem histamine levels, indicative of coercive wound.*

The description for wound number 2 read: *Superficial puncture on the lower left neck with ante-mortem histamine levels, indicative of coercive wound. This puncture measures 1 cm larger than wound No. 1.*

The descriptions meant the wounds had been inflicted while Martha Renteria was still alive. And that was likely why they had been the first wounds listed and described. The examiner had suggested it was likely that the wounds resulted from a knife being held to the victim's neck in a coercive manner. It was the killer's method of controlling her.

I turned back to the state's discovery file for the Campo case. I pulled the photographs of Reggie Campo and the report on her phys-ical examination at Holy Cross Medical Center. Campo had a small puncture wound on the lower left side of her neck and no wounds on her right side. I next scanned through her statement to the police until I found the part in which she described how she got the wound. She said that her attacker pulled her up off the floor of the living room and told her to lead him toward the bedroom. He controlled her from behind by gripping the bra strap across her back with his right hand and holding the knife point against the left side of her neck with his left hand. When she felt him momentarily rest his wrist on her shoulder she made her move, suddenly pivoting and pushing backwards, knocking her attacker into a large floor vase, and then breaking away.

I thought I understood now why Reggie Campo had only one wound on her neck, compared with the two Martha Renteria ended up with. If Campo's attacker had gotten her to the bedroom and put her down on the bed, he would have been facing her when he climbed on top of her. If he kept his knife in the same hand — the left — the blade would shift to the other side of her neck. When they found her dead in the bed, she'd have coercive punctures on both sides of her neck.

I put the files aside and sat cross-legged on the floor without moving for a long time. My thoughts were whispers in the darkness inside. In my mind I held the image of Jesus Menendez's tear-streaked face when he had told me that he was innocent — when he'd begged me to believe him — and I had told him that he must plead guilty. It had been more than legal advice I was dispensing. He had no money, no defense and no chance — in that order — and I told him he had no choice. And though ultimately it was his decision and from his mouth that the word *guilty* was uttered in front of the judge, it felt to me now as though it had been me, his own attorney, holding the knife of the system against his neck and forcing him to say it.

NINETEEN

I got out of the huge new rent-a-car facility at San Francisco International by one o'clock and headed north to the city. The Lincoln they gave me smelled like it had last been used by a smoker, maybe the renter or maybe just the guy who cleaned it up for me.

I don't know how to get anywhere in San Francisco. I just know how to drive through it. Three or four times a year I need to go to the prison by the bay, San Quentin, to talk to clients or witnesses. I could tell you how to get there, no sweat. But ask me how to get to Coit Tower or Fisherman's Wharf and we have a problem.

By the time I got through the city and over the Golden Gate it was almost two. I was in good shape. I knew from past experience that attorney visiting hours ended at four.

San Quentin is over a century old and looks as though the soul of every prisoner who lived or died there is etched on its dark walls. It was as foreboding a prison as I had ever visited, and at one time or another I had been to every one in California.

They searched my briefcase and made me go through a metal detector. After that they still passed a wand over me to make extra sure. Even then I wasn't allowed direct contact with Menendez because I had not formally scheduled the interview the required five days in advance. So I was put in a no-contact room — a Plexiglas wall between us with dime-size holes to speak through. I showed the guard the six-pack of photos I wanted to give Menendez and he told me I would have to show him the pictures through the Plexiglas. I sat down, put the photos away and didn't have to wait long until they brought Menendez in on the other side of the glass.

Two years ago, when he was shipped off to prison, Jesus Menendez had been a young man. Now he looked like he was already the forty years old I told him he could beat if he pleaded guilty. He looked at me with eyes as dead as the gravel stones out in the parking lot. He saw me and sat down reluctantly. He didn't have much use for me anymore.

We didn't bother with hellos and I got right into it.

"Look, Jesus, I don't have to ask you how you've been. I know. But something's come up and it could affect your case. I need to ask you a few questions. You understand me?"

"Why questions now, man? You had no questions before."

I nodded.

"You're right. I should've asked you more questions back then and I didn't. I didn't know then what I know now. Or at least what I think I know now. I am trying to make things right."

"What do you want?"

"I want you to tell me about that night at The Cobra Room."

He shrugged.

"The girl was there and I talked. She tol' me to follow her home."

He shrugged again.

"I went to her place, man, but I didn't kill her like that."

"Go back to the club. You told me that you had to impress the girl, that you had to show her the money and you spent more than you wanted to. You remember?"

"Is right."

"You said there was another guy trying to get with her. You remember that?"

"Si, he was there talking. She went to him but she came back to me."

"You had to pay her more, right?"

"Like that."

"Okay, do you remember that guy? If you saw a picture of him, would you remember him?"

"The guy who talked big? I think I 'member."

"Okay."

I opened my briefcase and took out the spread of mug shots. There were six photos and they included the booking photo of Louis Ross Roulet and five other men whose mug shots I had culled out of my archive boxes. I stood up and one by one started holding them up on the glass. I thought that by spreading my fingers I would be able to hold all six against the glass. Menendez stood up to look closely at the photos.

Almost immediately a voice boomed from an overhead speaker.

"Step back from the glass. Both of you step back from the glass and remain seated or the interview will be terminated."

I shook my head and cursed. I gathered the photos together and sat down. Menendez sat back down as well.

"Guard!" I said loudly.

I looked at Menendez and waited. The guard didn't enter the room.

"Guard!" I called again, louder.

Finally, the door opened and the guard stepped into my side of the interview room.

"You done?"

"No. I need him to look at these photos."

I held up the stack.

"Show him through the glass. He's not allowed to receive anything from you."

"But I'm going to take them right back."

"Doesn't matter. You can't give him anything."

"But if you don't let him come to the glass, how is he going to see them?"

"It's not my problem."

I waved in surrender.

"All right, okay. Then can you stay here for a minute?"

"What for?"

"I want you to watch this. I'm going to show him the photos and if he makes an ID, I want you to witness it."

"Don't drag me into your bullshit."

He walked to the door and left.

"Goddamn it," I said.

I looked at Menendez.

"All right, Jesus, I'm going to show you, anyway. See if you recognize any of them from where you are sitting."

One by one I held the photos up about a foot from the glass. Menendez leaned forward. As I showed each of the first five he looked, thought about it and then shook his head no. But on the sixth photo I saw his eyes flare. It seemed as though there was some life in them after all.

"That one," he said. "Is him."

I turned the photo toward me to be sure. It was Roulet.

"I 'member," Menendez said. "He's the one."

"And you're sure?"

Menendez nodded.

"What makes you so sure?"

"Because I know. In here I think on that night all of my time."

I nodded.

"Who is the man?" he asked.

"I can't tell you right now. Just know that I am trying to get you out of here."

"What do I do?"

"What you have been doing. Sit tight, be careful and stay safe."

"Safe?"

"I know. But as soon as I have something, you will know about it. I'm trying to get you out of here, Jesus, but it might take a little while."

"You were the one who tol' me to come here."

"At the time I didn't think there was a choice."

"How come you never ask me, did you murder this girl? You my lawyer, man. You din't care. You din't listen."

I stood up and loudly called for the guard. Then I answered his question.

"To legally defend you I didn't need to know the answer to that question. If I asked my clients if they were guilty of the crimes they were charged with, very few would tell me the truth. And if they did, I might not be able to defend them to the best of my ability."

The guard opened the door and looked in at me.

"I'm ready to go," I said.

I checked my watch and figured that if I was lucky in traffic I might be able to catch the five o'clock shuttle back to Burbank. The six o'clock at the latest. I dropped the photos into my briefcase and closed it. I looked back at Menendez, who was still in his chair on the other side of the glass.

"Can I just put my hand on the glass?" I asked the guard.

"Hurry up."

I leaned across the counter and put my hand on the glass, fingers spread. I waited for Menendez to do the same, creating a jailhouse handshake.

Menendez stood, leaned forward and spit on the glass where my hand was.

"You never shake my hand," he said. "I don't shake yours."

I nodded. I thought I understood just where he was coming from.

The guard smirked and told me to step through the door. In ten minutes I was out of the prison and crunching across the gravel to my rental car.

I had come four hundred miles for five minutes but those minutes were devastating. I think the lowest point of my life and professional career came an hour later when I was on the rent-a-car train being delivered back to the United terminal. No longer concentrating on the driving and making it back in time, I had only the case to think about. Cases, actually.

I leaned down, elbows on my knees and my face in my hands. My greatest fear had been realized, realized for two years but I hadn't known it. Not until now. I had been presented with innocence but I had not seen it or grasped it. Instead, I had thrown it into the maw of the machine like everything else. Now it was a cold, gray innocence, as dead as gravel and hidden in a fortress of stone and steel. And I had to live with it.

There was no solace to be found in the alternative, the knowledge that had we rolled the dice and gone to trial, Jesus would likely be on death row right now. There could be no comfort in knowing that fate was avoided, because I knew as sure as I knew anything else in the world that Jesus Menendez had been innocent. Something as rare as a true miracle — an innocent man — had come to me and I hadn't recognized it. I had turned away.

"Bad day?"

I looked up. There was a man across from me and a little bit further down the train car. We were the only ones on this link. He looked to be a decade older and had receding hair that made him look wise. Maybe he was even a lawyer, but I wasn't interested.

"I'm fine," I said. "Just tired."

And I held up a hand, palm out, a signal that I did not want conversation. I usually travel with a set of earbuds like Earl uses. I put them in and run the wire into a jacket pocket. It connects with nothing but it keeps people from talking to me. I had been in too much of a hurry this morning to think about them. Too much of a hurry to reach this point of desolation.

The man across the train got the message and said nothing else. I went back to my dark thoughts about Jesus Menendez. The bottom line was that I believed that I had one client who was guilty of the murder another client was serving a life sentence for. I could not help one without hurting the other. I needed an answer. I needed a plan. I needed proof. But for the moment on the train, I could only think of Jesus Menendez's dead eyes, because I knew I was the one who had killed the light in them.

TWENTY

As soon as I got off the shuttle at Burbank I turned on my cell. I had not come up with a plan but I had come up with my next step and that started with a call to Raul Levin. The phone buzzed in my hand, which meant I had messages. I decided I would get them after I set Levin in motion.

He answered my call and the first thing he asked was whether I had gotten his message.

"I just got off a plane," I said. "I missed it."

"A plane? Where were you?"

"Up north. What was the message?"

"Just an update on Corliss. If you weren't calling about that, what were you calling about?"

"What are you doing tonight?"

"Just hanging out. I don't like going out on Fridays and Saturdays. It's amateur hour. Too many drunks on the road."

"Well, I want to meet. I've got to talk to somebody. Bad things are happening."

Levin apparently sensed something in my voice because he immediately changed his stay-at-home-on-Friday-night policy and we agreed to meet at the Smoke House over by the Warner Studios. It was not far from where I was and not far from his home.

At the airport valet window I gave my ticket to a man in a red jacket and checked messages while waiting for the Lincoln.

Three messages had come in, all during the hour flight down from San Francisco. The first was from Maggie McPherson.

"Michael, I just wanted to call and say I'm sorry about how I was this morning. To tell you the truth, I was mad at myself for some of the things I said last night and the choices I made. I took it out on you and I should not have done that. Um, if you want to take Hayley out tomorrow or Sunday she would love it and, who knows, maybe I could come, too. Either way, just let me know."

She didn't call me Michael too often, even when we were married. She was one of those women who could use your last name and turn it into an endearment. That is, if she wanted to. She had always called me Haller. From the day we met in line to go through a metal detector at the CCB. She was headed to orientation at the DA's office and I was headed to misdemeanor arraignment court to handle a DUI.

I saved the message to listen to again sometime and went on to the next. I was expecting it to be from Levin but the automated voice reported the call came from a number with a 310 area code. The next voice I heard was Louis Roulet's.

"It's me, Louis. I was just checking in. I was just wondering after yesterday where things stood. I also have something I want to tell you."

I hit the erase button and moved on to the third and last message. This was Levin's.

"Hey, Bossman, give me a call. I have some stuff on Corliss. Anyway, the name is Dwayne Jeffery Corliss. That's Dwayne with a *D-W.* He's a hype and he's done the snitch thing a couple other times here in L.A. What's new, right? Anyway, he was actually arrested for stealing a bike he probably planned to trade for a little Mexican tar. He has parlayed snitching off Roulet into a ninety-day lockdown program at County-USC. So we won't be able to get to him and talk to him unless you got a judge that will set it up. Pretty shrewd move by the prosecutor. Anyway, I'm still running him down. Something came up on the Internet in Phoenix that looks pretty good for us if it was the same guy. Something that blew up in his face. I should be able to confirm it by Monday. So that's it for now. Give me a call over the weekend. I'm just hanging out."

I erased the message and closed the phone.

"Say no more," I said to myself.

Once I heard that Corliss was a hype, I needed to know nothing else. I understood why Maggie had not trusted the guy. Hypes — needle addicts — were the most desperate and unreliable people you could come across in the machine. Given the opportunity, they would snitch off their own mothers to get the next injection, or into the next methadone program. Every one of them was a liar and every one of them could easily be shown as such in court.

I was, however, puzzled by what the prosecutor was up to. The name Dwayne Corliss was not in the discovery material Minton had given me. Yet the prosecutor was making the moves he would make with a witness. He had stuck Corliss into a ninety-day program for safekeeping. The Roulet trial would come and go in that time. Was he hiding Corliss? Or was he simply putting the snitch on a shelf in the closet so he would know exactly where he was and where he'd been in case the time came in trial that his testimony would be needed? He was obviously operating under the belief that I didn't know about Corliss. And if it hadn't been for a slip by Maggie McPherson, I wouldn't. It was still a dangerous move, nevertheless. Judges do not look kindly on prosecutors who so openly flout the rules of discovery.

It led me to thinking of a possible strategy for the defense. If Minton was foolish enough to try to spring Corliss in trial, I might not even object under the rules of discovery. I might let him put the heroin addict on the stand so I would get the chance to shred him in front of the jury like a credit card receipt. It would all depend on what Levin could come up with. I planned to tell him to continue to dig into Dwayne Jeffery Corliss. To hold nothing back.

I also thought about Corliss being in a lockdown program at County-USC. Levin was wrong and so was Minton if he was thinking I couldn't reach his witness in lockdown. By coincidence, my client Gloria Dayton had been placed in a lockdown program at County-USC after she snitched off her drug-dealing client. While there were a number of such programs at County, it was likely that she shared group therapy sessions or even mealtime with Corliss. I might not be able to get directly to Corliss but as Dayton's attorney I could get to her, and she in turn could get a message to Corliss.

The Lincoln pulled up and I gave the man in the red jacket a couple dollars. I exited the airport and drove south on Hollywood Way toward the center of Burbank, where all the studios were. I got to the Smoke House ahead of Levin and ordered a martini at the bar. On the overhead TV was an update on the start of the college basketball tournament. Florida had defeated Ohio in the first round. The headline on the bottom of the screen said "March Madness" and I toasted my glass to it. I knew what real March Madness was beginning to feel like.

Levin came in and ordered a beer before we sat down to dinner. It was still green, left over from the night before. Must have been a slow night. Maybe everybody had gone to Four Green Fields.

"Nothing like hair of the dog that bit ya, as long as it's green hair," he said in that brogue that was getting old.

He sipped the level of the glass down so he could walk with it and we stepped out to the hostess station so we could go to a table. She led us to a red padded booth that was shaped like a U. We sat across from each other and I put my briefcase down next to me. When the waitress came for a cocktail order we ordered the whole shooting match: salads, steaks and potatoes. I also asked for an order of the restaurant's signature garlic cheese bread.

"Good thing you don't like going out on weekends," I said to Levin after she was gone. "You eat the cheese bread and your breath will probably kill anybody you come in contact with after this."

"I'll have to take my chances."

We were quiet for a long moment after that. I could feel the vodka working its way into my guilt. I would be sure to order another when the salads came.

"So?" Levin finally said. "You called the meeting."

I nodded.

"I want to tell you a story. Not all of the details are set or known. But I'll tell it to you in the way I think it goes and then you tell me what you think and what I should do. Okay?"

"I like stories. Go ahead."

"I don't think you'll like this one. It starts two years ago with —"

I stopped and waited while the waitress put down our salads and the cheese bread. I asked for another vodka martini even though I was only halfway through the one I had. I wanted to make sure there was no gap.

"So," I said after she was gone. "This whole thing starts two years ago with Jesus Menendez. You remember him, right?"

"Yeah, we mentioned him the other day. The DNA. He's the client you always say is in prison because he wiped his prick on a fluffy pink towel."

He smiled because it was true that I had often reduced Menendez's case to such an absurdly vulgar basis. I had often used it to get a laugh when trading war stories at Four Green Fields with other lawyers. That was before I knew what I now knew.

I did not return the smile.

"Yeah, well, it turns out Jesus didn't do it."

"What do you mean? Somebody else wiped his prick on the towel?"

This time Levin laughed out loud.

"No, you don't get it. I'm telling you Jesus Menendez was innocent."

Levin's face grew serious. He nodded, putting something together.

"He's in San Quentin. You were up at the Q today."

I nodded.

"Let me back up and tell the story," I said. "You didn't do much work for me on Menendez because there was nothing to be done. They had the DNA, his own incriminating statement and three witnesses who saw him throw a knife into the river. They never found the knife but they had the witnesses — his own roommates. It was a hopeless case. Truth is, I took it on the come line for publicity value. So basically all I did was walk him to a plea. He didn't like it, said he didn't do it, but there was no choice. The DA was going for the death penalty. He'd have gotten that or life without. I got him life with and I made the little fucker take it. I made him."

I looked down at my untouched salad. I realized I didn't feel like eating. I just felt like drinking and pickling the cork in my brain that contained all the guilt cells.

Levin waited me out. He wasn't eating, either.

"In case you don't remember, the case was about the murder of a woman named Martha Renteria. She was a dancer at The Cobra Room on East Sunset. You didn't end up going there on this, did you?"

Levin shook his head.

"They don't have a stage," I said. "They have like a pit in the center and for each number, these guys dressed like Aladdin come out carrying this big cobra basket between two bamboo poles. They put it down and the music starts. Then the top comes off the basket and the girl comes up dancing. Then her top comes off, too. Kind of a new take on the dancer coming out of the cake."

"It's Hollywood, baby," Levin said. "You gotta have a show."

"Well, Jesus Menendez liked the show. He had eleven hundred dollars his brother the drug dealer gave him and he took a fancy to Martha Renteria. Maybe because she was the only dancer who was shorter than him. Maybe because she spoke Spanish to him. After her set they sat and talked and then she circulated a little bit and came back and pretty soon he knew he was in competition with another guy in the club. He trumped the other guy by offering her five hundred if she'd take him home."

"But he didn't kill her when he got there?"

"Uh-uh. He followed her car in his. Got there, had sex, flushed the condom, wiped his prick on the towel and then he went home. The story starts after he left."

"The real killer."

"The real killer knocks on the door, maybe fakes like it's Jesus and that he's forgotten something. She opens the door. Or maybe it was an appointment. She was expecting the knock and she opens the door."

"The guy from the club? The one Menendez was bidding against?"

I nodded.

"Exactly. He comes in, punches her a few times to soften her up and then takes out his folding knife and holds it against her neck while he walks her to the bedroom. Sound familiar? Only she isn't lucky like Reggie Campo would be in a couple years. He puts her on the bed, puts on a condom and climbs on top. Now the knife is on the other side of her neck and he keeps it there while he rapes her. And when he's done, he kills her. He stabs her with that knife again and again. It's a case of overkill if there ever was one. He's working out something in his sick fucking mind while he's doing it."

My second martini came and I took it right from the waitress's hand and gulped half of it down. She asked if we were finished with our salads and we both waved them away untouched.

"Your steaks will be right out," she said. "Or do you want me to just dump them in the garbage and save you the time?"

I looked up at her. She was smiling but I was so caught up in the story I was telling that I had missed what it was she had said.

"Never mind," she said. "They'll be right out."

I got right back to the story. Levin said nothing.

"After she's dead the killer cleans up. He takes his time, because what's the hurry, she's not going anywhere or calling anybody. He wipes the place down to take care of any fingerprints he might have left. And in the process he wipes away Menendez's prints. This will look bad for Menendez when he later goes to the police to explain that he is the guy in the sketches but he didn't kill Martha. They'll look at him and say, 'Then why'd you wear gloves when you were there?'"

Levin shook his head.

"Oh man, if this is true . . ."

"Don't worry, it's true. Menendez gets a lawyer who once did a good job for his brother but this lawyer wouldn't know an innocent man if he kicked him in the nuts. This lawyer is all about the deal. He never even asks the kid if he did it. He just assumes he did it because they got his fucking DNA on the towel and the witnesses who saw him toss the knife. The lawyer goes to work and gets the best possible deal he could get. He actually feels pretty good about it because he's going to keep Menendez off death row and get him a shot at parole someday. So he goes to Menendez and brings down the hammer. He makes him take the deal and stand up there in court and say 'Guilty.' Jesus then goes off to prison and everybody's happy. The state's happy because it saves money on a trial and Martha Renteria's family is happy because they don't have to face a trial with all those autopsy photos and stories about their daughter dancing naked and taking men home for money. And the lawyer's happy because he got on TV with the case at least six times, plus he kept another client off death row."

I gulped down the rest of the martini and looked around for our waitress. I wanted another.

"Jesus Menendez goes off to prison a young man. I just saw him and he's twenty-six going on forty. He's a small guy. You know what happens to the little ones up there."

I was looking straight down at the empty space on the table in front of me when an egg-shaped platter with a sizzling steak and steaming potato was put down. I looked up at the waitress and told her to bring me another martini. I didn't say please.

"You better take it easy," Levin said after she was gone. "There probably isn't a cop in this county who wouldn't love to pull you over on a deuce, take you back to lockup and put the flashlight up your ass."

"I know, I know. It will be my last. And if it's too much I won't drive. They always have a cab out front of this place."

Deciding that food might help I cut into my steak and ate a piece. I then took a piece of cheese bread out of the napkin it was folded into a basket with, but it was no longer warm. I dropped it on my plate and put my fork down.

"Look, I know you're beating yourself up over this but you are forgetting something," Levin said.

"Yeah? What's that?"

"His exposure. He was facing the needle, man, and the case was a dog. I didn't work it for you because there was nothing to work. They had him and you saved him from the needle. That's your job and you did it well. So now you think you know what really went down. You can't beat yourself up for what you didn't know then."

I held my hand up in a *stop there* gesture.

"The guy was innocent. I should've seen it. I should've done something about it. Instead, I just did my usual thing and went through the motions with my eyes closed."

"Bullshit."

"No, no bullshit."

"Okay, go back to the story. Who was the second guy who came to her door?"

I opened my briefcase next to me and reached into it.

"I went up to San Quentin today and showed Menendez a six-pack. All mug shots of my clients. Mostly former clients. Menendez picked one out in less than ten seconds."

I tossed the mug shot of Louis Roulet across the table. It landed facedown. Levin picked it up and looked at it for a few moments, then put it back facedown on the table.

"Let me show you something else," I said.

My hand went back into the briefcase and pulled out the two folded photographs of Martha Renteria and Reggie Campo. I looked around to make sure the waitress wasn't about to deliver my martini and then handed them across the table.

"It's like a puzzle," I said. "Put them together and see what you get."

Levin put the one face together from the two and nodded as he understood the significance. The killer — Roulet — zeroed in on women that fit a model or profile he desired. I next showed him the weapon sketch drawn by the medical examiner on the Renteria autopsy and read him the description of the two coercive wounds found on her neck.

"You know that video you got from the bar?" I asked. "What it shows is a killer at work. Just like you, he saw that Mr. X was left-handed. When he attacked Reggie Campo he punched with his left and then held the knife with his left. This guy knows what he is doing. He saw an opportunity and took it. Reggie Campo is the luckiest woman alive."

"You think there are others? Other murders, I mean."

"Maybe. That's what I want you to look into. Check out all the knife murders of women in the last few years. Then get the victim's pictures and see if they match the physical profile. And don't look at unsolved cases only. Martha Renteria was supposedly among the closed cases."

Levin leaned forward.

"Look, man, I'm not going to throw a net over this like the police can. You have to bring the cops in on this. Or go to the FBI. They got their serial killer specialists."

I shook my head.

"Can't. He's my client."

"Menendez is your client, too, and you have to get him out."

"I'm working on that. And that's why I need you to do this for me, Mish."

We both knew that I called him Mish whenever I needed something that crossed the lines of our professional relationship into the friendship that was underneath it.

"What about a hitman?" Levin said. "That would solve our problems."

I nodded, knowing he was being facetious.

"Yeah, that would work," I said. "It would make the world a better place, too. But it probably wouldn't spring Menendez."

Levin leaned forward again. Now he was serious.

"I'll do what I can, Mick, but I don't think this is the right way to go. You can declare conflict of interest and dump Roulet. Then work on jumping Menendez out of the Q."

"Jump him out with what?"

"The ID he made on the six-pack. That was solid. He didn't know Roulet from a hole in the ground and he goes and picks him out of the pack."

"Who is going to believe that? I'm his lawyer! Nobody from the cops to the clemency board is going to believe I didn't set that up. This is all theory, Raul. You know it and I know it to be true but we can't prove a damn thing."

"What about the wounds? They could match the knife they got from the Campo case to Martha Renteria's wounds."

I shook my head.

"She was cremated. All they have is the descriptions and photos from the autopsy and it wouldn't be conclusive. It's not enough. Besides, I can't be seen as the guy pushing this on my own client. If I turn against a client, then I turn against all my clients. It can't look that way or I'll lose them all. I have to figure something else out."

"I think you're wrong. I think —"

"For now I go along as if I don't know any of this, you understand? But you look into it. All of it. Keep it separate from Roulet so I don't have a discovery issue. File it all under Jesus Menendez and bill the time to me on that case. You understand?"

Before Levin could answer, the waitress brought my third martini. I waved it away.

"I don't want it. Just the check."

"Well, I can't pour it back into the bottle," she said.

"Don't worry, I'll pay for it. I just don't want to drink it. Give it to the guy who makes the cheese bread and just bring me the check."

She turned and walked away, probably annoyed that I hadn't offered the drink to her. I looked back at Levin. He looked like he was pained by everything that had been revealed to him. I knew just how he felt.

"Some franchise I got, huh?"

"Yeah. How are you going to be able to act straight with this guy when you have to deal with him and meantime you're digging out this other shit on the side?"

"With Roulet? I plan to see him as little as possible. Only when it's necessary. He left me a message today, has something to tell me. But I'm not calling back."

"Why did he pick you? I mean, why would he pick the one lawyer who might put this thing together?"

I shook my head.

"I don't know. I thought about it the whole plane ride down. I think maybe he was worried I might hear about the case and put it together anyway. But if he was my client, then he knew I'd be ethically bound to protect him. At least at first. Plus there's the money."

"What money?"

"The money from Mother. The franchise. He knows how big a payday this is for me. My biggest ever. Maybe he thought I'd look the other way to keep the money coming in."

Levin nodded.

"Maybe I should, huh?" I said.

It was a vodka-spurred attempt at humor, but Levin didn't smile and then I remembered Jesus Menendez's face behind the prison Plexiglas and I couldn't even bring myself to smile.

"Listen, there's one other thing I need you to do," I said. "I want you to look at him, too. Roulet. Find out all you can without getting too close. And check out that story about the mother, about her getting raped in a house she was selling in Bel-Air."

Levin nodded.

"I'm on it."

"And don't farm it out."

This was a running joke between us. Like me, Levin was a one-man shop. He had no one to farm it out to.

"I won't. I'll handle it myself."

It was his usual response but this time it lacked the false sincerity and humor he usually gave it. He'd answered by habit.

The waitress moved by the table and put our check down without a thank you. I dropped a credit card on it without even looking at the damage. I just wanted to leave.

"You want her to wrap up your steak?" I asked.

"That's okay," Levin said. "I've kind of lost my appetite for right now."

"What about that attack dog you've got at home?"

"That's an idea. I forgot about Bruno."

He looked around for the waitress to ask for a box.

"Take mine, too," I said. "I don't have a dog."

TWENTY-ONE

Despite the vodka glaze, I made it through the slalom that was Laurel Canyon without cracking up the Lincoln or getting pulled over by a cop. My house is on Fareholm Drive, which terraces up off the southern mouth of the canyon. All the houses are built to the street line and the only problem I had coming home was when I found that some moron had parked his SUV in front of my garage and I couldn't get in. Parking on the narrow street is always difficult and the opening in front of my garage door was usually just too inviting, especially on a weekend night, when invariably someone on the street was throwing a party.

I motored by the house and found a space big enough for the Lincoln about a block and a half away. The further I had gotten from my house, the angrier I had gotten with the SUV. The fantasy grew from spitting on the windshield to breaking off the side mirror, flattening the tires and kicking in the side panels. But instead I wrote a sedate little note on a page of yellow legal paper: *This is not a parking space! Next time you will be towed.* After all, you never know who's driving an SUV in L.A., and if you threaten someone for parking in front of your garage, then they know where you live.

I walked back and was placing the note under the violator's windshield wiper when I noticed the SUV was a Range Rover. I put

my hand on the hood and it was cool to the touch. I looked up above
the garage to the windows of my house that I could see, but they were
dark. I slapped the folded note under the windshield wiper and
started up the stairs to the front deck and door. I half expected Louis
Roulet to be sitting in one of the tall director chairs, taking in the
twinkling view of the city, but he was not there.

Instead, I walked to the corner of the porch and looked out on
the city. It was this view that had made me buy the place. Everything
about the house once you went through the door was ordinary and
outdated. But the front porch and the view right above Hollywood
Boulevard could launch a million dreams. I had used money from
the last franchise case for a down payment. But once I was in and
there wasn't another franchise, I took the equity out in a second
mortgage. The truth was I struggled every month just to pay the nut.
I needed to get out from under it but that view off the front deck par-
alyzed me. I'd probably be staring out at the city when they came to
take the key and foreclose on the place.

I know the question my house prompts. Even with my struggles
to stay afloat with it, how fair is it that when a prosecutor and defense
attorney divorce, the defense attorney gets the house on the hill with
a million-dollar view while the prosecutor with the daughter gets the
two-bedroom apartment in the Valley. The answer is that Maggie
McPherson could buy a house of her choosing and I would help her
to my maximum ability. But she had refused to move while she
waited to be tapped for a promotion to the downtown office. Buying
a house in Sherman Oaks or anywhere else would send the wrong
message, one of sedentary contentment. She was not content to be
Maggie McFierce of the Van Nuys Division. She was not content to
be passed over by John Smithson or any of his young guns. She was
ambitious and wanted to get downtown, where supposedly the best
and brightest prosecuted the most important crimes. She refused to
accept the simple truism that the better you were, the bigger threat
you were to those at the top, especially if they are elected. I knew that
Maggie would never be invited downtown. She was too damn good.

Every now and then this realization would seep through and she would lash out in unexpected ways. She would make a cutting re-mark at a press conference or she would refuse to cooperate with a downtown investigation. Or she would drunkenly reveal to a crimi-nal defense attorney and ex-husband something about a case he shouldn't be told.

The phone started to ring from inside the house. I moved to the front door and fumbled with my keys to unlock it and get inside in time. My phone numbers and who has them could form a pyramid chart. The number in the yellow pages everybody has or could have. Next up the pyramid is my cell phone, which has been disseminated to key colleagues, investigators, bondsmen, clients and other cogs in the machine. My home phone — the land line — was the top of the pyramid. Very few had the number. No clients and no other lawyers except for one.

I got in and grabbed the phone off the kitchen wall before it went to message. The caller was that one other lawyer with the number. Maggie McPherson.

"Did you get my messages?"

"I got the one on my cell. What's wrong?"

"Nothing's wrong. I left one on this number a lot earlier."

"Oh, I've been gone all day. I just got in."

"Where have you been?"

"Well, I've been up to San Francisco and back and I just got in from having dinner with Raul Levin. Is all of that all right with you?"

"I'm just curious. What was in San Francisco?"

"A client."

"So what you really mean is you were up to San Quentin and back."

"You were always too smart for me, Maggie. I can never fool you. Is there a reason for this call?"

"I just wanted to see if you got my apology and I also wanted to find out if you were going to do something with Hayley tomorrow."

"Yes and yes. But Maggie, no apology is necessary and you should know that. I am sorry for the way I acted before I left. And if my daughter wants to be with me tomorrow, then I want to be with her. Tell her we can go down to the pier or to a movie if she wants. Whatever she wants."

"Well, she actually wants to go to the mall."

She said it as if she were stepping on glass.

"The mall? The mall is fine. I'll take her. What's wrong with the mall? Is there something in particular she wants?"

I suddenly noticed a foreign odor in the house. The smell of smoke. While standing in the middle of the kitchen I checked the oven and the stove. They were off. I was tethered to the kitchen because the phone wasn't cordless. I stretched it to the door and flicked on the light to the dining room. It was empty and its light was cast into the next room, the living room through which I had passed when I had entered. It looked empty as well.

"They have a place there where you make your own teddy bear and you pick the style and its voice box and you put a little heart in with the stuffing. It's all very cute."

I now wanted to get off the line and explore further into my house.

"Fine. I'll take her. What time is good?"

"I was thinking about noon. Maybe we could have lunch first."

"We?"

"Would that bother you?"

"No, Maggie, not at all. How about I come by at noon?"

"Great."

"See you then."

I hung the phone up before she could say good-bye. I owned a gun but it was a collector piece that hadn't been fired in my lifetime and was stored in a box in my bedroom closet at the rear of the house. So I quietly opened a kitchen drawer and took out a short but sharp steak knife. I then walked through the living room toward the hallway that led to the rear of the house. There were three doorways in the hall. They led to my bedroom, a bathroom and another bedroom I had turned into a home office, the only real office I had.

The desk light was on in the office. It was not visible from the angle I had in the hallway but I could tell it was on. I had not been home in two days but I did not remember leaving it on. I approached the open door to the room slowly, aware that this is what I may have been meant to do. Focus on the light in one room while the intruder is waiting in the darkness of the bedroom or bathroom.

"Come on back, Mick. It's just me."

I knew the voice but it didn't make me feel at ease. Louis Roulet was waiting in the room. I stepped to the threshold and stopped. He was sitting in the black leather desk seat. He swiveled it around so that he was facing me and crossed his legs. His pants rode up on his left leg and I could see the tracking bracelet that Fernando Valenzuela had made him wear. I knew that if Roulet had come to kill me, at least he would leave a trail. It wasn't all that comforting, though. I leaned against the door frame so that I could hold the knife behind my hip without being too obvious about it.

"So this is where you do your great legal work?" Roulet asked.

"Some of it. What are you doing here, Louis?"

"I came to see you. You didn't return my call and so I wanted to make sure we were still a team, you know?"

"I was out of town. I just got back."

"What about dinner with Raul? Isn't that what you said to your caller?"

"He's a friend. I had dinner on my way in from Burbank Airport. How did you find out where I live, Louis?"

He cleared his throat and smiled.

"I work in real estate, Mick. I can find out where anybody lives. In fact, I used to be a source for the *National Enquirer*. Did you know that? I could tell them where any celebrity lived, no matter what fronts and corporations they hid their purchases behind. But I gave it up after a while. The money was good but it was so . . . tawdry. You know what I mean, Mick? Anyway, I stopped. But I can still find out where anyone lives. I can also find out whether they've maxed the mortgage value out and even if they're making their payments on time."

He looked at me with a knowing smile. He was telling me he

knew the house was a financial shell, that I had nothing in the place and usually ran a month behind on the two mortgages. Fernando Valenzuela probably wouldn't even accept the place as collateral on a five-thousand-dollar bond.

"How'd you get in?" I asked.

"Well, that's the funny thing about this. It turns out I had a key. Back when this place was for sale — what was that, about eighteen months ago? Anyway, I wanted to see it because I thought I had a client who might be interested because of the view. So I came and got the key out of the realtor's combo box. I came in and looked around and knew immediately it wasn't right for my client — he wanted something nicer — so I left. And I forgot to put the key back. I have a bad habit of doing that. Isn't that strange that all this time later my lawyer would be living in this house? And by the way, I see you haven't done a thing with it. You have the view, of course, but you really need to do some updating."

I knew then that he had been keeping tabs on me since the Menendez case. And that he probably knew I had just been up to San Quentin visiting him. I thought about the man on the car-rental train. *Bad day?* I had later seen him on the shuttle to Burbank. Had he been following me? Was he working for Roulet? Was he the investigator Cecil Dobbs had tried to push onto the case? I didn't know all the answers but I knew that the only reason Roulet would be in my house waiting for me was because he knew what I knew.

"What do you really want, Louis? Are you trying to scare me?"

"No, no, I'm the one who should be scared. I assume you have a weapon of some sort behind your back there. What is it, a gun?"

I gripped the knife tighter but did not display it.

"What is it you want?" I repeated.

"I want to make you an offer. Not on the house. On your services."

"You already have my services."

He swiveled back and forth in the chair before responding. My eyes scanned the desk, checking if anything was missing. I noticed he had used a little pottery dish my daughter had made for me as an ash-tray. It was supposed to be for paperclips.

"I was thinking about our fee arrangement and the difficulties the case presents," he said. "Frankly, Mick, I think you are under-paid. So I want to set up a new fee schedule. You will be paid the amount already agreed upon and you will be paid in full before the trial begins. But I am now going to add a performance bonus. When I am found by a jury of my peers to be not guilty of this ugly crime, your fee automatically doubles. I will write the check in your Lincoln as we drive away from the courthouse."

"That's nice, Louis, but the California bar refuses to allow de-fense attorneys to accept bonuses based on results. I couldn't accept it. It's more than generous but I can't."

"But the California bar isn't here, Mick. And we don't have to treat it as a performance bonus. It's just part of the fee schedule. Because, after all, you will be successful in defending me, won't you?"

He looked intently at me and I read the threat.

"There are no guarantees in the courtroom. Things can always go badly. But I still think it looks good."

Roulet's face slowly broke into a smile.

"What can I do to make it look even better?"

I thought about Reggie Campo. Still alive and ready to go to trial. She had no idea whom she would be testifying against.

"Nothing," I answered. "Just sit tight and wait it out. Don't get any ideas. Don't do anything. The case is coming together and we'll be all right."

He didn't respond. I wanted to get him away from thoughts about the threat Reggie Campo presented.

"There is one thing that has come up, though," I said.

"Really? What's that?"

"I don't have the details. What I know I only know from a source who can't tell me any more. But it looks like the DA has a snitch from the jail. You didn't talk to anybody about the case when you were in there, did you? Remember, I told you not to talk to anybody."

"And I didn't. Whoever they have, he is a liar."

"Most of them are. I just wanted to be sure. I'll deal with it if it comes up."

"Good."

"One other thing. Have you talked to your mother about testifying about the attack in the empty house? We need it to set up the defense of you carrying the knife."

Roulet pursed his lips but didn't answer.

"I need you to work on her," I said. "It could be very important to establish that solidly with the jury. Besides that, it could swing sympathy toward you."

Roulet nodded. He saw the light.

"Can you please ask her?" I asked.

"I will. But she'll be tough. She never reported it. She never told anyone but Cecil."

"We need her to testify and then we can get Cecil to testify and back her up. It's not as good as a police report but it will work. We need her, Louis. I think if she testifies, she can convince them. Juries like old ladies."

"Okay."

"Did she ever tell you what the guy looked like or how old he was, anything like that?"

He shook his head.

"She couldn't tell. He wore a ski mask and goggles. He jumped on her as soon as she came in the door. He had been hiding behind it. It was very quick and very brutal."

His voice quavered as he described it. I became puzzled.

"I thought you said the attacker was a prospective buyer she was supposed to meet there," I said. "He was already in the house?"

He brought his eyes up to mine.

"Yes. Somehow he had already gotten in and was waiting for her. It was terrible."

I nodded. I didn't want to go further with him at the moment. I wanted him out of my house.

"Listen, thank you for your offer, Louis. Now if you would excuse me, I want to go to bed. It's been a long day."

I gestured with my free hand toward the hallway leading to the front of the house. Roulet got up from the desk chair and came toward me. I backed into the hallway and then into the open door of my bedroom. I kept the knife behind me and ready. But Roulet passed by without incident.

"And tomorrow you have your daughter to entertain," he said.

That froze me. He had listened to the call from Maggie. I didn't say anything. He did.

"I didn't know you had a daughter, Mick. That must be nice."

He glanced back at me, smiling as he moved down the hall.

"She's beautiful," he said.

My inertia turned to momentum. I stepped into the hall and started following him, anger building with each step. I gripped the knife tightly.

"How do you know what she looks like?" I demanded.

He stopped and I stopped. He looked down at the knife in my hand and then at my face. He spoke calmly.

"The picture of her on your desk."

I had forgotten about the photo. A small framed shot of her in a teacup at Disneyland.

"Oh," I said.

He smiled, knowing what I had been thinking.

"Good night, Mick. Enjoy your daughter tomorrow. You probably don't get to see her enough."

He turned and crossed the living room and opened the front door. He looked back at me before stepping out.

"What you need is a good lawyer," he said. "One that will get you custody."

"No. She's better off with her mother."

"Good night, Mick. Thanks for the conversation."

"Good night, Louis."

I stepped forward to close the door.

"Nice view," he said from out on the front porch.

"Yeah," I said as I closed and locked the door.

I stood there with my hand on the knob, waiting to hear his steps going down the stairs to the street. But a few moments later he knocked on the door. I closed my eyes, held the knife at the ready and opened it. Roulet raised his hand out. I took a step back.

"Your key," he said. "I figured you should have it."

I took the key off his outstretched palm.

"Thanks."

"Don't mention it."

I closed the door and locked it once again.

TWENTY-TWO

The day started better than any defense attorney could ask for. I had no courtroom to be in, no client to meet. I slept late, spent the morning reading the newspaper cover to cover and had a box ticket to the home opener of the Los Angeles Dodgers baseball season. It was a day game and a time-honored tradition among those on the defense side of the aisle to attend. My ticket had come from Raul Levin, who was taking five of the defense pros he did work for to the game as a gesture of thanks for their business. I was sure the others would grumble and complain at the game about how I was monopolizing Levin as I prepared for the Roulet trial. But I wasn't going to let it bother me.

We were in the outwardly slow time before trial, when the machine moves with a steady, quiet momentum. Louis Roulet's trial was set to begin in a month. As it was growing nearer I was taking on fewer and fewer clients. I needed the time to prepare and strategize. Though the trial was weeks away it would likely be won or lost with the information gathered now. I needed to keep my schedule clear for this. I took cases from repeat customers only — and only if the money was right and it came up front.

A trial was a slingshot. The key was in the preparation. Pretrial is when the sling is loaded with the proper stone and slowly the elastic is pulled back and stretched to its limit. Finally, at trial you let it go and the projectile shoots forward, unerringly at the target. The target is acquittal. Not guilty. You only hit that target if you have properly chosen the stone and pulled back carefully on the sling, stretching it as far as possible.

Levin was doing most of the stretching. He had continued to dig into the lives of the players in both the Roulet and Menendez cases. We had hatched a strategy and plan we were calling a "double sling-shot" because it had two intended targets. I had no doubt that when the trial began in May, we would be stretched back to the limit and ready to let go.

The prosecution did its part to help us load the slingshot, as well. In the weeks since Roulet's arraignment the state's discovery file grew thicker as scientific reports filtered in, further police investigations were carried out and new developments occurred.

Among the new developments of note was the identification of Mr. X, the left-handed man who had been with Reggie Campo at Morgan's the night of the attack. LAPD detectives, using the video I had alerted the prosecution to, were able to identify him by showing a frame taken off the video to known prostitutes and escorts when they were arrested by the Administrative Vice section. Mr. X was identified as Charles Talbot. He was known to many of the sex providers as a regular. Some said that he owned or worked at a convenience store on Reseda Boulevard.

The investigative reports forwarded to me through discovery requests revealed that detectives interviewed Talbot and learned that on the night of March 6 he left Reggie Campo's apartment shortly before ten and went to the previously mentioned twenty-four-hour convenience store. Talbot owned the business. He went to the store so that he could check on things and open a cigarette storage cabinet that only he carried the key for. Tape from surveillance cameras in the store confirmed that he was there from 10:09 to 10:51 P.M. restocking the cigarette bins beneath the front counter. The investigator's summary dismissed Talbot as having no bearing or part in the events that occurred after he left Campo's apartment. He was just one of her customers.

Nowhere in the state's discovery was there mention of Dwayne Jeffery Corliss, the jailhouse snitch who had contacted the prosecution with a tale to tell about Louis Roulet. Minton had either decided not to use him as a witness or was keeping him under wraps for emergency use only. I tended to think it was the latter. Minton had sequestered him in the lockdown program. He wouldn't have gone to the trouble unless he wanted to keep Corliss offstage but ready. This was fine with me. What Minton didn't know was that Corliss was the stone I was going to put into the slingshot.

And while the state's discovery contained little information on the victim of the crime, Raul Levin was vigorously pursuing Reggie Campo. He located a website called PinkMink.com on which she advertised her services. What was important about the discovery was not necessarily that it further established that she was engaged in prostitution but that the ad copy stated that she was "very open-minded and liked to get wild" and was "available for S&M role play — you spank me or I'll spank you." It was good ammunition to have. It was the kind of stuff that could help color a victim or witness in a jury's eyes. And she was both.

Levin also was digging deeper into the life and times of Louis Roulet and had learned that he had been a poor student who'd attended five different private schools in and around Beverly Hills as a youth. He did go on to attend and graduate from UCLA with a degree in English literature but Levin located fellow classmates who had said Roulet paid his way through by purchasing from other students completed class assignments, test answers and even a ninety-page senior thesis on the life and work of John Fante.

A far darker profile emerged of Roulet as an adult. Levin found numerous female acquaintances who said Roulet had mistreated them, either physically or mentally, or both. Two women who had known Roulet while they were students at UCLA told Levin that they suspected that Roulet had spiked their drinks at a fraternity party with a date-rape drug and then took sexual advantage of them.

Neither reported their suspicions to authorities but one woman had her blood tested the day after the party. She said traces of ketamine hydrochloride, a veterinary sedative, were found. Luckily for the defense, neither woman had so far been located by investigators for the prosecution.

Levin took a look at the so-called Real Estate Rapist cases of five years before as well. Four women — all realtors — reported being overpowered and raped by a man who was waiting inside when they entered homes they believed had been vacated by their owners for a showing. The attacks went unsolved but stopped eleven months after the first one was reported. Levin spoke to an LAPD sex crimes expert who worked the cases. He said that his gut instinct had always been that the rapist wasn't an outsider. The assailant seemed to know how to get into the houses and how to draw the female sales agents to them alone. The investigator was convinced the rapist was in the real estate community, but with no arrest ever made, he never proved his theory.

Added to this branch of his investigation, Levin could find little to confirm that Mary Alice Windsor had been one of the unreported victims of the rapist. She had granted us an interview and agreed to testify about her secret tragedy but only if her testimony was vitally needed. The date of the attack she provided fell within the dates of the documented assaults attributed to the Real Estate Rapist, and Windsor provided an appointment book and other documentation showing she was indeed the realtor on record in regard to the sale of the Bel-Air home where she said she was attacked. But ultimately we only had her word for it. There were no medical or hospital records indicative of treatment for a sexual assault. And no police record.

Still, when Mary Windsor recounted her story, it matched Roulet's telling of it in almost all details. Afterward, it had struck both Levin and me as odd that Louis had known so much about the attack. If his mother had decided to keep it secret and unreported, then why would she share so many details of her harrowing ordeal with her son? That question led Levin to postulate a theory that was as repulsive as it was intriguing.

"I think he knows all the details because he was there," Levin had said after the interview and we were by ourselves.

"You mean he watched it without doing anything to stop it?"

"No, I mean I think he was the man in the ski mask and goggles."

I was silent. I think on a subliminal level I may have been think- ing the same thing but the idea was too creepy to have broken through to the surface.

"Oh, man . . . ," I said.

Levin, thinking I was disagreeing, pressed his case forward.

"This is a very strong woman," he said. "She built that company from nothing and real estate in this town is cutthroat. She's a tough lady and I can't see her not reporting this, not wanting the guy who did it to be caught. I view people two ways. They're either eye-for- an-eye people or they are turn-the-cheek people. She's definitely an eye-for-an-eye person and I can't see her keeping it quiet unless she was protecting that guy. Unless that guy was our guy. I'm telling you, man, Roulet is evil. I don't know where it comes from or how he got it, but the more I look at him, the more I see the devil."

All of this backgrounding was completely sub rosa. It obviously was not the kind of background that would in any way be brought forward as a means of defense. It had to be hidden from discovery, so little of what Levin or I found was put down on paper. But it was still information that I had to know as I made my decisions and set up the trial and the play within it.

At 11:05 my home phone rang as I was standing in front of a mir- ror and fitting a Dodgers cap onto my head. I checked the caller ID before answering and saw that it was Lorna Taylor.

"Why is your cell phone off?" she asked.

"Because I'm off. I told you, no calls today. I'm going to the ball- game with Mish and I'm supposed to get going to meet him early."

"Who's Mish?"

"I mean Raul. Why are you bothering me?"

I said it good-naturedly.

"Because I think you are going to want to be bothered with this.

The mail came in a little early today and with it you got a notice from the Second."

The Second District Court of Appeal reviewed all cases emanating from L.A. County. They were the first appellate hurdle on the way to the Supreme Court. But I didn't think Lorna would be calling me to tell me I had lost an appeal.

"Which case?"

At any given time I usually have four or five cases on appeal to the Second.

"One of your Road Saints. Harold Casey. You won!"

I was shocked. Not at winning, but at the timing. I had tried to move quickly with the appeal. I had written the brief before the verdict had come in and paid extra for expedited daily transcripts from the trial. I filed the notice of appeal the day after the verdict and asked for an expedited review. Even still, I wasn't expecting to hear anything on Casey for another two months.

I asked Lorna to read the opinion and a smile widened on my face. The summary was literally a rewrite of my brief. The three-judge panel had agreed with me right down the line on my contention that the low flyover of the sheriff's surveillance helicopter above Casey's ranch constituted an invasion of privacy. The court overturned Casey's conviction, saying that the search that led to the discovery of the hydroponic pot farm was illegal.

The state would now have to decide whether to retry Casey and, realistically, a retrial was out of the question. The state would have no evidence, since the appeals court ruled everything garnered during the search of the ranch was inadmissible. The Second's ruling was clearly a victory for the defense, and they don't come that often.

"Man, what a day for the underdog!"

"Where is he, anyway?" Lorna asked.

"He may still be at the reception center but they were moving him to Corcoran. Here's what you do. Make about ten copies of the ruling and put them in an envelope and send it to Casey at Corcoran. You should have the address."

"Well, won't they be letting him go?"

"Not yet. His parole was violated after his arrest and the appeal doesn't affect that. He won't get out until he goes to the parole board and argues fruit of the poisonous tree, that he got violated because of an illegal search. It will probably take about six weeks for all that to work itself out."

"Six weeks? That's unbelievable."

"Don't do the crime if you can't do the time."

I sang it like Sammy Davis did on that old television show.

"Please don't sing to me, Mick."

"Sorry."

"Why are we sending ten copies to him? Isn't one enough?"

"Because he'll keep one for himself and spread the other nine around the prison and then your phone will start ringing. An attorney who can win on appeal is like gold in prison. They'll come calling and you're going to have to weed 'em out and find the ones who have family and can pay."

"You always have an angle, don't you?"

"I try to. Anything else happening?"

"Just the usual. The calls you told me you didn't want to hear about. Did you get in to see Glory Days yesterday at County?"

"It's Gloria Dayton and, yes, I got in to see her. She looks like she's over the hump. She's still got more than a month to go."

The truth was, Gloria Dayton looked better than over the hump. I hadn't seen her so sharp and bright-eyed in years. I'd had a purpose for going down to County-USC Medical Center to talk to her, but seeing her on the downhill side of recovery was a nice bonus.

As expected, Lorna was the doomsayer.

"And how long will it last this time before she calls your number again and says, 'I'm in jail. I need Mickey'?"

She said the last part with a whiny, nasal impression of Gloria Dayton. It was quite accurate but it annoyed me anyway. Then she topped it with a little song to the tune of the Disney classic.

"M-I-C . . . , see you real soon. K-E-Y . . . , why, because you never charge me! M-O-U-T-H. Mickey Mouth . . . Mickey Mouth, the lawyer every —"

"Please don't sing to me, Lorna."

She laughed into the phone.

"I'm just making a point."

I was smiling but trying to keep it out of my voice.

"Fine. I get it. I have to get going now."

"Well, have a great time . . . Mickey Mouth."

"You could sing that song all day and the Dodgers could lose twenty-zip to the Giants and I'd still have a great time. After hearing the news from you, what could go wrong?"

After ending the call I went into my home office and got a cell number for Teddy Vogel, the outside leader of the Saints. I gave him the good news and suggested that he could probably pass it on to Hard Case faster than I could. There are Road Saints in every prison. They have a communication system the CIA and FBI might be able to learn something from. Vogel said he'd handle it. Then he said the ten grand he gave me the month before on the side of the road near Vasquez Rocks was a worthy investment.

"I appreciate that, Ted," I said. "Keep me in mind next time you need an attorney."

"Will do, Counselor."

He clicked off and I clicked off. I then grabbed my first base-man's glove out of the hallway closet and headed out the front door.

Having given Earl the day off with pay, I drove myself toward downtown and Dodger Stadium. Traffic was light until I got close. The home opener is always a sell-out, even though it is a day game on a weekday. The start of baseball season is a rite of spring that draws downtown workers by the thousands. It's the only sporting event in laid-back L.A. where you see men all in stiff white shirts and ties. They're all playing hooky. There is nothing like the start of a season, before all the one-run losses, pitching breakdowns and missed oppor-tunities. Before reality sets in.

I was the first one to the seats. We were three rows from the field in seats added to the stadium during the off-season. Levin must have busted a nut buying the tickets from one of the local brokers. At least it was probably deductible as a business entertainment expense.

The plan was for Levin to get there early as well. He had called the night before and said he wanted some private time with me. Besides watching batting practice and checking out all the improvements the new owner had made to the stadium, we would discuss my visit with Gloria Dayton and Raul would give me the latest update on his various investigations relating to Louis Roulet.

But Levin never made it for BP. The other four lawyers showed up — three of them in ties, having come from court — and we missed our chance to talk privately.

I knew the other four from some of the boat cases we had tried together. In fact, the tradition of defense pros taking in Dodgers games together started with the boat cases. Under a wide-ranging mandate to stop drug flow to the United States, the U.S. Coast Guard had taken to stopping suspect vessels anywhere on the oceans. When they struck gold — or, that is, cocaine — they seized the vessels and crews. Many of the prosecutions were funneled to the U.S. District Court in Los Angeles. This resulted in prosecutions of sometimes twelve or more defendants at a time. Every defendant got his own lawyer, most of them appointed by the court and paid by Uncle Sugar. The cases were lucrative and steady and we had fun. Somebody had the idea of having case meetings at Dodger Stadium. One time we all pitched in and bought a private suite for a Cubs game. We actually did talk about the case for a few minutes during the seventh-inning stretch.

The pre-game ceremonies started and there was no sign of Levin. Hundreds of doves were released from baskets on the field and they formed up, circled the stadium to loud cheering and then flew up and away. Shortly after, a B-2 stealth bomber buzzed the stadium to even louder applause. That was L.A. Something for everyone and a little irony to boot.

The game started and still no Levin. I turned my cell phone on and tried to call him, even though it was hard to hear. The crowd was loud and boisterous, hopeful of a season that would not end in disappointment again. The call went to a message.

"Mish, where you at, man? We're at the game and the seats are fantastic, but we got one empty one. We're waiting on you."

I closed the phone, looked at the others and shrugged.

"I don't know," I said. "He didn't answer his cell."

I left my phone on and put it back on my belt.

Before the first inning was over I was regretting what I had said to Lorna about not caring if the Giants drilled us 20–zip. They built a 5–0 lead before the Dodgers even got their first bats of the season and the crowd grew frustrated early. I heard people complaining about the prices, the renovation and the overcommercialization of the stadium. One of the lawyers, Roger Mills, surveyed the surfaces of the stadium and remarked that the place was more crowded with corporate logos than a NASCAR race car.

The Dodgers were able to bite into the lead, but in the fourth inning the wheels came off and the Giants chased Jeff Weaver with a three-run shot over the centerfield wall. I used the downtime during the pitching change to brag about how fast I had heard from the Second on the Casey case. The other lawyers were impressed, though one of them, Dan Daly, suggested that I had only received the quick appellate review because the three judges were on my Christmas list. I remarked to Daly that he had apparently missed the bar memo regarding juries' distrust of lawyers with ponytails. His went halfway down his back.

It was also during this lull in the game that I heard my phone ringing. I grabbed it off my hip and flipped it open without looking at the screen.

"Raul?"

"No, sir, this is Detective Lankford with the Glendale Police Department. Is this Michael Haller?"

"Yes," I said.

"Do you have a moment?"

"I have a moment but I am not sure how well I'll be able to hear you. I'm at the Dodgers game. Can this wait until I can call you back?"

"No, sir, it can't. Do you know a man named Raul Aaron Levin? He's a —"

"Yes, I know him. What's wrong?"

"I'm afraid Mr. Levin is dead, sir. He's been the victim of a homicide in his home."

My head dropped so low and so forward that I banged it into the back of the man seated in front of me. I then pulled back and held one hand to one ear and pressed the phone against the other. I blanked out everything around me.

"What happened?"

"We don't know," Lankford said. "That's why we are here. It looks like he was working for you recently. Is there any chance you could come here to possibly answer some questions and assist us?"

I blew out my breath and tried to keep my voice calm and modulated.

"I'm on my way," I said.

TWENTY-THREE

Raul Levin's body was in the back room of his bungalow a few blocks off of Brand Boulevard. The room had likely been designed as a sunroom or maybe a TV room but Raul had turned it into his home office. Like me he'd had no need for a commercial space. His was not a walk-in business. He wasn't even in the yellow pages. He worked for attorneys and got jobs by word of mouth. The five lawyers that were to join him at the baseball game were testimony to his skill and success.

The uniformed cops who had been told to expect me made me wait in the front living room until the detectives could come from the back and talk to me. A uniformed officer stood by in the hallway in case I decided to make a mad dash for the back room or the front door. He was in position to handle it either way. I sat there waiting and thinking about my friend.

I had decided on the drive from the stadium that I knew who had killed Raul Levin. I didn't need to be led to the back room to see or hear the evidence to know who the killer was. Deep down I knew that Raul had gotten too close to Louis Roulet. And I was the one who had sent him. The only question left for me was what was I going to do about it.

After twenty minutes two detectives came from the back of the house and into the living room. I stood up and we talked while standing. The man identified himself as Lankford, the detective who had called me. He was older, the veteran. His partner was a woman named Sobel. She didn't look like she had been investigating homicides for very long.

We didn't shake hands. They were wearing rubber gloves. They also had paper booties over their shoes. Lankford was chewing gum.

"Okay, this is what we've got," he said gruffly. "Levin was in his office, sitting in his desk chair. The chair was turned from the desk, so he was facing the intruder. He was shot one time in the chest. Something small, looks like a twenty-two to me but we'll wait on the coroner for that."

Lankford tapped his chest dead center. I could hear the hard sound of a bullet-proof vest beneath his shirt.

I corrected him. He had pronounced the name here and on the phone earlier as Levine. I said the name rhymed with heaven.

"Levin, then," he said, getting it right. "Anyway, after the shot, he tried to get up or just fell forward to the floor. He expired face-down on the floor. The intruder ransacked the office and we are currently at a loss to determine what he was looking for or what he might have taken."

"Who found him?" I asked.

"A neighbor who found his dog running loose. The intruder must have let the dog out before or after the killing. The neighbor found it wandering around, recognized it and brought it back. She found the front door open, came in and found the body. It didn't look like much of a watchdog, you ask me. It's one of those little hair balls."

"A shih tzu," I said.

I had seen the dog before and heard Levin talk about it, but I couldn't remember its name. It was something like Rex or Bronco — a name that belied the dog's small stature.

Sobel referred to a notebook she was holding before continuing the questioning.

"We haven't found anything that can lead us to next of kin," she said. "Do you know if he had any family?"

"I think his mother lives back east. He was born in Detroit. Maybe she's there. I don't think they had much of a relationship."

She nodded.

"We have found his time and hours calendar. He's got your name on almost every day for the last month. Was he working on a specific case for you?"

I nodded.

"A couple different cases. One mostly."

"Do you care to tell us about it?" she asked.

"I have a case about to go to trial. Next month. It's an attempted rape and murder. He was running down the evidence and helping me to get ready."

"You mean helping you try to backdoor the investigation, huh?" Lankford said.

I realized then that Lankford's politeness on the phone was merely sweet talk to get me to come to the house. He would be different now. He even seemed to be chewing his gum more aggressively than when he had first entered the room.

"Whatever you want to call it, Detective. Everybody is entitled to a defense."

"Yeah, sure, and they're all innocent, only it's their parents' fault for taking them off the tit too soon," Lankford said. "Whatever. This guy Levin was a cop before, right?"

He was back to mispronouncing the name.

"Yes, he was LAPD. He was a detective on a Crimes Against Persons squad but he retired after twelve years on the force. I think it was twelve years. You'll have to check. And it's Levin."

"Right, as in heaven. I guess he couldn't hack working for the good guys, huh?"

"Depends on how you look at it, I guess."

"Can we get back to your case?" Sobel asked. "What is the name of the defendant?"

"Louis Ross Roulet. The trial's in Van Nuys Superior before Judge Fullbright."

"Is he in custody?"

"No, he's out on a bond."

"Any animosity between Roulet and Mr. Levin?"

"Not that I know of."

I had decided. I was going to deal with Roulet in the way I knew how. I was sticking with the plan I had concocted — with the help of Raul Levin. Drop a depth charge into the case and make sure to get clear. I felt I owed it to my friend Mish. He would have wanted it this way. I wouldn't farm it out. I would handle it personally.

"Could this have been a gay thing?" Lankford asked.

"What? Why do you say that?"

"Prissy dog and then all around the house, he's only got pictures of guys and the dog. Everywhere. On the walls, next to the bed, on the piano."

"Look closely, Detective. It is probably one guy. His partner died a few years ago. I don't think he's been with anybody since then."

"Died of AIDS, I bet."

I didn't confirm that for him. I just waited. On the one hand, I was annoyed with Lankford's manner. On the other hand, I figured that his torch-the-ground method of investigation would preclude him from being able to tag Roulet with this. That was fine with me. I only needed to stall him for five or six weeks and then I wouldn't care if they put it together or not. I'd be finished with my own play by then.

"Did this guy go out patrolling the gay joints?" Lankford asked.

I shrugged.

"I have no idea. But if it was a gay murder, why was his office ransacked and not the rest of the house?"

Lankford nodded. He seemed to be momentarily taken aback by the logic of my question. But then he hit me with a surprise punch.

"So where were you this morning, Counselor?"

"What?"

"It's just routine. The scene indicates the victim knew his killer. He let the shooter right into the back room. As I said before, he was probably sitting in his desk chair when he took the bullet. Looks to me like he was quite comfortable with his killer. We are going to have to clear all acquaintances, professional and social."

"Are you saying I'm a suspect in this?"

"No, I'm just trying to clear things up and tighten the focus."

"I was home all morning. I was getting ready to meet Raul at Dodger Stadium. I left for the stadium about twelve and that's where I was when you called."

"What about before that?"

"Like I said, I was home. I was alone. But I got a phone call about eleven that will put me in my house and I'm at least a half hour from here. If he was killed after eleven, then I'm clear."

Lankford didn't rise to the bait. He didn't give me the time of death. Maybe it was unknown at the moment.

"When was the last time you spoke to him?" he asked instead.

"Last night by telephone."

"Who called who and why?"

"He called me and asked if I could get to the game early. I said I could."

"How come?"

"He likes to — he liked to watch batting practice. He said we could jaw over the Roulet case a little bit. Nothing specific but he hadn't updated me in about a week."

"Thank you for your cooperation," Lankford said, sarcasm heavy in his voice.

"You realize that I just did what I tell every client and anybody who will listen not to do? I talked to you without a lawyer present, gave you my alibi. I must be out of my mind."

"I said thank you."

Sobel spoke up.

"Is there anything else you can tell us, Mr. Haller? About Mr. Levin or his work."

"Yeah, there is one other thing. Something you should probably check out. But I want to remain confidential on it."

I looked past them at the uniformed officer still standing in the hallway. Sobel followed my eyes and understood I wanted privacy.

"Officer, you can wait out front, please," she said.

The officer left, looking annoyed, probably because he had been dismissed by a woman.

"Okay," Lankford said. "What have you got?"

"I'll have to look up the exact dates but a few weeks ago, back in March, Raul did some work for me on another case that involved one of my clients snitching off a drug dealer. He made some calls, helped ID the guy. I heard afterward that the guy was a Colombian and he was pretty well connected. He could have had friends who . . ."

I left it for them to fill in the blanks.

"I don't know," Lankford said. "This was pretty clean. Doesn't look like a revenge deal. They didn't cut his throat or take his tongue. One shot, plus they ransacked the office. What would the dealer's people be looking for?"

I shook my head.

"Maybe my client's name. The deal I made kept it out of circulation."

Lankford nodded thoughtfully.

"What is the client's name?"

"I can't tell you. Attorney-client privilege."

"Okay, here we go with that bullshit. How are we going to investigate this if we don't even know your client's name? Don't you care about your friend in there on the floor with a piece of lead in his heart?"

"Yes, I care. I'm obviously the only one here who does care. But I am also bound by the rules and ethics of law."

"Your client could be in danger."

"My client is safe. My client is in lockdown."

"It's a woman, isn't it?" Sobel said. "You keep saying 'client' instead of he or she."

"I'm not talking to you about my client. If you want the name of the dealer, it's Hector Arrande Moya. He's in federal custody. I believe the originating charge came out of a DEA case in San Diego. That's all I can tell you."

Sobel wrote it all down. I believed I had now given them sufficient reason to look beyond Roulet and the gay angle.

"Mr. Haller, have you ever been in Mr. Levin's office before?" Sobel asked.

"A few times. Not in a couple months, at least."

"Do you mind walking back with us anyway? Maybe you'll see something out of place or notice something that's missing."

"Is he still back there?"

"The victim? Yes, he's still as he was found."

I nodded. I wasn't sure I wanted to see Raul Levin's body in the center of a murder scene. I then decided all at once that I must see him and I must not forget the vision. I would need it to fuel my resolve and my plan.

"Okay, I'll go back."

"Then put these on and don't touch anything while you're back there," Lankford said. "We're still processing the scene."

From his pocket he produced a folded pair of paper booties. I sat down on Raul's couch and put them on. Then I followed them down the hallway to the death room.

Raul Levin's body was in situ — as they had found it. He was chest-down on the floor, his face turned to his right, his mouth and eyes open. His body was in an awkward posture, one hip higher than the other and his arms and hands beneath him. It seemed clear that he had fallen from the desk chair that was behind him.

I immediately regretted my decision to come into the room. I suddenly knew that the final look on Raul's face would crowd out all other visual memories I had of him. I would be forced to try to forget him, so I would not have to look at those eyes in my mind again.

It was the same with my father. My only visual memory was of a man in a bed. He was a hundred pounds tops and was being ravaged from the inside out by cancer. All the other visuals I carried of him were false. They came from pictures in books I had read.

There were a number of people working in the room. Crime scene investigators and people from the medical examiner's office. My face must have shown the horror I was feeling.

"You know why we can't cover him up?" Lankford asked me. "Because of people like you. Because of O.J. It's what they call *evi-*

dence transference. Something you lawyers like to jump all over on. So no sheets over the body anymore. Not till we move it out of here."

I didn't say anything. I just nodded. He was right.

"Can you step over here to the desk and tell us if you see anything unusual?" Sobel asked, apparently having some sympathy for me.

I was thankful to do it because I could keep my back to the body. I walked over to the desk, which was a conjoining of three work-tables forming a turn in the corner of the room. It was furniture I recognized had come from the IKEA store in nearby Burbank. It was nothing fancy. It was simple and useful. The center table in the corner had a computer on top and a pull-out tray for a keyboard. The tables to either side looked like twin work spaces and possibly were used by Levin to keep separate investigations from mingling.

My eyes lingered on the computer as I wondered what Levin might have put on electronic files about Roulet. Sobel noticed.

"We don't have a computer expert," she said. "Too small a department. We've got a guy coming from the sheriff's office but it looks to me like the whole drive was pulled out."

She pointed with her pen under the table to where the PC unit was sitting upright but with one side of its plastic cowling having been removed and placed to the rear.

"Probably won't be anything there for us," she said. "What about the desks?"

My eyes moved over the table to the left of the computer first. Papers and files were spread across it in a haphazard way. I looked at some of the tabs and recognized the names.

"Some of these are my clients but they're old cases. Not active."

"They probably came from the file cabinets in the closet," Sobel said. "The killer could have dumped them here to confuse us. To hide what he was really looking for or taking. What about over here?"

We stepped over to the table to the right of the computer. This one was not in as much disarray. There was a calendar blotter on which it was clear Levin kept a running account of his hours and which attorney he was working for at the time. I scanned the blocks and saw my name numerous times going back five weeks. It was as they had told me, he had practically been working full-time for me.

"I don't know," I said. "I don't know what to look for. I don't see anything that could help."

"Well, most attorneys aren't that helpful," Lankford said from behind me.

I didn't bother to turn around to defend myself. He was by the body and I didn't want to see what he was doing. I reached out to turn the Rolodex that was on the table just so I could look through the names on the cards.

"Don't touch that!" Sobel said instantly.

I jerked my hand back.

"Sorry. I was just going to look through the names. I don't . . ."

I didn't finish. I was at sea here. I wanted to leave and get something to drink. I felt like the Dodger dog that had tasted so good back at the stadium was about to come up.

"Hey, check it out," Lankford said.

I turned with Sobel and saw that the medical examiner's people were slowly turning Levin's body over. Blood had stained the front of the Dodgers shirt he was wearing. But Lankford was pointing to the dead man's hands, which had not been visible beneath the body before. The two middle fingers of his left hand were folded down against the palm while the two outside fingers were fully extended.

"Was this guy a Texas Longhorns fan or what?" Lankford asked.

Nobody laughed.

"What do you think?" Sobel said to me.

I stared down at my friend's last gesture and just shook my head.

"Oh, I got it," Lankford said. "It's like a signal. A code. He's telling us that the devil did it."

I thought of Raul calling Roulet the devil, of having the proof that he was evil. And I knew what my friend's last message to me meant. As he died on the floor of his office, he tried to tell me. Tried to warn me.

TWENTY-FOUR

I went to Four Green Fields and ordered a Guinness but quickly escalated to vodka over ice. I didn't think there was any sense in delaying things. The Dodgers game was finishing up on the TV over the bar. The boys in blue were rallying, down now by just two with the bases loaded in the ninth. The bartender had his eyes glued to the screen but I didn't care anymore about the start of new seasons. I didn't care about ninth-inning rallies.

After the second vodka assault, I brought the cell phone up onto the bar and started making calls. First I called the four other lawyers from the game. We had all left when I had gotten the word but they went home only knowing that Levin was dead, none of the details. Then I called Lorna and she cried on the phone. I talked her through it for a little while and then she asked the question I was hoping to avoid.

"Is this because of your case? Because of Roulet?"

"I don't know," I lied. "I told the cops about it but they seemed more interested in him being gay than anything else."

"He was gay?"

I knew it would work as a deflection.

"He didn't advertise it."

"And you knew and didn't tell me?"

"There was nothing to tell. It was his life. If he wanted to tell people, he would have told people, I guess."

"The detectives said that's what happened?"

"What?"

"You know, that his being gay is how he got murdered."

"I don't know. They kept asking about it. I don't know what they think. They'll look at everything and hopefully it will lead to something."

There was silence. I looked up at the TV just as the winning run crossed the plate for the Dodgers and the stadium erupted in bedlam and joy. The bartender whooped and used a remote to turn up the broadcast. I looked away and put a hand over my free ear.

"Makes you think, doesn't it?" Lorna said.

"About what?"

"About what we do. Mickey, when they catch the bastard who did this, he might call me to hire you."

I got the bartender's attention by shaking the ice in my empty glass. I wanted a refill. What I didn't want was to tell Lorna that I believed I was already working for the bastard who had killed Raul.

"Lorna, take it easy. You're getting —"

"It could happen!"

"Look, Raul was my colleague and he was also my friend. But I'm not going to change what I do or what I believe in because —"

"Maybe you should. Maybe we all should. That's all I'm saying."

She started crying again. The bartender brought my fresh drink and I took a third of it down in one gulp.

"Lorna, do you want me to come over there?"

"No, I don't want anything. I don't know what I want. This is just so awful."

"Can I tell you something?"

"What? Of course you can."

"You remember Jesus Menendez? My client?"

"Yes, but what's he have —"

"He was innocent. And Raul was working on it. We were working on it. We're going to get him out."

"Why are you telling me this?"

"I'm telling you because we can't take what happened to Raul and just stop in our tracks. What we do is important. It's necessary."

The words sounded hollow as I said them. She didn't respond. I had probably confused her because I had confused myself.

"Okay?" I asked.

"Okay."

"Good. I have to make some more calls, Lorna."

"Will you tell me when you find out about the services?"

"I will."

After closing my phone I decided to take a break before making another call. I thought about Lorna's last question and realized I might be the one organizing the services she asked about. Unless an old woman in Detroit who had disowned Raul Levin twenty-five years ago stepped up to the plate.

I pushed my glass to the edge of the bar gutter and said to the bartender, "Gimme a Guinness and give yourself one, too."

I decided it was time to slow down and one way was to drink Guinness, since it took so long to fill a glass out of the tap. When the bartender finally brought it to me I saw that he had etched a harp in the foam with the tap nozzle. An angel's harp. I hoisted the glass before drinking from it.

"God bless the dead," I said.

"God bless the dead," the bartender said.

I drank heavily from the glass and the thick ale was like mortar I was sending down to hold the bricks together inside. All at once I felt like crying. But then my phone rang. I grabbed it up without looking at the screen and said hello. The alcohol had bent my voice into an unrecognizable shape.

"Is this Mick?" a voice asked.

"Yeah, who's this?"

"It's Louis. I just heard the news about Raul. I'm so sorry, man."

I pulled the phone away from my ear as if it were a snake about to bite me. I pulled my arm back, ready to throw it at the mirror behind the bar, where I saw my own reflection. Then I stopped and brought it back.

"Yeah, motherfucker, how did you —"

I broke off and started laughing as I realized what I had just called him and what Raul Levin's theory about Roulet had been.

"Excuse me," Roulet said. "Are you drinking?"

"You're damn right I'm drinking," I said. "How the fuck do you already know what happened to Mish?"

"If by Mish you mean Mr. Levin, I just got a call from the Glendale police. A detective said she wanted to speak to me about him."

That answer squeezed at least two of the vodkas right out of my liver. I straightened up on my stool.

"Sobel? Is that who called?"

"Yeah, I think so. She said she got my name from you. She said it would be routine questions. She's coming here."

"Where?"

"The office."

I thought about it for a moment but didn't think Sobel was in any kind of danger, even if she came without Lankford. Roulet wouldn't try anything with a cop, especially in his own office. My greater concern was that somehow Sobel and Lankford were already onto Roulet and I would be robbed of my chance to personally avenge Raul Levin and Jesus Menendez. Had Roulet left a fingerprint behind? Had a neighbor seen him go into Levin's house?

"That's all she said?"

"Yes. She said they were talking to all of his recent clients and I was the most recent."

"Don't talk to them."

"You sure?"

"Not without your lawyer present."

"Won't they get suspicious if I don't talk to them, like give them an alibi or something?"

"It doesn't matter. They don't talk to you unless I give my permission. And I'm not giving it."

I gripped my free hand into a fist. I couldn't stand the idea of giving legal advice to the man I was sure had killed my friend that very morning.

"Okay," Roulet said. "I'll send her on her way."

"Where were you this morning?"

"Me? I was here at the office. Why?"

"Did anybody see you?"

"Well, Robin came in at ten. Not before that."

I pictured the woman with the hair cut like a scythe. I didn't know what to tell Roulet because I didn't know what the time of death was. I didn't want to mention anything about the tracking bracelet he supposedly had on his ankle.

"Call me after Detective Sobel leaves. And remember, no matter what she or her partner says to you, do not talk to them. They can lie to you as much as they want. And they all do. Consider anything they tell you to be a lie. They're just trying to trick you into talking to them. If they tell you I said it was okay to talk, that is a lie. Pick up the phone and call me, I will tell them to get lost."

"All right, Mick. That's how I'll play it. Thanks."

He ended the call. I closed my phone and dropped it on the bar like it was something dirty and discarded.

"Yeah, don't mention it," I said.

I drained a good quarter of my pint, then picked up the phone again. Using speed dial I called Fernando Valenzuela's cell number. He was at home, having just gotten in from the Dodgers game. That meant that he had left early to beat the traffic. Typical L.A. fan.

"Do you still have a tracking bracelet on Roulet?"

"Yeah, he's got it."

"How's it work? Can you track where he's been or only where he's at?"

"It's global positioning. It sends up a signal. You can track it backwards to tell where somebody's been."

"You got it there or is it at the office?"

"It's on my laptop, man. What's up?"

"I want to see where he's been today."

"Well, let me boot it up. Hold on."

I held on, finished my Guinness and had the bartender start filling another before Valenzuela had his laptop fired up.

"Where're you at, Mick?"

"Four Green Fields."

"Anything wrong?"

"Yeah, something's wrong. Do you have it up or what?"

"Yeah, I'm looking at it right here. How far back do you want to check?"

"Start at this morning."

"Okay. He, uh . . . he hasn't done much today. I track it from his home to his office at eight. Looks like he took a little trip nearby — a couple blocks, probably for lunch — and then back to the office. He's still there."

I thought about this for a few moments. The bartender delivered my next pint.

"Val, how do you get that thing off your ankle?"

"You mean if you were him? You don't. You can't. It bolts on and the little wrench you use is unique. It's like a key. I got the only one."

"You're sure about that?"

"I'm sure. I got it right here on my key chain, man."

"No copies — like from the manufacturer?"

"Not supposed to be. Besides, it doesn't matter. If the ring is broken — like even if he did open it — I get an alarm on the system. It also has what's called a 'mass detector.' Once I put that baby around his ankle, I get an alarm on the computer the moment it reads that there is nothing there. That didn't happen, Mick. So you are talking about a saw being the only way. Cut off the leg, leave the bracelet on the ankle. That's the only way."

I drank the top off my new beer. The bartender hadn't bothered with any artwork this time.

"What about the battery? What if the battery's dead, you lose the signal?"

"No, Mick. I got that covered, too. He's got a charger and a receptacle on the bracelet. Every few days he's got to plug it in for a couple hours to juice it. You know, while he's at his desk or something or taking a nap. If the battery goes below twenty percent I get an alarm on my computer and I call him and say plug it in. If he doesn't do it then, I get another alarm at fifteen percent, and then at ten percent *he* starts beeping and he's got no way to take it off or turn it off. Doesn't make for a good getaway. And that last ten percent still gives me five hours of tracking. I can find him in five hours, no sweat."

"Okay, okay."

I was convinced by the science.

"What's going on?"

I told him about Levin and told him that the police would likely have to check out Roulet, and the ankle bracelet and tracking system would likely be our client's alibi. Valenzuela was stunned by the news. He might not have been as close to Levin as I had been, but he had known him just as long.

"What do you think happened, Mick?" he asked me.

I knew that he was asking if I thought Roulet was the killer or somehow behind the killing. Valenzuela was not privy to all that I knew or that Levin had found out.

"I don't know what to think," I said. "But you should watch yourself with this guy."

"And you watch yourself."

"I will."

I closed the phone, wondering if there was something Valenzuela didn't know. If Roulet had somehow found a way to take the ankle bracelet off or to subvert the tracking system. I was convinced by the science of it but not the human side of it. There are always human flaws.

The bartender sauntered over to my spot at the bar.

"Hey, buddy, did you lose your car keys?" he said.

I looked around to make sure he was talking to me and then shook my head.

"No," I said.

"Are you sure? Somebody found keys in the parking lot. You better check."

I reached into the pocket of my suit jacket, then brought my hand out and extended it, palm up. My key ring was displayed on my hand.

"See, I tol —"

In a quick and unexpected move, the bartender grabbed the keys off my hand and smiled.

"Falling for that should be a sobriety test in and of itself," he said. "Anyway, pal, you're not driving — not for a while. When you're ready to go, I'll call you a taxi."

He stepped back from the bar in case I had a violent objection to the ruse. But I just nodded.

"You got me," I said.

He tossed my keys onto the back counter, where the bottles were lined up. I looked at my watch. It wasn't even five o'clock. Embarrassment burned through the alcohol padding. I had taken the easy way out. The coward's way, getting drunk in the face of a terrible occurrence.

"You can take it," I said, pointing to my glass of Guinness.

I picked up the phone and punched in a speed-dial number. Maggie McPherson answered right away. The courts usually closed by four-thirty. The prosecutors were usually at their desks in that last hour or two before the end of the day.

"Hey, is it quitting time yet?"

"Haller?"

"Yeah."

"What's going on? Are you drinking? Your voice is different."

"I think I might need you to drive *me* home this time."

"Where are you?"

"For Greedy Fucks."

"What?"

"Four Green Fields. I've been here awhile."

"Michael, what is —"

"Raul Levin is dead."

"Oh my God, what —"

"Murdered. So this time can you drive *me* home? I've had too much."

"Let me call Stacey and get her to stay late with Hayley, then I'll be on my way. Do not try to leave there, okay? Just don't leave."

"Don't worry, the bartender isn't gonna let me."

TWENTY-FIVE

After closing my phone I told the bartender I had changed my mind and I'd have one more pint while waiting for my ride. I took out my wallet and put a credit card on the bar. He ran my tab first, then got me the Guinness. He took so long filling the glass, spooning foam over the side to give me a full pour, that I had barely tasted it by the time Maggie got there.

"That was too quick," I said. "You want a drink?"

"No, it's too early. Let's just get you home."

"Okay."

I got off the stool, remembered to collect my credit card and phone, and left the bar with my arm around her shoulders and feeling like I had poured more Guinness and vodka down the drain than my own throat.

"I'm right out front," Maggie said. "Four Greedy Fucks, how did you come up with that? Do four people own this place?"

"No, *for*, as in *for the people*. As in Haller *for the defense*. Not the number four. Greedy fucks as in lawyers."

"Thank you."

"Not you. You're not a lawyer. You're a prosecutor."

"How much did you drink, Haller?"

"Somewhere between too much and a lot."

"Don't puke in my car."

"I promise."

We got to the car, one of the cheap Jaguar models. It was the first car she had ever bought without me holding her hand and being involved in running down the choices. She'd gotten the Jag because it made her feel classy, but anybody who knew cars knew it was just a dressed-up Ford. I didn't spoil it for her. Whatever made her happy made me happy — except the time she thought divorcing me would make her life happier. That didn't do much for me.

She helped me in and then we were off.

"Don't pass out, either," she said as she pulled out of the parking lot. "I don't know the way."

"Just take Laurel Canyon over the hill. After that, it's just a left turn at the bottom."

Even though it was supposed to be a reverse commute, it took almost forty-five minutes in end-of-the-day traffic to get to Fareholm Drive. Along the way I told her about Raul Levin and what had happened. She didn't react like Lorna had because she had never known Levin. Though I had known him and used him as an investigator for years, he didn't become a friend until after we had divorced. In fact, it was Raul who had driven me home on more than one night from Four Green Fields as I was getting through the end of my marriage.

My garage opener was in the Lincoln back at the bar so I told her to just park in the opening in front of the garage. I also realized my front door key was on the ring that had the Lincoln's key and that had been confiscated by the bartender. We had to go down the side of the house to the back deck and get the spare key — the one Roulet had given me — from beneath an ashtray on the picnic table. We went in the back door, which led directly into my office. This was good because even in my inebriated state I was pleased that we avoided climbing the stairs to the front door. Not only would it have worn me out but she would have seen the view and been reminded of the inequities between life as a prosecutor and life as a greedy fuck.

"Ah, that's nice," she said. "Our little teacup."

I followed her eyes and saw she was looking at the photo of our daughter I kept on the desk. I thrilled at the idea I had inadvertently scored a point of some kind with her.

"Yeah," I said, fumbling any chance of capitalizing.

"Which way to the bedroom?" she asked.

"Well, aren't you being forward. To the right."

"Sorry, Haller, I'm not staying long. I only got a couple extra hours out of Stacey, and with that traffic, I've got to turn around and head back over the hill soon."

She walked me into the bedroom and we sat down next to each other on the bed.

"Thank you for doing this," I said.

"One good turn deserves another, I guess," she said.

"I thought I got my good turn that night I took you home."

She put her hand on my cheek and turned my face toward hers. She kissed me. I took this as confirmation that we actually had made love that night. I felt incredibly left out at not remembering.

"Guinness," she said, tasting her lips as she pulled away.

"And some vodka."

"Good combination. You'll be hurting in the morning."

"It's so early I'll be hurting tonight. Tell you what, why don't we go get dinner at Dan Tana's? Craig's on the door now and —"

"No, Mick. I have to go home to Hayley and you have to go to sleep."

I made a gesture of surrender.

"Okay, okay."

"Call me in the morning. I want to talk to you when you're sober."

"Okay."

"You want to get undressed and get under the covers?"

"No, I'm all right. I'll just . . ."

I leaned back on the bed and kicked my shoes off. I then rolled over to the edge and opened a drawer in the night table. I took out a bottle of Tylenol and a CD that had been given to me by a client named Demetrius Folks. He was a banger from Norwalk known on the street as Lil' Demon. He had told me once that he'd had a vision one night and that he knew he was destined to die young and violently. He gave me the CD and told me to play it when he was dead. And I did. Demetrius's prophecy came true. He was killed in a drive-by shooting about six months after he had given me the disc. In Magic Marker he had written *Wreckrium for Lil' Demon* on it. It was a collection of ballads he had burned off of Tupac CDs.

I loaded the CD into the Bose player on the night table and soon the rhythmic beat of "God Bless the Dead" started to play. The song was a salute to fallen comrades.

"You listen to this stuff?" Maggie asked, her eyes squinting at me in disbelief.

I shrugged as best I could while leaning on an elbow.

"Sometimes. It helps me understand a lot of my clients better."

"These are the people who should be in jail."

"Maybe some of them. But a lot of them have something to say. Some are true poets and this guy was the best of them."

"Was? Who is it, the one that got shot outside the car museum on Wilshire?"

"No, you're talking about Biggie Smalls. This is the late great Tupac Shakur."

"I can't believe you listen to this stuff."

"I told you. It helps me."

"Do me a favor. Do not listen to this around Hayley."

"Don't worry about it, I won't."

"I've gotta go."

"Just stay a little bit."

She complied but she sat stiffly on the edge of the bed. I could tell she was trying to pick up the lyrics. You needed an ear for it and it took some time. The next song was "Life Goes On," and I watched her neck and shoulders tighten as she caught some of the words.

"Can I please go now?" she asked.

"Maggie, just stay a few minutes."

I reached over and turned it down a little.

"Hey, I'll turn it off if you'll sing to me like you used to."

"Not tonight, Haller."

"Nobody knows the Maggie McFierce I know."

She smiled a little and I was quiet for a moment while I remembered those times.

"Maggie, why do you stay with me?"

"I told you, I can't stay."

"No, I don't mean tonight. I'm talking about how you stick with me, how you don't run me down with Hayley and how you're there when I need you. Like tonight. I don't know many people who have ex-wives who still like them."

She thought a little bit before answering.

"I don't know. I guess because I see a good man and a good father in there waiting to break out one day."

I nodded and hoped she was right.

"Tell me something. What would you do if you couldn't be a prosecutor?"

"Are you serious?"

"Yeah, what would you do?"

"I've never really thought about it. Right now I get to do what I've always wanted to do. I'm lucky. Why would I want to change?"

I opened the Tylenol bottle and popped two without a chaser. The next song was "So Many Tears," another ballad for all of those lost. It seemed appropriate.

"I think I'd be a teacher," she finally said. "Grade school. Little girls like Hayley."

I smiled.

"Mrs. McFierce, Mrs. McFierce, my dog ate my homework."

She slugged me on the arm.

"Actually, that's nice," I said. "You'd be a good teacher . . . except when you're sending kids off to detention without bail."

"Funny. What about you?"

I shook my head.

"I wouldn't be a good teacher."

"I mean what would you do if you weren't a lawyer."

"I don't know. But I've got three Town Cars. I guess I could start a limo service, take people to the airport."

Now she smiled at me.

"I'd hire you."

"Good. There's one customer. Give me a dollar and I'll tape it to the wall."

But the banter wasn't working. I leaned back, put my palms against my eyes and tried to push away the day, to push out the memory of Raul Levin on the floor of his house, eyes staring at a permanent black sky.

"You know what I used to be afraid of?" I asked.

"What?"

"That I wouldn't recognize innocence. That it would be there right in front of me and I wouldn't see it. I'm not talking about guilty or not guilty. I mean innocence. Just innocence."

She didn't say anything.

"But you know what I should have been afraid of?"

"What, Haller?"

"Evil. Pure evil."

"What do you mean?"

"I mean, most of the people I defend aren't evil, Mags. They're guilty, yeah, but they aren't evil. You know what I mean? There's a difference. You listen to them and you listen to these songs and you know why they make the choices they make. People are just trying to get by, just to live with what they're given, and some of them aren't given a damn thing in the first place. But evil is something else. It's different. It's like . . . I don't know. It's out there and when it shows up . . . I don't know. I can't explain it."

"You're drunk, that's why."

"All I know is I should have been afraid of one thing but I was afraid of the complete opposite."

She reached over and rubbed my shoulder. The last song was "to live & die in l.a.," and it was my favorite on the homespun CD. I started to softly hum and then I sang along with the refrain when it came up on the track.

to live & die in l.a.
it's the place to be
you got to be there to know it
ev'ybody wanna see

Pretty soon I stopped singing and pulled my hands down from my face. I fell asleep with my clothes on. I never heard the woman I had loved more than anyone else in my life leave the house. She would tell me later that the last thing I had mumbled before passing out was, "I can't do this anymore."

I wasn't talking about my singing.

slept almost ten hours but I still woke up in darkness. It said 5:18 on the Bose. I tried to go back to the dream but the door was closed. By 5:30 I rolled out of bed, struggled for equilibrium, and hit the shower. I stayed under the spray until the hot-water tank ran cold. Then I got out and got dressed for another day of fighting the machine.

It was still too early to call Lorna to check on the day's schedule but I keep a calendar on my desk that is usually up-to-date. I went into the home office to check it and the first thing I noticed was a dollar bill taped to the wall over the desk.

My adrenaline jogged up a couple notches as my mind raced and I thought an intruder had left the money on the wall as some sort of threat or message. Then I remembered.

"Maggie," I said out loud.

I smiled and decided to leave the dollar bill taped to the wall.

I got the calendar out of the briefcase and checked my schedule. It looked like I had the morning free until an 11 A.M. hearing in San Fernando Superior. The case was a repeat client charged with posses-sion of drug paraphernalia. It was a bullshit charge, hardly worth the time and money, but Melissa Menkoff was already on probation for a variety of drug offenses. If she took a fall for something as minor as drug paraphernalia, her probated sentence would kick in and she would end up behind a steel door for six to nine months.

That was all I had on the calendar. After San Fernando my day was clear and I silently congratulated myself for the foresight I must have used in keeping the day after opening day clear. Of course, I didn't know when I set up the schedule that the death of Raul Levin would send me into Four Green Fields so early, but it was good planning just the same.

The hearing on the Menkoff matter involved my motion to suppress the crack pipe found during a search of her vehicle after a reckless driving stop in Northridge. The pipe had been found in the closed center console of her car. She had told me that she had not given permission to the police to search the car but they did anyway. My argument was that there was no consent to search and no probable cause to search. If Menkoff had been pulled over by police for driving erratically, then there was no reason to search the closed compartments of her car.

It was a loser and I knew it, but Menkoff's father paid me well to do the best I could for his troubled daughter. And that was exactly what I was going to do at eleven o'clock in San Fernando Court.

For breakfast I had two Tylenols and chased them with fried eggs, toast and coffee. I doused the eggs liberally with pepper and salsa. It all hit the right spots and gave me the fuel to carry on the battle. I turned the pages of the *Times* as I ate, looking for a story on the murder of Raul Levin. Inexplicably, there was no story. I didn't understand this at first. Why would Glendale keep the wraps on this? Then I remembered that the *Times* put out several regional editions of the paper each morning. I lived on the Westside, and Glendale was considered part of the San Fernando Valley. News of a murder in the Valley may have been deemed by *Times* editors as unimportant to Westside readers, who had their own region's murders to worry about. I got no story on Levin.

I decided I would have to buy a second copy of the *Times* off a newsstand on the way to San Fernando Court and check again. Thoughts about which newsstand I would direct Earl Briggs to reminded me that I had no car. The Lincoln was in the parking lot at Four Green Fields — unless it had been stolen during the night — and I couldn't get my keys until the pub opened at eleven for lunch. I had a problem. I had seen Earl's car in the commuter lot where I picked him up each morning. It was a pimped-out Toyota with a low-rider profile and spinning chrome rims. My guess was that it had the permanent stink of weed in it, too. I didn't want to ride in it. In the north county it was an invitation to a police stop. In the south county it was an invitation to get shot at. I also didn't want Earl to pick me up at the house. I never let my drivers know where I live.

The plan I came up with was to take a cab to my warehouse in North Hollywood and use one of the new Town Cars. The Lincoln at Four Green Fields had over fifty thousand miles on it, anyway. Maybe breaking out the new wheels would help me get past the depression sure to set in because of Raul Levin.

After I had cleaned the frying pan and the dish in the sink I decided it was late enough to risk waking Lorna with a call to confirm my day's schedule. I went back into the home office and when I picked up the house phone to make the call I heard the broken dial tone that told me I had at least one message waiting.

I called the retrieval number and was told by an electronic voice that I had missed a call at 11:07 A.M. the day before. When the voice recited the number that the missed call had come from, I froze. The number was Raul Levin's cell phone. I had missed his last call.

"Hey, it's me. You probably left for the game already and I guess you got your cell turned off. If you don't get this I'll just catch you there. But I've got another ace for you. I guess you —"

He broke off for a moment at the background sound of a dog barking.

"— could say I've got Jesus's ticket out of the Q. I've gotta go, lad."

That was it. He hung up without a good-bye and had used that stupid brogue at the end. The brogue had always annoyed me. Now it sounded endearing. I missed it already.

I pushed the button to replay the message and listened again and then did it three more times before finally saving the message and hanging up. I then sat there in my desk chair and tried to apply the message to what I knew. The first puzzle involved the time of the call. I did not leave for the game until at least 11:30, yet I had somehow missed the call from Levin that had come in more than twenty minutes earlier.

This made no sense until I remembered the call from Lorna. At 11:07 I had been on the phone with Lorna. My home phone was used so infrequently and so few people had the number that I did not bother to have call waiting installed on the line. This meant that Levin's last call would have been kicked over to the voicemail system and I would have never known about it as I spoke to Lorna.

That explained the circumstances of the call but not its contents.

Levin had obviously found something. He was no lawyer but he certainly knew evidence and how to evaluate it. He had found something that could help me get Menendez out of prison. He had found Jesus's ticket out.

The last thing left to consider was the interruption of the dog barking and that was easy. I had been to Levin's home before and I knew the dog was a high-strung yapper. Every time I had come to the house, I had heard the dog start barking before I had even knocked on the door. The barking in the background on the phone message and Levin hurriedly ending the call told me someone was coming to his door. He had a visitor and it may very well have been his killer.

I thought about things for a few moments and decided that the timing of the call was something I could not in good conscience keep from the police. The contents of the message would raise new questions that I might have difficulty answering, but that was outweighed by the value of the call's timing. I went into the bedroom and dug through the pockets of the blue jeans I had worn the day before to the game. In one of the back pockets I found the ticket stub from the game and the business cards Lankford and Sobel had given me at the end of my visit to Levin's house.

I chose Sobel's card and noticed it only said *Detective Sobel* on it. No first name. I wondered why that was as I made the call. Maybe she was like me, with two different business cards in alternate pockets. One with her complete name in one, one with the more formal name in the other.

She answered the call right away and I decided to see what I could get from her before I gave her what I had.

"Anything new on the investigation?" I asked.

"Not a lot. Not a lot that I can share with you. We are sort of organizing the evidence we have. We got some ballistics back and —"

"They already did an autopsy?" I said. "That was quick."

"No, the autopsy won't be until tomorrow."

"Then how'd you get ballistics already?"

She didn't answer but then I figured it out.

"You found a casing. He was shot with an automatic that ejected the shell."

"You're good, Mr. Haller. Yes, we found a cartridge."

"I've done a lot of trials. And call me Mickey. It's funny, the killer ransacked the place but didn't pick up the shell."

"Maybe that's because it rolled across the floor and fell into a heating vent. The killer would have needed a screwdriver and a lot of time."

I nodded. It was a lucky break. I couldn't count the number of times clients had gone down because the cops had caught a lucky break. Then again, there were a lot of clients who walked because they caught the break. It all evened out in the end.

"So, was your partner right about it being a twenty-two?"

She paused before answering, deciding whether to cross some threshold of revealing case information to me, an involved party in the case but the enemy — a defense lawyer — nonetheless.

"He was right. And thanks to the markings on the cartridge, we even know the exact gun we are looking for."

I knew from questioning ballistics experts and firearms examiners in trials over the years that marks left on bullet casings during the firing process could identify the weapon even without the weapon in hand. With an automatic, the firing pin, breech block, ejector and extractor all leave signature marks on the bullet casing in the split second the weapon is fired. Analyzing the four markings in unison can lead to a specific make and model of the weapon being identified.

"It turns out that Mr. Levin owned a twenty-two himself," Sobel said. "But we found it in a closet safe in the house and it's not a Woodsman. The one thing we have not found is his cell phone. We know he had one but we —"

"He was talking to me on it right before he was killed."

There was a moment of silence.

"You told us yesterday that the last time you spoke to him was Friday night."

"That's right. But that's why I am calling. Raul called me yesterday morning at eleven-oh-seven and left me a message. I didn't get it until today because after I left you people yesterday I just went out and got drunk. Then I went to sleep and didn't realize I had a message from him till right now. He called about one of the cases he was working on for me sort of on the side. It's an appellate thing and the client's in prison. A no-rush thing. Anyway, the content of the message isn't important but the call helps with the timing. And get this, while he's leaving the message, you hear the dog start to bark. It did that whenever somebody came to the door. I know because I'd been there before and the dog always barked."

Again she hit me with some silence before responding.

"I don't understand something, Mr. Haller."

"What's that?"

"You told us yesterday you were at home until around noon before you left for the game. And now you say that Mr. Levin left a message for you at eleven-oh-seven. Why didn't you answer the phone?"

"Because I was on it and I don't have call waiting. You can check my records, you'll see I got a call from my office manager, Lorna Taylor. I was talking to her when Raul called. Without call waiting I didn't know. And of course he thought I had already left for the game so he just left a message."

"Okay, I understand. We'll probably want your permission in writing to look at those records."

"No problem."

"Where are you now?"

"I'm at home."

I gave her the address and she said that she and her partner were coming.

"Make it soon. I have to leave for court in about an hour."

"We're coming right now."

I closed the phone feeling uneasy. I had defended a dozen murderers over the years and that had brought me into contact with a number of homicide investigators. But I had never been questioned myself about a murder before. Lankford and now Sobel seemed to be suspicious of every answer I could give. It made me wonder what they knew that I didn't.

I straightened up things on the desk and closed my briefcase. I didn't want them seeing anything I didn't want them to see. I then walked through my house and checked every room. My last stop was the bedroom. I made the bed and put the CD case for *Wreckrium for Lil' Demon* back in the night table drawer. And then it hit me. I sat on the bed as I remembered something Sobel had said. She had made a slip and at first it had gone right by me. She had said that they had found Raul Levin's .22 caliber gun but it was not the murder weapon. She said it was not a Woodsman.

She had inadvertently revealed to me the make and model of the murder weapon. I knew the Woodsman was an automatic pistol manufactured by Colt. I knew this because I owned a Colt Woodsman Sport Model. It had been bequeathed to me many years ago by my father. Upon his death. Once old enough to handle it, I had never even taken it out of its wooden box.

I got up from the bed and went to the walk-in closet. I moved as if in a heavy fog. My steps were tentative and I put my hand out to the

wall and then the door casement as if needing my bearings. The polished wooden box was on the shelf where it was supposed to be. I
reached up with both hands to bring it down and then walked it out
to the bedroom.

I put the box down on the bed and flipped open the brass latch. I
raised the lid and pulled away the oilcloth covering.

The gun was gone.

PART TWO

— *A World Without Truth*

TWENTY-SEVEN

The check from Roulet cleared. On the first day of trial I had more money in my bank account than I'd ever had in my life. If I wanted, I could drop the bus benches and go with billboards. I could also take the back cover of the yellow pages instead of the half page I had inside. I could afford it. I finally had a franchise case and it had paid off. In terms of money, that is. The loss of Raul Levin would forever make this franchise a losing proposition.

We had been through three days of jury selection and were now ready to put on the show. The trial was scheduled for another three days at the most — two for the prosecution and one for the defense. I had told the judge that I would need a day to put my case before the jury, but the truth was, most of my work would be done during the prosecution's presentation.

There's always an electric feel to the start of a trial. A nervousness that attacks deep in the gut. So much is on the line. Reputation, personal freedom, the integrity of the system itself. Something about having those twelve strangers sit in judgment of your life and work always jumps things up inside. And I am referring to me, the defense attorney — the judgment of the defendant is a whole other thing. I've never gotten used to it, and the truth is, I never want to. I can only liken it to the anxiety and tension of standing at the front of a church on your wedding day. I'd had that experience twice and I was reminded of it every time a judge called a trial to order.

Though my experience in trial work severely outweighed my opponent's, there was no mistake about where I stood. I was one man standing before the giant maw of the system. Without a doubt I was the underdog. Yes, it was true that I faced a prosecutor in his first major felony trial. But that advantage was evened and then some by the power and might of the state. At the prosecutor's command were the forces of the entire justice system. And against this all I had was myself. And a guilty client.

I sat next to Louis Roulet at the defense table. We were alone. I had no second and no investigator behind me — out of some strange loyalty to Raul Levin I had not hired a replacement. I didn't really need one, either. Levin had given me everything I needed. The trial and how it played out would serve as a last testament to his skills as an investigator.

In the first row of the gallery sat C. C. Dobbs and Mary Alice Windsor. In accordance with a pretrial ruling, the judge was allowing Roulet's mother to be in the courtroom during opening statements only. Because she was listed as a defense witness, she would not be allowed to listen to any of the testimony that followed. She would remain in the hallway outside, with her loyal lapdog Dobbs at her side, until I called her to the stand.

Also in the first row but not seated next to them was my own support section: my ex-wife Lorna Taylor. She had gotten dressed up in a navy suit and white blouse. She looked beautiful and could have blended in easily with the phalanx of female attorneys who descended on the courthouse every day. But she was there for me and I loved her for it.

The rest of the rows in the gallery were sporadically crowded. There were a few print reporters there to grab quotes from the opening statements and a few attorneys and citizen onlookers. No TV had shown up. The trial had not yet drawn more than cursory attention from the public, and this was good. This meant our strategy of publicity containment had worked well.

Roulet and I were silent as we waited for the judge to take the bench and order the jury into the box so that we could begin. I was attempting to calm myself by rehearsing what I wanted to say to the jurors. Roulet was staring straight ahead at the State of California seal affixed to the front of the judge's bench.

The courtroom clerk took a phone call, said a few words and then hung up.

"Two minutes, people," he said loudly. "Two minutes."

When a judge called ahead to the courtroom, that meant people should be in their positions and ready to go. We were. I glanced over at Ted Minton at the prosecution's table and saw he was doing the same thing that I was doing. Calming himself by rehearsing. I leaned forward and studied the notes on the legal pad in front of me. Then Roulet unexpectedly leaned forward and almost right into me. He spoke in a whisper, even though it wasn't necessary yet.

"This is it, Mick."

"I know."

Since the death of Raul Levin, my relationship with Roulet had been one of cold endurance. I put up with him because I had to. But I saw him as little as possible in the days and weeks before the trial, and spoke to him as little as possible once it started. I knew the one weakness in my plan was my own weakness. I feared that any interaction with Roulet could lead me into acting out my anger and desire to personally, physically avenge my friend. The three days of jury selection had been torture. Day after day I had to sit right next to him and listen to his condescending comments about prospective jurors. The only way I got through it was to pretend he wasn't there.

"You ready?" he asked me.

"Trying to be," I said. "Are you?"

"I'm ready. But I wanted to tell you something before we began."

I looked at him. He was too close to me. It would have been invasive even if I loved him and not hated him. I leaned back.

"What?"

He followed me, leaning back next to me.

"You're my lawyer, right?"

I leaned forward, trying to get away.

"Louis, what is this? We've been together on this more than two months and now we're sitting here with a jury picked and ready for trial. You have paid me more than a hundred and fifty grand and you have to ask if I'm your lawyer? Of course I'm your lawyer. What is it? What is wrong?"

"Nothing's wrong."

He leaned forward and continued.

"I mean, like, if you're my lawyer, I can tell you stuff and you have to hold it as a secret, even if it's a crime I tell you about. More than one crime. It's covered by the attorney-client relationship, right?"

I felt the low rumbling of upset in my stomach.

"Yes, Louis, that's right — unless you are going to tell me about a crime about to be committed. In that case I can be relieved of the code of ethics and can inform the police so they can stop the crime. In fact, it would be my duty to inform them. A lawyer is an officer of the court. So what is it that you want to tell me? You just heard we got the two-minute warning. We're about to start here."

"I've killed people, Mick."

I looked at him for a moment.

"What?"

"You heard me."

He was right. I had heard him. And I shouldn't have acted surprised. I already knew he had killed people. Raul Levin was among them and he had even used my gun — though I hadn't figured out how he had defeated the GPS bracelet on his ankle. I was just surprised he had decided to tell me in such a matter-of-fact manner two minutes before his trial was called to order.

"Why are you telling me this?" I asked. "I'm about to try to defend you in this thing and you —"

"Because I know you already know. And because I know what your plan is."

"My plan? What plan?"

He smiled slyly at me.

"Come on, Mick. It's simple. You defend me on this case. You do your best, you get paid the big bucks, you win and I walk away. But then, once it's all over and you've got your money in the bank, you turn against me because I'm not your client anymore. You throw me to the cops so you can get Jesus Menendez out and redeem yourself."

I didn't respond.

"Well, I can't let that happen," he said quietly. "Now, I am yours forever, Mick. I am telling you I've killed people, and guess what? Martha Renteria was one of them. I gave her just what she deserved, and if you go to the cops or use what I've told you against me, then you won't be practicing law for very long. Yes, you might succeed in raising Jesus from the dead. But I'll never be prosecuted because of your misconduct. I believe it is called 'fruit of the poisonous tree,' and you are the tree, Mick."

I still couldn't respond. I just nodded again. Roulet had certainly thought it through. I wondered how much help he had gotten from Cecil Dobbs. He had obviously had somebody coach him on the law.

I leaned toward him and whispered.

"Follow me."

I got up and walked quickly through the gate and toward the rear door of the courtroom. From behind I heard the clerk's voice.

"Mr. Haller? We're about to start. The judge —"

"One minute," I called out without turning around.

I held one finger up as well. I then pushed through the doors into the dimly lit vestibule designed as a buffer to keep hallway sounds from the courtroom. A set of double doors on the other side led to the hallway. I moved to the side and waited for Roulet to step into the small space.

As soon as he came through the door I grabbed him and spun

him into the wall. I held him pressed against it with both of my hands on his chest.

"What the fuck do you think you are doing?"

"Take it easy, Mick. I just thought we should know where we both —"

"You son of a bitch. You killed Raul and all he was doing was working for you! He was trying to help you!"

I wanted to bring my hands up to his neck and choke him out on the spot.

"You're right about one thing. I am a son of a bitch. But you are wrong about everything else, Mick. Levin wasn't trying to help me. He was trying to bury me and he was getting too close. He got what he deserved for that."

I thought about Levin's last message on my phone at home. *I've got Jesus's ticket out of the Q.* Whatever it was that he had found, it had gotten him killed. And it had gotten him killed before he could deliver the information to me.

"How did you do it? You're confessing everything to me here, then I want to know how you did it. How'd you beat the GPS? Your bracelet showed you weren't even near Glendale."

He smiled at me, like a boy with a toy he wasn't going to share.

"Let's just say that is proprietary information and leave it at that. You never know, I may have to pull the old Houdini act again."

In his words I heard the threat and in his smile I saw the evil that Raul Levin had seen.

"Don't get any ideas, Mick," he said. "As you probably know, I do have an insurance policy."

I pressed harder against him and leaned in closer.

"Listen, you piece of shit. I want the gun back. You think you have this thing wired? You don't have shit. *I've* got it wired. And you won't make it through the week if I don't get that gun back. You got that?"

Roulet slowly reached up, grabbed my wrists and pulled my hands off his chest. He started straightening his shirt and tie.

"Might I suggest an agreement," he said calmly. "At the end of this trial I walk out of the courtroom a free man. I continue to maintain my freedom, and in exchange for this, the gun never falls into, shall we say, the wrong hands."

Meaning Lankford and Sobel.

"Because I'd really hate to see that happen, Mick. A lot of people depend on you. A lot of clients. And you, of course, wouldn't want to go where they are going."

I stepped back from him, using all my will not to raise my fists and attack. I settled for a voice that quietly seethed with all of my anger and hate.

"I promise you," I said, "if you fuck with me you will never be free of me. Are we clear on that?"

Roulet started to smile. But before he could respond the door from the courtroom opened and Deputy Meehan, the bailiff, looked in.

"The judge is on the bench," he said sternly. "She wants you in here. Now."

I looked back at Roulet.

"I said, are we clear?"

"Yes, Mick," he said good-naturedly. "We're crystal clear."

I stepped away from him and entered the courtroom, striding up the aisle to the gate. Judge Constance Fullbright was staring me down every step of the way.

"So nice of you to consider joining us this morning, Mr. Haller."

Where had I heard that before?

"I am sorry, Your Honor," I said as I came through the gate. "I had an emergency situation with my client. We had to conference."

"Client conferences can be handled right at the defense table," she responded.

"Yes, Your Honor."

"I don't think we are starting off correctly here, Mr. Haller. When my clerk announces that we will be in session in two minutes, then I expect everyone — including defense attorneys and their clients — to be in place and ready to go."

"I apologize, Your Honor."

"That's not good enough, Mr. Haller. Before the end of court today I want you to pay a visit to my clerk with your checkbook. I am fining you five hundred dollars for contempt of court. You are not in charge of this courtroom, sir. I am."

"Your Honor —"

"Now, can we please have the jury," she ordered, cutting off my protest.

The bailiff opened the jury room door and the twelve jurors and two alternates started filing into the jury box. I leaned over to Roulet, who had just sat down, and whispered.

"You owe me five hundred dollars."

TWENTY-EIGHT

ed Minton's opening statement was a by-the-numbers model of prosecutorial overkill. Rather than tell the jurors what evidence he would present and what it would prove, the prosecutor tried to tell them what it all meant. He was going for a big picture and this was almost always a mistake. The big picture involves inferences and suggestions. It extrapolates givens to the level of suspicions. Any experienced prosecutor with a dozen or more felony trials under his belt will tell you to keep it small. You want them to convict, not necessarily to understand.

"What this case is about is a predator," he told them. "Louis Ross Roulet is a man who on the night of March sixth was stalking prey. And if it were not for the sheer determination of a woman to survive, we would be here prosecuting a murder case."

I noticed early on that Minton had picked up a scorekeeper. This is what I call a juror who incessantly takes notes during trial. An opening statement is not an offer of evidence and Judge Fullbright had so admonished the jury, but the woman in the first seat in the front row had been writing since the start of Minton's statement. This was good. I like scorekeepers because they document just what the lawyers say will be presented and proved at trial and at the end they go back to check. They keep score.

I looked at the jury chart I had filled in the week before and saw that the scorekeeper was Linda Truluck, a homemaker from Reseda. She was one of only three women on the jury. Minton had tried hard to keep the female content to a minimum because, I believe, he feared that once it was established in trial that Regina Campo had been offering sexual services for money, he might lose the females' sympathy and ultimately their votes on a verdict. I believed he was probably correct in that assumption and I worked just as diligently to get women on the panel. We both ended up using all of our twenty challenges and it was probably the main reason it took three days to seat a jury. In the end I got three women on the panel and only needed one to head off a conviction.

"Now, you are going to hear testimony from the victim herself about her lifestyle being one that we would not condone," Minton told the jurors. "The bottom line is she was selling sex to the men she invited to her home. But I want you to remember that what the victim in this case did for a living is not what this trial is about. Anyone can be a victim of a violent crime. Anyone. No matter what someone does for a living, the law does not allow for them to be beaten, to be threatened at knifepoint or to be put in fear of their lives. It doesn't matter what they do to make money. They enjoy the same protections that we all do."

It was pretty clear to me that Minton didn't even want to use the word *prostitution* or *prostitute* for fear it would hurt his case. I wrote the word down on the legal pad I would take with me to the lectern when I made my statement. I planned to make up for the prosecutor's omissions.

Minton gave an overview of the evidence. He spoke about the knife with the defendant's initials on the blade. He talked about the blood found on his left hand. And he warned the jurors not to be fooled by the defense's efforts to confuse or muddle the evidence.

"This is a very clear-cut and straightforward case," he said as he was winding up. "You have a man who attacked a woman in her home. His plan was to rape and then kill her. It is only by the grace of God that she will be here to tell you the story."

With that he thanked them for their attention and took his seat at the prosecution table. Judge Fullbright looked at her watch and then looked at me. It was 11:40 and she was probably weighing whether to go to a break or let me proceed with my opener. One of the judge's chief jobs during trial is jury management. The judge's duty is to make sure the jury is comfortable and engaged. Lots of breaks, short and long, is often the answer.

I had known Connie Fullbright for at least twelve years, since long before she was a judge. She had been both a prosecutor and defense lawyer. She knew both sides. Aside from being overly quick with contempt citations, she was a good and fair judge — until it came to sentencing. You went into Fullbright's court knowing you were on an even level with the prosecution. But if the jury convicted your client, be prepared for the worst. Fullbright was one of the toughest sentencing judges in the county. It was as if she were punishing you and your client for wasting her time with a trial. If there was any room within the sentencing guidelines, she always went to the max, whether it was prison or probation. It had gotten her a telling sobriquet among the defense pros who worked the Van Nuys courthouse. They called her Judge Fullbite.

"Mr. Haller," she said, "are you planning to reserve your statement?"

"No, Your Honor, but I believe I am going to be pretty quick."

"Very good," she said. "Then we'll hear from you and then we'll take lunch."

The truth was I didn't know how long I would be. Minton had been about forty minutes and I knew I would take close to that. But I had told the judge I'd be quick simply because I didn't like the idea of the jury going to lunch with only the prosecutor's side of the story to think about as they chewed their hamburgers and tuna salads.

I got up and went to the lectern located between the prosecution and defense tables. The courtroom was one of the recently rehabbed spaces in the old courthouse. It had twin jury boxes on either side of the bench. Everything was done in a blond wood, including the rear wall behind the bench. The door to the judge's chambers was almost hidden in the wall, its lines camouflaged in the lines and grain of the wood. The doorknob was the only giveaway.

Fullbright ran her trials like a federal judge. Attorneys were not allowed to approach witnesses without permission and never allowed to approach the jury box. They were required to speak from the lectern only.

Standing now at the lectern, the jury was in the box to my right and closer to the prosecution table than to the defense's. This was fine with me. I didn't want them to get too close a look at Roulet. I wanted him to be a bit of a mystery to them.

"Ladies and gentlemen of the jury," I began, "my name is Michael Haller and I am representing Mr. Roulet during this trial. I am happy to tell you that this trial will most likely be a quick one. Just a few more days of your time will be taken. In the long run you will probably see that it took us longer to pick all of you than it will take to present both sides of the case. The prosecutor, Mr. Minton, seemed to spend his time this morning telling you about what he thinks all the evidence means and who Mr. Roulet really is. I would advise you to simply sit back, listen to the evidence and let your common sense tell you what it all means and who Mr. Roulet is."

I kept my eyes moving from juror to juror. I rarely looked down at the pad I had placed on the lectern. I wanted them to think I was shooting the breeze with them, talking off the top of my head.

"Usually, what I like to do is reserve my opening statement. In a criminal trial the defense always has the option of giving an opener at the start of the trial, just as Mr. Minton did, or right before presenting the defense's case. Normally, I would take the second option. I would wait and make my statement before trotting out all the defense's witnesses and evidence. But this case is different. It's different because the prosecution's case is also going to be the defense's case. You'll certainly hear from some defense witnesses, but the heart and soul of this case is going to be the prosecution's evidence and witnesses and how you decide to interpret them. I guarantee you that a version of the events and evidence far different from what Mr. Minton just outlined is going to emerge in this courtroom. And when it comes time to present the defense's case, it probably won't even be necessary."

I checked the scorekeeper and saw her pencil moving across the page of her notebook.

"I think that what you are going to find here this week is that this whole case will come down to the actions and motivations of one person. A prostitute who saw a man with outward signs of wealth and chose to target him. The evidence will show this clearly and it will be shown by the prosecution's own witnesses."

Minton stood up and objected, saying I was going out of bounds in trying to impeach the state's main witness with unsubstantiated accusations. There was no legal basis for the objection. It was just an amateurish attempt to send a message to the jury. The judge responded by inviting us to a sidebar.

We walked to the side of the bench and the judge flipped on a sound neutralizer which sent white noise from a speaker on the bench toward the jury and prevented them from hearing what was whispered in the sidebar. The judge was quick with Minton, like an assassin.

"Mr. Minton, I know you are new to felony trial work, so I see I will have to school you as we go. But don't you ever object during an opening statement in my courtroom. This isn't evidence he's presenting. I don't care if he says your own mother is the defendant's alibi witness, you don't object in front of my jury."

"Your Hon—"

"That's it. Go back."

She rolled her seat back to the center of the bench and flicked off the white noise. Minton and I returned to our positions without further word.

"Objection overruled," the judge said. "Continue, Mr. Haller, and let me remind you that you said you would be quick."

"Thank you, Your Honor. That is still my plan."

I referred to my notes and then looked back at the jury. Knowing that Minton would have been intimidated to silence by the judge, I decided to raise the rhetoric up a notch, go off notes and get directly to the windup.

"Ladies and gentlemen, in essence, what you will be deciding here is who the real predator was in this case. Mr. Roulet, a successful businessman with a spotless record, or an admitted prostitute with a successful business in taking money from men in exchange for sex. You will hear testimony that the alleged victim in this case was engaged in an act of prostitution with another man just moments before this supposed attack occurred. And you will hear testimony that within days of this supposedly life-threatening assault, she was back in business once again, trading sex for money."

I glanced at Minton and saw he was doing a slow burn. He had his eyes downcast on the table in front of him and he was slowly shaking his head. I looked up at the judge.

"Your Honor, could you instruct the prosecutor to refrain from demonstrating in front of the jury? I did not object or in any way try to distract the jury during his opening statement."

"Mr. Minton," the judge intoned, "please sit still and extend the courtesy to the defense that was extended to you."

"Yes, Your Honor," Minton said meekly.

The jury had now seen the prosecutor slapped down twice and we weren't even past openers. I took this as a good sign and it fed my momentum. I looked back at the jury and noticed that the score-keeper was still writing.

"Finally, you will receive testimony from many of the state's own witnesses that will provide a perfectly acceptable explanation for much of the physical evidence in this case. I am talking about the blood and about the knife Mr. Minton mentioned. Taken individually or as a whole, the prosecution's own case will provide you with more than reasonable doubt about the guilt of my client. You can mark it down in your notebooks. I guarantee you will find that you have only one choice at the end of this case. And that is to find Mr. Roulet not guilty of these charges. Thank you."

As I walked back to my seat I winked at Lorna Taylor. She nodded at me as if to say I had done well. My attention was then drawn to the two figures sitting two rows behind her. Lankford and Sobel. They had slipped in after I had first surveyed the gallery.

I took my seat and ignored the thumbs-up gesture given me by my client. My mind was on the two Glendale detectives, wondering what they were doing in the courtroom. Watching me? Waiting for me?

The judge dismissed the jury for lunch and everyone stood while the scorekeeper and her colleagues filed out. After they were gone Minton asked the judge for another sidebar. He wanted to try to explain his objection and repair the damage but not in open court. The judge said no.

"I'm hungry, Mr. Minton, and we're past that now. Go to lunch."

She left the bench, and the courtroom that had been so silent except for the voices of lawyers then erupted in chatter from the gallery and the court workers. I put my pad in my briefcase.

"That was really good," Roulet said. "I think we're already ahead of the game."

I looked at him with dead eyes.

"It's no game."

"I know that. It's just an expression. Listen, I am having lunch with Cecil and my mother. We would like you to join us."

I shook my head.

"I have to defend you, Louis, but I don't have to eat with you."

I took my checkbook out of my briefcase and left him there. I walked around the table to the clerk's station so that I could write out a check for five hundred dollars. The money didn't hurt as much as I knew the bar review that follows any contempt citation would.

When I was finished I turned back to find Lorna waiting for me at the gate with a smile. We planned to go to lunch and then she would go back to manning the phone in her condo. In three days I would be back in business and needed clients. I was depending on her to start filling in my calendar.

"Looks like I better buy you lunch today," she said.

I threw my checkbook into the briefcase and closed it. I joined her at the gate.

"That would be nice," I said.

I pushed through the gate and checked the bench where I had seen Lankford and Sobel sitting a few moments before.

They were gone.

TWENTY-NINE

The prosecution began presenting its case to the jury in the afternoon session and very quickly Ted Minton's strategy became clear to me. The first four witnesses were a 911 dispatch operator, the patrol officers who responded to Regina Campo's call for help and the paramedic who treated her before she was transported to the hospital. In anticipation of the defense strategy, it was clear that Minton wanted to firmly establish that Campo had been brutally assaulted and was indeed the victim in this crime. It wasn't a bad strategy. In most cases it would get the job done.

The dispatch operator was essentially used as the warm body needed to introduce a recording of Campo's 911 call for help. Printed transcripts of the call were handed out to jurors so they could read along with a scratchy audio playback. I objected on the grounds that it was prejudicial to play the audio recording when the transcript would suffice but the judge quickly overruled me before Minton even had to counter. The recording was played and there was no doubt that Minton had started out of the gate strong as the jurors sat raptly listening to Campo scream and beg for help. She sounded genuinely distraught and scared. It was exactly what Minton wanted the jurors to hear and they certainly got it. I didn't dare question the dispatcher on cross-examination because I knew it might give Minton the opportunity to play the recording again on redirect.

The two patrol officers who followed offered different testimony because they did separate things upon arriving at the Tarzana apartment complex in response to the 911 call. One primarily stayed with the victim while the other went up to the apartment and handcuffed the man Campo's neighbors were sitting on — Louis Ross Roulet.

Officer Vivian Maxwell described Campo as disheveled, hurt and frightened. She said Campo kept asking if she was safe and if the intruder had been caught. Even after she was assured on both questions, Campo remained scared and upset, at one point telling the officer to unholster her weapon and have it ready in case the attacker broke free. When Minton was through with this witness, I stood up to conduct my first cross-examination of the trial.

"Officer Maxwell," I asked, "did you at any time ask Ms. Campo what had happened to her?"

"Yes, I did."

"What exactly did you ask her?"

"I asked what had happened and who did this to her. You know, who had hurt her."

"What did she tell you?"

"She said a man had come to her door and knocked and when she opened it he punched her. She said he hit her several times and then took out a knife."

"She said he took the knife out after he punched her?"

"That's how she said it. She was upset and hurt at the time."

"I understand. Did she tell you who the man was?"

"No, she said she didn't know the man."

"You specifically asked if she knew the man?"

"Yes. She said no."

"So she just opened her door at ten o'clock at night to a stranger."

"She didn't say it that way."

"But you said she told you she didn't know him, right?"

"That is correct. That is how she said it. She said, 'I don't know who he is.'"

"And did you put this in your report?"

"Yes, I did."

I introduced the patrol officer's report as a defense exhibit and had Maxwell read parts of it to the jury. These parts involved Campo saying that the attack was unprovoked and at the hands of a stranger.

"'The victim does not know the man who assaulted her and did not know why she was attacked,'" she read from her own report.

Maxwell's partner, John Santos, testified next, telling jurors that Campo directed him to her apartment, where he found a man on the floor near the entrance. The man was semiconscious and was being held on the ground by two of Campo's neighbors, Edward Turner and Ronald Atkins. One man was straddling the man's chest and the other was sitting on his legs.

Santos identified the man being held on the floor as the defendant, Louis Ross Roulet. Santos described him as having blood on his clothes and his left hand. He said Roulet appeared to be suffering from a concussion or some sort of head injury and initially was not responsive to commands. Santos turned him over and handcuffed his hands behind his back. The officer then put a plastic evidence bag he carried in a compartment on his belt over Roulet's bloody hand.

Santos testified that one of the men who had been holding Roulet handed over a folding knife that was open and had blood on its handle and blade. Santos told jurors he bagged this item as well and turned it over to Detective Martin Booker as soon as he arrived on the scene.

On cross-examination I asked Santos only two questions.

"Officer, was there blood on the defendant's right hand?"

"No, there was no blood on his right hand or I would have bagged that one, too."

"I see. So you have blood on the left hand only and a knife with blood on the handle. Would it then appear to you that if the defendant had held that knife, then he would have to have held it in his left hand?"

Minton objected, saying that Santos was a patrol officer and that the question was beyond the scope of his expertise. I argued that the question required only a commonsense answer, not an expert. The judge overruled the objection and the court clerk read the question back to the witness.

"It would seem that way to me," Santos answered.

Arthur Metz was the paramedic who testified next. He told jurors about Campo's demeanor and the extent of her injuries when he treated her less than thirty minutes after the attack. He said that it appeared to him that she had suffered at least three significant impacts to the face. He also described a small puncture wound to her neck. He described all the injuries as superficial but painful. A large blowup of the same photograph of Campo's face I had seen on the first day I was on the case was displayed on an easel in front of the jury. I objected to this, arguing that the photo was prejudicial because it had been blown up to larger-than-life size, but I was overruled by Judge Fullbright.

Then, when it was my turn to cross-examine Metz, I used the photo I had just objected to.

"When you tell us that it appeared that she suffered at least three impacts to the face, what do you mean by 'impact'?" I asked.

"She was struck with something. Either a fist or a blunt object."

"So basically someone hit her three times. Could you please use this laser pointer and show the jury on the photograph where these impacts occurred."

From my shirt pocket I unclipped a laser pointer and held it up for the judge to see. She granted me permission to carry it to Metz. I turned it on and handed it to him. He then put the red eye of the laser beam on the photo of Campo's battered face and drew circles in the three areas where he believed she had been struck. He circled her right eye, her right cheek and an area encompassing the right side of her mouth and nose.

"Thank you," I said, taking the laser back from him and returning to the lectern. "So if she was hit three times on the right side of her face, the impacts would have come from the left side of her attacker, correct?"

Minton objected, once more saying the question was beyond the scope of the witness's expertise. Once more I argued common sense and once more the judge overruled the prosecutor.

"If the attacker was facing her, he would have punched her from the left, unless it was a backhand," Metz said. "Then it could have been a right."

He nodded and seemed pleased with himself. He obviously thought he was helping the prosecution but his effort was so disingenuous that he was actually probably helping the defense.

"You are suggesting that Ms. Campo's attacker hit her three times with a backhand and caused this degree of injury?"

I pointed to the photo on the exhibit easel. Metz shrugged, realizing he had probably not been so helpful to the prosecution.

"Anything is possible," he said.

"Anything is possible," I repeated. "Well, is there any other possibility you can think of that would explain these injuries as coming from anything other than direct left-handed punches?"

Metz shrugged again. He was not an impressive witness, especially following two cops and a dispatcher who had been very precise in their testimony.

"What if Ms. Campo were to have hit her face with her own fist? Wouldn't she have used her right —"

Minton jumped up immediately and objected.

"Your Honor, this is outrageous! To suggest that this victim did this to herself is not only an affront to this court but to all victims of violent crime everywhere. Mr. Haller has sunk to —"

"The witness said anything is possible," I argued, trying to knock Minton off the soapbox. "I am trying to explore what —"

"Sustained," Fullbright said, ending it. "Mr. Haller, don't go there unless you are making more than an exploratory swing through the possibilities."

"Yes, Your Honor," I said. "No further questions."

I sat down and glanced at the jurors and knew from their faces that I had made a mistake. I had turned a positive cross into a negative. The point I had made about a left-handed attacker was obscured by the point I had lost with the suggestion that the injuries to the victim's face were self-inflicted. The three women on the panel looked particularly annoyed with me.

Still, I tried to focus on a positive aspect. It was good to know the jury's feelings on this now, before Campo was in the witness box and I asked the same thing.

Roulet leaned toward me and whispered, "What the fuck was that?"

Without responding I turned my back to him and took a scan around the courtroom. It was almost empty. Lankford and Sobel had not returned to the courtroom and the reporters were gone as well. That left only a few other onlookers. They appeared to be a disparate collection of retirees, law students and lawyers resting their feet until their own hearings began in other courtrooms. But I was counting on one of these onlookers being a plant from the DA's office. Ted Minton might be flying solo but my guess was that his boss would have a means of keeping tabs on him and the case. I knew I was playing as much to the plant as I was to the jury. By the trial's end I needed to send a note of panic down to the second floor that would then echo back to Minton. I needed to push the young prosecutor toward taking a desperate measure.

The afternoon dragged on. Minton still had a lot to learn about pacing and jury management, knowledge that comes only with courtroom experience. I kept my eyes on the jury box — where the real judges sat — and saw the jurors were growing bored as witness after witness offered testimony that filled in small details in the prosecutor's linear presentation of the events of March 6. I asked few questions on cross and tried to keep a look on my face that mirrored those I saw in the jury box.

Minton obviously wanted to save his most powerful stuff for day two. He would have the lead investigator, Detective Martin Booker, to bring all the details together, and then the victim, Regina Campo, to bring it all home to the jury. It was a tried-and-true formula — ending with muscle and emotion — and it worked ninety percent of the time, but it was making the first day move like a glacier.

Things finally started to pop with the last witness of the day.

Minton brought in Charles Talbot, the man who had picked up Regina Campo at Morgan's and gone with her to her apartment on the night of the sixth. What Talbot had to offer to the prosecution's case was negligible. He was basically hauled in to testify that Campo had been in good health and uninjured when he left her. That was it. But what caused his arrival to rescue the trial from the pit of boredom was that Talbot was an honest-to-God alternate lifestyle man and jurors always loved visiting the other side of the tracks.

Talbot was fifty-five years old with dyed blond hair that wasn't fooling anyone. He had blurred Navy tattoos on both forearms. He was twenty years divorced and owned a twenty-four-hour convenience store called Kwik Kwik. The business gave him a comfortable living and lifestyle with an apartment in the Warner Center, a late-model Corvette and a nightlife that included a wide sampling of the city's professional sex providers.

Minton established all of this in the early stages of his direct examination. You could almost feel the air go still in the courtroom as the jurors plugged into Talbot. The prosecutor then brought him quickly to the night of March 6, and Talbot described hooking up with Reggie Campo at Morgan's on Ventura Boulevard.

"Did you know Ms. Campo before you met her in the bar that night?"

"No, I did not."

"How did it come about that you met her there?"

"I just called her up and said I wanted to get together with her and she suggested we meet at Morgan's. I knew the place, so I said sure."

"And how did you call her up?"

"With the telephone."

Several jurors laughed.

"I'm sorry. I understand that you used a telephone to call her. I meant how did you know *how* to contact her?"

"I saw her ad on the website and I liked what I saw and so I went ahead and called her up and we made a date. It's as simple as that. Her number is on her website ad."

"And you met at Morgan's."

"Yes, that's where she meets her dates, she told me. So I went there and we had a couple drinks and we talked and we liked each other and that was that. I followed her back to her place."

"When you went to her apartment did you engage in sexual relations?"

"Sure did. That's what I was there for."

"And you paid her?"

"Four hundred bucks. It was worth it."

I saw a male juror's face turning red and I knew I had pegged him perfectly during selection the week before. I had wanted him because he had brought a Bible with him to read while other prospective jurors were being questioned. Minton had missed it, focusing only on the candidates as they were being questioned. But I had seen the Bible and asked few questions of the man when it was his turn. Minton accepted him on the jury and so did I. I figured he would be easy to turn against the victim because of her occupation. His reddening face confirmed it.

"What time did you leave her apartment?" Minton asked.

"About five minutes before ten," Talbot answered.

"Did she tell you she was expecting another date at the apartment?"

"No, she didn't say anything about that. In fact, she was sort of acting like she was done for the night."

I stood up and objected.

"I don't think Mr. Talbot is qualified here to interpret what Ms. Campo was thinking or planning by her actions."

"Sustained," the judge said before Minton could offer an argument.

The prosecutor moved right along.

"Mr. Talbot, could you please describe the physical state Ms. Campo was in when you left her shortly before ten o'clock on the night of March sixth?"

"Completely satisfied."

There was a loud blast of laughter in the courtroom and Talbot beamed proudly. I checked the Bible man and it looked like his jaw was tightly clenched.

"Mr. Talbot," Minton said. "I mean her physical state. Was she hurt or bleeding when you left her?"

"No, she was fine. She was okay. When I left her she was fit as a fiddle and I know because I had just played her."

He smiled, proud of his use of language. This time there was no laughter and the judge had finally had enough of his use of the double entendre. She admonished him to keep his more off-color remarks to himself.

"Sorry, Judge," he said.

"Mr. Talbot," Minton said. "Ms. Campo was not injured in any way when you left her?"

"Nope. No way."

"She wasn't bleeding?"

"No."

"And you didn't strike her or physically abuse her in any way?"

"No again. What we did was consensual and pleasurable. No pain."

"Thank you, Mr. Talbot."

I looked at my notes for a few moments before standing up. I wanted a break of time to clearly mark the line between direct and cross-examination.

"Mr. Haller?" the judge prompted. "Do you wish to cross-examine the witness?"

I stood up and moved to the lectern.

"Yes, Your Honor, I do."

I put my pad down and looked directly at Talbot. He was smiling pleasantly at me but I knew he wouldn't like me for very long.

"Mr. Talbot, are you right- or left-handed?"

"I'm left-handed."

"Left-handed," I echoed. "And isn't it true that on the night of the sixth, before leaving Regina Campo's apartment, she asked you to strike her with your fist repeatedly in the face?"

Minton stood up.

"Your Honor, there is no basis for this sort of questioning. Mr. Haller is simply trying to muddy the waters by taking outrageous statements and turning them into questions."

The judge looked at me and waited for a response.

"Judge, it is part of the defense theory as outlined in my opening statement."

"I am going to allow it. Just be quick about it, Mr. Haller."

The question was read to Talbot and he smirked and shook his head.

"That is not true. I've never hurt a woman in my life."

"You struck her with your fist three times, didn't you, Mr. Talbot?"

"No, I did not. That is a lie."

"You said you have never hurt a woman in your life."

"That's right. Never."

"Do you know a prostitute named Shaquilla Barton?"

Talbot had to think before answering.

"Doesn't ring a bell."

"On the website where she advertises her services she uses the name Shaquilla Shackles. Does that ring a bell now, Mr. Talbot?"

"Okay, yeah, I think so."

"Have you ever engaged in acts of prostitution with her?"

"One time, yes."

"When was that?"

"Would've been at least a year ago. Maybe longer."

"And did you hurt her on that occasion?"

"No."

"And if she were to come to this courtroom and say that you did hurt her by punching her with your left hand, would she be lying?"

"She damn sure would be. I tried her out and didn't like that rough stuff. I'm strictly a missionary man. I didn't touch her."

"You didn't touch her?"

"I mean I didn't punch her or hurt her in any way."

"Thank you, Mr. Talbot."

I sat down. Minton did not bother with a redirect. Talbot was ex-

cused and Minton told the judge that he had only two witnesses re-
maining to present in the case but that their testimony would be
lengthy. Judge Fullbright checked the time and recessed court for the
day.

Two witnesses left. I knew that had to be Detective Booker and
Reggie Campo. It looked like Minton was going to go without the
testimony of the jailhouse snitch he had stashed in the PTI program
at County-USC. Dwayne Corliss's name had never appeared on any
witness list or any other discovery document associated with the
prosecution of the case. I thought maybe Minton had found out what
Raul Levin had found out about Corliss before Raul was murdered.
Either way, it seemed apparent that Corliss had been dropped by the
prosecution. And that was what I needed to change.

As I gathered my papers and documents in my briefcase, I also
gathered the resolve to talk to Roulet. I glanced over at him. He was
sitting there waiting to be dismissed by me.

"So what do you think?" I asked.

"I think you did very well. More than a few moments of reasonable doubt."

I snapped the latches on the briefcase closed.

"Today I was just planting seeds. Tomorrow they'll sprout and
on Wednesday they'll bloom. You haven't seen anything yet."

I stood up and lifted the briefcase off the table. It was heavy with
all the case documents and my computer.

"See you tomorrow."

I walked out through the gate. Cecil Dobbs and Mary Windsor
were waiting for Roulet in the hallway near the courtroom door. As I
came out they turned to speak to me but I walked on by.

"See you tomorrow," I said.

"Wait a minute, wait a minute," Dobbs called to my back.

I turned around.

"We're stuck out here," he said as he and Windsor walked to me.
"How is it going in there?"

I shrugged.

"Right now it's the prosecution's case," I answered. "All I'm doing is bobbing and weaving, trying to protect. I think tomorrow will be our round. And Wednesday we go for the knockout. I've got to go prepare."

As I headed to the elevator, I saw that a number of the jurors from the case had beaten me to it and were waiting to go down. The scorekeeper was among them. I went into the restroom next to the bank of elevators so I didn't have to ride down with them. I put my briefcase on the counter between the sinks and washed my face and hands. As I stared at myself in the mirror I looked for signs of stress from the case and everything associated with it. I looked reasonably sane and calm for a defense pro who was playing both his client and the prosecution at the same time.

The cold water felt good and I felt refreshed as I came out of the restroom, hoping the jurors had cleared out.

The jurors were gone. But standing in the hallway by the elevator were Lankford and Sobel. Lankford was holding a folded sheaf of documents in one hand.

"There you are," he said. "We've been looking for you."

THIRTY

The document Lankford handed me was a search warrant granting the police the authority to search my home, office and car for a .22 caliber Colt Woodsman Sport Model pistol with the serial number 656300081-52. The authorization said the pistol was believed to have been the murder weapon in the April 12 homicide of Raul A. Levin. Lankford had handed the warrant to me with a proud smirk on his face. I did my best to act like it was business as usual, the kind of thing I handled every other day and twice on Fridays. But the truth was, my knees almost buckled.

"How'd you get this?" I said.

It was a nonsensical response to a nonsensical moment.

"Signed, sealed and delivered," Lankford said. "So where do you want to start? You have your car here, right? That Lincoln you're chauffeured around in like a high-class hooker."

I checked the judge's signature on the last page and saw it was a Glendale muni-court judge I had never heard of. They had gone to a local who probably knew he'd need the police endorsement come election time. I started to recover from the shock. Maybe the search was a front.

"This is bullshit," I said. "You don't have the PC for this. I could have this thing quashed in ten minutes."

"It looked pretty good to Judge Fullbright," Lankford said.

"Fullbright? What does she have to do with this?"

"Well, we knew you were in trial, so we figured we ought to ask her if it was okay to drop the warrant on you. Don't want to get a lady like that mad, you know. She said after court was over was fine by her — and she didn't say shit about the PC or anything else."

They must have gone to Fullbright on the lunch break, right after I had seen them in the courtroom. My guess was, it had been Sobel's idea to check with the judge first. A guy like Lankford would have enjoyed pulling me right out of court and disrupting the trial.

I had to think quickly. I looked at Sobel, the more sympathetic of the two.

"I'm in the middle of a three-day trial," I said. "Any way we can put this on hold until Thursday?"

"No fucking way," Lankford answered before his partner could. "We're not letting you out of our sight until we execute the search. We're not going to give you the time to dump the gun. Now where's your car, Lincoln lawyer?"

I checked the authorization of the warrant. It had to be very specific and I was in luck. It called for the search of a Lincoln with the California license plate NT GLTY. I realized that someone must have written the plate down on the day I was called to Raul Levin's house from the Dodgers game. Because that was the old Lincoln — the one I was driving that day.

"It's at home. Since I'm in trial I don't use the driver. I got a ride in with my client this morning and I was just going to ride back with him. He's probably waiting down there."

I lied. The Lincoln I had been driving was in the courthouse parking garage. But I couldn't let the cops search it because there was a gun in a compartment in the backseat armrest. It wasn't the gun they were looking for but it was a replacement. After Raul Levin was murdered and I'd found my pistol box empty, I asked Earl Briggs to get me a gun for protection. I knew that with Earl there would be no ten-day waiting period. But I didn't know the gun's history or registration and I didn't want to find out through the Glendale Police Department.

But I was in luck because the Lincoln with the gun inside wasn't the one described in the warrant. That one was in my garage at home, waiting on the buyer from the limo service to come by and take a look at. And that would be the Lincoln that would be searched.

Lankford grabbed the warrant out of my hand and shoved it into an inside coat pocket.

"Don't worry about your ride," Lankford said. "We're your ride. Let's go."

On the way down and out of the courthouse, we didn't run into Roulet or his entourage. And soon I was riding in the back of a Grand Marquis, thinking that I had made the right choice when I had gone with the Lincoln. There was more room in the Lincoln and the ride was smoother.

Lankford did the driving and I sat behind him. The windows were up and I could hear him chewing gum.

"Let me see the warrant again," I said.

Lankford made no move.

"I'm not letting you inside my house until I've had a chance to completely study the warrant. I could do it on the way and save you some time. Or . . ."

Lankford reached inside his jacket and pulled out the warrant. He handed it over his shoulder to me. I knew why he was hesitant. Cops usually had to lay out their whole investigation in the warrant application in order to convince a judge of probable cause. They didn't like the target reading it, because it gave away the store.

I glanced out the window as we were passing the car lots on Van Nuys Boulevard. I saw a new model Town Car on a pedestal in front of the Lincoln dealership. I looked back down at the warrant, opened it to the summary section and read.

Lankford and Sobel had started out doing some good work. I had to give them that. One of them had taken a shot — I was guessing Sobel — and put my name into the state's Automated Firearm System and hit the lotto. The AFS computer said I was the registered owner of a pistol of the same make and model as the murder weapon.

It was a smooth move but it still wasn't enough to make probable cause. Colt made the Woodsman for more than sixty years. That meant there were probably a million of them out there and a million suspects who owned them.

They had the smoke. They then rubbed other sticks together to make the required fire. The application summary stated that I had hidden from the investigators the fact that I owned the gun in question. It said I had also fabricated an alibi when initially interviewed about Levin's death, then attempted to throw detectives off the track by giving them a phony lead on the drug dealer Hector Arrande Moya.

Though motivation was not necessarily a subject needed to obtain a search warrant, the PC summary alluded to it anyway, stating that the victim — Raul Levin — had been extorting investigative assignments from me and that I had refused to pay him upon completion of those assignments.

The outrage of such an assertion aside, the alibi fabrication was the key point of probable cause. The statement said that I had told the detectives I was home at the time of the murder, but a message on my home phone was left just before the suspected time of death and this indicated that I was not home, thereby collapsing my alibi and proving me a liar at the same time.

I slowly read the PC statement twice more but my anger did not subside. I tossed the warrant onto the seat next to me.

"In some ways it's really too bad I am not the killer," I said.

"Yeah, why is that?" Lankford said.

"Because this warrant is a piece of shit and you both know it. It won't stand up to challenge. I told you that message came in when I was already on the phone and that can be checked and proven, only you were too lazy or you didn't want to check it because it would have made it a little difficult to get your warrant. Even with your pocket judge in Glendale. You lied by omission and commission. It's a bad-faith warrant."

Because I was sitting behind Lankford I had a better angle on Sobel. I watched her for signs of doubt as I spoke.

"And the suggestion that Raul was extorting business from me and that I wouldn't pay is a complete joke. Extorted me with what? And what didn't I pay him for? I paid him every time I got a bill. Man, I tell you, if this is how you work all your cases, I gotta open up an office in Glendale. I'm going to shove this warrant right up your police chief's ass."

"You lied about the gun," Lankford said. "And you owed Levin money. It's right there in his accounts book. Four grand."

"I didn't lie about anything. You never asked if I owned a gun."

"Lied by omission. Right back at ya."

"Bullshit."

"Four grand."

"Oh yeah, the four grand — I killed him because I didn't want to pay him four grand," I said with all the sarcasm I could muster. "You got me there, Detective. Motivation. But I guess it never occurred to you to see if he had even billed me for the four grand yet, or to see if I hadn't just paid an invoice from him for six thousand dollars a week before he was murdered."

Lankford was undaunted. But I saw the doubt start to creep into Sobel's face.

"Doesn't matter how much or when you paid him," Lankford said. "A blackmailer is never satisfied. You never stop paying until you reach the point of no return. That's what this is about. The point of no return."

I shook my head.

"And what exactly was it that he had on me that made me give him jobs and pay him until I reached the point of no return?"

Lankford and Sobel exchanged a look and Lankford nodded. Sobel reached down to a briefcase on the floor and took out a file. She handed it over the seat to me.

"Take a look," Lankford said. "You missed it when you were ransacking his place. He'd hidden it in a dresser drawer."

I opened the file and saw that it contained several 8 × 10 color photos. They were taken from afar and I was in each one of them. The photographer had trailed my Lincoln over several days and several miles. Each image a frozen moment in time, the photos showed me with various individuals whom I easily recognized as clients. They were prostitutes, street dealers and Road Saints. The photos could be interpreted as suspicious because they showed one split second of time. A male prostitute in mini-shorts alighting from the backseat of the Lincoln. Teddy Vogel handing me a thick roll of cash through the back window. I closed the file and tossed it back over the seat.

"You're kidding me, right? You're saying Raul came to me with that? He extorted me with that? Those are my clients. Is this a joke or am I just missing something?"

"The California bar might not think it's a joke," Lankford said. "We hear you're on thin ice with the bar. Levin knew it. He worked it."

I shook my head.

"Incredible," I said.

I knew I had to stop talking. I was doing everything wrong with these people. I knew I should just shut up and ride it out. But I felt an almost overpowering need to convince them. I began to understand why so many cases were made in the interview rooms of police stations. People just can't shut up.

I tried to place the photographs that were in the file. Vogel giving me the roll of cash was in the parking lot outside the Saints' strip club on Sepulveda. That happened after Harold Casey's trial and Vogel was paying me for filing the appeal. The prostitute was named Terry Jones and I handled a soliciting charge for him the first week of April. I'd had to find him on the Santa Monica Boulevard stroll the night before a hearing to make sure he was going to show up.

It became clear that the photos had all been taken between the morning I had caught the Roulet case and the day Raul Levin was murdered. They were then planted at the crime scene by the killer — all part of Roulet's plan to set me up so that he could control me. The police would have everything they needed to put the Levin murder on me — except the murder weapon. As long as Roulet had the gun, he had me.

I had to admire the plan and the ingenuity at the same time that it made me feel the dread of desperation. I tried to put the window down but the button wouldn't work. I asked Sobel to open a window and she did. Fresh air started blowing into the car.

After a while Lankford looked at me in the rearview and tried to jump-start the conversation.

"We ran the history on that Woodsman," he said. "You know who owned it once, don't you?"

"Mickey Cohen," I answered matter-of-factly, staring out the window at the steep hillsides of Laurel Canyon.

"How'd you end up with Mickey Cohen's gun?"

I answered without turning from the window.

"My father was a lawyer. Mickey Cohen was his client."

Lankford whistled. Cohen was one of the most famous gangsters to ever call Los Angeles home. He was from back in the day when the gangsters competed with movie stars for the gossip headlines.

"And what? He just gave your old man a gun?"

"Cohen was charged in a shooting and my father defended him. He claimed self-defense. There was a trial and my father got a not-guilty verdict. When the weapon was returned Mickey gave it to my father. Sort of a keepsake, you could say."

"Your old man ever wonder how many people the Mick whacked with it?"

"I don't know. I didn't really know my father."

"What about Cohen? You ever meet him?"

"My father represented him before I was even born. The gun came to me in his will. I don't know why he picked me to have it. I was only five years old when he died."

"And you grew up to be a lawyer like dear old dad, and being a good lawyer you registered it."

"I thought if it was ever stolen or something I would want to be able to get it back. Turn here on Fareholm."

Lankford did as I instructed and we started climbing up the hill to my home. I then gave them the bad news.

"Thanks for the ride," I said. "You guys can search my house and my office and my car for as long as you want, but I have to tell you, you are wasting your time. Not only am I the wrong guy for this, but you aren't going to find that gun."

I saw Lankford's head jog up and he was looking at me in the rearview again.

"And why is that, Counselor? You already dumped it?"

"Because the gun was stolen out of my house and I don't know where it is."

Lankford started laughing. I saw the joy in his eyes.

"Uh-huh, stolen. How convenient. When did this happen?"

"Hard to tell. I hadn't checked on the gun in years."

"You make a police report on it or file an insurance claim?"

"No."

"So somebody comes in and steals your Mickey Cohen gun and you don't report it. Even after you just told us you registered it in case this very thing happened. You being a lawyer and all, doesn't that sound a little screwy to you?"

"It does, except I knew who stole it. It was a client. He told me he took it and if I were to report it, I would be violating a client trust because my police report would lead to his arrest. Kind of a catch-twenty-two, Detective."

Sobel turned and looked back at me. I think maybe she thought I was making it up on the spot, which I was.

"That sounds like legal jargon and bullshit, Haller," Lankford said.

"But it's the truth. We're here. Just park in front of the garage."

Lankford pulled the car into the space in front of my garage and killed the engine. He turned to look back at me before getting out.

"Which client stole the gun?"

"I told you, I can't tell you."

"Well, Roulet's your only client right now, isn't he?"

"I have a lot of clients. But I told you, I can't tell you."

"Think maybe we should run the charts from his ankle bracelet and see if he's been to your place lately?"

"Do whatever you want. He actually has been here. We had a meeting here once. In my office."

"Maybe that's when he took it."

"I'm not telling you he took it, Detective."

"Yeah, well, that bracelet gives Roulet a pass on the Levin thing, anyway. We checked the GPS. So I guess that leaves you, Counselor."

"And that leaves you wasting your time."

I suddenly realized something about Roulet's ankle bracelet but tried not to show it. Maybe a line on the trapdoor to his Houdini act. It was something I would need to check into later.

"Are we just going to sit here?"

Lankford turned and got out. He then opened my door because the inside handle had been disabled for transporting suspects and custodies. I looked at the two detectives.

"You want me to show you the gun box? Maybe when you see it is empty, you can just leave and save us all the time."

"Not quite, Counselor," Lankford said. "We're going through this whole place. I'll take the car and Detective Sobel will start in the house."

I shook my head.

"Not quite, Detective. It doesn't work that way. I don't trust you. Your warrant is bent, so as far as I'm concerned, you're bent. You stay together so I can watch you both or we wait until I can get a second observer up here. My case manager could be here in ten minutes. I could bring her up here to watch and you could also ask her about calling me on the morning Raul Levin got killed."

Lankford's face grew dark with insult and anger that he looked like he was having trouble controlling. I decided to push it. I took out my cell phone and opened it.

"I'm going to call your judge right now and see if he —"

"Fine," Lankford said. "We'll start with the car. Together. We'll work our way inside the house."

I closed the phone and put it back in my pocket.

"Fine."

I walked over to a keypad on the wall outside the garage. I tapped in the combination and the garage door started to rise, revealing the blue-black Lincoln awaiting inspection. Its license plate read NT GLTY. Lankford looked at it and shook his head.

"Yeah, right."

He stepped into the garage, his face still tight with anger. I decided to ease things a little bit.

"Hey, Detective," I said. "What's the difference between a catfish and a defense attorney?"

He didn't respond. He stared angrily at the license plate on my Lincoln.

"One's a bottom-feeding shit sucker," I said. "And the other one's a fish."

For a moment his face remained frozen. Then a smile creased it and he broke into a long and hard laugh. Sobel stepped into the garage, having not heard the joke.

"What?" she said.

"I'll tell you later," Lankford said.

THIRTY-ONE

It took them a half hour to search the Lincoln and then move into the house, where they started with the office. I watched the whole time and only spoke when offering explanation about something that gave them pause in their search. They didn't talk much to each other and it was becoming increasingly clear that there was a rift between the two partners over the direction Lankford had taken the investigation.

At one point Lankford got a call on his cell phone and he went out the front door onto the porch to talk privately. I had the shades up and if I stood in the hallway I could look one way and see him out there and the other way and see Sobel in my office.

"You're not too happy about this, are you?" I said to Sobel when I was sure her partner couldn't hear.

"It doesn't matter how I am. We're following the case and that's it."

"Is your partner always like that, or only with lawyers?"

"He spent fifty thousand dollars on a lawyer last year, trying to get custody of his kids. He didn't. Before that we lost a big case — a murder — on a legal technicality."

I nodded.

"And he blamed the lawyer. But who broke the rules?"

She didn't respond and that as much as confirmed it had been Lankford who had made the technical misstep.

"I get the picture," I said.

I checked on Lankford on the porch again. He was gesturing impatiently like he was trying to explain something to a moron. Must have been his custody lawyer. I decided to change the subject with Sobel.

"Do you think you are being manipulated at all on this case?"

"What are you talking about?"

"The photos stashed in the bureau, the bullet casing in the floor vent. Pretty convenient, don't you think?"

"What are you saying?"

"I'm not saying anything. I'm asking questions your partner doesn't seem interested in."

I checked on Lankford. He was tapping in numbers on his cell, making a new call. I turned and stepped into the open doorway of the office. Sobel was looking behind the files in a drawer. Finding no gun, she closed the drawer and stepped over to the desk. I spoke in a low voice.

"What about Raul's message to me?" I said. "About finding Jesus Menendez's ticket out, what do you think he meant?"

"We haven't figured that out yet."

"Too bad. I think it's important."

"Everything's important until it isn't."

I nodded, not sure what she meant by that.

"You know, the case I'm trying is pretty interesting. You ought to come back by and watch. You might learn something."

She looked from the desk to me. Our eyes held for a moment. Then she squinted with suspicion, like she was trying to judge whether a supposed murder suspect was actually coming on to her.

"Are you serious?"

"Yeah, why not?"

"Well, for one thing, you might have trouble getting to court if you're in lockup."

"Hey, no gun, no case. That's why you're here, right?"

She didn't answer.

"Besides, this is your partner's thing. You're not riding with him on this. I can tell."

"Typical lawyer. You think you know all the angles."

"No, not me. I'm finding out I don't know any of them."

She changed the subject.

"Is this your daughter?"

She pointed to the framed photograph on the desk.

"Yeah. Hayley."

"Nice alliteration. Hayley Haller. Named after the comet?"

"Sort of. Spelled differently. My ex-wife came up with it."

Lankford came in then, talking to Sobel loudly about the call he had gotten. It had been from a supervisor telling them that they were back in play and would handle the next Glendale homicide whether the Levin case was still active or not. He didn't say anything about the call he had made.

Sobel told him she had finished searching the office. No gun.

"I'm telling you, it's not here," I said. "You are wasting your time. And mine. I have court tomorrow and need to prepare for witnesses."

"Let's do the bedroom next," Lankford said, ignoring my protest.

I backed up into the hallway to give them space to come out of one room and go into the next. They walked down the sides of the bed to where twin night tables waited. Lankford opened the top drawer of his table and lifted out a CD.

"*Wreckrium for Lil' Demon,*" he read. "You have to be fucking kidding me."

I didn't respond. Sobel quickly opened the two drawers of her table and found them empty except for a strip of condoms. I looked the other way.

"I'll take the closet," Lankford said after he had finished with his night table — leaving the drawers open in typical police search fashion. He walked into the closet and soon spoke from inside it.

"Here we go."

He stepped back out of the closet holding the wooden gun box.

"Bingo," I said. "You found an empty gun box. You must be a detective."

Lankford shook the box in his hands before putting it down on the bed. Either he was trying to play with me or the box had a solid heft to it. I felt a little charge go down the back of my neck as I realized that Roulet could have just as easily snuck back into my house to return the gun. It would have been the perfect hiding place for it. The last place I might think to check again once I had determined that the gun was gone. I remembered the odd smile on Roulet's face when I had told him I wanted my gun back. Was he smiling because I already had the gun back?

Lankford flipped the box's latch and lifted the top. He pulled back the oilcloth covering. The cork cutout which once held Mickey Cohen's gun was still empty. I breathed out so heavily it almost came out as a sigh.

"What did I tell you?" I said quickly, trying to cover up.

"Yeah, what did you tell us," Lankford said. "Heidi, you got a bag? We're going to take the box."

I looked at Sobel. She didn't look like a Heidi to me. I wondered if it was some sort of a squad room nickname. Or maybe it was the reason she didn't put her first name on her business card. It didn't sound homicide tough.

"In the car," she said.

"Go get it," Lankford said.

"You are going to take an empty gun box?" I asked. "What good does it do you?"

"All part of the chain of evidence, Counselor. You should know that. Besides, it will come in handy, since I have a feeling we'll never find the gun."

I shook my head.

"Maybe handy in your dreams. The box is evidence of nothing."

"It's evidence that you had Mickey Cohen's gun. Says it right on this little brass plaque your daddy or somebody had made."

"So fucking what?"

"Well, I just made a call while I was out on your front porch, Haller. See, we had somebody checking on Mickey Cohen's self-defense case. Turns out that over there in LAPD's evidence archive they still have all the ballistic evidence from that case. That's a lucky break for us, the case being, what, fifty years old?"

I understood immediately. They would take the bullet slugs and casings from the Cohen case and compare them with the same evidence recovered in the Levin case. They would match the Levin murder to Mickey Cohen's gun which they would then tie to me with the gun box and the state's AFS computer. I doubted Roulet could have realized how the police would be able to make a case without even having the gun when he thought out his scheme to control me.

I stood there silently. Sobel left the room without a glance at me and Lankford looked up from the box at me with a killer smile.

"What's the matter, Counselor?" he asked. "Evidence got your tongue?"

I finally was able to speak.

"How long will ballistics take?" I managed to ask.

"Hey, for you, we're going to put a rush on it. So get out there and enjoy yourself while you can. But don't leave town."

He laughed, almost giddy with himself.

"Man, I thought they only said that in movies. But there, I just said it! I wish my partner had been here."

Sobel came back in with a large brown bag and a roll of red evidence tape. I watched her put the gun box into the bag and then seal it with the tape. I wondered how much time I had and if the wheels had just come off of everything I had put into motion. I started to feel as empty as the wooden box Sobel had just sealed inside the brown paper bag.

THIRTY-TWO

F ernando Valenzuela lived out in Valencia. From my home it was easily an hour's drive north in the last remnants of rush-hour traffic. Valenzuela had moved out of Van Nuys a few years earlier because his three daughters were nearing high school age and he feared for their safety and education. He moved into a neighborhood filled with people who had also fled from the city and his commute went from five minutes to forty-five. But he was happy. His house was nicer and his children safer. He lived in a Spanish-style house with a red tile roof in a planned community full of Spanish-style houses with red tile roofs. It was more than a bail bondsman could ever dream of having, but it came with a stiff monthly price tag.

It was almost nine by the time I got there. I pulled up to the garage, which had been left open. One space was taken by a minivan and the other by a pickup. On the floor between the pickup and a fully equipped tool bench was a large cardboard box that said SONY on it. It was long and thin. I looked closer and saw it was a box for a fifty-inch plasma TV. I got out and went to the front door and knocked. Valenzuela answered after a long wait.

"Mick, what are you doing up here?"

"Do you know your garage door is open?"

"Holy shit! I just had a plasma delivered."

He pushed by me and ran across the yard to look into the garage. I closed his front door and followed him to the garage. When I got there he was standing next to his TV, smiling.

"Oh, man, you know that would've never happened in Van Nuys," he said. "That sucker woulda been long gone. Come on, we'll go in through here."

He headed toward a door that would take us from the garage into the house. He hit a switch that made the garage door start to roll down.

"Hey, Val, wait a minute," I said. "Let's just talk out here. It's more private."

"But Maria probably wants to say hello."

"Maybe next time."

He came back over to me, concern in his eyes.

"What's up, Boss?"

"What's up is I spent some time today with the cops working on Raul's murder. They said they cleared Roulet on it because of the ankle bracelet."

Valenzuela nodded vigorously.

"Yeah, yeah, they came to see me a few days after it happened. I showed them the system and how it works and I pulled up Roulet's track for that day. They saw he was at work. And I also showed them the other bracelet I got and explained how it couldn't be tampered with. It's got a mass detector. Bottom line is you can't take it off. It would know and then I would know."

I leaned back against the pickup and folded my arms.

"So did those two cops ask where *you* were on that Saturday?"

It hit Valenzuela like a punch.

"What did you say, Mick?"

My eyes lowered to the plasma TV box and then back up to his.

"Somehow, some way, he killed Raul, Val. Now my ass is on the line and I want to know how he did it."

"Mick, listen to me, he's clear. I'm telling you, that bracelet didn't come off his ankle. The machine doesn't lie."

"Yeah, I know, the machine doesn't lie . . ."

After a moment he got it.

"What are you saying, Mick?"

He stepped in front of me, his body posture stiffening aggressively. I stopped leaning on the truck and dropped my hands to my sides.

"I'm asking, Val. Where were you on that Tuesday morning?"

"You son of a bitch, how could you ask me that?"

He had moved into a fight stance. I was momentarily taken off guard as I thought about him calling me what I had called Roulet earlier in the day.

Valenzuela suddenly lunged at me and shoved me hard against his truck. I shoved him back harder and he went backwards into the TV box. It tipped over and hit the floor with a loud, heavy *whump* and then he came down on it in a seated position. There was a sharp snap sound from inside the box.

"Oh, fuck!" he cried. "Oh, fuck! You broke the screen!"

"You pushed me, Val. I pushed back."

"Oh, fuck!"

He scrambled to the side of the box and tried to lift it back up but it was too heavy and unwieldy. I walked over to the other side and helped him right it. As the box came upright we heard small bits of material inside it slide down. It sounded like glass.

"Motherfuck!" Valenzuela yelled.

The door leading into the house opened and his wife, Maria, looked out.

"Hi, Mickey. Val, what is all the noise?"

"Just go inside," her husband ordered.

"Well, what is —"

"Shut the fuck up and go inside!"

She paused for a moment, staring at us, then closed the door. I heard her lock it. It looked like Valenzuela was sleeping with the broken TV tonight. I looked back at him. His mouth was spread in shock.

"That was eight thousand dollars," he whispered.

"They make TVs that cost eight thousand dollars?"

I was shocked. What was the world coming to?

"That was with a discount."

"Val, where'd you get the money for an eight-thousand-dollar TV?"

He looked at me and the fire came back.

"Where the fuck do you think? Business, man. Thanks to Roulet I'm having a hell of a year. But goddamn, Mick, I didn't cut him loose from the bracelet so he could go out and kill Raul. I knew Raul just as long as you did. I did not do that. I did not put the bracelet on and wear it while he went to kill Raul. And I did not go and kill Raul for him for a fucking TV. If you can't believe that, then just get the hell out of here and out of my life!"

He said it all with the desperate intensity of a wounded animal. A flash thought of Jesus Menendez came to my mind. I had failed to see the innocence in his pleas. I didn't want that to ever happen again.

"Okay, Val," I said.

I walked over to the house door and pushed the button that raised the garage door. When I turned back I saw he had taken a box cutter from the tool bench and was cutting the tape on the top of the TV box. It looked like he was trying to confirm what we already knew about the plasma. I walked past him and out of the garage.

"I'll split it with you, Val," I said. "I'll have Lorna send you a check in the morning."

"Don't bother. I'll tell them it was delivered this way."

I got to my car door and looked back at him.

"Then give me a call when they arrest you for fraud. After you bail yourself out."

I got in the Lincoln and backed out of the driveway. When I glanced back into the garage, I saw Valenzuela had stopped cutting open the box and was just standing there looking at me.

Traffic going back into the city was light and I made good time. I was just coming in through the front door when the house phone started to ring. I grabbed it in the kitchen, thinking maybe it was Valenzuela calling to tell me he was taking his business to another defense pro. At the moment I didn't care.

Instead, it was Maggie McPherson.

"Everything all right?" I asked. She usually didn't call so late.

"Fine."

"Where's Hayley?"

"Asleep. I didn't want to call until she went down."

"What's up?"

"There was a strange rumor about you floating around the office today."

"You mean the one about me being Raul Levin's murderer?"

"Haller, is this serious?"

The kitchen was too small for a table and chairs. I couldn't go far with the phone cord tether so I hoisted myself up onto the counter. Through the window over the sink I could see the lights of downtown twinkling in the distance and a glow on the horizon that I knew came from Dodger Stadium.

"I would say, yes, the situation is serious. I am being set up to take the fall for Raul's murder."

"Oh my God, Michael, how is this possible?"

"A lot of different ingredients — evil client, cop with a grudge, stupid lawyer, add sugar and spice and everything nice."

"Is it Roulet? Is he the one?"

"I can't talk about my clients with you, Mags."

"Well, what are you planning to do?"

"Don't worry, I've got it covered. I'll be okay."

"What about Hayley?"

I knew what she was saying. She was warning me to keep it away from Hayley. Don't let her go to school and hear kids talking about her father the murder suspect with a face and name splashed across the news.

"Hayley will be fine. She'll never know. Nobody will ever know if I play this thing right."

She didn't say anything and there was nothing else I could do to reassure her. I changed the subject. I tried to sound confident, even cheerful.

"How did your boy Minton look after court today?"

She didn't answer at first, probably reluctant to change the subject.

"I don't know. He looked fine. But Smithson sent an observer up because it's his first solo."

I nodded. I was counting on Smithson, who ran the DA's Van Nuys branch, having sent somebody to keep a watch on Minton.

"Any feedback?"

"No, not yet. Nothing that I heard. Look, Haller, I am really worried about this. The rumor was that you were served a search warrant in the courthouse. Is that true?"

"Yeah, but don't worry about it. I'm telling you, I have things under control. It will all come out okay. I promise."

I knew I had not quelled her fears. She was thinking about our daughter and the possible scandal. She was probably also thinking a little bit about herself and what having an ex-husband disbarred or accused of murder would do to her chances of advancement.

"Besides, if it all goes to shit, you're still going to be my first customer, right?"

"What are you talking about?"

"The Lincoln Lawyer Limousine Service. You're in, right?"

"Haller, it doesn't sound like this is a time to be making jokes."

"It's no joke, Maggie. I've been thinking about quitting. Even before all of this bullshit came up. It's like I told you that night, I can't do this anymore."

There was a long silence before she responded.

"Whatever you want to do is going to be fine by me and Hayley."

I nodded.

"You don't know how much I appreciate that."

She sighed into the phone.

"I don't know how you do it, Haller."

"Do what?"

"You're a sleazy defense lawyer with two ex-wives and an eight-year-old daughter. And we all still love you."

Now I was silent. Despite everything I smiled.

"Thank you, Maggie McFierce," I finally said. "Good night."

And I hung up the phone.

THIRTY-THREE

The second day of trial began with a forthwith to the judge's chambers for Minton and me. Judge Fullbright wanted only to speak to me but the rules of trial made it improper for her to meet privately with me about any matter and exclude the prosecution. Her chambers were spacious, with a desk and separate seating area surrounded by three walls of shelves containing law books. She told us to sit in the seats in front of her desk.

"Mr. Minton," she began, "I can't tell you not to listen but I'm going to have a conversation with Mr. Haller that I don't expect you to join or interrupt. It doesn't concern you or, as far as I know, the Roulet case."

Minton, taken by surprise, didn't quite know how to react other than to drop his jaw a couple inches and let light into his mouth. The judge turned in her desk chair toward me and clasped her hands together on the desk.

"Mr. Haller, is there anything you need to bring up with me? Keeping in mind that you are sitting next to a prosecutor."

"No, Judge, everything's fine. Sorry if you were bothered yesterday."

I did my best to put a rueful smile on my face, as if to show the search warrant had been nothing more than an embarrassing inconvenience.

"It is hardly a bother, Mr. Haller. We've invested a lot of time on this case. The jury, the prosecution, all of us. I am hoping that it is not going to be for naught. I don't want to do this again. My calendar is already overflowing."

"Excuse me, Judge Fullbright," Minton said. "Could I just ask what —"

"No, you may not," she said, cutting him off. "What we are talking about does not concern the trial other than the timing of it. If Mr. Haller is assuring me that we don't have a problem, then I will take him at his word. You need no further explanation than that."

She looked pointedly at me.

"Do I have your word on this, Mr. Haller?"

I hesitated before nodding. What she was telling me was that there would be hell to pay if I broke my word and the Glendale investigation caused a disruption or mistrial in the Roulet case.

"You've got my word," I said.

She immediately stood up and turned toward the hat rack in the corner. Her black robe hung there on a hanger.

"Okay, then, gentlemen, let's get to it. We've got a jury waiting."

Minton and I left the chambers and entered the courtroom through the clerk's station. Roulet was seated in the defendant's chair and waiting.

"What the hell was that all about?" Minton whispered to me.

He was playing dumb. He had to have heard the same rumors my ex-wife had picked up in the halls of the DA's office.

"Nothing, Ted. Just some bullshit involving another case of mine. You going to wrap it up today?"

"Depends on you. The longer you take, the longer I take cleaning up the bullshit you sling."

"Bullshit, huh? You're bleeding to death and don't even know it."

He smiled confidently at me.

"I don't think so."

"Call it death by a thousand razor blades, Ted. One doesn't do it. They all do it. Welcome to felony practice."

I separated from him and went to the defense table. As soon as I sat down, Roulet was in my ear.

"What was that about with the judge?" he whispered.

"Nothing. She was just warning me about how I handle the victim on cross."

"Who, the woman? She actually called her a victim?"

"Louis, first of all, keep your voice down. And second, she *is* the victim in this thing. You may have that rare ability to convince yourself of almost anything, but we still — no, make that I — still need to convince the jury."

He took the rebuke like I was blowing bubbles in his face and moved on.

"Well, what did she say?"

"She said she isn't going to allow me a lot of freedom in cross-examination. She reminded me that Regina Campo is a victim."

"I'm counting on you to rip her to shreds, to borrow a quote from you on the day we met."

"Yeah, well, things are a lot different than on the day we met, aren't they? And your little scheme with my gun is about to blow up in my face. And I'm telling you right now, I'm not going down for it. If I have to drive people to the airport the rest of my life, I will do that and do it gladly if it's my only way out from this. You understand, Louis?"

"I understand, Mick," he said glibly. "I'm sure you'll figure something out. You're a smart man."

I turned and looked at him. Luckily, I didn't have to say anything further. The bailiff called the court to order and Judge Fullbright took the bench.

Minton's first witness of the day was LAPD Detective Martin Booker. He was a solid witness for the prosecution. A rock. His answers were clear and concise and given without hesitation. Booker introduced the key piece of evidence, the knife with my client's initials on it, and under Minton's questioning he took the jury through his entire investigation of the attack on Regina Campo.

He testified that on the night of March 6 he had been working night duty out of Valley Bureau in Van Nuys. He was called to Regina Campo's apartment by the West Valley Division watch commander, who believed, after being briefed by his patrol officers, that the attack on Campo merited immediate attention from an investigator. Booker explained that the six detective bureaus in the Valley were only staffed during daytime hours. He said the night-duty detective was a quick-response position and often assigned cases of a pressing nature.

"What made this case of pressing nature, Detective?" Minton asked.

"The injuries to the victim, the arrest of a suspect and the belief that a greater crime had probably been averted," Booker answered.

"That greater crime being what?"

"Murder. It sounded like the guy was planning to kill her."

I could have objected but I planned to exploit the exchange on cross-examination, so I let it go.

Minton walked Booker through the investigative steps he took at the crime scene and later while interviewing Campo as she was being treated at a hospital.

"Before you got to the hospital you had been briefed by Officers Maxwell and Santos on what the victim had reported had happened, correct?"

"Yes, they gave me an overview."

"Did they tell you that the victim was engaged in selling sex to men for a living?"

"No, they didn't."

"When did you find that out?"

"Well, I was getting a pretty good sense of it when I was in her apartment and I saw some of the property she had there."

"What property?"

"Things I would describe as sex aids, and in one of the bedrooms, there was a closet that only had negligees and clothing of a sexually provocative nature in it. There was also a television in that room and a collection of pornographic tapes in the drawers beneath it. I had been told that she did not have a roommate but it looked to me like both bedrooms were in active use. I started to think that one room was hers, like it was the one she slept in when she was alone, and the other was for her professional activities."

"A trick pad?"

"You could call it that."

"Did it change your opinion of her as a victim of this attack?"

"No, it didn't."

"And why not?"

"Because anybody can be a victim. Prostitute or pope, doesn't matter. A victim is a victim."

Spoken just as rehearsed, I thought. Minton made a check mark on his pad and moved on.

"Now, when you got to the hospital, did you ask the victim about your theory in regard to her bedrooms and what she did for a living?"

"Yes, I did."

"What did she tell you?"

"She flat out said she was a working girl. She didn't try to hide it."

"Did anything she said to you differ from the accounts of the attack you had already gathered at the crime scene?"

"No, not at all. She told me she opened the door to the defendant and he immediately punched her in the face and drove her backwards into the apartment. He assaulted her further and produced a knife. He told her he was going to rape her and then kill her."

Minton continued to probe the investigation in more detail and to the point of boring the jury. When I was not writing down questions to ask Booker during cross, I watched the jurors and saw their attention lag under the weight of so much information.

Finally, after ninety minutes of direct examination it was my turn with the police detective. My goal was to get in and get out.

While Minton performed the whole case autopsy, I only wanted to go in and scrape cartilage out of the knees.

"Detective Booker, did Regina Campo explain why she lied to the police?"

"She didn't lie to me."

"Maybe not to you but she told the first officers on the scene, Maxwell and Santos, that she did not know why the suspect had come to her apartment, didn't she?"

"I wasn't present when they spoke to her so I can't testify to that. I do know that she was scared, that she had just been beaten and threatened with rape and death at the time of the first interview."

"So you are saying that under those circumstances it is acceptable to lie to the police."

"No, I did not say that."

I checked my notes and moved on. I wasn't going for a linear continuum of questions. I was potshotting, trying to keep him off balance.

"Did you catalog the clothing you found in the bedroom you said Ms. Campo used for her prostitution business?"

"No, I did not. It was just an observation I made. It was not important to the case."

"Would any of the outfits you saw in the closet have been appropriate to sadomasochistic sexual activities?"

"I wouldn't know that. I am not an expert in that field."

"How about the pornographic videos? Did you write down the titles?"

"No, I did not. Again, I did not believe that it was pertinent to the investigation of who had brutally assaulted this woman."

"Do you recall if the subject matter of any of the videos involved sadomasochism or bondage or anything of that nature?"

"No, I do not."

"Now, did you instruct Ms. Campo to get rid of those tapes and the clothing from the closet before members of Mr. Roulet's defense team could view the apartment?"

"I certainly did not."

I checked that one off my list and moved on.

"Have you ever spoken to Mr. Roulet about what happened in Ms. Campo's apartment that night?"

"No, he lawyered up before I got to him."

"Do you mean he exercised his constitutional right to remain silent?"

"Yes, that's exactly what he did."

"So, as far as you know, he never spoke to the police about what happened."

"That is correct."

"In your opinion, was Ms. Campo struck with great force?"

"I would say so, yes. Her face was very badly cut and swollen."

"Then please tell the jury about the impact injuries you found on Mr. Roulet's hands."

"He had wrapped a cloth around his fist to protect it. There were no injuries on his hands that I could see."

"Did you document this lack of injury?"

Booker looked puzzled by the question.

"No," he said.

"So you had Ms. Campo's injuries documented by photographs but you didn't see the need to document Mr. Roulet's lack of injuries, correct?"

"It didn't seem to me to be necessary to photograph something that wasn't there."

"How do you know he wrapped his fist in a cloth to protect it?"

"Ms. Campo told me she saw that his hand was wrapped right before he punched her at the door."

"Did you find this cloth he supposedly wrapped his hand in?"

"Yes, it was in the apartment. It was a napkin, like from a restaurant. It had her blood on it."

"Did it have Mr. Roulet's blood on it?"

"No."

"Was there anything that identified it as belonging to the defendant?"

"No."

"So we have Ms. Campo's word for it, right?"

"That's right."

I let some time pass while I scribbled a note on my pad. I then continued to question the detective.

"Detective, when did you learn that Louis Roulet denied assaulting or threatening Ms. Campo and that he would be vigorously defending himself against the charges?"

"That would have been when he hired you, I guess."

There was a murmur of laughter in the courtroom.

"Did you pursue other explanations for Ms. Campo's injuries?"

"No, she told me what happened. I believed her. He beat her and was going to —"

"Thank you, Detective Booker. Just try to answer the question I ask."

"I was."

"If you looked for no other explanation because you believed the word of Ms. Campo, is it safe to say that this whole case relies upon her word and what she said occurred in her apartment on the night of March sixth?"

Booker deliberated a moment. He knew I was leading him into a trap of his own words. As the saying goes, there is no trap so deadly as the one you set for yourself.

"It's not just her word," he said after thinking he saw a way out. "There is physical evidence. The knife. Her injuries. More than just her word on this."

He nodded affirmatively.

"But doesn't the state's explanation for her injuries and the other evidence begin with her telling of what happened?"

"You could say that, yes," he said reluctantly.

"She is the tree on which all of these fruits grow, is she not?"

"I probably wouldn't use those words."

"Then what words would you use, Detective?"

I had him now. Booker was literally squirming in his seat. Minton stood up and objected, saying I was badgering the witness. It must have been something he had seen on TV or in a movie. He was told to sit down by the judge.

"You can answer the question, Detective," the judge said.

"What was the question?" Booker asked, trying to buy some time.

"You disagreed with me when I characterized Ms. Campo as the tree from which all the evidence in the case grows," I said. "If I am wrong, how would you describe her position in this case?"

Booker raised his hands in a quick gesture of surrender.

"She's the victim! Of course she's important because she told us what happened. We have to rely on her to set the course of the investigation."

"You rely on her for quite a bit in this case, don't you? Victim and chief witness against the defendant, correct?"

"That's right."

"Who else saw the defendant attack Ms. Campo?"

"Nobody else."

I nodded, to underline the answer for the jury. I looked over and exchanged eye contact with those in the front row.

"Okay, Detective," I said. "I want to ask you about Charles Talbot now. How did you find out about this man?"

"Uh, the prosecutor, Mr. Minton, told me to find him."

"And do you know how Mr. Minton came to know about his existence?"

"I believe you were the one who informed him. You had a videotape from a bar that showed him with the victim a couple hours before the attack."

I knew this could be the point to introduce the video but I wanted to wait on that. I wanted the victim on the stand when I showed the tape to the jury.

"And up until that point you didn't think it was important to find this man?"

"No, I just didn't know about him."

"So when you finally did know about Talbot and you located him, did you have his left hand examined to determine if he had any injuries that could have been sustained while punching someone re-peatedly in the face?"

"No, I didn't."

"Is that because you were confident in your choice of Mr. Roulet as the person who punched Regina Campo?"

"It wasn't a choice. It was where the investigation led. I didn't lo-cate Charles Talbot until more than two weeks after the crime oc-curred."

"So what you are saying is that if he'd had injuries, they would have been healed by then, correct?"

"I'm no expert on it but that was my thinking, yes."

"So you never looked at his hand, did you?"

"Not specifically, no."

"Did you question any coworkers of Mr. Talbot about whether they saw bruising or other injuries on his hand around the time of the crime?"

"No, I did not."

"So you never really looked beyond Mr. Roulet, did you?"

"That is wrong. I come into every case with an open mind. But Roulet was there and in custody from the start. The victim identified him as her attacker. He was obviously a focus."

"Was he *a* focus or *the* focus, Detective Booker?"

"He was both. At first he was *a* focus and later — after we found his initials on the weapon that had been held to Reggie Campo's throat — he became *the* focus, you could say."

"How do you know that knife was held to Ms. Campo's throat?"

"Because she told us and she had the puncture wound to show for it."

"Are you saying there was some sort of forensic analysis that matched the knife to the wound on her neck?"

"No, that was impossible."

"So again we have Ms. Campo's word that the knife was held to her throat by Mr. Roulet."

"I had no reason to doubt her then. I have none now."

"Now without any explanation for it, I guess you would consider the knife with the defendant's initials on it to be a highly important piece of evidence of guilt, wouldn't you?"

"Yes. Even with explanation, I would say. He brought that knife in there with one purpose in mind."

"You are a mind reader, are you, Detective?"

"No, I'm a detective. And I am just saying what I think."

"Accent on *think*."

"It's what I know from the evidence in the case."

"I'm glad you are so confident, sir. I have no further questions at this time. I reserve the right to recall Detective Booker as a witness for the defense."

I had no intention of calling Booker back to the stand but I thought the threat might sound good to the jury.

I returned to my seat while Minton tried to bandage up Booker on redirect. The damage was in perceptions and there wasn't a lot that he could do with that. Booker had only been a setup man for the defense. The real damage would come later.

After Booker stepped down, the judge called for the mid-morning break. She told the jurors to be back in fifteen minutes but I knew the break would last longer. Judge Fullbright was a smoker and had already faced highly publicized administrative charges for sneaking smokes in her chambers. That meant that for her to take care of her habit and avoid further scandal, she had to take the elevator down and leave the building and stand in the entry port where the jail buses come in. I figured I had at least a half hour.

I went out into the hallway to talk to Mary Alice Windsor and work my cell phone. It looked like I would be putting on witnesses in the afternoon session.

I was first approached by Roulet, who wanted to talk about my cross-examination of Booker.

"It looked to me like it went really well for us," he said.

"Us?"

"You know what I mean."

"You can't tell whether it's gone well until you get the verdict. Now leave me alone, Louis. I have to make some calls. And where is your mother? I am probably going to need her this afternoon. Is she going to be here?"

"She had an appointment this morning but she'll be here. Just call Cecil and he'll bring her in."

After he walked away Detective Booker took his place, walking up to me and pointing a finger in my face.

"It's not going to fly, Haller," he said.

"What's not going to fly?" I asked.

"Your whole bullshit defense. You're going to crash and burn."

"We'll see."

"Yeah, we'll see. You know, you have some balls trying to trash Talbot with this. Some balls. You must need a wheelbarrow to carry them around in."

"I'm just doing my job, Detective."

"And some job it is. Lying for a living. Tricking people from looking at the truth. Living in a world without truth. Let me ask you something. You know the difference between a catfish and a lawyer?"

"No, what's the difference?"

"One's a bottom-feeding, shit-eating scum sucker. The other's a fish."

"That's a good one, Detective."

He left me then and I stood there smiling. Not because of the joke or the understanding that Lankford had probably been the one to elevate the insult from defense attorneys to all of lawyerdom when he had retold the joke to Booker. I smiled because the joke was confirmation that Lankford and Booker were in communication. They were talking and it meant that things were moving and in play. My plan was still holding together. I still had a chance.

THIRTY-FOUR

Every trial has a main event. A witness or a piece of evidence that becomes the fulcrum upon which everything swings one way or the other. In this case the main event was billed as Regina Campo, victim and accuser, and the case would seem to rest upon her performance and testimony. But a good defense attorney always has an understudy and I had mine, a witness secretly waiting in the wings upon whom I hoped to shift the weight of the trial.

Nevertheless, when Minton called Regina Campo to the stand after the break, it was safe to say all eyes were on her as she was led in and walked to the witness box. It was the first time anyone in the jury had seen her in person. It was also the first time I had ever seen her. I was surprised, but not in a good way. She was diminutive and her hesitant walk and slight posture belied the picture of the scheming mercenary I had been building in the jury's collective consciousness.

Minton was definitely learning as he was going. With Campo he seemed to have arrived at the conclusion that less was more. He economically led her through the testimony. He first started with personal background before moving on to the events of March 6.

Regina Campo's story was sadly unoriginal and that was what Minton was counting on. She told the story of a young, attractive woman coming to Hollywood from Indiana a decade before with hopes of celluloid glory. There were starts and stops to a career, an appearance on a television show here and there. She was a fresh face and there were always men willing to put her in small meaningless parts. But when she was no longer a fresh face, she found work in a series of straight-to-cable films which often required her to appear nude. She supplemented her income with nude modeling jobs and slipped easily into a world of trading sex for favors. Eventually, she skipped the façade altogether and started trading sex for money. It finally brought her to the night she encountered Louis Roulet.

Regina Campo's courtroom version of what happened that night did not differ from the accounts offered by all previous witnesses in the trial. But where it was dramatically different was in the delivery. Campo, with her face framed by dark, curly hair, seemed like a little girl lost. She appeared scared and tearful during the latter half of her testimony. Her lower lip and finger shook with fear as she pointed to the man she identified as her attacker. Roulet stared right back, a blank expression on his face.

"It was him," she said in a strong voice. "He's an animal who should be put away!"

I let that go without objection. I would get my chance with her soon enough. Minton continued the questioning, taking Campo through her escape, and then asked why she had not told the responding officers the truth about knowing who the man who attacked her was and why he was there.

"I was scared," she said. "I wasn't sure they would believe me if I told them why he was there. I wanted to make sure they arrested him because I was very afraid of him."

"Do you regret that decision now?"

"Yes, I do because I know it might help him get free to do this again to somebody."

I did object to that answer as prejudicial and the judge sustained it. Minton threw a few more questions at his witness but seemed to know he was past the apex of the testimony and that he should stop before he obscured the trembling finger of identification.

Campo had testified on direct examination for slightly less than an hour. It was almost 11:30 but the judge did not break for lunch as I had expected. She told the jurors she wanted to get as much testimony in as possible during the day and that they would go to a late, abbreviated lunch. This made me wonder if she knew something I didn't. Had the Glendale detectives called her during the mid-morning break to warn of my impending arrest?

"Mr. Haller, your witness," she said to prompt me and keep things going.

I went to the lectern with my legal pad and looked at my notes. If I was engaged in a defense of a thousand razors, I had to use at least half of them on this witness. I was ready.

"Ms. Campo, have you engaged the services of an attorney to sue Mr. Roulet over the alleged events of March sixth?"

She looked as though she had expected the question, but not as the first one out of the shoot.

"No, I haven't."

"Have you talked to an attorney about this case?"

"I haven't hired anybody to sue him. Right now, all I am interested in is seeing that justice is —"

"Ms. Campo," I interrupted. "I didn't ask whether you hired an attorney or what your interests are. I asked if you had *talked* to an attorney — any attorney — about this case and a possible lawsuit against Mr. Roulet."

She was looking closely at me, trying to read me. I had said it with the authority of someone who knew something, who had the goods to back up the charge. Minton had probably schooled her on the most important aspect of testifying: don't get trapped in a lie.

"Talked to an attorney, yes. But it was nothing more than talk. I didn't hire him."

"Is that because the prosecutor told you not to hire anybody until the criminal case was over?"

"No, he didn't say anything about that."

"Why did you talk to an attorney about this case?"

She had dropped into a routine of hesitating before every answer.

This was fine with me. The perception of most people is that it takes time to tell a lie. Honest responses come easily.

"I talked to him because I wanted to know my rights and to make sure I was protected."

"Did you ask him if you could sue Mr. Roulet for damages?"

"I thought what you say to your attorney is private."

"If you wish, you can tell the jurors what you spoke to the attorney about."

There was the first deep slash with the razor. She was in an untenable position. No matter how she answered she would not look good.

"I think I want to keep it private," she finally said.

"Okay, let's go back to March sixth, but I want to go a little further back than Mr. Minton did. Let's go back to the bar at Morgan's when you first spoke to the defendant, Mr. Roulet."

"Okay."

"What were you doing at Morgan's that night?"

"I was meeting someone."

"Charles Talbot?"

"Yes."

"Now, you were meeting him there to sort of size up whether you wanted to lead him back to your place to engage in sex for hire, correct?"

She hesitated but then nodded.

"Please answer verbally," the judge told her.

"Yes."

"Would you say that practice is a safety precaution?"

"Yes."

"A form of safe sex, right?"

"I guess so."

"Because in your profession you deal intimately with strangers, so you must protect yourself, correct?"

"Yes, correct."

"People in your profession call this the 'freak test,' don't they?"

"I've never called it that."

"But it is true that you meet your prospective clients in a public place like Morgan's to test them out and make sure they aren't freaks or dangerous before you take them to your apartment. Isn't that right?"

"You could say that. But the truth is, you can never be sure about somebody."

"That is true. So when you were at Morgan's you noticed Mr. Roulet sitting at the same bar as you and Mr. Talbot?"

"Yes, he was there."

"And had you ever seen him before?"

"Yes, I had seen him there and a few other places before."

"Had you ever spoken to him?"

"No, we never talked."

"Had you ever noticed that he wore a Rolex watch?"

"No."

"Had you ever seen him drive up or away from one of these places in a Porsche or a Range Rover?"

"No, I never saw him driving."

"But you had seen him before in Morgan's and other places like it."

"Yes."

"But never spoke to him."

"Correct."

"Then, what made you approach him?"

"I knew he was in the life, that's all."

"What do you mean by 'in the life'?"

"I mean that the other times I had seen him I could tell he was a player. I'd seen him leave with girls that do what I do."

"You saw him leave with other prostitutes?"

"Yes."

"Leave to where?"

"I don't know, leave the premises. Go to a hotel or the girl's apartment. I don't know that part."

"Well, how do you know they even left the premises? Maybe they went outside for a smoke."

"I saw them get into his car and drive away."

"Ms. Campo, you testified a minute ago that you never saw Mr. Roulet's cars. Now you are saying that you saw him get into his car with a woman who is a prostitute like yourself. Which is it?"

She realized her misstep and froze for a moment until an answer came to her.

"I saw him get into a car but I didn't know what kind it was."

"You don't notice things like that, do you?"

"Not usually."

"Do you know the difference between a Porsche and a Range Rover?"

"One's big and one's small, I guess."

"What kind of car did you see Mr. Roulet get into?"

"I don't remember."

I paused a moment and decided I had milked her contradiction for all it was worth. I looked down at my list of questions and moved on.

"These women that you saw leave with Mr. Roulet, were they ever seen again?"

"I don't understand."

"Did they disappear? Did you ever see them again?"

"No, I saw them again."

"Had they been beaten or injured?"

"Not that I know of but I didn't ask."

"But all of this added up to you believing that you were safe as far as approaching and soliciting him, correct?"

"I don't know about safe. I just knew he was probably there looking for a girl and the man I was with already told me he would be finished by ten because he had to go to his business."

"Well, can you tell the jury why it was that you did not have to sit with Mr. Roulet like you did with Mr. Talbot and subject him to a freak test?"

Her eyes drifted over to Minton. She was hoping for a rescue but none was coming.

"I just thought he was a known quantity, that's all."

"You thought he was safe."

"I guess so. I don't know. I needed the money and I made a mistake with him."

"Did you think he was rich and could solve your need for money?"

"No, nothing like that. I saw him as a potential customer who wasn't new to the game. Somebody who knew what he was doing."

"You testified that on prior occasions you had seen Mr. Roulet with other women who practice the same profession as yourself?"

"Yes."

"They're prostitutes."

"Yes."

"Do you know them?"

"We're acquaintances."

"And do you extend professional courtesy to these women in terms of alerting them to customers who might be dangerous or unwilling to pay?"

"Sometimes."

"And they extend the same professional courtesy to you, right?"

"Yes."

"How many of them warned you about Louis Roulet?"

"Well, nobody did, or I wouldn't have gone with him."

I nodded and looked at my notes for a long moment before continuing. I then led her in more detail through the events at Morgan's and then introduced the video surveillance tape from the bar's overhead camera. Minton objected to it being shown to the jury without proper foundation but he was overruled. A television on an industrial stand was wheeled in front of the jury and the video was played. I could tell by the rapt attention they paid to it that they were enamored with the idea of watching a prostitute at work as well as the aspect of seeing the two main players in the case in unguarded moments.

"What did the note say that you passed him?" I asked after the television was pushed to the side of the courtroom.

"I think it just said my name and address."

"You didn't quote him a price for the services you would perform?"

"I may have. I don't remember."

"What is the going rate that you charge?"

"Usually I get four hundred dollars."

"Usually? What would make you differentiate from that?"

"Depends on what the client wants."

I looked over at the jury box and saw that the Bible man's face was getting tight with discomfort.

"Do you ever engage in bondage and domination with your clients?"

"Sometimes. It's only role playing, though. Nobody ever gets hurt. It's just playacting."

"Are you saying that before the night of March sixth, you have never been hurt by a client?"

"Yes, that's what I am saying. That man hurt me and tried to kill —"

"Please just answer the question I ask, Ms. Campo. Thank you. Now, let's go back to Morgan's. Yes or no, at the moment you gave Mr. Roulet the napkin with your address and price on it, you were confident that he would not be a danger to you and that he was carrying sufficient cash funds to pay the four hundred dollars you demand for your services?"

"Yes."

"So, why didn't Mr. Roulet have any cash on him when the police searched him?"

"I don't know. I didn't take it."

"Do you know who did?"

"No."

I hesitated for a long moment, preferring to punctuate my shifts in questioning streams with an underscore of silence.

"Now, uh, you are still working as a prostitute, correct?" I asked.

Campo hesitated before saying yes.

"And are you happy working as a prostitute?" I asked.

Minton stood.

"Your Honor, what does this have to do with —"

"Sustained," the judge said.

"Okay," I said. "Then, isn't it true, Ms. Campo, that you have told several of your clients that your hope is to leave the business?"

"Yes, that's true," she answered without hesitation for the first time in many questions.

"Isn't it also true that you see the potential financial aspects of this case as a means of getting out of the business?"

"No, that's not true," she said forcefully and without hesitation. "That man attacked me. He was going to kill me! That's what this is about!"

I underlined something on my pad, another punctuation of silence.

"Was Charles Talbot a repeat customer?" I asked.

"No, I met him for the first time that night at Morgan's."

"And he passed your safety test."

"Yes."

"Was Charles Talbot the man who punched you in the face on March sixth?"

"No, he was not," she answered quickly.

"Did you offer to split the profits you would receive from a lawsuit against Mr. Roulet with Mr. Talbot?"

"No, I did not. That's a lie!"

I looked up at the judge.

"Your Honor, can I ask my client to stand up at this time?"

"Be my guest, Mr. Haller."

I signaled Roulet to stand at the defense table and he obliged. I looked back at Regina Campo.

"Now, Ms. Campo, are you sure that this is the man who struck you on the night of March sixth?"

"Yes, it's him."

"How much do you weigh, Ms. Campo?"

She leaned back from the microphone as if put out by what was an invasive question, even coming after so many questions pertaining to her sex life. I noticed Roulet start to sit back down and I signaled him to remain standing.

"I'm not sure," Campo said.

"On your ad on the website you list your weight at one hundred and five pounds," I said. "Is that correct?"

"I think so."

"So if the jury is to believe your story about March sixth, then they must believe that you were able to overpower and break free of Mr. Roulet."

I pointed to Roulet, who was easily six feet and outweighed her by at least seventy-five pounds.

"Well, that's what I did."

"And this was while he supposedly was holding a knife to your throat."

"I wanted to live. You can do some amazing things when your life is in danger."

She used her last defense. She started crying, as if my question had reawakened the horror of coming so close to death.

"You can sit down, Mr. Roulet. I have nothing else for Ms. Campo at this time, Your Honor."

I took my seat next to Roulet. I felt the cross had gone well. My razor work had opened up a lot of wounds. The state's case was bleeding. Roulet leaned over and whispered one word to me. *"Brilliant!"*

Minton went back in for a redirect but he was just a gnat flitting around an open wound. There was no going back on some of the answers his star witness had given, and there was no way to change some of the images I had planted in the jurors' minds.

In ten minutes he was through and I waived off a recross, feeling that Minton had accomplished little during his second effort and I could leave well enough alone. The judge asked the prosecutor if he had any further witnesses and Minton said he would like to think about it through lunch before deciding whether to rest the state's case.

Normally, I would have objected to this because I would want to know if I had to put a witness on the stand directly after lunch. But I let it go. I believed that Minton was feeling the pressure and was wavering. I wanted to push him toward a decision and thought maybe giving him the lunch hour would help.

The judge excused the jury to lunch, giving them only an hour instead of the usual ninety minutes. She was going to keep things moving. She said court would recess until 1:30 and then abruptly left the bench. She probably needed a cigarette, I guessed.

I asked Roulet if his mother could join us for lunch so that we could talk about her testimony, which I thought would come in the afternoon if not directly after lunch. He said he would arrange it and suggested we meet at a French restaurant on Ventura Boulevard. I told him we had less than an hour and that his mother should meet us at Four Green Fields. I didn't like the idea of bringing them into my sanctuary but I knew we could eat there quickly and be back to court on time. The food probably wasn't up to the standards of the French bistro on Ventura but I wasn't worried about that.

When I got up and turned from the defense table, I saw the rows of the gallery were empty. Everybody had hustled out to lunch. Only Minton was waiting by the rail for me.

"Can I talk to you for a minute?" he asked.

"Sure."

We waited until Roulet had gone through the gate and left the courtroom before either one of us spoke. I knew what was coming. It was customary for the prosecutor to throw out a low-ball disposition at the first sign of trouble. Minton knew he had trouble. The main-event witness was a draw at best.

"What's up?" I said.

"I was thinking about what you said about the thousand razors."

"And?"

"And, well, I want to make you an offer."

"You're new at this, kid. Don't you need somebody in charge to approve a plea agreement?"

"I have some authority."

"Okay, then give me what you are authorized to offer."

"I'll drop it all down to an aggravated assault with GBI."

"And?"

"I'll go down to four."

The offer was a substantial reduction but Roulet, if he took it, would still be sentenced to four years in prison. The main concession was that it knocked the case out of sex crime status. Roulet would not have to register with local authorities as a sex offender after he got out of prison.

I looked at him as if he had just insulted my mother's memory.

"I think that's a little strong, Ted, considering how your ace just held up on the stand. Did you see the juror who is always carrying the Bible? He looked like he was about to shit the Good Book when she was testifying."

Minton didn't respond. I could tell he hadn't even noticed a juror carrying a Bible.

"I don't know," I said. "It's my duty to bring your offer to my client and I will do that. But I'm also going to tell him he'd be a fool to take it."

"Okay, then, what do you want?"

"A case like this, there's only one verdict, Ted. I'm going to tell him he should ride it out. I think it's clear sailing from here. Have a good lunch."

I left him there at the gate, halfway expecting him to shout a new offer to my back as I went down the center aisle of the gallery. But Minton held his ground.

"That offer's good only until one-thirty, Haller," he called after me, an odd tone in his voice.

I raised a hand and waved without looking back. As I went through the courtroom door, I was sure that what I had heard was the sound of desperation creeping into his voice.

THIRTY-FIVE

After we came back into court from Four Green Fields I purposely ignored Minton. I wanted to keep him guessing as long as possible. It was all part of the plan to push him in a direction I wanted him and the trial to go. When we were all seated at the tables and ready for the judge, I finally looked over at him, waited for the eye contact, and then just shook my head. No deal. He nodded, trying his best to give me a show of confidence in his case and confusion over my client's decision. One minute later the judge took the bench, brought out the jury, and Minton promptly folded his tent.

"Mr. Minton, do you have another witness?" the judge asked.

"Your Honor, at this time the state rests."

There was the slightest hesitation in Fullbright's response. She stared at Minton for just a second longer than she should have. I think it sent a message of surprise to the jury. She then looked over at me.

"Mr. Haller, are you ready to proceed?"

The routine procedure would be to ask the judge for a directed verdict of acquittal at the end of the state's case. But I didn't, fearing that this could be the rare occasion that the request was granted. I couldn't let the case end yet. I told the judge I was ready to proceed with a defense.

My first witness was Mary Alice Windsor. She was escorted into

the courtroom by Cecil Dobbs, who then took a seat in the front row
of the gallery. Windsor was wearing a powder blue suit with a chif-
fon blouse. She had a regal bearing as she crossed in front of the
bench and took a seat in the witness box. Nobody would have
guessed she had eaten shepherd's pie for lunch. I very quickly went
through the routine identifiers and established her relationship by
both blood and business to Louis Roulet. I then asked the judge for
permission to show the witness the knife the prosecution had entered
as evidence in the case.

Permission granted, I went to the court clerk to retrieve the
weapon, which was still wrapped in a clear plastic evidence bag. It
was folded so that the initials on the blade were visible. I took it to the
witness box and put it down in front of the witness.

"Mrs. Windsor, do you recognize this knife?"

She picked up the evidence bag and attempted to smooth the
plastic over the blade so she could look for and read the initials.

"Yes, I do," she finally said. "It's my son's knife."

"And how is it that you would recognize a knife owned by your
son?"

"Because he showed it to me on more than one occasion. I knew
he always carried it and sometimes it came in handy at the office
when our brochures came in and we needed to cut the packing
straps. It was very sharp."

"How long did he have the knife?"

"Four years."

"You seem pretty exact about that."

"I am."

"How can you be so sure?"

"Because he got it for protection four years ago. Almost exactly."

"Protection from what, Mrs. Windsor?"

"In our business we often show homes to complete strangers.
Sometimes we are the only ones in the home with these strangers.
There has been more than one incident of a realtor being robbed or
hurt . . . or even murdered or raped."

"As far as you know, was Louis ever the victim of such a crime?"

"Not personally, no. But he knew someone who had gone into a home and that happened to them . . ."

"What happened?"

"She got raped and robbed by a man with a knife. Louis was the one who found her after it was over. The first thing he did was go out and get a knife for protection after that."

"Why a knife? Why not a gun?"

"He told me that at first he was going to get a gun but he wanted something he could always carry and not be noticeable with. So he got a knife and he got me one, too. That's how I know it was almost exactly four years ago that he got this."

She held the bag up containing the knife.

"Mine's exactly the same, only the initials are different. We both have been carrying them ever since."

"So would it seem to you that if your son was carrying that knife on the night of March sixth, then that would be perfectly normal behavior from him?"

Minton objected, saying I had not built the proper foundation for Windsor to answer the question and the judge sustained it. Mary Windsor, being unschooled in criminal law, assumed that the judge was allowing her to answer.

"He carried it every day," she said. "March sixth would have been no dif —"

"Mrs. Windsor," the judge boomed. "I sustained the objection. That means you do not answer. The jury will disregard her answer."

"I'm sorry," Windsor said in a weak voice.

"Next question, Mr. Haller," the judge ordered.

"That's all I have, Your Honor. Thank you, Mrs. Windsor."

Mary Windsor started to get up but the judge admonished her again, telling her to stay seated. I returned to my seat as Minton got up from his. I scanned the gallery and saw no recognizable faces save that of C. C. Dobbs. He gave me an encouraging smile, which I ignored.

Mary Windsor's direct testimony had been perfect in terms of her adhering to the choreography we had worked up at lunch. She had succinctly delivered to the jury the explanation for the knife, yet she had also left in her testimony a minefield that Minton would have to cross. Her direct testimony had covered no more than I had provided Minton in a discovery summary. If he strayed from it he would quickly hear the deadly *click* under his foot.

"This incident that inspired your son to start carrying around a five-inch folding knife, when exactly was that?"

"It happened on June ninth in two thousand and one."

"You're sure?"

"Absolutely."

I turned in my seat so I could more fully see Minton's face. I was reading him. He thought he had something. Windsor's exact memory of a date was obvious indication of planted testimony. He was excited. I could tell.

"Was there a newspaper story about this supposed attack on a fellow realtor?"

"No, there wasn't."

"Was there a police investigation?"

"No, there wasn't."

"And yet you know the exact date. How is that, Mrs. Windsor? Were you given this date before testifying here?"

"No, I know the date because I will never forget the day I was attacked."

She waited a moment. I saw at least three of the jurors open their mouths silently. Minton did the same. I could almost hear the *click*.

"My son will never forget it, either," Windsor continued. "When he came looking for me and found me in that house, I was tied up, naked. There was blood. It was traumatic for him to see me that way. I think that was one of the reasons he took to carrying a knife. I think in some ways he wished he had gotten there earlier and been able to stop it."

"I see," Minton said, staring down at his notes.

He froze, unsure how to proceed. He didn't want to raise his foot for fear that the mine would detonate and blow it off.

"Mr. Minton, anything else?" the judge asked, a not so well disguised note of sarcasm in her voice.

"One moment, Your Honor," Minton said.

Minton gathered himself, reviewed his notes and tried to salvage something.

"Mrs. Windsor, did you or your son call the police after he found you?"

"No, we didn't. Louis wanted to but I did not. I thought that it would only further the trauma."

"So we have no official police documentation of this crime, correct?"

"That's correct."

I knew that Minton wanted to carry it further and ask if she had sought medical treatment after the attack. But sensing another trap, he didn't ask the question.

"So what you are saying here is that we only have your word that this attack even occurred? Your word and your son's, if he chooses to testify."

"It did occur. I live with it each and every day."

"But we only have you who says so."

She looked at the prosecutor with deadpan eyes.

"Is that a question?"

"Mrs. Windsor, you are here to help your son, correct?"

"If I can. I know him as a good man who would not have committed this despicable crime."

"You would be willing to do anything and everything in your power to save your son from conviction and possible prison, wouldn't you?"

"But I wouldn't lie about something like this. Oath or no oath, I wouldn't lie."

"But you want to save your son, don't you?"

"Yes."

"And saving him means lying for him, doesn't it?"

"No. It does not."

"Thank you, Mrs. Windsor."

Minton quickly returned to his seat. I had only one question on redirect.

"Mrs. Windsor, how old were you when this attack occurred?"

"I was fifty-four."

I sat back down. Minton had nothing further and Windsor was excused. I asked the judge to allow her to sit in the gallery for the remainder of the trial, now that her testimony was concluded. Without an objection from Minton the request was granted.

My next witness was an LAPD detective named David Lambkin, who was a national expert on sex crimes and had worked on the Real Estate Rapist investigation. In brief questioning I established the facts of the case and the five reported cases of rape that were investigated. I quickly got to the five key questions I needed to bolster Mary Windsor's testimony.

"Detective Lambkin, what was the age range of the known victims of the rapist?"

"These were all professional women who were pretty successful. They tended to be older than your average rape victim. I believe the youngest was twenty-nine and the oldest was fifty-nine."

"So a woman who was fifty-four years old would have fallen within the rapist's target profile, correct?"

"Yes."

"Can you tell the jury when the first reported attack occurred and when the last reported attack occurred?"

"Yes. The first was October one, two thousand, and the last one was July thirtieth of two thousand and one."

"So June ninth of two thousand and one was well within the span of this rapist's attacks on women in the real estate business, correct?"

"Yes, correct."

"In the course of your investigation of this case, did you come to a conclusion or belief that there were more than five rapes committed by this individual?"

Minton objected, saying the question called for speculation. The judge sustained the objection but it didn't matter. The question was what was important and the jury seeing the prosecutor keeping the answer from them was the payoff.

Minton surprised me on cross. He recovered enough from the misstep with Windsor to hit Lambkin with three solid questions with answers favorable to the prosecution.

"Detective Lambkin, did the task force investigating these rapes issue any kind of warning to women working in the real estate business?"

"Yes, we did. We sent out fliers on two occasions. The first went to all licensed real estate businesses in the area and the next mail-out went to all licensed real estate brokers individually, male and female."

"Did these mail-outs contain information about the rapist's description and methods?"

"Yes, they did."

"So if someone wished to concoct a story about being attacked by this rapist, the mail-outs would have provided all the information needed, correct?"

"That is a possibility, yes."

"Nothing further, Your Honor."

Minton proudly sat down and Lambkin was excused when I had nothing further. I asked the judge for a few minutes to confer with my client and then leaned in close to Roulet.

"Okay, this is it," I said. "You're all we have left. Unless there's something you haven't told me, you're clean and there isn't much Minton can come back at you with. You should be safe up there unless you let him get to you. Are you still cool with this?"

Roulet had said all along that he would testify and deny the charges. He had reiterated his desire again at lunch. He demanded it. I always viewed the risks of letting a client testify as evenly split. Anything he said could come back to haunt him if the prosecution could bend it to the state's favor. But I also knew that no matter what admonishments were given to a jury about a defendant's right to remain silent, the jury always wanted to hear the defendant say he didn't do it. You take that away from the jury and they might hold a grudge.

"I want to do it," Roulet whispered. "I can handle the prosecutor."

I pushed my chair back and stood up.

"The defense calls Louis Ross Roulet, Your Honor."

THIRTY-SIX

Louis Roulet moved toward the witness box quickly, like a basketball player pulled off the bench and sent to the scorer's table to check into the game. He looked like a man anxious for the opportunity to defend himself. He knew this posture would not be lost on the jury.

After dispensing with the preliminaries, I got right down to the issues of the case. Under my questioning Roulet freely admitted that he had gone to Morgan's on the night of March 6 to seek female companionship. He said he wasn't specifically looking to engage the services of a prostitute but was not against the possibility.

"I had been with women I had to pay before," he said. "So I wouldn't have been against it."

He testified that he had no conscious eye contact with Regina Campo before she approached him at the bar. He said that she was the aggressor but at the time that didn't bother him. He said the solicitation was open-ended. She said she would be free after ten and he could come by if he was not otherwise engaged.

Roulet described efforts made over the next hour at Morgan's and then at the Lamplighter to find a woman he would not have to pay but said he was unsuccessful. He then drove to the address Campo had given him and knocked on the door.

"Who answered?"

"She did. She opened the door a crack and looked out at me."

"Regina Campo? The woman who testified this morning?"

"Yes, that's right."

"Could you see her whole face through the opening in the door?"

"No. She only opened up a crack and I couldn't see her. Only her left eye and a little bit of that side of her face."

"How did the door open? Was this crack through which you could see her on the right or left side?"

"As I was looking at the door the opening would have been on the right."

"So let's make sure we make this clear. The opening was on the right, correct?"

"Correct."

"So if she were standing behind the door and looking through the opening, she would be looking at you with her left eye."

"That is correct."

"Did you see her right eye?"

"No."

"So if she had a bruise or a cut or any damage on the right side of her face, could you have seen it?"

"No."

"Okay. So what happened next?"

"She saw it was me and she said come in. She opened the door wider but still sort of stood behind it."

"You couldn't see her?"

"Not completely. She was using the edge of the door as sort of a block."

"What happened next?"

"Well, it was kind of like an entry area, a vestibule, and she pointed through an archway to the living room. I went the way she pointed."

"Did this mean that she was then behind you?"

"Yes, when I turned toward the living room she was behind me."

"Did she close the door?"

"I think so. I heard it close."

"And then what?"

"Something hit me on the back of my head and I went down. I blacked out."

"Do you know how long you were out?"

"No. I think it was a while but none of the police or anybody ever told me."

"What do you remember when you regained consciousness?"

"I remember having a hard time breathing and when I opened my eyes, there was somebody sitting on me. I was on my back and he was sitting on me. I tried to move and that was when I realized somebody was sitting on my legs, too."

"What happened next?"

"They took turns telling me not to move and one of them told me they had my knife and if I tried to move or escape he would use it on me."

"Did there come a time that the police came and you were arrested?"

"Yes, a few minutes later the police were there. They handcuffed me and made me stand up. That was when I saw I had blood on my jacket."

"What about your hand?"

"I couldn't see it because it was handcuffed behind my back. But I heard one of the men who had been sitting on me tell the police officer that there was blood on my hand and then the officer put a bag over it. I felt that."

"How did the blood get on your hand and jacket?"

"All I know is that somebody put it on there because I didn't."

"Are you left-handed?"

"No, I am not."

"You didn't strike Ms. Campo with your left fist?"

"No, I did not."

"Did you threaten to rape her?"

"No, I did not."

"Did you tell her you were going to kill her if she didn't cooperate with you?"

"No, I did not."

I was hoping for some of the fire I had seen on that first day in C. C. Dobbs's office but Roulet was calm and controlled. I decided that before I finished with him on direct I needed to push things a little to get some of that anger back. I had told him at lunch I wanted to see it and wasn't sure what he was doing or where it had gone.

"Are you angry about being charged with attacking Ms. Campo?"

"Of course I am."

"Why?"

He opened his mouth but didn't speak. He seemed outraged that I would ask such a question. Finally, he responded.

"What do you mean, why? Have you ever been accused of something you didn't do and there's nothing you can do about it but wait? Just wait for weeks and months until you finally get a chance to go to court and say you've been set up. But then you have to wait even longer while the prosecutor puts on a bunch of liars and you have to listen to their lies and just wait your chance. Of course it makes you angry. I am innocent! I did not do this!"

It was perfect. To the point and playing to anybody who had ever been falsely accused of anything. There was more I could ask but I reminded myself of the rule: get in and get out. Less is always more. I sat down. If I decided there was anything I had missed I would clean it up on redirect.

I looked at the judge.

"Nothing further, Your Honor."

Minton was up and ready before I even got back to my seat. He moved to the lectern without breaking his steely glare away from Roulet. He was showing the jury what he thought of this man. His eyes were like lasers shooting across the room. He gripped the sides of the lectern so hard his knuckles were white. It was all a show for the jury.

"You deny touching Ms. Campo," he said.

"That's right," Roulet retorted.

"According to you she just punched herself or had a man she had never met before that night punch her lights out for her as part of this setup, is that correct?"

"I don't know who did it. All I know is that I didn't."

"But what you are saying is that this woman, Regina Campo, is lying. She came into this courtroom today and flat out lied to the judge and the jury and the whole wide world."

Minton punctuated the sentence by shaking his head with disgust.

"All I know is that I did not do the things she said I did. The only explanation is that one of us is lying. It's not me."

"That will be for the jury to decide, won't it?"

"Yes."

"And this knife you supposedly got for your own protection. Are you telling this jury that the victim in this case somehow knew you had a knife and used it as part of the setup?"

"I don't know what she knew. I had never shown the knife to her or in a bar where she would have been. So I don't see how she could have known about it. I think that when she went into my pocket for the money she found the knife. I always keep my knife and money in the same pocket."

"Oh, so now you have her stealing money out of your pocket as well. When does this end with you, Mr. Roulet?"

"I had four hundred dollars with me. When I was arrested it was gone. Someone took it."

Rather than try to pinpoint Roulet on the money, Minton was wise enough to know that no matter how he handled it, he would be facing a break-even proposition at best. If he tried to make a case that Roulet never had the money and that his plan was to attack and rape Campo rather than pay her, then he knew I would trot out Roulet's tax returns, which would throw serious doubt on the idea that he couldn't afford to pay a prostitute. It was an avenue of testimony

commonly referred to by lawyers as a "cluster fuck" and he was staying away. He moved on to his finish.

In dramatic style Minton held up the evidence photo of Regina
Campo's beaten and bruised face.

"So Regina Campo is a liar," he said.

"Yes."

"She had this done to her or maybe even did it herself."

"I don't know who did it."

"But not you."

"No, it wasn't me. I wouldn't do that to a woman. I wouldn't
hurt a woman."

Roulet pointed to the photo Minton had continued to hold up.

"No woman deserves that," he said.

I leaned forward and waited. Roulet had just said the line I had
told him to somehow find a way of putting into one of his answers
during testimony. *No woman deserves that.* It was now up to Minton
to take the bait. He was smart. He had to understand that Roulet had
just opened a door.

"What do you mean by *deserves?* Do you think crimes of violence
come down to a matter of whether a victim gets what they deserve?"

"No. I didn't mean it that way. I meant that no matter what she
does for a living, she shouldn't have been beaten like that. Nobody
deserves to have that happen to them."

Minton brought down the arm that held the photo. He looked at
it himself for a moment and then looked back up at Roulet.

"Mr. Roulet, I have nothing more to ask you."

THIRTY-SEVEN

I still felt that I was winning the razor fight. I had done everything possible to maneuver Minton into a position in which he had only one choice. It was now time to see if doing everything possible had been enough. After the young prosecutor sat down, I chose not to ask my client another question. He had held up well under Minton's attack and I felt the wind was in our sails. I stood up and looked back at the clock on the upper rear wall of the courtroom. It was only three-thirty. I then looked back at the judge.

"Your Honor, the defense rests."

She nodded and looked over my head at the clock. She told the jury to take the mid-afternoon break. Once the jurors were out of the courtroom, she looked at the prosecution table where Minton had his head down and was writing.

"Mr. Minton?"

The prosecutor looked up.

"We're still in session. Pay attention. Does the state have rebuttal?"

Minton stood.

"Your Honor, I would ask that we adjourn for the day so that the state has time to consider rebuttal witnesses."

"Mr. Minton, we still have at least ninety minutes to go today. I told you I wanted to be productive today. Where are your witnesses?"

"Frankly, Your Honor, I was not anticipating the defense resting after only three witnesses and I —"

"He gave fair warning of that in his opening statement."

"Yes, but still the case has moved faster than anticipated. We're a half day ahead. I would beg the court's indulgence. I would be hard-pressed to get the rebuttal witness I am considering even into court before six o'clock tonight."

I turned and looked at Roulet, who had returned to the seat next to mine. I nodded to him and winked with my left eye so the judge would not see the gesture. It looked like Minton had swallowed the bait. Now I just had to make sure the judge didn't make him spit it out. I stood up.

"Your Honor, the defense has no objection to the delay. Maybe we can use the time to prepare closing arguments and instructions to the jury."

The judge first looked at me with a puzzled frown. It was a rarity that the defense would not object to prosecutorial foot dragging. But then the seed I had planted began to bloom.

"You may have an idea there, Mr. Haller. If we adjourn early today I will expect that we will go to closing statements directly after rebuttal. No further delays except to consider jury instructions. Is that understood, Mr. Minton?"

"Yes, Your Honor, I will be ready."

"Mr. Haller?"

"It was my idea, Judge. I'll be ready."

"Very well, then. We have a plan. As soon as the jurors are back I will dismiss them for the day. They'll beat the traffic and tomorrow things will run so smoothly and quickly that I have no doubt they will be deliberating by the afternoon session."

She looked at Minton and then me, as if daring one of us to disagree with her. When we didn't, she got up and left the bench, probably in pursuit of a cigarette.

Twenty minutes later the jury was heading home and I was

gathering my things at the defense table. Minton stepped over and said, "Can I talk to you?"

I looked at Roulet and told him to head out with his mother and Dobbs and that I would call him if I needed him for anything.

"But I want to talk to you, too," he said.

"About what?"

"About everything. How do you think I did up there?"

"You did good and everything is going good. I think we're in good shape."

I then nodded my head toward the prosecution table where Minton had returned and dropped my voice to a whisper.

"He knows it, too. He's about to make another offer."

"Should I stick around to hear what it is?"

I shook my head.

"No, it doesn't matter what it is. There's only one verdict, right?"

"That's right."

He patted my shoulder when he got up and I had to steady myself not to shrink away from the touch.

"Don't touch me, Louis," I said. "You want to do something for me, then give me my fucking gun back."

He didn't reply. He just smiled and moved toward the gate. After he was gone I turned to look at Minton. He now had the gleam of desperation in his eye. He needed a conviction — any conviction — on this case.

"What's up?"

"I have another offer."

"I'm listening."

"I'll drop it down further. Take it down to simple assault. Six months in county. The way they empty that place out at the end of every month, he probably won't do sixty days actual."

I nodded. He was talking about the federal mandate to stop overcrowding in the county jail system. It didn't matter what was handed down in a courtroom; out of necessity, sentences were often drastically cut. It was a good offer but I didn't show anything. I knew the offer had to have come from the second floor. Minton wouldn't have had the authority to go so low.

"He takes that and she'll rob him blind in civil," I said. "I doubt he'll go for it."

"That's a damn good offer," Minton said.

There was a hint of outrage in his voice. My guess was that the observer's report card on Minton was not good and he was under orders to close the case out with a guilty plea. Trash the trial and the judge's and jury's time, just get that plea. The Van Nuys office didn't like losing cases and we were only two months removed from the Robert Blake fiasco. It pleaded them out when the going got rough. Minton could go as low as he needed to go, just as long as he got something. Roulet had to go down — even if it was only for sixty days actual.

"Maybe from your side of things it's a damn good offer. But it still means I have to convince a client to plead to something he says he didn't do. Then on top of that, the dispo still opens the door to civil liability. So while he's sitting up there in county trying to protect his asshole for sixty days, Reggie Campo and her lawyer are down here taking him to the cleaners. You see? It's not so good when you look at it from his angle. If it was left to me, I'd ride the trial out. I think we're winning. I know we've got the Bible guy, so we've got a hanger at minimum. But who knows, maybe we've got all twelve."

Minton slapped his hand down on his table.

"What the fuck are you talking about? You know he did this thing, Haller. And six months — let alone sixty days — for what he did to that woman is a joke. It's a fucking travesty that I'll lose sleep over, but they've been watching and think you've got the jury, so I have to do it."

I closed my briefcase with an authoritative snap and stood up.

"Then I hope you got something good for rebuttal, Ted. Because you're going to get your wish for a jury verdict. And I have to tell you, man, you're looking more and more like a guy who came naked to a razor fight. Better get your hands off your nuts and fight back."

I headed through the gate. Halfway to the doors at the back of the courtroom I stopped and looked back at him.

"Hey, you know something? If you lose sleep over this or any other case, then you gotta quit the job and go do something else. Because you're not going to make it, Ted."

Minton sat at his table, staring straight ahead at the empty bench. He didn't acknowledge what I had said. I left him there thinking about it. I thought I had played it right. I'd find out in the morning.

I went back over to Four Green Fields to work on my closing. I wouldn't need the two hours the judge had given us. I ordered a Guinness at the bar and took it over to one of the tables to sit by myself. Table service didn't start again until six. I sketched out some basic notes but I instinctively knew I would largely be reacting to the state's presentation. In pretrial motions, Minton had already asked and received permission from Judge Fullbright to use a PowerPoint presentation to illustrate the case to the jury. It had become all the rage with young prosecutors to put up the screen and flash computer graphics on it, as if the jurors couldn't be trusted to think and make connections on their own. It now had to be fed to them like TV.

My clients rarely had the money to pay my fees, let alone for PowerPoint presentations. Roulet was an exception. Through his mother he could afford to hire Francis Ford Coppola to put together a PowerPoint for him if he wanted it. But I never even brought it up. I was strictly old school. I liked going into the ring on my own. Minton could throw whatever he wanted up on the big blue screen. When it was my turn I wanted the jury looking only at me. If I couldn't convince them, nothing from a computer could, either.

At 5:30 I called Maggie McPherson at her office.

"It's quitting time," I said.

"Maybe for big-shot defense pros. Us public servants have to work till after dark."

"Why don't you take a break and come meet me for a Guinness and some shepherd's pie, then you can go back to work and finish up."

"No, Haller. I can't do that. Besides, I know what you want."

I laughed. There was never a time that she didn't think she knew what I wanted. Most of the time she was right but not this time.

"Yeah? What do I want?"

"You're going to try to corrupt me again and find out what Minton is up to."

"Not a chance, Mags. Minton is an open book. Smithson's observer is giving him bad marks. So Smithson's told him to fold the tent, get something and get out. But Minton's been working on his little PowerPoint closing and wants to gamble, take it all the way to the house. Besides that, he's got genuine outrage in his blood, so he doesn't like the idea of folding up."

"Neither do I. Smithson's always afraid of losing — especially since Blake. He always wants to sell short. You can't be that way."

"I always said they lost the Blake case the minute they passed you over. You tell 'em, Maggie."

"If I ever get the chance."

"Someday."

She didn't like dwelling on her own stalled career. She moved on.

"So you sound chipper," she said. "Yesterday you were a murder suspect. Today you've got the DA by the short hairs. What changed?"

"Nothing. It's just the calm before the storm, I guess. Hey, let me ask you something. Have you ever put a rush on ballistics?"

"What kind of ballistics?"

"Matching casing to casing and slug to slug."

"Depends on who is doing it — which department, I mean. But if they put a real rush on it, they could have something in twenty-four hours."

I felt the dull thud of dread drop into my stomach. I knew I could be on borrowed time.

"Most of the time, though, that doesn't happen," she continued. "Two or three days is what it will usually take on a rush. And if you want the whole package — casing and slug comparisons — it could take longer because the slug could be damaged and tough to read. They have to work with it."

I nodded. I didn't think any of that could help me. I knew they had recovered a bullet casing at the crime scene. If Lankford and Sobel got a match on that to the casing of a bullet fired fifty years ago from Mickey Cohen's gun, they would come for me and worry about the slug comparison later.

"You still there?" Maggie asked.

"Yeah. I was just thinking of something."

"You don't sound so chipper anymore. You want to talk about this, Michael?"

"No, not right now. But if I end up needing a good lawyer, you know who I'll call."

"That'll be the day."

"You might be surprised."

I let some more silence into the conversation. Just having her on the other end of the line was a calming comfort. I liked it.

"Haller, I should get back to my job now."

"Okay, Maggie, put those bad guys away."

"I will."

"Good night."

I closed the phone and thought about things for a few moments, then opened it up again and called the Sheraton Universal to see if they had a room available. I had decided that as a precaution I would not go home this night. There might be two detectives from Glendale waiting for me.

THIRTY-EIGHT

After a sleepless night in a bad hotel bed I got to the courthouse early on Wednesday morning and found no welcoming party, no Glendale detectives waiting with smiles and a warrant for my arrest. A flash of relief went through me as I made my way through the metal detector. I was wearing the same suit I had worn the day before but was hoping no one would notice. I did have a fresh shirt and tie on. I keep spares in the trunk of the Lincoln for summer days when I'm working up in the desert and the car's air conditioner can get overwhelmed.

When I got to Judge Fullbright's courtroom I was surprised to find I was not the first of the trial's players to arrive. Minton was in the gallery, setting up the screen for his PowerPoint presentation. Because the courtroom had been designed before the era of computer-enhanced presentations, there was no place to put a twelve-foot screen in comfortable view of the jury, the judge, and the lawyers. A good chunk of the gallery space would be taken up by the screen, and any spectator who sat behind it wouldn't get to see the show.

"Bright and early," I said to Minton.

He looked over from his work and seemed a bit surprised to see me in early as well.

"Have to work out the logistics of this thing. It's kind of a pain."

"You could always do it the old-fashioned way and just look at the jury and talk directly to them."

"No, thanks. I like this better. Did you talk to your client about the offer?"

"Yeah, no sale. Looks like we ride this one to the end."

I put my briefcase down on the defense table and wondered if the fact that Minton was setting up for his closing argument meant he had decided against mounting any kind of rebuttal. A sharp jab of panic went through me. I looked over at the state's table and saw nothing that gave me a clue to what Minton was planning. I knew I could flat out ask him but I did not want to give away my appearance of disinterested confidence.

Instead, I sauntered over to the bailiff's desk to talk to Bill Meehan, the deputy who ran Fullbright's court. I saw on his desk a spread of paperwork. He would have the courtroom calendar as well as the list of custodies bused to the courthouse that morning.

"Bill, I'm going to grab a cup of coffee. You want something?"

"No, man, but thanks. I'm set on caffeine. For a while, at least."

I smiled and nodded.

"Hey, is that the custody list? Can I take a look and see if any of my clients are on it?"

"Sure."

Meehan handed me several pages that were stapled together. It was a listing by name of every inmate that was now housed in the courthouse's jails. Following the name was the courtroom each prisoner was headed to. Acting as nonchalant as I could I scanned the list and quickly found the name Dwayne Jeffery Corliss on it. Minton's snitch was in the building and was headed to Fullbright's court. I almost let out a sigh of relief but kept it all inside. It looked like Minton was going to play things the way I had hoped and planned.

"Something wrong?" Meehan asked.

I looked at him and handed back the list.

"No, why?"

"I don't know. You look like something happened, is all."

"Nothing's happened yet but it will."

I left the courtroom and went down to the cafeteria on the second floor. When I was in line paying for my coffee I saw Maggie McPherson walk in and go directly to the coffee urns. After I paid I walked up behind her as she was mixing powder from a pink packet into her coffee.

"Sweet 'N Low," I said. "My ex-wife used to tell me that's how she liked it."

She turned and saw me.

"Stop, Haller."

But she smiled.

"Stop, Haller, or I'll holler," I said. "She used to have to say that, too. A lot."

"What are you doing? Shouldn't you be up on six getting ready to pull the plug on Minton's PowerPoint?"

"I'm not worried. In fact, you ought to come up and check it out. Old school versus new school, a battle for the ages."

"Hardly. By the way, isn't that the same suit you were wearing yesterday?"

"Yeah, it's my lucky suit. But how do you know what I was wearing yesterday?"

"Oh, I popped my head in Fullbite's court for a couple minutes yesterday. You were too busy questioning your client to notice."

I was secretly pleased that she would even notice my suits. I knew it meant something.

"So, then, why don't you pop your head in again this morning?"

"Today I can't. I'm too busy."

"What've you got?"

"I'm taking over a murder one for Andy Seville. He's quitting to go private and yesterday they divided up his cases. I got the good one."

"Nice. Does the defendant need a lawyer?"

"No way, Haller. I'm not losing another one to you."

"Just kidding. I've got my hands full."

She snapped a top onto her cup and picked it up off the counter, using a layer of napkins as insulation against its heat.

"Same here. So I'd wish you good luck today but I can't."

"Yeah, I know. Gotta keep the company line. Just cheer up Minton when he comes down with his hat in his hand."

"I'll try."

She left the cafeteria and I walked over to an empty table. I still had fifteen minutes before the trial was supposed to start up again. I pulled out my cell and called my second ex-wife.

"Lorna, it's me. We're in play with Corliss. Are you set?"

"I'm ready."

"Okay, I'm just checking. I'll call you."

"Good luck today, Mickey."

"Thanks. I'll need it. You be ready for the next call."

I closed the phone and was about to get up when I saw LAPD Detective Howard Kurlen cutting through the tables toward me. The man who put Jesus Menendez in prison didn't look like he was stopping in for a peanut butter and sardine sandwich. He was carrying a folded document. He got to my table and dropped it in front of my coffee cup.

"What is this shit?" he demanded.

I started unfolding the document, even though I knew what it was.

"Looks like a subpoena, Detective. I would've thought you'd know what it is."

"You know what I mean, Haller. What's the game? I've got nothing to do with that case up there and I don't want to be a part of your bullshit."

"It's no game and it's no bullshit. You've been subpoenaed as a re-buttal witness."

"To rebut what? I told you and you already know, I didn't have a goddamn thing to do with that case. It's Marty Booker's and I just talked to him and he said it's gotta be a mistake."

I nodded like I wanted to be accommodating.

"I'll tell you what, go on up to the courtroom and take a seat. If it's a mistake I'll get it straightened out as soon as I can. I doubt you'll be here another hour. I'll get you out of there and back chasing the bad guys."

"How about this? I leave now and you straighten it out whenever the fuck you want."

"I can't do that, Detective. That is a valid and lawful subpoena and you must appear in that courtroom unless otherwise discharged. I told you, I will do that as soon as I can. The state's got one witness and then it's my turn and I'll take care of it."

"This is such bullshit."

He turned from me and stalked back through the cafeteria toward the doorway. Luckily, he had left the subpoena with me, because it was phony. I had never registered it with the court clerk and the scribbled signature at the bottom was mine.

Bullshit or not, I didn't think Kurlen was leaving the courthouse. He was a man who understood duty and the law. He lived by it. It was what I was counting on. He would be in the courtroom until discharged. Or until he understood why I had called him there.

THIRTY-NINE

A t 9:30 the judge put the jury in the box and immediately pro- ceeded with the day's business. I glanced back at the gallery and caught sight of Kurlen in the back row. He had a pensive, if not angry, cast to his face. He was close to the door and I didn't know how long he would last. I was figuring I would need that whole hour I had told him about.

I glanced further around the room and saw that Lankford and Sobel were sitting on a bench next to the bailiff's desk that was desig- nated for law enforcement personnel. Their faces revealed nothing but they still put the pause in me. I wondered if I would even get the hour I needed.

"Mr. Minton," the judge intoned, "does the state have any rebut- tal?"

I turned back to the court. Minton stood up, adjusted his jacket and then seemed to hesitate and brace himself before responding.

"Yes, Your Honor, the state calls Dwayne Jeffery Corliss as a re- buttal witness."

I stood up and noticed to my right that Meehan, the bailiff, had stood up as well. He was going to go into the courtroom lockup to re- trieve Corliss.

"Your Honor?" I said. "Who is Dwayne Jeffery Corliss and why wasn't I told about him before now?"

"Deputy Meehan, hold on a minute," Fullbright said.

Meehan stood frozen with the key to the lockup door poised in his hand. The judge then apologized to the jury but told them they had to go back into the deliberation room until recalled. After they filed through the door behind the box, the judge turned her focus onto Minton.

"Mr. Minton, do you want to tell us about your witness?"

"Dwayne Corliss is a cooperating witness who spoke with Mr. Roulet when he was in custody following his arrest."

"Bullshit!" Roulet barked. "I didn't talk to —"

"Be quiet, Mr. Roulet," the judge boomed. "Mr. Haller, instruct your client on the danger of outbursts in my courtroom."

"Thank you, Your Honor."

I was still standing. I leaned down to whisper in Roulet's ear.

"That was perfect," I said. "Now be cool and I'll take it from here."

He nodded and leaned back. He angrily folded his arms across his chest. I straightened up.

"I'm sorry, Your Honor, but I do share my client's outrage over this last-ditch effort by the state. This is the first we have heard of Mr. Corliss. I would like to know when he came forward with this supposed conversation."

Minton had remained standing. I thought it was the first time in the trial that we had stood side by side and argued to the judge.

"Mr. Corliss first contacted the office through a prosecutor who handled the first appearance of the defendant," Minton said. "However, that information was not passed on to me until yesterday when in a staff meeting I was asked why I had never acted on the information."

This was a lie but not one I wanted to expose. To do so would reveal Maggie McPherson's slip on St. Patrick's Day and it might also derail my plan. I had to be careful. I needed to argue vigorously against Corliss taking the stand but I also needed to lose the argument.

I put my best look of outrage on my face.

"This is incredible, Your Honor. Just because the DA's office has a communication problem, my client has to suffer the consequences of not being informed that the state had a witness against him? This man should clearly not be allowed to testify. It's too late to bring him in now."

"Your Honor," Minton said, jumping in quickly. "I have had no time to interview or depose Mr. Corliss myself. Because I was preparing my closing I simply made arrangements for him to be brought here today. His testimony is key to the state's case because it serves as rebuttal to Mr. Roulet's self-serving statements. To not allow his testimony is a serious disservice to the state."

I shook my head and smiled in frustration. With his last line Minton was threatening the judge with the loss of the DA's backing should she ever face an election with an opposing candidate.

"Mr. Haller?" the judge asked. "Anything before I rule?"

"I just want my objection on the record."

"So noted. If I were to give you time to investigate and interview Mr. Corliss, how much would you need?"

"A week."

Now Minton put on the fake smile and shook his head.

"That's ridiculous, Your Honor."

"Do you want to go back and talk to him?" the judge asked me. "I'll allow it."

"No, Your Honor. As far as I'm concerned all jailhouse snitches are liars. It would do me no good to interview him because anything that comes out of his mouth would be a lie. Anything. Besides, it's not what he has to say. It's what others have to say about him. That's what I would need time for."

"Then I am going to rule that he can testify."

"Your Honor," I said. "If you are going to allow him into this courtroom, could I ask one indulgence for the defense?"

"What is that, Mr. Haller?"

"I would like to step into the hallway and make a quick phone call to an investigator. It will take me less than a minute."

The judge thought for a moment and then nodded.

"Go ahead. I will bring the jury in while you do it."

"Thank you."

I hurried through the gate and down the middle aisle. My eyes caught those of Howard Kurlen and he gave me one of his best smirks.

In the hallway I speed-dialed Lorna Taylor's cell phone and she answered right away.

"Okay, how far away are you?"

"About fifteen minutes."

"Did you remember the printout and the tape?"

"Got it all right here."

I looked at my watch. It was a quarter to ten.

"Okay, well, we're in play here. Don't delay getting here but then I want you to wait out in the hall outside the courtroom. Then at ten-fifteen come into court and give it to me. If I'm crossing the witness, just sit in the first row and wait until I notice you."

"Got it."

I closed the phone and went back into the courtroom. The jury was seated and Meehan was leading a man in a gray jumpsuit through the lockup door. Dwayne Corliss was a thin man with stringy hair that wasn't getting washed enough in the lockdown drug program at County-USC. He wore a blue plastic hospital ID band on his wrist. I recognized him. He was the man who had asked me for a business card when I interviewed Roulet in the holding cell my first day on the case.

Corliss was led by Meehan to the witness box and the court clerk swore him in. Minton took over the show from there.

"Mr. Corliss, were you arrested on March fifth of this year?"

"Yes, the police arrested me for burglary and possession of drugs."

"Are you incarcerated now?"

Corliss looked around.

"Um, no, I don't think so. I'm just in the courtroom."

I heard Kurlen's coarse laugh behind me but nobody joined in.

"No, I mean are you currently being held in jail? When you are not here in court."

"I'm in a lockdown drug treatment program in the jail ward at Los Angeles County–USC Medical Center."

"Are you addicted to drugs?"

"Yes. I'm addicted to heroin but at the moment I am straight. I haven't had any since I got arrested."

"More than sixty days."

"That's right."

"Do you recognize the defendant in this case?"

Corliss looked over at Roulet and nodded.

"Yes, I do."

"Why is that?"

"Because I met him in lockup after I got arrested."

"You are saying that after you were arrested you came into close proximity to the defendant, Louis Roulet?"

"Yes, the next day."

"How did that happen?"

"Well, we were both in Van Nuys jail but in different wards. Then, when we got bused over here to the courts, we were together, first in the bus and then in the tank and then when we were brought into the courtroom for first appearance. We were together all of that time."

"When you say 'together,' what do you mean?"

"Well, we sort of stuck close because we were the only white guys in the group we were in."

"Now, did you talk at all while you were together for all of that time?"

Corliss nodded his head and at the same time Roulet shook his. I touched my client's arm to caution him to make no demonstrations.

"Yes, we talked," Corliss said.

"About what?"

"Mostly about cigarettes. We both needed them but they don't let you smoke in the jail."

Corliss made a what-are-you-going-to-do gesture with both hands and a few of the jurors — probably smokers — smiled and nodded.

"Did you reach a point where you asked Mr. Roulet what got him into jail?" Minton asked.

"Yes, I did."

"What did he say?"

I quickly stood up and objected but just as quickly was overruled.

"What did he tell you, Mr. Corliss?" Minton prompted.

"Well, first he asked me why I was there and I told him. So then I asked him why he was in and he said, 'For giving a bitch exactly what she deserved.'"

"Those were his words?"

"Yes."

"Did he elaborate further on what he meant by that?"

"No, not really. Not on that."

I leaned forward, waiting for Minton to ask the next obvious question. But he didn't. He moved on.

"Now, Mr. Corliss, have you been promised anything by me or the district attorney's office in return for your testimony?"

"Nope. I just thought it was the right thing to do."

"What is the status of your case?"

"I still got the charges against me, but it looks like if I complete my program I'll be able to get a break on them. The drugs, at least. I don't know about the burglary yet."

"But I have made no promise of help in that regard, correct?"

"No, sir, you haven't."

"Has anyone else from the district attorney's office made any promises?"

"No, sir."

"I have no further questions."

I sat unmoving and just staring at Corliss. My pose was that of a man who was angry but didn't know exactly what to do about it. Finally, the judge prompted me into action.

"Mr. Haller, cross-examination?"

"Yes, Your Honor."

I stood up, glancing back at the door as if hoping a miracle would walk through it. I then checked the big clock on the back door and saw it was five minutes after ten. I noticed as I turned back to the witness that I had not lost Kurlen. He was still in the back row and he still had the same smirk on his face. I realized that it might have been his natural look.

I turned to the witness.

"Mr. Corliss, how old are you?"

"Forty-three."

"You go by Dwayne?"

"That's right."

"Any other names?"

"People called me D.J. when I was growing up. Everybody called me that."

"And where did you grow up?"

"Mesa, Arizona."

"Mr. Corliss, how many times have you been arrested before?"

Minton objected but the judge overruled. I knew she was going to give me a lot of room with this witness since I was the one who had supposedly been sandbagged.

"How many times have you been arrested before, Mr. Corliss?" I asked again.

"I think about seven."

"So you've been in a number of jails in your time, haven't you?"

"You could say that."

"All in Los Angeles County?"

"Mostly. But I got arrested over in Phoenix before, too."

"So you know how the system works, don't you?"

"I just try to survive."

"And sometimes surviving means ratting out your fellow inmates, doesn't it?"

"Your Honor?" Minton said, standing to object.

"Take a seat, Mr. Minton," Fullbright said. "I gave you a lot of
leeway bringing this witness in. Mr. Haller gets his share of it now.
The witness will answer the question."

The stenographer read the question back to Corliss.

"I suppose so."

"How many times have you snitched on another inmate?"

"I don't know. A few times."

"How many times have you testified in a court proceeding for
the prosecution?"

"Would that include my own cases?"

"No, Mr. Corliss. For the prosecution. How many times have
you testified against a fellow inmate for the prosecution?"

"I think this is my fourth time."

I looked surprised and aghast, although I was neither.

"So you are a pro, aren't you? You could almost say your occupation is drug-addicted jailhouse snitch."

"I just tell the truth. If people tell me things that are bad, then I
feel obligated to report it."

"But you try to get people to tell you things, don't you?"

"No, not really. I guess I'm just a friendly guy."

"A friendly guy. So what you expect this jury to believe is that a
man you didn't know would just come out of the blue and tell you —
a perfect stranger — that he gave a bitch exactly what she deserved.
Is that correct?"

"It's what he said."

"So he just mentioned that to you and then you both just went
back to talking about cigarettes after that, is that right?"

"Not exactly."

"Not exactly? What do you mean by 'not exactly'?"

"He also told me he did it before. He said he got away with it before and he would get away with it now. He was bragging about it

because with the other time, he said he killed the bitch and got away
with it."

I froze for a moment. I then glanced at Roulet, who sat as still as a
statue with surprise on his face, and then back at the witness.

"You . . ."

I started and stopped, acting like I was the man in the minefield
who had just heard the *click* come from beneath my foot. In my pe-
ripheral vision I noticed Minton's body posture tightening.

"Mr. Haller?" the judge prompted.

I broke my stare from Corliss and looked at the judge.

"Your Honor, I have no further questions at this time."

FORTY

Minton came up from his seat like a boxer coming out of his corner at his bleeding opponent.

"Redirect, Mr. Minton?" Fullbright asked.

But he was already at the lectern.

"Absolutely, Your Honor."

He looked at the jury as if to underline the importance of the upcoming exchange and then at Corliss.

"You said he was bragging, Mr. Corliss. How so?"

"Well, he told me about this time he actually killed a girl and got away with it."

I stood up.

"Your Honor, this has nothing to do with the case at hand and it is rebuttal to no evidence previously offered by the defense. The witness can't —"

"Your Honor," Minton cut in, "this is information brought forward by defense counsel. The prosecution is entitled to pursue it."

"I will allow it," Fullbright said.

I sat down and appeared dejected. Minton plowed ahead. He was going just where I wanted him to go.

"Mr. Corliss, did Mr. Roulet offer any of the details of this previous incident in which he said he got away with killing a woman?"

"He called the girl a snake dancer. She danced in some joint where she was like in a snake pit."

I felt Roulet wrap his fingers around my biceps and squeeze. His hot breath came into my ear.

"What the fuck is this?" he whispered.

I turned to him.

"I don't know. What the hell did you tell this guy?"

He whispered back through gritted teeth.

"I didn't tell him anything. This is a setup. You set me up!"

"Me? What are you talking about? I told you, I couldn't get to this guy in lockdown. If you didn't tell him this shit, then somebody else did. Start thinking. Who?"

I turned and looked up at Minton standing at the lectern and continuing his questioning of Corliss.

"Did Mr. Roulet say anything else about the dancer he said he murdered?" he asked.

"No, that's all he really told me."

Minton checked his notes to see if there was anything else, then nodded to himself.

"Nothing further, Your Honor."

The judge looked at me. I could almost see sympathy on her face.

"Any recross from the defense with this witness?"

Before I could answer, there was a noise from the rear of the courtroom and I turned to see Lorna Taylor entering. She hurriedly walked down the aisle toward the gate.

"Your Honor, can I have a moment to confer with my staff?"

"Hurry, Mr. Haller."

I met Lorna at the gate and took from her a videotape with a single piece of paper wrapped around it with a rubber band. As she had been told to do earlier, she whispered in my ear.

"This is where I act like I am whispering something very important into your ear," she said. "How is it going?"

I nodded as I took the rubber band off the tape and looked at the piece of paper.

"Perfect timing," I whispered back. "I'm good to go."

"Can I stay and watch?"

"No, I want you out of here. I don't want anybody talking to you after this goes down."

I nodded and she nodded and then she left. I went back to the lectern.

"No recross, Your Honor."

I sat down and waited. Roulet grabbed my arm.

"What are you doing?"

I pushed him away.

"Stop touching me. We have new information we can't bring up on cross."

I focused on the judge.

"Any other witnesses, Mr. Minton?" she asked.

"No, Your Honor. No further rebuttal."

The judge nodded.

"The witness is excused."

Meehan started crossing the courtroom to Corliss. The judge looked at me and I started to stand.

"Mr. Haller, surrebuttal?"

"Yes, Your Honor, the defense would like to call D.J. Corliss back to the stand as surrebuttal."

Meehan stopped in his tracks and all eyes were on me. I held up the tape and the paper Lorna had brought me.

"I have new information on Mr. Corliss, Your Honor. I could not have brought it up on cross."

"Very well. Proceed."

"Can I have a moment, Judge?"

"A short one."

I huddled with Roulet again.

"Look, I don't know what is going on but it doesn't matter," I whispered.

"What do you mean it doesn't matter? Are you —"

"Listen to me. It doesn't matter because I can still destroy him. Doesn't matter if he says you killed twenty women. If he's a liar, he's a liar. If I destroy him, none of it counts. You understand?"

Roulet nodded and seemed to calm as he considered this.

"Then destroy him."

"I will. But I have to know. Is there anything else he knows that could come out? Is there anything I need to stay away from?"

Roulet whispered slowly, as if explaining something to a child.

"I don't know because I never talked to him. I'm not that stupid as to have a discussion about cigarettes and murder with a total fucking stranger!"

"Mr. Haller," the judge prompted.

I looked up at her.

"Yes, Your Honor."

Carrying the tape and the paper that came with it, I stood up to go back to the lectern. On the way I took a quick glance across the gallery and saw that Kurlen was gone. I had no way of knowing how long he had stayed and what he had heard. Lankford was gone as well. Only Sobel remained and she averted her eyes from mine. I turned my attention to Corliss.

"Mr. Corliss, can you tell the jury exactly where you were when Mr. Roulet supposedly made these revelations to you about murder and assault?"

"When we were together."

"Together where, Mr. Corliss?"

"Well, on the bus ride we didn't talk because we were in different seats. But when we got to the courthouse, we were in the same holding cell with about six other guys and we sat together there and we talked."

"And those six other men all witnessed you and Mr. Roulet talking, correct?"

"They woulda had to. They were there."

"So what you are saying is that if I brought them in here one by one and asked them if they observed you and Mr. Roulet talking, they would confirm that?"

"Well, they should. But . . ."

"But what, Mr. Corliss?"

"It's just that they probably wouldn't talk, that's all."

"Is it because nobody likes a snitch, Mr. Corliss?"

Corliss shrugged.

"I guess so."

"Okay, so let's make sure we have all of this straight. You didn't talk with Mr. Roulet on the bus but you did talk to him when you were in the holding cell together. Anywhere else?"

"Yeah, we talked when they moved us on out into the courtroom. They stick you in this glassed-in area and you wait for your case to be called. We talked some in there, too, until his case got called. He went first."

"This is in the arraignment court where you had your first appearance before a judge?"

"That's right."

"So you two were talking in the court and this is where Mr. Roulet would have revealed his part in these crimes you described."

"That's right."

"Do you remember specifically what he told you when you were in the courtroom?"

"No, not really. Not specifics. I think that might have been when he told me about the girl who was a dancer."

"Okay, Mr. Corliss."

I held the videotape up, described it as video of Louis Roulet's first appearance, and asked to enter it as a defense exhibit. Minton tried to block it as something I had not produced during discovery, but that was easily and quickly shot down by the judge without my having to argue the point. He then objected again, citing the lack of authentication of the tape.

"I am just trying to save the court some time," I said. "If needed I can have the man who took the film here in about an hour to authenticate it. But I think that Your Honor will be able to authenticate it herself with just one look."

"I am going to allow it," the judge said. "Once we see it the prosecution can object again if so inclined."

The television and video unit I had used previously was rolled into the courtroom and placed at an angle viewable by Corliss, the jury and the judge. Minton had to move to a chair to the side of the jury box to fully see it. The tape was played. It lasted twenty minutes and showed Roulet from the moment he entered the courtroom custody area until he was led out after the bail hearing. At no time did Roulet talk to anyone but me. When the tape was over I left the television in its place in case it was needed again. I addressed Corliss with a tinge of outrage in my voice.

"Mr. Corliss, did you see a moment anywhere on that tape where you and Mr. Roulet were talking?"

"Uh, no. I —"

"Yet, you testified under oath and penalty of perjury that he confessed crimes to you while you were both in the courtroom, didn't you?"

"I know I said that but I must have been mistaken. He must have told me everything when we were in the holding cell."

"You lied to the jury, didn't you?"

"I didn't mean to. That was the way I remembered it but I guess I was wrong. I was coming off a high that morning. Things got confused."

"It would seem that way. Let me ask you, were things confused when you testified against Frederic Bentley back in nineteen eighty-nine?"

Corliss knitted his eyebrows together in concentration but didn't answer.

"You remember Frederic Bentley, don't you?"

Minton stood.

"Objection. Nineteen eighty-nine? Where is he going with this?"

"Your Honor," I said. "This goes to the veracity of the witness. It is certainly at issue here."

"Connect the dots, Mr. Haller," the judge ordered. "In a hurry."

"Yes, Your Honor."

I picked up the piece of paper and used it as a prop during my final questions of Corliss.

"In nineteen eighty-nine Frederic Bentley was convicted, with your help, of raping a sixteen-year-old girl in her bed in Phoenix. Do you remember this?"

"Barely," Corliss said. "I've done a lot of drugs since then."

"You testified at his trial that he confessed the crime to you while you were both together in a police station holding cell. Isn't that correct?"

"Like I said, it's hard for me to remember back then."

"The police put you in that holding cell because they knew you were willing to snitch, even if you had to make it up, didn't they?"

My voice was rising with each question.

"I don't remember that," Corliss responded. "But I don't make things up."

"Then, eight years later, the man who you testified had told you he did it was exonerated when a DNA test determined that the semen from the girl's attacker came from another man. Isn't that correct, sir?"

"I don't . . . I mean . . . that was a long time ago."

"Do you remember being questioned by a reporter for the *Arizona Star* newspaper following the release of Frederic Bentley?"

"Vaguely. I remember somebody calling but I didn't say anything."

"He told you that DNA tests exonerated Bentley and asked you whether you fabricated Bentley's confession, didn't he?"

"I don't know."

I held the paper I was clutching up toward the bench.

"Your Honor, I have an archival story from the *Arizona Star* newspaper here. It is dated February ninth, nineteen ninety-seven. A member of my staff came across it when she Googled the name D.J. Corliss on her office computer. I ask that it be marked as a defense exhibit and admitted into evidence as a historical document detailing an admission by silence."

My request set off a brutal clash with Minton about authenticity and proper foundation. Ultimately, the judge ruled in my favor. She was showing some of the same outrage I was manufacturing, and Minton didn't stand much of a chance.

The bailiff took the computer printout to Corliss, and the judge instructed him to read it.

"I'm not too good at reading, Judge," he said.

"Try, Mr. Corliss."

Corliss held the paper up and leaned his face into it as he read.

"Out loud, please," Fullbright barked.

Corliss cleared his throat and read in a halting voice.

"'A man wrongly convicted of rape was released Saturday from the Arizona Correctional Institution and vowed to seek justice for other inmates falsely accused. Frederic Bentley, thirty-four, served almost eight years in prison for attacking a sixteen-year-old Tempe girl. The victim of the assault identified Bentley, a neighbor, and blood tests matched his type to semen recovered from the victim after the attack. The case was bolstered at trial by testimony from an informant who said Bentley had confessed the crime to him while they were housed together in a holding cell. Bentley always maintained his innocence during the trial and even after his conviction. Once DNA testing was accepted as valid evidence by courts in the state, Bentley hired attorneys to fight for such testing of semen collected from the victim of the attack. A judge ordered the testing earlier this year, and the resulting analysis proved Bentley was not the attacker.

"'At a press conference yesterday at the Arizona Biltmore the newly freed Bentley railed against jailhouse informants and called for a state law that would put strict guidelines on police and prosecutors who wish to use them.

"'The informant who claimed in sworn testimony that Bentley admitted the rape was identified as D.J. Corliss, a Mesa man who had been arrested on drug charges. When told of Bentley's exoneration and asked whether he fabricated his testimony against Bentley, Corliss declined comment Saturday. At his press conference, Bentley charged that Corliss was well known to the police as a snitch and was used in several cases to get close to suspects. Bentley claimed that Corliss's practice was to make up confessions if he could not draw them out of the suspects. The case against Bentley —'"

"Okay, Mr. Corliss," I said. "I think that is enough."

Corliss put the printout down and looked at me like a child who has opened the door of a crowded closet and sees everything about to fall out on top of him.

"Were you ever charged with perjury in the Bentley case?" I asked him.

"No, I wasn't," he said forcefully, as if that fact exonerated him of wrongdoing.

"Was that because the police were complicit with you in setting up Mr. Bentley?"

Minton objected, saying, "I am sure Mr. Corliss would have no idea what went into the decision of whether or not to charge him with perjury."

Fullbright sustained it but I didn't care. I was so far ahead on this witness that there was no catching up. I just moved on to the next question.

"Did any prosecutor or police officer ask you to get close to Mr. Roulet and get him to confide in you?"

"No, it was just luck of the draw, I guess."

"You were not told to get a confession from Mr. Roulet?"

"No, I was not."

I stared at him for a long moment with disgust in my eyes.

"I have nothing further."

I carried the pose of anger with me to my seat and dropped the tape box angrily down in front of me before sitting down.

"Mr. Minton?" the judge asked.

"I have nothing further," he responded in a weak voice.

"Okay," Fullbright said quickly. "I am going to excuse the jury for an early lunch. I would like you all back here at one o'clock sharp."

She put on a strained smile and directed it at the jurors and kept it there until they had filed out of the courtroom. It dropped off her face the moment the door was closed.

"I want to see counsel in my chambers," she said. "Immediately."

She didn't wait for any response. She left the bench so fast that her robe flowed up behind her like the black gown of the grim reaper.

FORTY-ONE

Judge Fullbright had already lit a cigarette by the time Minton and I got back to her chambers. After one long drag she put it out against a glass paperweight and then put the butt into a Ziploc bag she had taken out of her purse. She closed the bag, folded it and re-placed it in the purse. She would leave no evidence of her transgression for the night cleaners or anyone else. She exhaled the smoke toward a ceiling intake vent and then brought her eyes down to Minton's. Judging by the look in them I was glad I wasn't him.

"Mr. Minton, what the fuck have you done to my trial?"

"Your —"

"Shut up and sit down. Both of you."

We did as we were told. The judge composed herself and leaned forward across her desk. She was still looking at Minton.

"Who did the due diligence on this witness of yours?" she asked calmly. "Who did the background?"

"Uh, that would have — actually, we only did a background on him in L.A. County. There were no cautions, no flags. I checked his name on the computer but I didn't use the initials."

"How many times had he been used in this county before today?"

"Only one previous time in court. But he had given information on three other cases I could find. Nothing about Arizona came up."

"Nobody thought to check to see if this guy had been anywhere else or used variations of his name?"

"I guess not. He was passed on to me by the original prosecutor on the case. I just assumed she had checked him out."

"Bullshit," I said.

The judge turned her eyes to me. I could have sat back and watched Minton go down but I wasn't going to let him try to take Maggie McPherson with him.

"The original prosecutor was Maggie McPherson," I said. "She had the case all of about three hours. She's my ex-wife and she knew as soon as she saw me at first apps that she was gone. And you got the case that same day, Minton. Where in there was she supposed to background your witnesses, especially this guy who didn't come out from under his rock until after first appearance? She passed him on and that was it."

Minton opened his mouth to say something but the judge cut him off.

"It doesn't matter who should have done it. It wasn't done properly and, either way, putting that man on the stand in my opinion was gross prosecutorial misconduct."

"Your Honor," Minton barked. "I did —"

"Save it for your boss. He's the one you'll need to convince. What was the last offer the state made to Mr. Roulet?"

Minton seemed frozen and unable to respond. I answered for him.

"Simple assault, six months in county."

The judge raised her eyebrows and looked at me.

"And you didn't take it?"

I shook my head.

"My client won't take a conviction. It will ruin him. He'll gamble on a verdict."

"You want a mistrial?" she asked.

I laughed and shook my head.

"No, I don't want a mistrial. All that will do is give the prose-cution time to clean up its mess, get it all right and then come back at us."

"Then what do you want?" she asked.

"What do I want? A directed verdict would be nice. Something with no comebacks from the state. Other than that, we'll ride it out."

The judge nodded and clasped her hands together on the desk.

"A directed verdict would be ridiculous, Your Honor," Minton said, finally finding his voice. "We're at the end of trial, anyway. We might as well take it to a verdict. The jury deserves it. Just because one mistake was made by the state, there is no reason to subvert the whole process."

"Don't be stupid, Mr. Minton," the judge said dismissively. "It's not about what the jury deserves. And as far as I am concerned, one mistake like you have made is enough. I don't want this kicked back at me by the Second and that is surely what they will do. Then I am holding the bag for your miscon —"

"I didn't know Corliss's background!" Minton said forcefully. "I swear to God I didn't know."

The intensity of his words brought a momentary silence to the chambers. But soon I slipped into the void.

"Just like you didn't know about the knife, Ted?"

Fullbright looked from Minton to me and then back at Minton.

"What knife?" she asked.

Minton said nothing.

"Tell her," I said.

Minton shook his head.

"I don't know what he's talking about," he said.

"Then you tell me," the judge said to me.

"Judge, if you wait on discovery from the DA, you might as well hang it up at the start," I said. "Witnesses disappear, stories change, you can lose a case just sitting around waiting."

"All right, so what about the knife?"

"I needed to move on this case. So I had my investigator go through the back door and get reports. It's fair game. But they were waiting for him and they phonied up a report on the knife so I wouldn't know about the initials. I didn't know until I got the formal discovery packet."

The judge formed a hard line with her lips.

"That was the police, not the DA's office," Minton said quickly.

"Thirty seconds ago you said you didn't know what he was talking about," Fullbright said. "Now suddenly you do. I don't care who did it. Are you telling me that this did in fact occur?"

Minton reluctantly nodded.

"Yes, Your Honor. But I swear, I didn't —"

"You know what this tells me?" the judge said, cutting him off. "It tells me that from start to finish the state has not played fair in this case. It doesn't matter who did what or that Mr. Haller's investigator may have been acting improperly. The state must be above that. And as evidenced today in my courtroom it has been anything but that."

"Your Honor, that's not —"

"No more, Mr. Minton. I think I've heard enough. I want you both to leave now. In half an hour I'll take the bench and announce what we'll do about this. I am not sure yet what that will be but no matter what I do, you aren't going to like what I have to say, Mr. Minton. And I am directing you to have your boss, Mr. Smithson, in the courtroom with you to hear it."

I stood up. Minton didn't move. He still seemed frozen to the seat.

"I said you can go!" the judge barked.

FORTY-TWO

I followed Minton through the court clerk's station and into the courtroom. It was empty except for Meehan, who sat at the bailiff's desk. I took my briefcase off the defense table and headed toward the gate.

"Hey, Haller, wait a second," Minton said, as he gathered files from the prosecution table.

I stopped at the gate and looked back.

"What?"

Minton came to the gate and pointed to the rear door of the courtroom.

"Let's go out here."

"My client is going to be waiting out there for me."

"Just come here."

He headed to the door and I followed. In the vestibule where I had confronted Roulet two days earlier Minton stopped to confront me. But he didn't say anything. He was putting words together. I decided to push him even further.

"While you go get Smithson I think I'll stop by the *Times* office on two and make sure the reporter down there knows there'll be some fireworks up here in a half hour."

"Look," Minton sputtered. "We have to work this out."

"We?"

"Just hold off on the *Times,* okay? Give me your cell number and give me ten minutes."

"For what?"

"Let me go down to my office and see what I can do."

"I don't trust you, Minton."

"Well, if you want what's best for your client instead of a cheap headline, you're going to have to trust me for ten minutes."

I looked away from his face and acted like I was considering the offer. Finally, I looked back at him. Our faces were only two feet apart.

"You know, Minton, I could've put up with all your bullshit. The knife and the arrogance and everything else. I'm a pro and I have to live with that shit from prosecutors every day of my life. But when you tried to put Corliss on Maggie McPherson in there, that's when I decided not to show you any mercy."

"Look, I did nothing to intentionally —"

"Minton, look around. There's nobody here but us. No cameras, no tape, no witnesses. Are you going to stand there and tell me you never heard of Corliss until a staff meeting yesterday?"

He responded by pointing an angry finger in my face.

"And you're going to stand there and tell me you never heard of him until this morning?"

We stared at each other for a long moment.

"I may be green but I'm not stupid," he said. "The strategy of your whole case was to push me toward using Corliss. You knew all along what you could do with him. And you probably got it from your ex."

"If you can prove that, then prove it," I said.

"Oh, don't worry, I could . . . if I had the time. But all I've got is a half hour."

I slowly raised my arm and checked my watch.

"More like twenty-six minutes."

"Give me your cell number."

I did and then he was gone. I waited in the vestibule for fifteen seconds before stepping through the door. Roulet was standing close to the glass wall that looked down at the plaza below. His mother and C. C. Dobbs were sitting on a bench against the opposite wall. Further down the hallway I saw Detective Sobel lingering in the hallway.

Roulet noticed me and started walking quickly toward me. Soon his mother and Dobbs followed.

"What's going on?" Roulet asked first.

I waited until they were all gathered close to me before answering.

"I think it's all about to blow up."

"What do you mean?" Dobbs asked.

"The judge is considering a directed verdict. We'll know pretty soon."

"What is a directed verdict?" Mary Windsor asked.

"It's when the judge takes it out of the jury's hands and issues a verdict of acquittal. She's hot because she says Minton engaged in misconduct with Corliss and some other things."

"Can she do that? Just acquit him."

"She's the judge. She can do what she wants."

"Oh my God!"

Windsor brought one hand to her mouth and looked like she might burst into tears.

"I said she is considering it," I cautioned. "It doesn't mean it will happen. But she did offer me a mistrial already and I turned that down flat."

"You turned it down?" Dobbs yelped. "Why on earth did you do that?"

"Because it's meaningless. The state could come right back and try Louis again — this time with a better case because they'll know our moves. Forget the mistrial. We're not going to educate the prosecution. We want something with no comebacks or we ride with this jury to a verdict today. Even if it goes against us we have solid grounds for appeal."

"Isn't that a decision for Louis to make?" Dobbs asked. "After all, he's —"

MICHAEL CONNELLY

"Cecil, shut up," Windsor snapped. "Just shut up and stop second-guessing everything this man does for Louis. He's right. We're not going through this again!"

Dobbs looked like he had been slapped by her. He seemed to shrink back from the huddle. I looked at Mary Windsor and saw a different face. It was the face of the woman who had started a business from scratch and had taken it to the top. I also looked at Dobbs differently, realizing that he had probably been whispering sweet negatives about me in her ear all along.

I let it go and focused on what was at hand.

"There's only one thing the DA's office hates worse than losing a verdict," I said. "That's getting embarrassed by a judge with a directed verdict, especially after a finding of prosecutorial misconduct. Minton went down to talk to his boss and he's a guy who is very political and always has his finger in the wind. We might know something in a few minutes."

Roulet was directly in front of me. I looked over his shoulder to see that Sobel was still standing in the hallway. She was talking on a cell phone.

"Listen," I said. "All of you just sit tight. If I don't hear from the DA, then we go back into court in twenty minutes to see what the judge wants to do. So stay close. If you will excuse me, I'm going to go to the restroom."

I stepped away from them and walked down the hallway toward Sobel. But Roulet broke away from his mother and her lawyer and caught up to me. He grabbed me by the arm to stop me.

"I still want to know how Corliss got that shit he was saying," he demanded.

"What does it matter? It's working for us. That's what matters."

Roulet brought his face in close to mine.

"The guy calls me a murderer on the stand. How is that working for us?"

"Because no one believed him. And that's why the judge is so pissed, because they used a professional liar to get up there on the stand and say the worst things about you. To put that in front of the jury and then have the guy revealed as a liar, that's the misconduct. Don't you see? I had to heighten the stakes. It was the only way to push the judge into pushing the prosecution. I am doing exactly what you wanted me to do, Louis. I'm getting you off."

I studied him as he computed this.

"So let it go," I said. "Go back to your mother and Dobbs and let me go take a piss."

He shook his head.

"No, I'm not going to let it go, Mick."

He poked a finger into my chest.

"Something else is going on here, Mick, and I don't like it. You have to remember something. I have your gun. And you have a daughter. You have to —"

I closed my hand over his hand and finger and pushed it away from my chest.

"Don't you ever threaten my family," I said with a controlled but angry voice. "You want to come at me, fine, then come at me and let's do it. But if you *ever* threaten my daughter again, I will bury you so deep you will never be found. You understand me, Louis?"

He slowly nodded and a smile creased his face.

"Sure, Mick. Just so we understand each other."

I released his hand and left him there. I started walking toward the end of the hallway where the restrooms were and where Sobel seemed to be waiting while talking on a cell. I was walking blind, my thoughts of the threat to my daughter crowding my vision. But as I got close to Sobel I shook it off. She ended her call when I got there.

"Detective Sobel," I said.

"Mr. Haller," she said.

"Can I ask why you are here? Are you going to arrest me?"

"I'm here because you invited me, remember?"

"Uh, no, I don't."

She narrowed her eyes.

"You told me I ought to check out your trial."

I suddenly realized she was referring to the awkward conversation in my home office during the search of my house on Monday night.

"Oh, right, I forgot about that. Well, I'm glad you took me up on it. I saw your partner earlier. What happened to him?"

"Oh, he's around."

I tried to read something in that. She had not answered the question about whether she was going to arrest me. I gestured back up the hallway toward the courtroom.

"So what did you think?"

"Interesting. I wish I could have been a fly on the wall in the judge's chambers."

"Well, stick around. It ain't over yet."

"Maybe I will."

My cell phone started to vibrate. I reached under my jacket and pulled it off my hip. The caller ID readout said the call was coming from the district attorney's office.

"I have to take this," I said.

"By all means," Sobel said.

I opened the phone and started walking back up the hallway toward where Roulet was pacing.

"Hello?"

"Mickey Haller, this is Jack Smithson in the DA's office. How's your day going?"

"I've had better."

"Not after you hear what I'm offering to do for you."

"I'm listening."

FORTY-THREE

The judge did not come out of chambers for fifteen minutes on top of the thirty she had promised. We were all waiting, Roulet and I at the defense table, his mother and Dobbs behind us in the first row. At the prosecution table Minton was no longer flying solo. Next to him sat Jack Smithson. I was thinking that it was probably the first time he had actually been inside a courtroom in a year.

Minton looked downcast and defeated. Sitting next to Smithson, he could have been taken as a defendant with his attorney. He looked guilty as charged.

Detective Booker was not in the courtroom and I wondered if he was working on something or simply if no one had bothered to call him with the bad news.

I turned to check the big clock on the back wall and to scan the gallery. The screen for Minton's PowerPoint presentation was gone now, a hint of what was to come. I saw Sobel sitting in the back row, but her partner and Kurlen were still nowhere to be seen. There was nobody else but Dobbs and Windsor, and they didn't count. The row reserved for the media was empty. The media had not been alerted. I was keeping my side of the deal with Smithson.

Deputy Meehan called the courtroom to order and Judge Fullbright took the bench with a flourish, the scent of lilac wafting toward the tables. I guessed that she'd had a cigarette or two back there in chambers and had gone heavy with the perfume as cover.

"In the matter of the state versus Louis Ross Roulet, I understand from my clerk that we have a motion."

Minton stood.

"Yes, Your Honor."

He said nothing further, as if he could not bring himself to speak.

"Well, Mr. Minton, are you sending it to me telepathically?"

"No, Your Honor."

Minton looked down at Smithson and got the go-ahead nod.

"The state moves to dismiss all charges against Louis Ross Roulet."

The judge nodded as though she had expected the move. I heard a sharp intake of breath behind me and knew it was from Mary Windsor. She knew what was going to happen but had held her emotions in check until she had actually heard it in the courtroom.

"Is that with or without prejudice?" the judge asked.

"Dismiss with prejudice."

"Are you sure about that, Mr. Minton? That means no comebacks from the state."

"Yes, Your Honor, I know," Minton said with a note of annoyance at the judge's need to explain the law to him.

The judge wrote something down and then looked back at Minton.

"I believe for the record the state needs to offer some sort of explanation for this motion. We have chosen a jury and heard more than two days of testimony. Why is the state doing this at this stage, Mr. Minton?"

Smithson stood. He was a tall and thin man with a pale complexion. He was a prosecutorial specimen. Nobody wanted a fat man as district attorney and that was exactly what he hoped one day to be. He wore a charcoal gray suit with what had become his trademark: a maroon bow tie with matching handkerchief peeking from the suit's breast pocket. The word among the defense pros was that a political advisor had told him to start building a recognizable media image so that when the time came to run, the voters would think they already knew him. This was one situation where he didn't want the media carrying his image to the voters.

"If I may, Your Honor," he said.

"The record will note the appearance of Assistant District Attorney John Smithson, head of the Van Nuys Division. Welcome, Jack. Go right ahead, please."

"Judge Fullbright, it has come to my attention that in the interest of justice, the charges against Mr. Roulet should be dropped."

He pronounced Roulet's name wrong.

"Is that all the explanation you can offer, Jack?" the judge asked.

Smithson deliberated before answering. While there were no reporters present, the record of the hearing would be public and his words viewable later.

"Judge, it has come to my attention that there were some irregularities in the investigation and subsequent prosecution. This office is founded upon the belief in the sanctity of our justice system. I personally safeguard that in the Van Nuys Division and take it very, very seriously. And so it is better for us to dismiss a case than to see justice possibly compromised in any way."

"Thank you, Mr. Smithson. That is refreshing to hear."

The judge wrote another note and then looked back down at us.

"The state's motion is granted," she said. "All charges against Louis Roulet are dismissed with prejudice. Mr. Roulet, you are discharged and free to go."

"Thank you, Your Honor," I said.

"We still have a jury returning at one o'clock," Fullbright said. "I will gather them and explain that the case has been resolved. If any of you attorneys wish to come back then, I am sure they will have questions for you. However, it is not required that you be back."

I nodded but didn't say I would be back. I wouldn't be. The twelve people who had been so important to me for the last week had just dropped off the radar. They were now as meaningless to me as the drivers going the other way on the freeway. They had gone by and I was finished with them.

The judge left the bench and Smithson was the first one out of the courtroom. He had nothing to say to Minton or me. His first priority was to distance himself from this prosecutorial catastrophe. I looked over and saw Minton's face had lost all color. I assumed that I would soon see his name in the yellow pages. He would not be retained by the DA and he would join the ranks of the defense pros, his first felony lesson a costly one.

Roulet was at the rail, leaning over to hug his mother. Dobbs had a hand on his shoulder in a congratulatory gesture, but the family lawyer had not recovered from Windsor's harsh rebuke in the hallway.

When the hugs were over, Roulet turned to me and with hesitation shook my hand.

"I wasn't wrong about you," he said. "I knew you were the one."

"I want the gun," I said, deadpan, my face showing no joy in the victory just achieved.

"Of course you do."

He turned back to his mother. I hesitated a moment and then turned back to the defense table. I opened my briefcase to return all the files to it.

"Michael?"

I turned and it was Dobbs reaching a hand across the railing. I shook it and nodded.

"You did good," Dobbs said, as if I needed to hear it from him. "We all appreciate it greatly."

"Thanks for the shot. I know you were shaky about me at the start."

I was courteous enough not to mention Windsor's outburst in the hallway and what she had said about him backstabbing me.

"Only because I didn't know you," Dobbs said. "Now I do. Now I know who to recommend to my clients."

"Thank you. But I hope your kind of clients never need me."

He laughed.

"Me, too!"

Then it was Mary Windsor's turn. She extended her hand across the bar.

"Mr. Haller, thank you for my son."

"You're welcome," I said flatly. "Take care of him."

"I always do."

I nodded.

"Why don't you all go out to the hallway and I'll be out in a minute. I have to finish up some things here with the clerk and Mr. Minton."

I turned back to the table. I then went around it and approached the clerk.

"How long before I can get a signed copy of the judge's order?"

"We'll enter it this afternoon. We can send you a copy if you don't want to come back."

"That would be great. Could you also fax one?"

She said she would and I gave her the number to the fax in Lorna Taylor's condominium. I wasn't sure yet how it could be used but I had to believe that an order to dismiss could somehow help me get a client or two.

When I turned back to get my briefcase and leave I noticed that Detective Sobel had left the courtroom. Only Minton remained. He was standing and gathering his things.

"Sorry I never got the chance to see your PowerPoint thing," I said.

He nodded.

"Yeah, it was pretty good. I think it would have won them over."

I nodded.

"What are you going to do now?"

"I don't know. See if I can ride this out and somehow hold on to my job."

He put his files under his arm. He had no briefcase. He only had to go down to the second floor. He turned and gave me a hard stare.

"The only thing I know is that I don't want to cross the aisle. I don't want to become like you, Haller. I think I like sleeping at night too much for that."

With that he headed through the gate and strode out of the courtroom. I glanced over at the clerk to see if she had heard what he had said. She acted like she hadn't.

I took my time following Minton out. I picked up my briefcase and turned backwards as I pushed through the gate. I looked at the judge's empty bench and the state seal on the front panel. I nodded at nothing in particular and then walked out.

FORTY-FOUR

Roulet and his entourage were waiting for me in the hallway. I looked both ways and saw Sobel down by the elevators. She was on her cell phone and it seemed as though she was waiting for an elevator but it didn't look like the down button was lit.

"Michael, can you join us for lunch?" Dobbs said upon seeing me. "We are going to celebrate!"

I noticed that he was now calling me by my given name. Victory made everybody friendly.

"Uh . . . ," I said, still looking down at Sobel. "I don't think I can make it."

"Why not? You obviously don't have court in the afternoon."

I finally looked at Dobbs. I felt like saying that I couldn't have lunch because I never wanted to see him or Mary Windsor or Louis Roulet again.

"I think I'm going to stick around and talk to the jurors when they come back at one."

"Why?" Roulet asked.

"Because it will help me to know what they were thinking and where we stood."

Dobbs gave me a clap on the upper arm.

"Always learning, always getting better for the next one. I don't blame you."

He looked delighted that I would not be joining them. And for good reason. He probably wanted me out of the way now so he could work on repairing his relationship with Mary Windsor. He wanted that franchise account just to himself again.

I heard the muted bong of the elevator and looked back down the hall. Sobel was standing in front of the opening elevator. She was leaving.

But then Lankford, Kurlen and Booker stepped out of the elevator and joined Sobel. They turned and started walking toward us.

"Then we'll leave you to it," Dobbs said, his back to the approaching detectives. "We have a reservation at Orso and I'm afraid we're already going to be late getting back over the hill."

"Okay," I said, still looking down the hall.

Dobbs, Windsor and Roulet turned to walk away just as the four detectives got to us.

"Louis Roulet," Kurlen announced. "You are under arrest. Turn around, please, and place your hands behind your back."

"No!" Mary Windsor shrieked. "You can't —"

"What is this?" Dobbs cried out.

Kurlen didn't answer or wait for Roulet to comply. He stepped forward and roughly turned Roulet around. As he made the forced turn, Roulet's eyes came to mine.

"What's going on, Mick?" he said in a calm voice. "This shouldn't be happening."

Mary Windsor moved toward her son.

"Take your hands off of my son!"

She grabbed Kurlen from behind but Booker and Lankford quickly moved in and detached her, handling her gently but strongly.

"Ma'am, step back," Booker commanded. "Or I will put you in jail."

Kurlen started giving Roulet the Miranda warning. Windsor stayed back but was not silent.

"How dare you? You cannot do this!"

Her body moved in place and she looked as though unseen hands were keeping her from charging at Kurlen again.

"Mother," Roulet said in a tone that carried more weight and control than any of the detectives.

Windsor's body relented. She gave up. But Dobbs didn't.

"You're arresting him for what?" he demanded.

"Suspicion of murder," Kurlen said. "The murder of Martha Renteria."

"That's impossible!" Dobbs cried. "Everything that witness Corliss said in there was proven to be a lie. Are you crazy? The judge dismissed the case because of his lies."

Kurlen broke from his recital of Roulet's rights and looked at Dobbs.

"If it was all a lie, how'd you know he was talking about Martha Renteria?"

Dobbs realized his mistake and took a step back from the gathering. Kurlen smiled.

"Yeah, I thought so," he said.

He grabbed Roulet by an elbow and turned him back around.

"Let's go," he said.

"Mick?" Roulet said.

"Detective Kurlen," I said. "Can I talk to my client for a moment?"

Kurlen looked at me, seemed to measure something in me and then nodded.

"One minute. Tell him to behave himself and it will all go a lot easier for him."

He shoved Roulet toward me. I took him by one arm and walked him a few paces away from the others so we would have privacy if we kept our voices down. I stepped close to him and began in a whisper.

"This is it, Louis. This is good-bye. I got you off. Now you're on your own. Get yourself a new lawyer."

The shock showed in his eyes. Then his face clouded over with a tightly focused anger. It was pure rage and I realized it was the same rage Regina Campo and Martha Renteria must have seen.

"I won't need a lawyer," he said to me. "You think they can make a case off of what you somehow fed to that lying snitch in there? You better think again."

"They won't need the snitch, Louis. Believe me, they'll find more. They probably already have more."

"What about you, Mick? Aren't you forgetting something? I have —"

"I know. But it doesn't matter anymore. They don't need my gun. They've already got all they need. But whatever happens to me, I'll know that I put you down. At the end, after the trial and all the appeals, when they finally stick that needle in your arm, that will be me, Louis. Remember that."

I smiled with no humor and moved in closer.

"This is for Raul Levin. You might not go down for him but make no mistake, you are going down."

I let that register for a moment and then stepped back and nodded to Kurlen. He and Booker came up on either side of Roulet and took hold of his upper arms.

"You set me up," Roulet said, somehow maintaining his calm. "You aren't a lawyer. You work for them."

"Let's go," Kurlen said.

They started moving him but he shook them off momentarily and put his raging eyes right back into mine.

"This isn't the end, Mick," he said. "I'll be out by tomorrow morning. What will you do then? Think about it. What are you going to do then? You can't protect everybody."

They took a tighter hold of him and roughly turned him toward the elevators. This time Roulet went without a struggle. Halfway down the hall toward the elevator, his mother and Dobbs trailing behind, he turned his head to look back over his shoulder at me. He smiled and it sent something right through me.

You can't protect everybody.

A cold shiver of fear pierced my chest.

Someone was waiting for the elevator and it opened just as the entourage got there. Lankford signaled the person back and took the elevator. Roulet was hustled in. Dobbs and Windsor were about to follow when they were halted by Lankford's hand extended in a stop signal. The elevator door started to close and Dobbs angrily and impotently pushed on the button next to it.

My hope was that it would be the last I would ever see of Louis Roulet, but the fear stayed locked in my chest, fluttering like a moth caught inside a porch light. I turned away and almost walked right into Sobel. I hadn't noticed that she had stayed behind the others.

"You have enough, don't you?" I said. "Tell me you wouldn't have moved so quickly if you didn't have enough to keep him."

She looked at me a long moment before answering.

"We won't decide that. The DA will. Probably depends on what they get out of him in interrogation. But up till now he's had a pretty smart lawyer. He probably knows not to say a word to us."

"Then why didn't you wait?"

"Wasn't my call."

I shook my head. I wanted to tell her that they had moved too fast. It wasn't part of the plan. I wanted to plant the seed, that's all. I wanted them to move slowly and get it right.

The moth fluttered inside and I looked down at the floor. I couldn't shake the idea that all of my machinations had failed, leaving me and my family exposed in the hard-eyed focus of a killer. *You can't protect everybody.*

It was as if Sobel read my fears.

"But we're going to try to keep him," she said. "We have what the snitch said in court and the ticket. We're working on witnesses and the forensics."

My eyes came up to hers.

"What ticket?"

A look of suspicion entered her face.

"I thought you had it figured out. We put it together as soon as the snitch mentioned the snake dancer."

"Yeah. Martha Renteria. I got that. But what ticket? What are you talking about?"

I had moved in too close to her and Sobel took a step back from me. It wasn't my breath. It was my desperation.

"I don't know if I should tell you, Haller. You're a defense lawyer. You're *his* lawyer."

"Not anymore. I just quit."

"Doesn't matter. He —"

"Look, you just took that guy down because of me. I might get disbarred because of it. I might even go to jail for a murder I didn't commit. What ticket are you talking about?"

She hesitated and I waited, but then she finally spoke.

"Raul Levin's last words. He said he found Jesus's ticket out."

"Which means what?"

"You really don't know, do you?"

"Look, just tell me. Please."

She relented.

"We traced Levin's most recent movements. Before he was murdered he had made inquiries about Roulet's parking tickets. He even pulled hard copies of them. We inventoried what he had in the office and eventually compared it with what's on the computer. He was missing one ticket. One hard copy. We didn't know if his killer took it that day or if he had just missed pulling it. So we went and pulled a copy ourselves. It was issued two years ago on the night of April eighth. It was a citation for parking in front of a hydrant in the sixty-seven-hundred block of Blythe Street in Panorama City."

It all came together for me, like the last bit of sand dropping through the middle of an hourglass. Raul Levin really had found Jesus Menendez's salvation.

"Martha Renteria was murdered two years ago on April eighth," I said. "She lived on Blythe in Panorama City."

"Yes, but we didn't know that. We didn't see the connection. You told us that Levin was working separate cases for you. Jesus Menendez and Louis Roulet were separate investigations. Levin had them filed that way, too."

"It was a discovery issue. He kept the cases separate so I wouldn't have to turn over anything on Roulet that he came up with on Menendez."

"One of your lawyer angles. Well, it stopped us from putting it together until that snitch in there mentioned the snake dancer. That connected everything."

I nodded.

"So whoever killed Raul Levin took the hard copy?"

"We think."

"Did you check Raul's phones for a tap? Somehow somebody knew he found the ticket."

"We did. They were clear. Bugs could have been removed at the time of the murder. Or maybe it was someone else's phone that was tapped."

Meaning mine. Meaning it might explain how Roulet knew so many of my moves and was even conveniently waiting for me in my home the night I had come home from seeing Jesus Menendez.

"I will have them checked," I said. "Does all of this mean I am clear on Raul's murder?"

"Not necessarily," Sobel said. "We still want to see what comes back from ballistics. We're hoping for something today."

I nodded. I didn't know how to respond. Sobel lingered, looking like she wanted to tell me or ask me something.

"What?" I said.

"I don't know. Is there anything you want to tell me?"

"I don't know. There's nothing to tell."

"Really? In the courtroom it seemed like you were trying to tell us a lot."

I was silent a moment, trying to read between the lines.

"What do you want from me, Detective Sobel?"

"You know what I want. I want Raul Levin's killer."

"Well, so do I. But I couldn't give you Roulet on Levin even if I wanted to. I don't know how he did it. And that's off the record."

"So that still leaves you in the crosshairs."

She looked down the hall at the elevators, her implication clear.

If the ballistics matched, I could still have a problem on Levin. They would use it as leverage. Give up how Roulet did it or go down for it myself. I changed the subject.

"How long do you think before Jesus Menendez gets out?" I asked.

She shrugged.

"Hard to say. Depends on the case they build against Roulet — if they have a case. But I know one thing. They can't prosecute Roulet as long as another man is in prison for the same crime."

I turned and walked over to the glass wall. I put my free hand on the railing that ran along the glass. I felt a mixture of elation and dread and that moth still batting around in my chest.

"That's all I care about," I said quietly. "Getting him out. That and Raul."

She came over and stood next to me.

"I don't know what you are doing," she said. "But leave the rest for us."

"I do that and your partner will probably put me in jail for a murder I didn't commit."

"You are playing a dangerous game," she said. "Leave it alone."

I looked at her and then back down at the plaza.

"Sure," I said. "I'll leave it alone now."

Having heard what she needed to, she made a move to go.

"Good luck," she said.

I looked at her again.

"Same to you."

She left then and I stayed. I turned back to the window and looked down into the plaza. I saw Dobbs and Windsor crossing the concrete squares and heading toward the parking garage. Mary Windsor was leaning against her lawyer for support. I doubted they were still headed to lunch at Orso.

FORTY-FIVE

By that night the word had begun to spread. Not the secret details but the public story. The story that I had won the case, gotten a DA's motion to dismiss with no comebacks, only to have my client arrested for a murder in the hallway outside the courtroom where I had just cleared him. I got calls from every other defense pro I knew. I got call after call until my cell phone finally died. My colleagues were all congratulating me. In their eyes, there was no downside. Roulet was the ultimate franchise. I got schedule A fees for one trial and then I would get schedule A fees for the next one. It was a double-dip most defense pros could only dream about. And, of course, when I told them I would not be handling the defense of the new case, each one of them asked if I could refer him to Roulet.

It was the one call that came in on my home line that I wanted the most. It was from Maggie McPherson.

"I've been waiting for your call all night," I said.

I was pacing in the kitchen, tethered by the phone cord. I had checked my phones when I had gotten home and found no evidence of bugging devices.

"Sorry, I've been in the conference room," she said.

"I heard you were pulled in on Roulet."

"Yes, that's why I'm calling. They're going to cut him loose."

"What are you talking about? They're letting him go?"

"Yes. They've had him for nine hours in a room and he hasn't broken. Maybe you taught him too well not to talk, because he's a rock and they got nothing and that means they don't have enough."

"You're wrong. There is enough. They have the parking ticket and there have to be witnesses who can put him in The Cobra Room. Even Menendez can ID him there."

"You know as well as I do that Menendez is a scratch. He'd identify anybody to get out. And if there are other wits from The Cobra Room, then it's going to take some time to run them down. The parking ticket puts him in the neighborhood but it doesn't put him inside her apartment."

"What about the knife?"

"They're working on it but that's going to take time, too. Look, we want to do this right. It was Smithson's call and, believe me, he wanted to keep him, too. It would make that fiasco you created in court today a little more palatable. But it's just not there. Not yet. They're going to kick him loose and work the forensics and look for the witnesses. If Roulet's good for this, then we will get him, and your other client will get out. You don't have to worry. But we have to do it right."

I swung a fist impotently through the air.

"They jumped the gun. Damn it, they shouldn't have made the move today."

"I guess they thought nine hours in interrogation would do the trick."

"They were stupid."

"Nobody's perfect."

I was annoyed by her attitude but held my tongue on that. I needed her to keep me in the loop.

"When exactly will they let him go?" I asked.

"I don't know. This all just went down. Kurlen and Booker

came over here to present it and Smithson just sent them back to the PD. When they get back, I assume they'll kick him loose."

"Listen to me, Maggie. Roulet knows about Hayley."

There was a horribly long moment of silence before she answered.

"What are you saying, Haller? You let our daughter into —"

"I didn't let anything happen. He broke into my house and saw her picture. It doesn't mean he knows where she lives or even what her name is. But he knows about her and he wants to get back at me. So you have to go home right now. I want you to be with Hayley. Get her and get out of the apartment. Just play it safe."

Something made me hold back on telling her everything, that I felt that Roulet had specifically threatened my family in the courthouse. *You can't protect everybody.* I would only use that if she refused to do what I wanted her to do with Hayley.

"I'm leaving now," she said. "And we're coming to you."

I knew she would say that.

"No, don't come to me."

"Why not?"

"Because *he* might come to me."

"This is crazy. What are you going to do?"

"I'm not sure yet. Just go get Hayley and get somewhere safe. Then call me on your cell, but don't tell me where you are. It will be better if I don't even know."

"Haller, just call the police. They can —"

"And tell them what?"

"I don't know. Tell them you've been threatened."

"A defense lawyer telling the police he feels threatened . . . yeah, they'll jump all over that. Probably send out a SWAT team."

"Well, you have to do something."

"I thought I did. I thought he was going to be in jail for the rest of his life. But you people moved too fast and now you have to let him go."

"I told you, it wasn't enough. Even knowing now about the possible threat to Hayley, it's still not enough."

"Then go to our daughter and take care of her. Leave the rest to me."

"I'm going."

But she didn't hang up. It was like she was giving me the chance to say something more.

"I love you, Mags," I said. "Both of you. Be careful."

I closed the phone before she could respond. Almost immediately I opened it again and called Fernando Valenzuela's cell phone number. After five rings he answered.

"Val, it's me, Mick."

"Shit. If I'd known it was you I wouldn't have answered."

"Look, I need your help."

"My help? You're asking for my help after what you asked me the other night? After you accused me?"

"Look, Val, this is an emergency. What I said the other night was out of line and I apologize. I'll pay for your TV, I'll do whatever you want, but I need your help right now."

I waited. After a pause he responded.

"What do you want me to do?"

"Roulet still has the bracelet on his ankle, right?"

"That's right. I know what happened in court but I haven't heard from the guy. One of my courthouse people said the cops picked him up again so I don't know what's going on."

"They picked him up but he's about to be kicked loose. He'll probably be calling you so he can get the bracelet taken off."

"I'm already home, man. He can find me in the morning."

"That's what I want. Make him wait."

"That ain't no favor, man."

"This is. I want you to open your laptop and watch him. When he leaves the PD, I want to know where he's going. Can you do that for me?"

"You mean right now?"

"Yeah, right now. You got a problem with that?"

"Sort of."

I got ready for another argument. But I was surprised.

"I told you about the battery alarm on the bracelet, right?" Valenzuela said.

"Yeah, I remember."

"Well, I got the twenty percent alarm about an hour ago."

"So how much longer can you track him until the battery's dead?"

"Probably about six to eight hours' active tracking before it goes on low pulse. Then he'll come up every fifteen minutes for another five hours."

I thought about all of this. I just needed to make it through the night and to know that Maggie and Hayley were safe.

"The thing is, when he is on low pulse he beeps," Valenzuela said. "You'll hear him coming. Or he'll get tired of the noise and juice the battery."

Or maybe he'll pull the Houdini act again, I thought.

"Okay," I said. "You told me that there were other alarms that you could build into the tracking program."

"That's right."

"Can you set it so you get an alarm if he comes near a specific target?"

"Yeah, like if it's on a child molester you can set an alarm if he gets close to a school. Stuff like that. It's got to be a fixed target."

"Okay."

I gave him the address of the apartment on Dickens in Sherman Oaks where Maggie and my daughter lived.

"If he comes within ten blocks of that place you call me. Doesn't matter what time, call me. That's the favor."

"What is this place?"

"It's where my daughter lives."

There was a long silence before Valenzuela responded.

"With Maggie? You think this guy's going to go there?"

"I don't know. I'm hoping that as long as he's got the tracker on his ankle he won't be stupid."

"Okay, Mick. You got it."

"Thanks, Val. And call my home number. My cell is dead."

I gave him the number and then was silent for a moment, wondering what else I could say to make up for my betrayal two nights earlier. Finally, I let it go. I had to focus on the current threat.

I moved from the kitchen and down the hallway to my office. I rolled through the Rolodex on my desk until I found a number and then grabbed the desk phone.

I dialed and waited. I looked out the window to the left of my desk and noticed for the first time that it was raining. It looked like it was going to come down hard and I wondered if the weather would affect the satellite tracking of Roulet. I dropped the thought when my call was answered by Teddy Vogel, the leader of the Road Saints.

"Speak to me."

"Ted, Mickey Haller."

"Counselor, how are you?"

"Not so good tonight."

"Then I am glad you called. What can I do for you?"

I looked out the window at the rain before answering. I knew that if I continued I would be indebted to people I never wanted to be on the hook with.

But there was no choice.

"You happen to have anybody down my way tonight?" I asked.

There was a hesitation before Vogel answered. I knew he had to be curious about his lawyer calling him for help. I was obviously asking about the kind of help that came with muscles and guns.

"Got a few guys watching things at the club. What's up?"

The club was the strip bar on Sepulveda, not too far from Sherman Oaks. I was counting on that.

"There's a threat to my family, Ted. I need some warm bodies to put up a front, maybe grab a guy if needed."

"Armed and dangerous?"

I hesitated but not too long.

"Yeah, armed and dangerous."

"Sounds like our kind of move. Where do you want them?"

He was immediately ready to act. He knew the value of having me under his thumb instead of on retainer. I gave him the address of the apartment on Dickens. I also gave him a description of Roulet and what he had been wearing in court that day.

"If he shows up at that apartment, I want him stopped," I said. "And I need your people to go now."

"Done," Vogel said.

"Thank you, Ted."

"No, thank you. We're glad to help you out, seeing as how you've helped us out so much."

Yeah, right, I thought. I hung the phone up, knowing I had just crossed one of those lines you hope to never see let alone have to step across. I looked out the window again. Outside, the rain was now coming down hard off the roof. I had no gutter in the back and it was coming down in a translucent sheet that blurred the lights out there. Nothing but rain this year, I thought. Nothing but rain.

I left the office and went back to the front of the house. On the table in the dining alcove was the gun Earl Briggs had given me. I contemplated the weapon and all the moves I had made. The bottom line was I had been flying blind and in the process had endangered more than just myself.

Panic started to set in. I grabbed the phone off the kitchen wall and called Maggie's cell. She answered right away. I could tell she was in her car.

"Where are you?"

"I'm just getting home now. I'll get some things together and we'll get out."

"Good."

"What do I tell Hayley, that her father put her life in danger?"

"It's not like that, Maggie. It's him. It's Roulet. I couldn't control him. One night I came home and he was sitting in my house. He's a real estate guy. He knows how to find places. He saw her picture on my desk. What was I —"

"Can we talk about this later? I have to go in now and get my daughter."

Not *our* daughter. *My* daughter.

"Sure. Call me when you're in a new place."

She disconnected without further word and I slowly hung the phone back on the wall. My hand was still on the phone. I leaned forward until my forehead touched the wall. I was out of moves. I could only wait on Roulet to make the next one.

The phone's ring startled me and I jumped back. The phone fell to the floor and I pulled it up by the cord. It was Valenzuela.

"You get my message? I just called."

"No, I've been on the phone. What?"

"Glad I called back, then. He's moving."

"Where?"

I shouted it too loud into the phone. I was losing it.

"He's heading south on Van Nuys. He called me and said he wanted to lose the bracelet. I told him I was already home and that he could call me tomorrow. I told him he had better juice the battery so he wouldn't start beeping in the middle of the night."

"Good thinking. Where's he now?"

"Still on Van Nuys."

I tried to build an image of Roulet driving. If he was going south on Van Nuys that meant he was heading directly toward Sherman Oaks and the neighborhood where Maggie and Hayley lived. But he could also be headed right through Sherman Oaks on his way south over the hill and to his home. I had to wait to be sure.

"How up to the moment is the GPS on that thing?" I asked.

"It's real time, man. This is where he's at. He just crossed under the one-oh-one. He might be just going home, Mick."

"I know, I know. Just wait till he crosses Ventura. The next street is Dickens. If he turns there, then he's not going home."

I stood up and didn't know what to do. I started pacing, the phone pressed tightly to my ear. I knew that even if Teddy Vogel had immediately put his men in motion they were still minutes away. They were no good to me now.

"What about the rain? Does it affect the GPS?"

"It's not supposed to."

"That's comforting."

"He stopped."

"Where?"

"Must be a light. I think that's Moorpark Avenue there."

That was a block before Ventura and two before Dickens. I heard a beeping sound come over the phone.

"What's that?"

"The ten-block alarm you asked me to set."

The beeping sound stopped.

"I turned it off."

"I'll call you right back."

I didn't wait for a response. I hung up and called Maggie's cell. She answered right away.

"Where are you?"

"You told me not to tell you."

"You're out of the apartment?"

"No, not yet. Hayley's picking the crayons and coloring books she wants to take."

"Goddamn it, get out of there! Now!"

"We're going as fast as —"

"Just get out! I'll call you back. Make sure you answer."

I hung up and called Valenzuela back.

"Where is he?"

"He's now at Ventura. Must've caught another light, because he's not moving."

"You're sure he's on the road and not just parked there?"

"No, I'm not sure. He could — never mind, he's moving. Shit, he turned on Ventura."

"Which way?"

I started pacing, the phone pressed so hard against my ear that it hurt.

"Right — uh, west. He's going west."

He was now driving parallel to Dickens, one block away, in the direction of my daughter's apartment.

"He just stopped again," Valenzuela announced. "It's not an

intersection. It looks like he's in the middle of the block. I think he parked it."

I ran my free hand through my hair like a desperate man.

"Fuck it, I've gotta go. My cell's dead. Call Maggie and tell her he's heading her way. Tell her to just get in the car and get out of there!"

I shouted Maggie's number into the phone and dropped it as I headed out of the kitchen. I knew it would take me a minimum of twenty minutes to get to Dickens — and that was hitting the curves on Mulholland at sixty in the Lincoln — but I couldn't stand around shouting orders on the phone while my family was in danger. I grabbed the gun off the table and went to the door. I was shoving it into the side pocket of my jacket as I opened the door.

Mary Windsor was standing there, her hair wet from the rain.

"Mary, what —"

She raised her hand. I looked down to see the metal glint of the gun in it just as she fired.

FORTY-SIX

The sound was loud and the flash as bright as a camera's. The impact of the bullet tearing into me was like what I imagine a kick from a horse would feel like. In a split second I went from standing still to moving backwards. I hit the wood floor hard and was propelled into the wall next to the living room fireplace. I tried to reach both hands to the hole in my gut but my right hand was hung up in the pocket of my jacket. I held myself with the left and tried to sit up.

Mary Windsor stepped forward and into the house. I had to look up at her. Through the open door behind her I could see the rain coming down. She raised the weapon and pointed it at my forehead. In a flash moment my daughter's face came to me and I knew I wasn't going to let her go.

"You tried to take my son from me!" Windsor shouted. "Did you think I could allow you to do that and just walk away?"

And then I knew. Everything crystallized. I knew she had said similar words to Raul Levin before she had killed him. And I knew that there had been no rape in an empty house in Bel-Air. She was a mother doing what she had to do. Roulet's words came back to me then. *You're right about one thing. I am a son of a bitch.*

And I knew, too, that Raul Levin's last gesture had not been to make the sign of the devil, but to make the letter *M* or *W,* depending on how you looked at it.

Windsor took another step toward me.

"You go to hell," she said.

She steadied her hand to fire. I raised my right hand, still wrapped in my jacket. She must have thought it was a defensive gesture because she didn't hurry. She was savoring the moment. I could tell. Until I fired.

Mary Windsor's body jerked backwards with the impact and she landed on her back in the threshold of the door. Her gun clattered to the floor and I heard her make a high-pitched whining noise. Then I heard the sound of running feet on the steps up to the front deck.

"Police!" a woman shouted. "Put your weapons down!"

I looked through the door and didn't see anyone.

"Put your weapons down and come out with your hands in full view!"

This time it was a man who had yelled and I recognized the voice.

I pulled the gun out of my jacket pocket and put it on the floor. I slid it away from me.

"The weapon's down," I called out, as loud as the hole in my stomach allowed me to. "But I'm shot. I can't get up. We're both shot."

I first saw the barrel of a pistol come into view in the doorway. Then a hand and then a wet black raincoat containing Detective Lankford. He moved into the house and was quickly followed by his partner, Detective Sobel. Lankford kicked the gun away from Windsor as he came in. He kept his own weapon pointed at me.

"Anybody else in the house?" he asked loudly.

"No," I said. "Listen to me."

I tried to sit up but pain shot through my body and Lankford yelled.

"Don't move! Just stay there!"

"Listen to me. My fam —"

Sobel yelled a command into a handheld radio, ordering paramedics and ambulance transport for two people with gunshot wounds.

"One transport," Lankford corrected. "She's gone."

He pointed his gun at Windsor.

Sobel shoved the radio into her raincoat pocket and came to me. She knelt down and pulled my hand away from my wound. She pulled my shirt out of my pants so she could lift it and see the damage. She then pressed my hand back down on the bullet hole.

"Press down as hard as you can. It's a bleeder. You hear me, hold your hand down tight."

"Listen to me," I said again. "My family's in danger. You have to —"

"Hold on."

She reached inside her raincoat and pulled a cell phone off her belt. She flipped it open and hit a speed-dial button. Whoever she called answered right away.

"It's Sobel. You better bring him back in. His mother just tried to hit the lawyer. He got her first."

She listened for a moment and asked, "Then, where is he?"

She listened some more and then said good-bye. I stared at her as she closed her phone.

"They'll pick him up. Your daughter is safe."

"You're watching him?"

She nodded.

"We piggy-backed on your plan, Haller. We have a lot on him but we were hoping for more. I told you, we want to clear Levin. We were hoping that if we kicked him loose he'd show us his trick, show us how he got to Levin. But the mother sort of just solved that mystery for us."

I understood. Even with the blood and life running out of the hole in my gut I was able to put it together. Releasing Roulet had been a play. They were hoping that he'd go after me, revealing the method he had used to defeat the GPS ankle bracelet when he had killed Raul Levin. Only he hadn't killed Raul. His mother had done it for him.

"Maggie?" I asked weakly.

Sobel shook her head.

"She's fine. She had to play along because we didn't know if Roulet had a tap on your line or not. She couldn't tell you that she and Hayley were safe."

I closed my eyes. I didn't know whether just to be thankful that they were okay or to be angry that Maggie had used her daughter's father as bait for a killer.

I tried to sit up.

"I want to call her. She —"

"Don't move. Just stay still."

I leaned my head back on the floor. I was cold and on the verge of shaking, yet I also felt as though I were sweating. I could feel myself getting weaker as my breathing grew shallow.

Sobel pulled the radio out of her pocket again and asked dispatch for an ETA on the paramedics. The dispatcher reported back that the medical help was still six minutes away.

"Hang in there," Sobel said to me. "You'll be all right. Depending on what the bullet did inside, you should be all right."

"Gray . . ."

I meant to say *great* with full sarcasm attached. But I was fading.

Lankford came up next to Sobel and looked at me. In a gloved hand he held up the gun Mary Windsor had shot me with. I recognized the pearl grips. Mickey Cohen's gun. My gun. The gun she shot Raul with.

He nodded and I took it as some sort of signal. Maybe that in his eyes I had stepped up, that he knew I had done their work by drawing the killer out. Maybe it was even the offering of a truce and maybe he wouldn't hate lawyers so much after this.

Probably not. But I nodded back at him and the small movement made me cough. I tasted something in my mouth and knew it was blood.

"Don't flatline on us now," Lankford ordered. "If we end up giving a defense lawyer mouth-to-mouth, we'll never live it down."

He smiled and I smiled back. Or tried to. Then the blackness started crowding my vision. Pretty soon I was floating in it.

PART THREE

— Postcard from Cuba

FORTY-SEVEN

I t has been five months since I was in a courtroom. In that time I have had three surgeries to repair my body, been sued in civil court twice and been investigated by both the Los Angeles Police Department and the California Bar Association. My bank accounts have been bled dry by medical expenses, living expenses, child support and, yes, even my own kind — the lawyers.

But I have survived it all and today will be the first day since I was shot by Mary Alice Windsor that I will walk without a cane or the numbing of painkillers. To me it is the first real step toward getting back. The cane is a sign of weakness. Nobody wants a defense attorney who looks weak. I must stand upright, stretch the muscles the surgeon cut through to get to the bullet, and walk on my own before I feel I can walk into a courtroom again.

I have not been in a courtroom but that does not mean I am not the subject of legal proceedings. Jesus Menendez and Louis Roulet are both suing me and the cases will likely follow me for years. They are separate claims but both of my former clients charge me with malpractice and violation of legal ethics. For all the specific accusations in his lawsuit, Roulet has not been able to learn how I supposedly got to Dwayne Jeffery Corliss at County-USC and fed him privileged information. And it is unlikely he ever will. Gloria Dayton is long gone. She finished her program, took the $25,000 I gave her and moved to Hawaii to start life again. And Corliss, who probably knows better than anyone the value of keeping one's mouth shut, has divulged nothing other than what he testified to in court — maintaining that while in custody Roulet told him about the murder of the snake dancer. He has avoided perjury charges because pursuing them would undermine the case against Roulet and be an act of self-flagellation by the DA's office. My lawyer tells me Roulet's lawsuit against me is a face-saving effort without merit and that it will eventually go away. Probably when I have no more money to pay my lawyer his fees.

But Menendez will never go away. He is the one who gets to me at night when I sit on the deck and watch the million-dollar view from my house with the million-one mortgage. He was pardoned by the governor and released from San Quentin two days after Roulet was charged with Martha Renteria's murder. But he only traded one life sentence for another. It was revealed that he contracted HIV in prison and the governor doesn't have a pardon for that. Nobody does. Whatever happens to Jesus Menendez is on me. I know this. I live with it every day. My father was right. There is no client as scary as an innocent man. And no client as scarring.

Menendez wants to spit on me and take my money as punishment for what I did and didn't do. As far as I am concerned he is entitled. But no matter what my failings of judgment and ethical lapses were, I know that by the end, I bent things in order to do the right thing. I traded evil for innocence. Roulet is in because of me. Menendez is out because of me. Despite the efforts of his new attorneys — it has now taken the partnership of Dan Daly and Roger Mills to replace me — Roulet will not see freedom again. From what I have heard from Maggie McPherson, prosecutors have built an impenetrable case against him for the Renteria murder. They have also followed Raul Levin's steps and connected Roulet to another killing: the follow-home rape and stabbing of a woman who tended bar in a Hollywood club. The forensic profile of his knife was matched to the fatal wounds inflicted on this other woman. For Roulet, the science will be the iceberg spotted too late. His ship will founder and go down. The battle for him now lies in just staying alive. His lawyers are engaged in plea negotiations to keep him from a lethal injection. They are hinting at other murders and rapes that he would be willing to clear up in exchange for his life. Whatever the outcome, alive or dead, he is surely gone from this world and I take my salvation in that. It is what has mended me better than any surgeon.

Maggie McPherson and I are attempting to mend our wounds, too. She brings my daughter to visit me every weekend and often stays for the day. We sit on the deck and talk. We both know our daughter will be what saves us. I can no longer hold anger for being used as bait for a killer. I think Maggie no longer holds anger for the choices I have made.

The California bar looked at all of my actions and sent me on a vacation to Cuba. That's what defense pros call being suspended for conduct unbecoming an attorney. CUBA. I was shelved for ninety days. It was a bullshit finding. They could prove no specific ethical violations in regard to Corliss, so they hit me for borrowing a gun from my client Earl Briggs. I got lucky there. It was not a stolen or unregistered gun. It belonged to Earl's father, so my ethical infraction was minor.

I didn't bother contesting the bar reprimand or appealing the suspension. After taking a bullet in the gut, ninety days on the shelf didn't look so bad to me. I served the suspension during my recovery, mostly in a bathrobe while watching Court TV.

Neither the bar nor the police found ethical or criminal violation on my part in the killing of Mary Alice Windsor. She entered my home with a stolen weapon. She shot first and I shot last. From a block away Lankford and Sobel watched her take that first shot at my front door. Self-defense, cut and dried. But what has not been so clear-cut are the feelings I have for what I did. I wanted to avenge my friend Raul Levin, but I didn't want to see it done in blood. I am a killer now. Being state sanctioned only tempers slightly the feelings that come with that.

All investigations and official findings aside, I think now that in the whole matter of Menendez and Roulet I was guilty of conduct unbecoming myself. And the penalty for that is harsher than anything the state or the bar could ever throw at me. No matter. I will carry all of it with me as I go back to work. My work. I know my place in this world and on the first day of court next year I will pull the Lincoln out of the garage, get back on the road and go looking for the underdog. I don't know where I will go or what cases will be mine. I just know I will be healed and ready to stand once again in the world without truth.

ACKNOWLEDGMENTS

This novel was inspired by a chance meeting and conversation with attorney David Ogden many years ago at a Los Angeles Dodgers baseball game. For that, the author will always be grateful. Though the character and exploits of Mickey Haller are fictitious and wholly of the author's imagination, this story could not have been written without the tremendous help and guidance of attorneys Daniel F. Daly and Roger O. Mills, both of whom allowed me to watch them work and strategize cases and were tireless in their efforts to make sure the world of criminal defense law was depicted accurately in these pages. Any errors or exaggerations in the law or the practice of it are purely the fault of the author.

Superior Court Judge Judith Champagne and her staff in Department 124 in the Criminal Courts Building in downtown Los Angeles allowed the author complete access to her courtroom, chambers and holding cells and answered any question posed. To the judge, Joe, Marianne, and Michelle a great debt of thanks is owed.

Also of great help to the author and contribution to the story were Asya Muchnick, Michael Pietsch, Jane Wood, Terrill Lee Lankford, Jerry Hooten, David Lambkin, Lucas Foster, Carolyn Chriss, and Pamela Marshall.

Last but not least, the author wishes to thank Shannon Byrne, Mary Elizabeth Capps, Jane Davis, Joel Gotler, Philip Spitzer, Lukas Ortiz, and Linda Connelly for their help and support during the writing of this story.

ABOUT THE AUTHOR

Michael Connelly is the author of twenty-eight previous novels, including #1 *New York Times* bestsellers *The Crossing* and *The Burning Room*. His books, which include the Harry Bosch series and Lincoln Lawyer series, have sold more than sixty million copies worldwide. Connelly is a former newspaper reporter who has won numerous awards for his journalism and his novels and is the executive producer of *Bosch*, starring Titus Welliver. He spends his time in California and Florida.

New job. Same Bosch.

Don't miss THE WRONG SIDE OF GOODBYE.

Available November 2016.

Please turn the page for a preview.

*T*hey charged from the cover of the elephant grass toward the LZ, five of them swarming the slick on both sides, one among them yelling, "Go! Go! Go!"—as if each man needed to be prodded and reminded that these were the most dangerous seconds of their lives.

The rotor wash bent the grass back and blew the marker smoke in all directions. The noise was deafening as the turbine geared up for a heavy liftoff. The door gunners pulled everyone in by their pack straps and the chopper was quickly in the air again, having alighted no longer than a dragonfly on water.

The tree line could be seen through the portside door as the craft rose and started to bank. Then came the muzzle flashes from the banyan trees. Somebody yelled, "Snipers!"—as if the door gunner had to be told what he had out there.

It was an ambush. Three distinct flashpoints, three snipers. They had waited until the helicopter was up and flying fat, an easy target from six hundred feet.

The gunner opened up his M60, sending a barrage of fire into the treetops, shredding them. But the sniper rounds kept coming. The slick had no armor plating, a decision made nine thousand miles away to take speed and maneuverability over the burden of weight and protection.

One shot hit the turbine cowling, a *thock* sound reminding one of the helpless men on board of a fouled-off baseball hitting the hood of a car in the parking lot. Then came the snap of glass shattering as the next round tore through the cockpit. It was a million-to-one shot, hitting both the pilot and copilot at once. The pilot was killed instantly, and the copilot clamped his hands to his neck in an instinctive but helpless move to keep blood inside his body. The helicopter yawed into a clockwise spin and was soon hurtling out of control. It spun away from the trees and across the rice paddies. The men in the back started to yell helplessly. The man who had just had a memory of baseball tried to orient himself. The world outside the slick was spinning. He kept his eyes on a single word imprinted on the metal wall separating the cockpit from the cargo hold. It said ADVANCE. The letter A with a crossbar was an arrow pointed forward.

He kept his eyes on the word even as the screaming intensified and he could feel the craft losing altitude. Seven months backing recon and now on short time. He knew he wasn't going to make it back. This was the end.

The last thing he heard was someone yell "Brace! Brace! Brace!"— as if there was a possibility that anybody on board had a shot at surviving the impact, never mind the fire that would come after. While the others screamed in panic he whispered a name to himself.

"Vibiana..."

He knew he would never see her.

"Vibiana..."

The helicopter dove into one of the rice paddy dikes and exploded into a million metal parts. A moment later the spilled fuel caught fire and burned through the wreckage and spread flames across the surface of the paddy water. Black smoke rose into the air, marking the wreckage like an LZ marker.

The snipers reloaded and waited for the rescue choppers to come next.

ONE

B osch didn't mind the wait. The view was spectacular. He didn't
bother with the waiting room couch. Instead he stood with his
face a foot from the glass and took in the view that ranged
from rooftops of downtown to the Pacific Ocean. He was fifty-nine
floors up in the U.S. Bank Tower, and Creighton was making him
wait because it was something he always did going all the way back
to his days at Parker Center, where the waiting room only had a
low-angle view of the back side of City Hall. Creighton had moved
a mere five blocks west since his days with the Los Angeles Police
Department, but he certainly had risen far beyond that measure if
you were going upward to the lofty heights of the city's financial
gods.

Still, view or no view, Bosch didn't know why anyone would
keep offices in the tower. The tallest building west of the Mississippi,
it had been the target of two foiled terrorist plots previously. That
didn't count the ones unknown or still being planned. Bosch imagined there had to be a general uneasiness added to the daily pressures
of work for every soul who entered its glass doors each morning.
Relief might soon come in the form of the Wilshire Grand, a glass-
sheathed spire rising to the sky a few blocks away. When finished it
would take the distinction of tallest building west of the Mississippi
from the U.S. Bank Tower. It would probably take the target as well.

Bosch loved any opportunity to see his city from up high.

When he was a young detective he would often take extra shifts as a spotter in one of the department's airships just to take a ride above the city and be reminded of its seemingly infinite vastness.

He looked down at the 110 freeway and saw it was backed up all the way down through South-Central. He also noted the number of helipads on the tops of the buildings below him. The helicopter had become the commuter vessel of the elite. He had heard that even some of the higher-contract players on the Lakers took choppers to work at the Staples Center.

The glass was thick enough to cut off the penetration of any sound. The city below was silent. The only thing Bosch heard was the receptionist behind him answering the phone with same greeting over and over: "Trident Security, how can I help you?"

Bosch's eye held on a fast-moving patrol car going south on Figueroa toward L.A. Live. He saw the 01 painted large on the trunk and knew that the car was from Central Division. Soon it was followed in the air by an LAPD airship that moved at a lower altitude than the fifty-ninth floor. Bosch tracked it but was pulled away by a voice from behind.

"Mr. Bosch?"

He turned to see a woman standing in the middle of the waiting room. She wasn't the receptionist.

"I'm Gloria. We spoke on the phone," she said.

"Right, yes," Bosch said. "Mr. Creighton's assistant."

"Yes, nice to meet you. You can come back now."

"Good. Any longer and I was going to jump."

She didn't smile. She led Bosch through a door into a hallway with framed watercolors perfectly spaced on the walls.

"It's impact-resistant glass," she said. "It can take the force of a category 5 hurricane."

"Good to know," Bosch said. "And I was only joking. Your boss had a history of keeping people waiting—back when he was a deputy chief with the police department."

"Oh, really? I haven't noticed it here."

This made no sense to Bosch since she had just fetched him from the waiting room fifteen minutes after the appointed meeting time.

"He must've read it in a management book back when he was climbing the ranks," Bosch said. "You know, keep 'em waiting even if they're on time. Gives you the upper hand when you finally bring them into the room, lets them know you are a busy man."

"I'm not familiar with that business philosophy."

"Probably more of a cop philosophy."

They entered an office suite where there were two separate desk arrangements, one occupied by a man in his twenties wearing a suit and the other empty and most likely belonging to Gloria. They walked between the desks to a door. Gloria opened it and then stepped to the side.

"Go on in," she said. "Can I bring you a bottle of water?"

"No thanks," Bosch said. "I'm fine."

Bosch entered an even larger room with a desk area to the left and an informal seating area on the right with a couple of couches facing each other across a glass-topped coffee table. Creighton was sitting behind his desk—with Bosch it was going to be formal.

It had been more than a decade since Bosch had seen Creighton in person. He could not remember the occasion but assumed it was a squad meeting where Creighton came in and made an announcement concerning the overtime budget or the department's travel protocols. Back then Creighton was the head bean counter—in charge of budgeting for the department among his other management duties. He was known for instituting strict policies on overtime that required detailed explanations to be written on green cards that were subject to supervisor approval. Since that approval or disapproval usually came after the extra hours were already worked, the new system was viewed by the rank and file as an effort to dissuade cops from working overtime or, worse yet, get them to work overtime and then deny authorization or replace it with comp time. It was during this posting that Creighton became universally known as "Cretin" by the rank and file. Though Creighton left the department for the private sector not long after, the "greenies" were still in use.

"Harry, come in," Creighton said. "Sit down."

Bosch moved to the desk. Creighton was a few years older but in good shape. He stood behind the desk with his hand held forward. He wore a gray suit that was tailor-cut to his wiry frame. He looked good. He looked like money. Bosch shook his hand and then sat down in front of the desk. He hadn't gotten dressed up for the appointment. He was in blue jeans, a blue denim shirt, and a charcoal corduroy jacket he'd had for at least twelve years. These days Bosch's work suits from his days with the department were wrapped in plastic. He didn't want to pull one of them out just for a meeting with Cretin.

"Chief, how are you?" he said.

"It's not 'chief' anymore," Creighton said with a laugh. "Those days are long ago. Call me John."

"John then."

"Sorry to keep you waiting out there. I had a client on the phone and, well, the client always comes first. Am I right?"

"Sure, no problem. I enjoyed the view."

The view through the window behind Creighton was in the opposite direction, stretching northeasterly across the Civic Center and to the snow-capped mountains in San Bernardino. But Bosch guessed that the mountains weren't the reason Creighton picked this office. It was the Civic Center. From his desk Creighton looked down on the spire of City Hall, the Police Administration Building, and the Los Angeles Times. Creighton was above them all.

"It is truly spectacular seeing the world from this angle," Creighton said.

Bosch nodded and got down to business.

"So," he said. "What can I do for you...John?"

"Well, first of all, I appreciate you coming in without really knowing why I wished to see you. Gloria told me she had a difficult time convincing you to come in."

"Yeah, well, I'm sorry about that. But like I told her, if this is about a job I'm not interested. I've got a job."

"I've heard. San Fernando. But that's gotta be part time, right?"

He said it with a slightly mocking tone and Bosch remembered a line from a movie he once saw: "If you're not cop, you're little people." It also held that if you worked for a little department you were still little people.

"It keeps me as busy as I want to be," he said. "I also have a private ticket. I pick up stuff from time to time on that."

"All referrals, correct?" Creighton said.

Bosch looked at him a moment.

"Am I supposed to be impressed that you checked me out?" he finally said. "I'm not interested in working here. I don't care what the pay is, I don't care what the cases are."

"Well, let me just ask you something, Harry," Creighton said. "Do you know what we do here?"

For a moment Bosch looked over Creighton's shoulder and out at the mountains before answering.

"I know you are high-level security for those who can afford it," he said.

"Exactly," Creighton said.

He held up three fingers on his right hand in what Bosch assumed was supposed to be a trident.

"Trident Security," Creighton said. "Specializing in financial, technological, and personal security. I started the California branch ten years ago. We have bases here, New York, Boston, Chicago, Miami, London, and Frankfurt. We are about to open in Istanbul. We are a very large operation with thousands of clients and even more connections in the fields of our expertise."

"Good for you," Bosch said.

He had spent about ten minutes on his laptop reading up on Trident before coming in. The upscale security venture was founded in New York in 1996 by a shipping magnate named Dennis Laughton, who had been abducted and ransomed in the Philippines. Laughton first hired a former NYPD police commissioner to be his front man and had followed suit in every city where he opened a base, plucking a local chief or high-ranking commander from the local police department to make a media splash and secure the absolute musthave of local police cooperation. The word was that ten years ago

Laughton had tried to hire L.A.'s police chief but was turned down and then went to Creighton as a second choice.

"I told your assistant I wasn't interested in a job with Trident," Bosch said. "She said it wasn't about that. So why don't you tell me what it is about so we can both get on with our days."

"I can assure you, I am not offering you a job with Trident," Creighton said. "To be honest, we must have full cooperation and respect from the LAPD to do what we do and to handle the delicate matters that involve our clients and the police. If we were to bring you in as a Trident associate there could be a problem."

"You are talking about the LAPD lawsuit."

"Exactly."

For most of the last year Bosch had been in the middle of a protracted lawsuit against the department where he had worked for more than thirty years. He sued because he believed he had been illegally forced into retirement by the department. The case had drawn ill will from the department toward Bosch. It did not seem to matter that during his time with a badge that he had brought more than a hundred murderers to justice. The lawsuit was settled, but the ill will continued from some quarters of the department, mostly the quarter at the top.

"So if you brought me into Trident that would not be good for your relations with the LAPD," Bosch said. "I get that. But you want me for something. What is it?"

Creighton nodded. It was time to get down to it.

"Do you know the name Whitney Vance?" he asked.

Bosch nodded.

"Of course I do," he said.

"Yes, well, he is a client," Creighton said. "As is his company, Advance Engineering."

"Whitney Vance has got to be eighty years old."

"Eighty-five next month. And..."

Creighton opened the top middle drawer of his desk and removed a document. He put it on the desk between them. Bosch could see it was a printed check with an attached receipt. He wasn't wearing his glasses and was unable to read the amount or the other details.

"He wants to speak to you," Creighton finished.

"About what?" Bosch asked.

"I don't know. He said it was a private matter and he specifically asked for you by name. He said he would discuss the matter privately with you. He had this certified check drawn for ten thousand dollars. It is yours to keep for meeting him, whether the appointment leads to further work or not."

Bosch didn't know what to say. At the moment he was flush because of the lawsuit settlement, but he had put most of the money into long-term investment accounts designed to carry him comfortably into old age with a solid stake left over for his daughter. Meantime she still had three years of college and then graduate school tuition ahead of her, and he was on the hook for a good chunk of it. There was no doubt in his mind that 10K could be put to good use.

"When and where is this appointment going to be?" he finally said.

"Tomorrow morning at nine at Mr. Vance's home in Pasadena," Creighton said. "The address is on the check receipt. You might want to dress a little nicer than that."

Bosch ignored the sartorial jab. From an inside jacket pocket he took out his eyeglasses. He put them on as he reached across the desk and took the check. He studied it for a moment. It was made out to his full name, and Bosch wondered how Vance or Creighton knew about that.

There was a perforated line running across the bottom of the check. Below it was the address and appointment time as well as the admonition; "Don't bring a firearm." Bosch folded the check along the perforation line and looked at Creighton as he put it into his jacket.

"I'm going to go to the bank from here," he said. "I'll deposit this and if it clears I'll be there tomorrow."

Creighton smirked.

"That will not be a problem."

Bosch nodded.

"I guess that's it then," he said.

He stood up to go.

"There is one thing, Bosch," Creighton said.

Bosch noted that he had dropped from first name to last name status with Creighton inside of ten minutes.

"What's that?" he asked.

"I have no idea what the old man is going to ask you, but I'm very protective of him," Creighton said. "He is more than a client and I don't want to see him taken for a ride at this point in his life. Whatever the task is he wants you to perform, I want to be in the loop."

"A ride? Unless I missed something, you called me, Creighton. If anybody's being taken for a ride, it will be me. It doesn't matter how much he's paying me."

"I can assure you that's not the case. The only ride is the ride out to Pasadena for which you just received ten thousand dollars."

"Good. I'm going to hold you to that. I'm going to go see the 'old man' tomorrow and see what this is about. But if he becomes my client then that business, whatever it is, will be between him and me. There won't be any loop that includes you unless Vance tells me there is. That's how I work."

Bosch turned toward the door. When he got there he looked back at Creighton.

"Thanks for the view."

He left and closed the door behind him. On the way out he stopped at the receptionist's desk and got his parking receipt validated. He wanted to be sure Creighton ate the thirty bucks for that.

TWO

T he Vance estate was on San Rafael near the Annandale Country Club. It was a neighborhood of old money, homes and
estates that had been passed down generations like money in
the bank and guarded just like it behind stone walls and black iron
fences. It was a far cry from the Hollywood Hills, where the new
money went and the rich left their trash cans out on the street all
week. There were no for sale signs here. You had to know somebody, maybe even share their blood, to buy in here.

Bosch parked against the curb about a hundred yards from the
gate that guarded entrance to the Vance estate. There were spikes
ornately disguised as flowers atop it. For a few moments he studied
the curve of the driveway beyond the gate as it wound and rose into
the cleft of two rolling green hills and then disappeared. There was
no sign of any structure, not even a garage. All of that would be
well back from the street, buffered by geography, iron, and money.
But Bosch knew that Whitney Vance, eighty-four years old, was up
there somewhere beyond those money-colored hills waiting for him.

He was twenty minutes early for the appointment and decided
to use the time to review several stories he had found on the Internet
and printed out that morning. They were all about the man who the
day before had paid Bosch ten thousand dollars to pay him a visit.

The general contours of Whitney Vance's life were known to
Bosch, as they were most likely known to most Californians. But he

still found the details fascinating and even admirable in that Vance
was the rare recipient of a rich inheritance who had turned his silver
spoon into gold. He was the fourth-generation Pasadena scion of a
mining family that extended all the way back to the California gold
rush. Gold was what drew Vance's great-grandfather west but not
what the family fortune was founded on. Frustrated by the hunt for
gold, the great-grandfather established the state's first strip mining
operation, extracting millions of tons of iron ore out of the earth
in San Bernardino County. Vance's grandfather then followed that
with a second strip mine further south in Imperial County, and his
father parlayed that success into a steel mill and fabrication plant
that helped support the dawning aviation industry. At the time the
face of that industry belonged to Howard Hughes, and he counted
Nelson Vance as first a contractor and then a partner in many different aviation endeavors. Hughes would become godfather to Nelson Vance's only child.

Whitney Vance was born in 1931 and as a young man apparently set out to blaze a unique path for himself. He initially went off
to the University of Southern California to study filmmaking but
eventually dropped out and came back to the family fold, transferring to California Institute of Technology in Pasadena, the school
"Uncle Howard" had attended. It was Hughes who urged young
Whitney to study aeronautical engineering at Caltech.

As with the elders of his family, when it was his turn Vance
pushed the family business in new and ever increasingly successful
directions, always with a continuing thread to the family's original product: steel. He won numerous government contracts for
the manufacture of aircraft parts and mechanisms and founded
Advance Engineering, which held the patents on many of them.
Couplings that were used for the safe fueling of aircraft were per-
fected in the family steel mill and are still used today at every airport in the world. Ferrite extracted from the iron ore culled from
Vance mining operations was used in the earliest efforts to build
aircraft that avoided radar detection. These processes were meticulously patented and protected by Vance and guaranteed his com-

pany participation in in the decades-long development of stealth technologies. Vance and his company were part of the so-called military-industrial complex, and the Vietnam War saw their value grow exponentially. Every mission in or out of that country over the entire length of the war involved equipment that came from Advance Engineering. Bosch remembered seeing the company logo—an arrow through the middle of the A—imprinted on the steel walls of every helicopter he had ever flown on in Vietnam.

Bosch was startled by a sharp rap on the window beside him. He looked up to see a uniformed Pasadena patrol officer. He checked the rearview and saw the black and white parked behind him. He realized he had become so engrossed in his reading that he had not even heard the cop car come up on him.

He had to turn on the Cherokee's engine to lower the window. He knew what this was about. A twenty-year-old vehicle in need of paint parked outside the estate of a family that helped build the state of California constituted a suspicious activity. It didn't matter that Bosch was white, his hair was combed, and he was wearing a crisp suit and tie rescued from a plastic storage bag. It had taken less than fifteen minutes for the police to respond to his intrusion into the neighborhood.

"I know how this looks, officer," he began. "But I have an appointment across the street in about five minutes and I was just—"

"That's wonderful," the cop said. "Do you mind stepping out of the car?"

Bosch looked at him for a moment. He saw the nameplate above his breast pocket said Cooper.

"You're kidding, right?" he asked.

"No, sir, I'm not," Cooper said. "Please step out of the car."

Bosch took a deep breath, opened the door, and did as he was told. He raised his hands to shoulder height and said, "I'm a police officer."

Cooper immediately tensed as Bosch knew he would.

"I'm unarmed," Bosch said quickly. "My weapon's in the glove box."

At that moment he was thankful for the edit typed on the check stub telling him to come to the Vance appointment unarmed.

"Let me some ID," Cooper demanded.

Bosch carefully reached into an inside pocket in his suit coat and pulled his badge case. Cooper studied the detective's badge and then the ID.

"This says you're a reserve officer," he said.

"Yep," Bosch said. "Part timer."

"About fifteen miles off your reservation, aren't you? What are you doing here, Detective Bosch?"

He handed the badge case back and Bosch put it away.

"Well, I was trying to tell you," he said. "I have an appointment—which you are going to make me late for—with Mr. Vance, who I'm guessing you know lives right over there."

Bosch pointed toward the black gate.

"Is this appointment police business?" Cooper asked.

"It's actually none of your business," Bosch replied.

They held each other's cold stare for a long moment, neither man blinking. Finally Bosch spoke.

"Mr. Vance is waiting for me," he said. "Guy like that, he'll probably ask why I'm late, and he'll probably do something about it. You got a first name, Cooper?"

Cooper blinked.

"Yeah, it's fuck you," he said. "Have a nice day."

He turned and started back toward the patrol car.

"Thank you, officer," Bosch called after him.

Bosch got back into his car and immediately turned the ignition, then pulled away from the curb. If the old car still had the juice to leave rubber, he would have done so. But the most he could show Cooper, who remained parked at the curb, was a plume of blue smoke from the exhaust pipe.

He pulled into the entrance channel at the gate to the Vance estate and up to a camera and communication box. Almost immediately he was greeted by a voice.

"Yes?"

It was male, young and tiredly arrogant. Bosch leaned out the window even though he knew he probably didn't have to. He spoke loudly even though he didn't have to.

"Harry Bosch to see Mr. Vance. I have an appointment."

After a moment the gate in front of him started to automatically roll open.

"Follow the driveway to the parking apron by the security post," the voice said. "I will meet you there at the metal detector. Leave all weapons and recording devices in the glove compartment of your vehicle."

"Done," Bosch said.

"Drive up," the voice said.

The gate was all the way open now and Bosch drove through. He followed the cobblestone driveway through a finely manicured set of rolling emerald hills until he came to a second fence line and a guard shack. The double-fencing security measures at the estate were similar to those employed at most prisons Bosch had visited—of course, with the opposite intention of keeping people out instead of in.

The second gate rolled open and a uniformed guard stepped out of a booth to signal Bosch through and to the parking apron. As he passed Bosch waved a hand and noticed the Trident Security patch on the shoulder of the guard's navy blue uniform.

After parking Bosch was instructed to place his keys, phone, watch, and belt in a plastic tub and then walk through an air-port-style metal detector while two more Trident men watched. They returned everything but the phone, which they explained would be placed in the glove box of his car.

"Anybody else get the irony here?" he asked as he put his belt back on. "You know, the family made their money on metal—now you have to go through a metal detector to get inside the house."

Neither of the guards said anything.

"Okay, I guess it's just me then," Bosch said.

Once he buckled his belt he was passed off to the next level of security, a man in a suit with the requisite earbud and wrist mike and the dead-eyed stare to go with it. He did not say his name. He escorted Bosch wordlessly through the delivery entrance of a massive gray stone mansion that Bosch guessed would rival anything the du Ponts or Vanderbilts had to offer. According to Wikipedia, he was calling on six billion dollars. There was no doubt in Bosch as he entered that this would be the closest to American royalty he would ever get.

He was led to a room paneled in dark wood with dozens of framed eight-by-ten photographs hung in four rows across one wall. There were a couple of couches and a bar at the end of the room. The escort in the suit pointed Bosch to one of the couches.

"Sir, have a seat and Mr. Vance's secretary will come for you when he is ready to see you."

Bosch took a seat on the couch facing the wall of photos.

"Would you like some water?" the suit asked.

"No, I'm fine," Bosch said.

The suit took a position next to the door they had entered through and clasped one wrist with the other hand in a posture that said he was alert and ready for anything.

Bosch used the waiting time to study the photographs. They offered a record of Whitney Vance's life and the people he had met over the course of it. The first photo depicted Howard Hughes and a young teenager he assumed was Vance. They were leaning against the unpainted metal skin of a plane. From there the photos appeared to run left to right in chronological order. They depicted Vance with numerous well-known figures of industry and politics and the media. Bosch couldn't put a name to every person Vance posed with, but from Lyndon Johnson to Larry King he knew who most of them were. In all the photos Vance displayed the same half smile, the corner of his mouth on the left side curled up, as if to communicate to the camera lens that it wasn't his idea to pose for a picture. The face grew older picture to picture, the eyelids more hooded, but the smile was always the same.

In the photo with Larry King, Vance and King were seated across from each other on the TV set where King had conducted interviews on CNN for more than two decades. Bosch could see that there was a book standing up on the counter between them.

He got up and went to the wall to look more closely at the book in the photo. He took a pair of glasses out of his jacket pocket, put them on and leaned in close to read the book's title.

STEALTH: The Making of the Disappearing Plane
By Whitney P. Vance

The title jogged loose a memory and Bosch recalled something about Whitney Vance writing a family history that the critics trashed more for what was left out than left in. His father, Nelson Vance, had been a brutal businessman and controversial political figure in his day. He was said but never proven to be a member of a cabal of wealthy industrialists who were supporters of eugenics— the so-called science of improving the human race through controlled breeding that would eliminate undesirable attributes. After the Nazis employed a similar but perverted doctrine to carry out genocide in World War II, eugenics fell into disfavor and people like Nelson Vance hid their beliefs and affiliations.

His son's book amounted to little more than a vanity project full of hero worship and little mention of the negatives. Whitney Vance had become such a recluse in his later life that the book was merely just a reason to bring him out into public light and ask him about the things left out. Once he had him on live TV, King probably asked Vance little about what was in the book.

"Mr. Bosch?"

Bosch turned from the photo to a woman standing by the entrance to a hallway on the other side of the room. She looked like she was at least seventy years old, and Bosch guessed she was a valued, long-time employee.

"I'm Mr. Vance's secretary, Ida," she said. "He will see you now."

Bosch stood up and followed her into the hallway. They walked for a distance that seemed like a city block before going up a short set of stairs to another hallway, this one traversing a wing of the mansion built on a higher slope of the hill. Finally they arrived at a set of double doors and Ida ushered Bosch into Whitney Vance's home office.

The man Bosch had come to see was sitting behind a desk, his back to an empty fireplace big enough to take shelter in during a tornado. He motioned for Bosch to come forward with a thin hand so white it looked like he was wearing a latex glove.

Bosch stepped up to the desk and Vance pointed to the lone leather chair in front of it. He made no offer to shake Bosch's hand. As he sat, Bosch noticed that Vance was in a wheelchair with electric controls extending from the left armrest. He saw the desk was clear except for a single white piece of paper that was either blank or had its contents facedown on the polished dark wood.

"Mr. Vance," Bosch said. "How are you?"

"I'm old—that's how I am," Vance said. "I have fought like hell to defeat time, but some things can't be beat. It is hard for a man in my position to accept, but I am resigned, Mr. Bosch."

He gestured with that bony, white hand again, taking all of the room in with a sweep.

"All of this will soon be meaningless," he said.

He offered the smile Bosch had seen on the photos in the waiting room, the upward curve on only one side. He believed it might have been caused by nerve damage. Vance couldn't complete a smile. According to the photos Bosch had seen, he never could.

Bosch didn't quite know how to respond to the old man's words. Instead, he pressed on with words he had thought about repeatedly since meeting with Creighton.

"Well, Mr. Vance, I was told you wanted to see me and you have paid me quite of bit of money to be here. It may not be a lot to you but it is to me. What can I do for you, sir?"

Vance cut the smile and nodded.

"A man who gets right to the point," he said. "I like that. I read about you in the newspaper. Last year, I believe. The case with that doctor in Beverly Hills and the shootout. You seemed to me like a man who stands his ground, Mr. Bosch. They put a lot of pressure on you but you stood up to it. I like that. I need that. There's not a lot of that around anymore."

"What do you want me to do?" Bosch asked again.

"I want you to find someone for me," Vance said. "Someone who might not have ever existed."

THREE

A fter intriguing Bosch with his request Vance flipped over the piece of paper on his desk and told Bosch he would have to sign it before they discussed anything further.

"It is a nondisclosure form," he explained. "My lawyer said it is ironclad. Your signature guarantees that you will not reveal the contents of our discussion or your subsequent investigation to anyone but me. Not even an employee of mine, not even someone who says they have come to you on my behalf. Only me, Mr. Bosch. If you sign this document you answer only to me. You report any findings of your investigation only to me. Do you understand?"

"Yes, I understand," Bosch said. "I have no problem signing it."

"Very good then. I have a pen here."

Vance pushed the document across the desk, then opened a drawer and withdrew a pen. It was a fountain pen that felt heavy in Bosch's hand because it was thick and made of what he presumed was real gold. He signed the document without reading it, put the pen down on top of it and pushed both across the desk back to Vance. He put the document in the desk drawer and closed it. He held the pen up for Bosch to study.

"This pen was made with gold my great-great-grandfather prospected in the Sierra Nevada goldfields in eighteen fifty-two," he said. "That was before the competition up there forced him to head south. Before he realized that there was more to be made from iron than gold."

He looked at the pen himself, turning it in his hand.

"It was passed on generation to generation," he said. "I've had it all of my life."

Vance studied the pen as if seeing it for the first time. Bosch said nothing. He wondered if Vance suffered from any sort of diminished mental capacity. He seemed to be wandering. Bosch wondered if the old man's desire to have him find somebody who may never have existed was some sort of figment of a failing mind.

"Mr. Vance?" he asked.

Vance put the pen into the desk drawer and looked at Bosch.

"I have no one to give it to," he said. "No one to give any of this to."

It was true. The biographical data Bosch had looked up said Vance was never married and childless. Several of the summaries he had read suggested obliquely that he was homosexual, but there was never any confirmation of this. Other biographical extracts suggested that he was simply too driven by his work to keep a steady relationship, let alone establish a family. There were a few brief romances reported, primarily with Hollywood starlets of the moment—a date for the cameras that put off speculation. But nothing in more than forty years that Bosch could find.

"Do you have children, Mr. Bosch?" Vance asked.

"A daughter," Bosch answered.

"Where?"

"In school. Chapman University down in Orange County."

"Good school. Is she a film student?"

"Psychology."

Vance leaned back in his chair and looked off at the past.

"I wanted to study film when I was a young man," he said. "The dreams of youth..."

He didn't finish his thought. Bosch realized he would have to give the money back. This was all some kind of derangement and there was no problem and no job and he could not take the money from this man even if it was only an infinitesimal drop in his money bucket. Bosch didn't take money from damaged people, no matter how rich they were.

Vance broke away from his stare into the abyss of memory and looked at Bosch. He nodded, seeming to know Harry's thoughts. He gripped the armrests of his chair and leaned forward.

"I guess I need to tell you what this is about," he said.

Bosch nodded.

"That would be good, yes."

Vance nodded back and for a moment offered the half smile again. He looked down for a moment and then back up at Bosch, his eyes deeply set and shiny behind rimless glasses.

"A long time ago I made a mistake," he said. "I never corrected it, I never looked back. I now want to find out if I had a child. A child I could give my gold pen to."

Bosch stared at him for a long moment, hoping he might continue. But when he did he seemed to have picked up another string of memory.

"When I was eighteen years old I wanted nothing to do with my father's business," Vance said. "I was more interested in being the next Orson Welles. I wanted to make films, not airplane parts. I was full of myself, as young men often are at that age."

Bosch thought of himself at that age. His desire to blaze his own path had led him into the tunnels of Vietnam.

"I insisted on film school," Vance said. "I enrolled at USC in nineteen forty-nine."

Bosch nodded. He knew from his prior reading that Vance would only spend a year at USC before changing paths and transferring to Caltech and furthering the family dynasty. There had been no explanation found in his Internet search. Bosch now believed he was going to find out why.

"I met a girl," Vance said. "A Mexican girl. And soon after she became pregnant. It was the second worst thing that ever happened to me. The first was telling my father."

Vance grew quiet, his eyes down on the desk in front of him. It wasn't difficult to fill in the blanks, but Bosch needed to hear as much of the story from Vance as he could.

"What happened?" he asked.

"He sent people," Vance said. "People to convince her not to have the child. People who would take her to Mexico to take care of it."

"Did she go?"

"If she did, it was not with my father's people. She disappeared from my life and I never saw her again. And I was too much of a coward to go find her. I had given my father all he needed to control me. The potential embarrassment and disgrace. I transferred to Caltech, and that was the end of it."

Vance nodded, as though confirming something for himself.

"It was a different time then ... for me and for her."

Vance looked up now and held Bosch's eyes for a long moment before continuing.

"But now I want to know. It's when you reach the end of things that you want to go back ... Can you help me, Mr. Bosch?"

Bosch nodded. He believed the pain in Vance's eyes was real.

"I can try," Bosch said. "Do you mind if I ask a few questions and take some notes?"

"Take your notes," Vance said. "But I warn you again that everything about this must remain completely confidential. Lives could be in danger. Every move you make, you must look over your shoulder. I have no doubt that efforts will be made to find out why I wanted to see you and what you are doing for me. I have a cover story for that, which we can get to later. For now, ask your questions."

Bosch pulled a small notebook from the inside pocket of his suit coat. He pulled out a pen. It was made of plastic, not gold. He'd bought it at a drugstore.

"You just said lives could be in danger. Whose lives? Why?"

"Don't be naïve, Mr. Bosch. I am sure you conducted a modicum of research before coming to see me. I have no heirs—at least, known heirs. When I die, control of Advance Engineering will go to a board of directors who will continue to line their pockets with millions while fulfilling government contracts. A valid heir could change all of that. Billions could be at stake. You don't think people and entities would kill for that?"

Bosch nodded. "It's been my experience that people will kill for any reason and no reason at all," he said. "If I find you have heirs, are you sure you want to possibly make them targets?"

"I would give them the choice," Vance said. "I believe I owe that. And I would protect them as well as is possible."

"What was her name? The girl you got pregnant."

"Vibiana Abas. You spell it A-B-A-S."

Bosch wrote it down on his pad.

"You know her birthdate by any chance?"

"I can't remember it."

"She was a student at USC?"

"No, I met her at the EVK. She worked there."

"EVK?"

"The student cafeteria was called Everybody's Kitchen. EVK, for short."

Bosch immediately knew this eliminated the prospect of tracing Vibiana Abas through student records, which were usually very helpful since most schools kept close track of alumni. It meant the search for the woman would most likely be more difficult and more of a long shot.

"You said she was Mexican," he said. "Was she a U.S. citizen?"

"I don't know. I don't think she was. My father—"

He didn't finish.

"Your father what?" Bosch asked.

"I don't know if it was the truth but my father said that that was her plan," Vance said. "To get pregnant so I would have to marry her and she would become a citizen. But my father said a lot of things to me that weren't true, and he believed a lot of things that were...out of step. So I don't know."

Bosch thought about what he had read about Nelson Vance and eugenics. He pressed on.

"By any chance, do you have a photograph of Vibiana?" he asked.

"No," Vance said. "You don't know how many times I've wished for a photograph. That I could just look at her one more time."

"Where did she live?"

"By the school. Just a few blocks away. She walked to work."

"Do you remember the address? The street maybe?"

"No, I don't remember. It was so long ago and I spent so many years trying to block it out. But the truth is I never really loved anybody again after that."

It was the first time Vance mentioned love or gave an indication of how deep the relationship had been. It had been Bosch's experience that when you looked back at a life you used a magnifying glass. Everything was bigger, amplified. A college tryst could become the love of a lifetime in memory. Still, Vance's pain seemed real so many decades after the events he was describing.

"How long were you together with her before all of this happened?" he asked.

"Eight months between the first and last times I ever saw her," Vance said. "Eight months."

"Do you remember when she told you she was pregnant? I mean, what month or time of year?"

"It was at the end of the school year. May. I had started in September the year before. I noticed her right away working at the EVK. I didn't get the courage to talk to her for a couple months."

The old man looked down at the desk, to see a memory from that time.

"What else do you remember?" Bosch prompted. "Did you ever meet her family? Do you remember any names?"

"No, I didn't," Vance said. "She told me her father was very strict and they were Catholic and I was not. You know, like Romeo and Juliet."

"You know what church she went to?"

Vance looked up, his eyes sharp.

"She told me she was named after the church the family attended, where she was baptized. St. Vibiana."

Bosch nodded. The original St. Vibiana's was downtown, just a block from the LAPD headquarters where he used to work. More than a hundred years old, it was badly damaged in the 1994 earthquake. A new church was built nearby and the old structure was donated to the city and preserved. Bosch wasn't sure but he believed it was an event hall and library now. But the connection to Vibiana Abas was a good one. Catholic churches kept records of births and baptisms. He felt this bit of good information countered the bad news that Vibiana had not been a USC student. It also was a strong indication that she might have been a U.S. citizen, whether her parents were or not.

"If the pregnancy was carried to full term, when would the child have been born?" he asked.

It was a delicate question but Bosch needed to narrow the timing down if he was going to wade into records.

"She told me in May," Vance said. "I would say December would be the birth. Maybe January."

Bosch wrote it down.

"How old was she when you knew her?" he asked.

"She was sixteen when we met," Vance said. "I was eighteen."

It was another reason for the reaction of Vance's father. Vibiana was underage. Getting a sixteen-year-old pregnant in 1950 could have gotten Whitney into minor but embarrassing legal trouble.

"Was she in high school?" Bosch asked.

He knew the area around USC. The high school would have been Manual Arts—another shot at traceable records.

"She had dropped out to work," Vance said. "The family needed the money."

"Did she ever say what her father did for a living?" Bosch asked.

"I don't recall."

"Okay, going back to her birthday, you don't remember the date but do you remember ever celebrating it with her during those seven months?"

Vance thought a moment and then shook his head.

"No, I can't remember a birthday occurring," he said.

"And if I have this right, you were together from October to May, so her birthday would have likely been somewhere in June to September. Roughly."

Vance nodded. Narrowing it to five months might help at

some point when Bosch was going through records. Attaching a birth date to the name Vibiana Abas would be a key starting point. He wrote the spread of months down and then looked up at Vance.

"Do you think your father paid her or her family off?" he asked. "So they would keep quiet and just go away?"

"If he did he never told me that," Vance said. "I was the one who went away. An act of cowardice I have always regretted."

"Have you ever looked for her before now? Ever paid anybody else to?"

"No, sadly, I have not. I can't say if anyone else has."

"Meaning what?"

"Meaning that is quite possible such a search was conducted as a preemptive move in preparation for my death."

Bosch nodded and thought about that for a long moment. He then looked down at the few notes he had written down. He felt he had enough to start.

"You said you had a cover story for me?"

"Yes, James Louis Aldridge."

"Who is he?"

"My first roommate. He was dismissed from school in the first semester."

"For academics?"

"No, for something else. Your cover is that I asked you to find my college roommate because I want to make amends for something we both did but he took the blame for. This way, if you are looking at records from that time it will seem plausible."

Bosch nodded.

"It might work. Is it a true story?"

"It is."

"I should probably know what it is you both did."

"You don't need to know that to find him."

Bosch waited a moment but that was all that Vance had to say on the subject. Harry wrote the name down after checking the spelling of Louis with Vance and then closed his notebook.

"Last question—for now. The odds are Vibiana Abas is dead by now. But what if she had the child and I find living heirs, what do you want me to do? Do I make contact?"

"No, absolutely not. You make no contact until you report to me. I'll need thorough confirmation before any approach will be made."

"DNA confirmation?"

Vance nodded and studied Bosch for a long moment before once more going to the desk drawer. He removed a padded white envelope with nothing written on it. He slid it across the desk to Bosch.

"I am trusting you, Mr. Bosch. I have now given you all you need to trick an old man if you want. I trust you won't."

Bosch picked up the envelope. It wasn't sealed. He looked into it and saw a clear glass test tube containing a swab used to collect saliva. It was Vance's DNA sample.

"This is where you could be tricking me, Mr. Vance."

"How so?"

"It would have been better if I had swabbed you, collected this myself."

"You have my word."

"And you have mine."

Vance nodded and there did not seem to be anything else to say.

"I think I have what I need to start."

"Then I have a final question for you, Mr. Bosch."

"Go ahead."

"I'm curious because it wasn't mentioned in the newspaper stories I read about you. But you appear to be the right age. What was your status during the Vietnam War?"

Bosch paused a moment before answering.

"I was over there," he finally said. "Two tours. I probably flew more times on the helicopters you helped build than you ever did."

Vance nodded. "Probably so," he said.

Bosch stood up. "How do I reach you if I have more questions or want to report what I find out?"

"Of course." Vance opened his desk drawer a final time and

removed a business card. He handed it to Bosch with a shaking hand. There was a phone number printed on it, nothing else.

"Call that number and you will get to me. If it's not me then something is wrong. Don't trust who you speak to."

Bosch looked from the number on the card to Vance, sitting in his wheelchair, his papier-mâché skin and wispy hair looking as frail as dried leaves. He wondered if his caution was paranoia or there was a real danger to the information he would be seeking.

"I'll get back to you soon," he said.

"We have not discussed payment for your services," Vance said.

"You've paid me enough already."

"That was only to get you to come here."

"It's more than enough, Mr. Vance. All right if I find my way out? Or will that set off a security breach?"

"As soon as you leave this room they'll know it and come to meet you."

Vance registered Bosch's puzzled look.

"It is only room in the house not under camera," he explained. "There are cameras even in my bedroom to watch over me. But I insisted on privacy here. As soon as you leave, they will come."

Bosch nodded.

"I understand," he said. "Talk to you soon."

He stepped through the door and started down the hallway. Soon enough Bosch was met by the nameless man in the suit and escorted wordlessly through the house and out to his car.

FOUR

Working cold cases had made Bosch proficient in time travel. He knew how to go back into the past to find people. Going back to 1951 would be the farthest and likely the most difficult trek he had ever made, but he believed he was up to it, and that made him excited about the challenge.

The starting point was finding the birthdate of Vibiana Abas, and he believed he knew the best way to accomplish that. Rather than go home after his meeting with Vance, Bosch took the 210 freeway across the northern rim of the Valley and headed toward the city of San Fernando.

Barely bigger than two square miles in size, San Fernando was an island city within the megalopolis of Los Angeles. A hundred years earlier all of the small towns and cities that comprised the San Fernando Valley were annexed into Los Angeles because of one reason. The newly built Los Angeles Aqueduct offered bountiful supplies of water that would keep their rich agricultural fields from drying up and blowing away. One by one they annexed and Los Angeles grew and spread north, eventually taking in the entire sprawl of the San Fernando Valley. All except for the 2.3 square miles of the Valley's namesake, the city of San Fernando. The little town didn't need L.A.'s water. Its ground supplies were more than adequate. It avoided the overture of the big city that now surrounded it and stayed independent.

A hundred years later it remained so. The Valley's agriculture pedigree may have long given way to urban sprawl and urban blight, but the city of San Fernando remained a quaint throwback to small-town sensibilities. Of course, urban issues and crime were unavoidable but nothing the tiny town's tiny police department couldn't routinely take care of.

That is, until the financial crash of 2008. When the banking crisis occurred and economies constricted and spiraled downward around the world, it was only a few years before the tidal wave of financial pain hit tiny San Fernando. Deep budget cuts occurred and then occurred again. Police Chief Anthony Valdez saw his department shrink from thirty-nine sworn officers, including himself, in 2010 to thirty officers by 2016. He saw his detective squad of five investigators shrink to just two—one detective to handle property crimes and one to handle crimes against persons. Valdez saw cases start to pile up unsolved, some not even investigated fully and properly.

Valdez was born and raised in San Fernando but was seasoned as a cop with the LAPD, putting in twenty years and rising to the rank of captain before taking his pension and checking out before landing the top spot at his hometown's department. His connections to the bigger department that surrounded his own ran deep and his solution to the budgetary crisis was to expand SFPD's reserve program and bring in more officers who worked part time hours but who worked for free.

And it was this expansion that led Chief Valdez to Harry Bosch. One of his early assignments when he was with the LAPD had been in a gang suppression unit in the Hollywood Division, where he ran afoul of a lieutenant named Pounds, who filed an internal complaint and unsuccessfully attempted to have Valdez demoted or even fired.

Valdez avoided both and just a few months later he heard about a detective named Bosch who got into an altercation with Pounds himself and ended up throwing him through a plate glass window at Hollywood Station. Valdez always remembered that name, and years later when he read about a now-retired Harry Bosch suing the LAPD for forcing him out of his job on the cold case squad, he picked up the phone.

Valdez couldn't offer Bosch a paycheck, but he could offer him a detective's badge and access to the cell in the old city jail where the files from all the open and unsolved cases were stored. The SFPD's reserve unit had only three requirements: its officers had to maintain their state training standards as law enforcement officers, had to qualify once a month at the department's indoor shooting range, and had to work at least two shifts a month.

It was a no-brainer for Bosch. The LAPD didn't want or need him anymore but the little town up in the Valley certainly did. And there was work to be done and victims waiting for justice. Bosch took the job the moment it was offered. He knew it was the way. It would allow him to continue his life's mission, and there was no paycheck needed for that.

The reserve officer minimums were easily met and surpassed by Bosch. It was rare that he didn't put in at least two shifts a week, let alone a month, in the detective bureau. He was there so often that he was permanently assigned one of the cubicles in the detective bureau that had been left open when the squad was trimmed in the budget crunch.

Most days he was working in the cubicle or across First Street from the police station where the cells of the old city jail were repurposed as storage rooms. The former drunk tank now housed three rows of standing shelves stocked with open case files going back decades.

Because of the statute of limitations on all crimes but murder, the wide majority of these cases would never be solved or even examined by Bosch. There weren't a lot of murders because the city was small, but Bosch was meticulously going through them looking for ways of applying new technologies to old evidence. He also took on a review of all sexual assaults, nonfatal shootings, and GBI cases within the statute of limitations for those crimes.

The job came with no pay but it had a lot of freedom to it. Bosch

could set his own hours and could always take time away from it if
a paying job came up for him in private investigation. Chief Valdez
knew he was asking a lot to have a detective with Bosch's experience
working for him for nothing. He never wanted to impinge on Bosch
ability to take on a paying job. He just stressed to Bosch that the two
could never mix. Harry couldn't use his badge and access as a San
Fernando cop to facilitate or further any private investigation.

Murder knows no bounds or city limits. Most of the cases
Bosch reviewed and pursued took him into LAPD turf. It was
only expected. Two of the big city's police divisions bordered San
Fernando, Mission Division on one half and Foothill Division on
the other. In four months Bosch had cleared two unsolved gang
murders, connecting them through ballistics to murders in L.A.
in which the perpetrators were already in prison, and he had connected a third to a pair of suspects already being sought for murder
by the larger department.

Additionally, Bosch had used MO and then DNA to connect
four sexual assault cases in San Fernando over a five-year period
and was in the process of trying to determine if the attacker was
responsible for rapes in Los Angeles as well.

Driving the 210 away from Pasadena allowed Bosch to check for
a tail. Midday traffic was light and by alternately driving five miles
below the speed limit and then taking it up to fifteen above it, he
could check the mirrors for vehicles following the same pattern. He
wasn't sure how to take Whitney Vance's concerns about the secrecy
of Bosch's investigation, but it didn't hurt to be alert to a tail. He
didn't see anything on the road behind him. Of course, he knew
that his car could have been tagged with a GPS tracker while he
was in the mansion with Vance. He would need to check for that
later.

In fifteen minutes he had crossed the top of the Valley and was
back in L.A. He took the Maclay Street exit and dropped down
into San Fernando, where he turned on to First Street. The SFPD
was located in a single-story building with white stucco walls and a
red barrel tile roof. The population of the tiny town was 90 percent

Latino, and its municipal structures were all designed with a nod to Mexican culture.

Bosch parked in the employee lot and used an electronic key to enter the station through the side door. He nodded to a couple of uniformed cops through the window of the report room and followed the back hallway past the chief's office to the detective bureau.

By LAPD or any standards, the bureau was quite small. It had once consisted of two rooms, but one room had been subleased to the county coroner's office as a satellite office for two of its investigators. Now there were three detective cubicles crammed into one room with a closet-size supervisor's office adjoining.

Bosch's cubicle had five-foot walls that allowed him privacy from three sides. But the fourth side was open to the door of the supervisor's office. The supervisor was a lieutenant named Trevino, who had so far not been convinced that having Bosch on premises was a good thing. He seemed suspicious of Bosch's motives for working so many hours for no pay and kept a careful watch over him. The only thing that alleviated this unwanted attention for Bosch was that Trevino wore two hats in the department, as is often the case with supervisors in small agencies. He ran the detective bureau and was also in charge of interior operations in the station, including the dispatch center, the firing range, and the sixteen-bed jail built to replace the aging facility across the street.

Bosch checked his mail slot upon entering and found a reminder notice that he was overdue qualifying this month on the range. He moved into his cubicle and sat down at his desk.

He checked his back and saw that Trevino's door was closed. This meant that the lieutenant was most likely in another part of the building carrying out one of his other duties. Bosch had settled on an understanding about Trevino's suspicion and lack of welcome to Bosch. He knew that any success Bosch might have in clearing cases could be seen as a failing on Trevino's part. After all, the detective bureau was his domain. Bosch believed that Trevino's fear of Bosch's success might have set the tone of a relationship. And it wasn't helped any when word got around that Bosch had once thrown a detective lieutenant through a plate glass window.

Still, there was nothing Trevino could do about Bosch's placement in the office because he was a Valdez guy and part of the police chief's effort to overcome personnel cuts.

Bosch turned on his computer terminal and waited for it to boot. It had been four days since he was last in the office. He saw that a flyer for a department bowling night had been left on his desk and he immediately transferred this to the recycle bin beneath it. He liked the people he worked with in the new department, but he wasn't much of a bowler.

He sat up straight to look over the partitions and saw that both of the other cubicles were empty. Lourdes, the CAPs investigator, and Sisto, who handled property crimes, were probably out in the field following up on weekend reports.

Once he was logged into the department's computer system, Bosch opened up the law enforcement databases. He got out his notebook and began the search for Vibiana Abas, knowing he was breaking the one rule the police chief had given him; using his SFPD access to supplement a private investigation. It was not only a firing offense at SFPD but also a crime in California to access a law enforcement database for information not pertaining to a police investigation. If Trevino ever decided to audit Bosch's use of the computer there would be a problem. But Bosch figured that would not happen. Trevino would know that if he made a move against Bosch then he was making a move against the police chief, and that was career suicide.

The search for Vibiana Abas was short. There was no listing of her ever having a driver's license in California, no record of her ever committing a crime or even getting a parking ticket. Of course, the digital databases were less complete the further back the search went, but Bosch knew from experience that it was rare not to find any reference to an entered name. It furthered his speculation that Abas had been an illegal immigrant and possibly returned to Mexico in 1950 after becoming pregnant. Abortion was illegal in California back then. She may have crossed the border to have her baby or to have the pregnancy aborted in one of the backroom clinics in Tijuana.

Bosch knew the law on abortion back then because he had been born in 1950 to an unmarried woman. Soon after becoming a cop he had looked up the laws and the options so that he would better understand the choices his mother faced and had made.

What he was not familiar with was the California penal code in 1950. He accessed it next and looked up the codes for sexual assault. He pretty quickly learned that in 1950 under penal code section 261, sexual intercourse with a female under age eighteen was considered a chargeable offense of rape. Consensual relations were not listed as an exclusion to prosecution. The only exclusion offered in the code was if the female was the wife of the offender.

Bosch thought about what Vance had told him about his father believing the pregnancy was a trap set by Abas to force a marriage that would bring her citizenship and money. If that were the case the penal code gave her a solid piece of leverage. But the lack of any record of Abas in California seemed to belie that angle. Rather than use her leverage, Abas had disappeared, possibly back to Mexico.

Immediately Bosch felt like calling Vance on the number he had given, but decided against it. There would probably be more questions, and he would wait until he had an accumulation. He switched the screen and went back to the DMV interface and typed in "James Louis Aldridge," the cover name Vance had given him. Before the results came up he saw Lt. Trevino enter the squad carrying a cup of coffee from Starbucks. Bosch knew there was a franchise located a few blocks away on Truman.

"Harry, I wasn't expecting you in today," he said.

Trevino always greeted him cordially and by his first name.

"I was in the neighborhood," Bosch said. "Thought I'd check email and send out few more alerts on Screen Cutter."

As he spoke he killed the DMV screen and pulled up the email account he had been given by the department. He didn't turn around as Trevino went to the door behind him and unlocked it.

Bosch heard the door open but then felt Trevino's presence behind him in the cubicle.

"In the neighborhood?" Trevino said. "All the way up here?"

"Well, actually, I was in Pasadena seeing somebody and then I just took the Foothill across," Bosch said. "Thought I'd just send out a few emails, then get out of here."

"Your name's not on the board, Harry. You have to sign in to get credit for your hours."

"Sorry, I was only going to be here a few minutes. And I don't have to worry about making my hours. I put in twenty-four last week alone."

There was a duty board by the entrance to the detective bureau in which Bosch had been instructed to sign in and out so Trevino could chart his hours and make sure he hit the reserve officer minimum.

"I still want you signing in and out," Trevino said.

"You got it, LT," Bosch said.

Trevino stepped into his office and Bosch heard the door close. He turned and checked to make sure, then turned back to his terminal and went back to work. He reopened the DMV portal to run Aldridge's name. He soon pulled up a history that showed Aldridge had a California driver's license from 1948 until 2002, at which point it was surrendered when the license holder moved to Florida. He wrote down Aldridge's date of birth and then entered it with his name on a check of the Florida DMV database. This determined that Aldridge had surrendered his license at age eighty in Florida. The last address listed was in a place called the Villages.

After writing down the information, Bosch checked for a website and found that the Villages was a massive retirement community in Sumter County, Florida. Further searching of online records found an address for Aldridge and no indication of a death record or obituary. He had likely surrendered his driver's license because he no longer could or needed to drive, but it appeared that George Louis Aldridge was still alive.

Content that he had sufficiently chased down the name as needed for a possible cover story, Bosch decided to check through the email that had accumulated on the Screen Cutter case. It was the investigation that had consumed most of his time since he had joined the ranks of the San Fernando Police Department.

FIVE

"Screen Cutter" was the case name for a serial rapist Bosch had identified among the department's open sexual assault reports. Combing through the files in the old city jail Bosch had found four cases since 2012 that were seemingly related by MO—modus operandi—but previously not seen as connected. The cases shared four suspect behaviors that alone were not unusual but when taken as a whole indicated the strong possibility of one perpetrator at work. In each case the rapist had entered the victim's home through a rear door or window after cutting the screen rather than removing it. All four assaults occurred during the day and within fifty minutes before or after noon. The rapist used the knife to cut the victim's clothes off rather than ordering her to remove them. And finally the rapist used no condom or other method to avoid leaving his DNA behind.

With these commonalities in hand, Bosch had focused an investigation on the four cases and soon learned that while the suspect's semen had been collected in rape kits in three of the four cases, only in one instance had the material actually been analyzed in the L.A. County Sheriff's crime lab and submitted for comparison to state and national DNA databases, where it found no match. Analysis in the two most recent cases had been delayed because of the massive backlog of rape kits submitted to the county lab for examination. In the fourth case, which was actually the first reported rape, DNA was not collected because the victim had showered and douched before calling police to report the assault.

The county lab and the LAPD lab shared the same building at Cal State LA, and Bosch used his connections from his cold case days to put an urgent push on analysis of the two recent cases. While he awaited results he thought would solidly connect the cases he began follow up interviews of the victims. On two of the cases he had to turn over the questioning to Anabella Lourdes, the department's CAPs detective, because the victims preferred to do the interviews in Spanish. It underlined the one drawback for Bosch in working cases in a city where nine out of every ten citizens were Latino and had varying capabilities when it came to English. He spoke Spanish passably, but for an interview with a crime victim where subtle nuances of storytelling might be important, he needed Lourdes, who understood it as a first language.

What emerged from the four victims—three women in their twenties and a now eighteen-year-old—was a story that was equal parts sad and terrifying. These were undoubtedly stranger rapes, and the attacks had left each woman recovering both mentally and physically even as long as four years after the crime. All of them lived in fear of their attacker returning; none had recovered the confidence they once had. One of them had been married and at the time was trying to conceive a child with her husband. The attack changed things in the marriage, and at the time of the follow-up interview the couple was in the midst of divorce proceedings.

After each interview Bosch felt depressed and couldn't help but think about his own daughter and what sort of impact such an assault would have on her. Each time he called her within the hour to check that she was safe and okay, unable to tell her the true reason he was calling.

But the follow-up interviews did more than reopen wounds for the victims. They help focus the investigation and underline the urgent need to identify and arrest the Screen Cutter.

Lt. Trevino had granted Bosch's request to call in a sketch artist from the Sheriff's Department. The drawings that were produced in separate sessions with the victims were remarkably similar and furthered Bosch's suspicion that one man was responsible for all four attacks. It was while interviewing the first victim, who had showered and cleaned herself directly after the attack, that a detail emerged that would later put the investigation on a level of psychological horror Bosch had never encountered before.

The woman explained that she had taken a shower and cleaned herself immediately after the attack out of fear that she would become pregnant. She and her husband at the time were trying to conceive a child. She had an app on her phone that tracked her menstrual cycle and told her the day of the month she was most likely to conceive. She had checked the app the morning of the attack and knew it was her most fertile day. Knowing this left her unwilling to allow the semen of the man who attacked her to be inside her body while she waited for the police to respond and then went to the hospital for medical care and evidence collection.

When Bosch and Lourdes conducted an interview of the second victim, the woman added details that were not in the original case summaries. She said that she was surprised by the attacker, who was waiting inside her apartment when she came home from work for lunch. She then revealed that in the course of the assault she attempted to dissuade the suspect from raping her by lying and saying she was having her menstrual period.

The woman told Bosch and Lourdes that the man replied, "No, you're not."

When pressed as to whether the attacker could have actually known that she was not menstruating, the victim said she kept a calendar in her bedside table where she kept track of her cycle because she and her boyfriend did not use birth control and employed the rhythm method to keep an active sex life while attempting to avoid pregnancy. The attacker could have found the calendar while waiting for her to arrive home. She provided the calendar to the investigators and they noted that on the day of her assault, she was in the most fertile part of her cycle.

Two interviews, two women who tracked their menstrual

cycles, two assaults on the most fertile day of each woman's cycle. It was a coincidence too eerie to be dismissed. Bosch told Lourdes he didn't believe in coincidences.

The final two victims preferred to speak in Spanish, and their interviews were handled by Lourdes. Both victims revealed under questioning that they also kept track of their menstrual cycles. One victim charted her cycle on a laptop calendar because her doctor had told her that her frequent migraine headaches might be tied to the fluctuations of hormones that occurred during her menstrual period. She tracked her cycle to know when to take a prescribed migraine inhibitor.

The last interview was with the eighteen-year-old, who had been sixteen when attacked on a summer day when she was home alone while her parents were at work. The girl reported that at fourteen she had been diagnosed with juvenile diabetes and her menstrual cycle affected her insulin needs. She tracked the cycle on a calendar on the door of the refrigerator so she and her mother could prepare the proper insulin therapy.

Further questioning revealed that the two victims, like the two before them, were attacked during a day in their menstrual cycle when they were most fertile and likely to conceive.

Bosch and Lourdes drew a number of conclusions from the interviews. The rapist had obviously carefully chosen the day of each attack. While charting of each victim's cycle could be found inside her home, the attacker had to have had this information beforehand. This meant he had stalked his victims and likely had been in their homes previously in an effort to determine the day he would come back for the assault. His cutting of the screens on the day of the attack but not during the early reconnaissance was subterfuge—designed to hide the planning of each assault.

The connection between the cases was stunning and soon confirmed when the DNA results came back linking the three cases in which semen had been collected. There was now no doubt that a serial rapist had struck at least four times in four years in tiny San Fernando.

Bosch had no doubt that there were more victims. In San Fernando alone there was an estimated population of five thousand illegal immigrants, many of whom would not call the police if victimized by crime. It was also ridiculous to consider that such a predator would operate only within the bounds of the tiny city. The four known victims were Latinas and shared common physical appearances: long brown hair, dark eyes, and a small build—none of them weighed more than 110 pounds. The two contiguous LAPD geographic divisions had majority Latino populations, and there was no doubt in Bosch's mind that there were more victims to be found there.

Since discovering the connection between the cases he had been spending almost all of his time on the SFPD job making contact with investigators from LAPD's burglary and sexual assault squads throughout the Valley as well as the nearby departments in Burbank, Glendale, and Pasadena. He was interested in any open cases involving screen cutting. So far nothing had come back, but he knew it was a matter of getting detectives interested and looking, maybe getting the message to the right detective who would remember something.

Bosch had also contacted an old friend who had been a senior profiler with the FBI's Behavioral Analysis Unit. Bosch had worked with Jennifer McKay on several different occasions while he was with the LAPD and she was with the bureau. She was now retired from the FBI and working as a professor of forensic psychology at the John Jay College of Criminal Justice in New York. She also kept her hand in profiling as a private consultant. She agreed to look at Bosch's case pro bono, and he sent her a package on the Screen Cutter. He was keenly interested in knowing the motivation and psychology behind the attacks. Why was the Screen Cutter's stalking pattern geared toward determining fertility dates? Was he trying to impregnate his victims? Was that part of the control and terror he drew fulfillment from?

McKay took two weeks to get back to Bosch and her assessment was surprising to him. She concluded that the perpetrator was not choosing the attack dates because he wished to impregnate his victims. Quite the opposite. The details of the stalking and subsequent attacks revealed a subject with a deep-seated hatred of women and disgust toward the bodily ritual of bleeding. The day of the attack is chosen because the victim is considered by him to be at the most clean part of her cycle. It is the psychologically safest moment for him to attack.

McKay's profile ended with an ominous warning: "If you discount the idea that the perpetrator's motive is to give life (impregnate) and realize that the attack is urged by hate, then it is clear this subject has not concluded his evolution as predator. It is only a matter of time before these rapes become kills."

The warning resulted in Bosch and Lourdes upping their game and sending out another set of emails to local law enforcement agencies with McKay's assessment and the composite drawing attached. This was followed up with phone calls from Bosch and Lourdes in an effort to break through the typical law enforcement inertia that descends on investigators who have too many cases and too little time.

The response was close to nothing. One burglary detective from LAPD's North Hollywood Division reported that he had an open burglary case involving a screen cutting but there was no rape involved. The detective said the victim was a male Hispanic, twenty-six years old. Bosch urged the investigator to go back to the case and the victim to see if he had a wife or girlfriend who may have been attacked but afraid or embarrassed to report the assault. A week later the LAPD detective reported back and said there was no female in the apartment. The case was unconnected.

Bosch was now playing a waiting game. The rapist's DNA was not in the databanks. He had never been swabbed. He had left no fingerprints or other evidence behind other than his semen. Bosch found no other connecting cases in San Fernando or elsewhere. The debate over whether to go public with the case and ask for the help of citizens was simmering on the back burner in the office of Chief Valdez. It was an age-old law enforcement question: Go public and possibly draw a lead that leads to an arrest? Or go public and possibly alert the predator, who then changes up his patterns or moves on and visits his terror on an unsuspecting community somewhere else?

There was no right answer and the chief appeared to be waiting, hoping that Bosch would come through and break the case before another victim was attacked. Bosch was happy not to have the decision on his shoulders. This was why the chief made the big bucks and Bosch made none.

Bosch checked his email now and saw he had no new messages in his queue with "Screen Cutter" in the subject line. Disappointed, he shut down the computer. He put his notebook back in his pocket and wondered if Trevino had looked down on it while hovering in the cubicle. It had been opened to the page with James Louis Aldridge's name written on it.

He left the squad room without bothering to say goodbye to Trevino or write his time down on the board at the front door.

SIX

After leaving the station Bosch got on the 5 freeway and back onto the Whitney Vance case. Not coming up with any birth date or other information on Vibiana Abas on the DMV base was disappointing but no more than a temporary setback. Bosch was headed south to Norwalk, where the time travel goldmine was housed: the Los Angeles County Department of Public Health, where he used to spend so much time as a cold case investigator in the Vital Records office that he knew exactly how the clerks liked their coffee. He felt confident he would be able to answer some questions about Vibiana Abas there.

Bosch put a CD in the Jeep's music slot and started listening to a young horn player named Christian Scott. The first track up, "Litany Against Fear," had a relentless sound and drive to it and that's what Bosch felt he needed at the moment. It took him an hour to get down to Norwalk after a slow crawl around the east edge of downtown. He pulled into the lot fronting the seven-story county building and killed the engine while Scott was in the middle of "Naima," which Bosch thought compared favorably with John Handy's classic version record fifty years earlier.

Just as he stepped out of the car his cell phone buzzed and he checked the screen. It said UNKNOWN CALLER but he took it anyway. It was John Creighton and the call was not a surprise.

"So, you saw Mr. Vance?" he asked.

"I did," Bosch answered.

"Well, how did it go?"

"It went fine. He's a nice man."

Bosch was going to make Creighton dig for it. It might be considered passive-aggressive behavior on his part, but he was keeping the wishes of his client in mind.

"Is there anything we can help with?"

"Uh, no, I think I can handle it. Mr. Vance wants it kept confidential so I'll just leave it at that."

There was a long silence before Creighton spoke next.

"Harry," he said, "you and I go way back to the department, and of course Mr. Vance and I go way back as well. As I said yesterday before hiring you, he's an important client of this firm, and if there is anything I need to know regarding his comfort and security, then I need to know it. I was hoping as former brothers in blue you might share with me what is going on. Mr. Vance is an old man, I don't want him taken advantage of."

"By 'taken advantage of,' are you talking about me?" Bosch asked.

"Of course not, Harry. Poor choice of words. What I mean is if the old man is being extorted or otherwise facing any sort of trouble involving the need for a private detective, well we are here and we have enormous resources at our fingertips. We need to be brought in."

Bosch nodded. He expected this sort of play from Creighton, once Vance had warned him.

"Well," he said. "All I can tell you is that first of all, you didn't hire me. You delivered money to me. Mr. Vance hired me and that's who I work for. Mr. Vance was very specific. He told me not to share what I am doing or why I am doing it with anybody. That would include you. If you want me to break from that, I need to call him back and ask for his per—"

"That won't be necessary," Creighton said quickly. "If that is how Mr. Vance wants it, that is fine. Just know, we are here to help if needed."

"Absolutely," Bosch said in an upbeat but phony voice. "I'll call you if needed, John, and thanks for checking in."

He disconnected the call and headed through the parking lot toward the seven-story building that contained the records of all official births and deaths in L.A. County. All records of marriage and divorce were recorded here as well. The building in front of him was massive and rectangular in dimensions. It always reminded Bosch of a giant treasure chest. The information was in there if you knew where to look—or knew somebody who did. For those who didn't, the front steps of the building were where hawkers stood by ready to counsel the uninitiated on how to fill out request forms—all for the price of a few dollars.

Bosch jogged up the steps, ignoring those who came at him asking if he was applying for a fictitious business name or a marriage licenses. He entered and walked past the information booth and then toward the stairs. He knew from experience that waiting for an elevator in the building could suck the will to live out of a person. He took the stairs down to the basement level, where the BDM section of the Register-Recorder's office was located. As he pushed through the glass door there was a shriek from one of the desks lined along the wall on the other side of the public counter. A woman stood up and smiled broadly at Bosch. She was Asian and her name was Flora. She had always been most helpful to Bosch when he had carried a badge.

"Harry Bosch!" she called out.

"Flora!" he called right back.

Along the counter there was a window for law enforcement requests, which were always given priority, and two windows for citizen requests. There was a man standing at one of the citizen windows. Bosch stepped up to the other. Flora was already heading to the law enforcement window.

"No, you come down here," she instructed.

Bosch did as instructed and then leaned over the counter for an awkward embrace.

"I knew you'd come back to us here," Flora said.

"Sooner or later, right?" he said. "But, hey, I'm here as a citizen right now. I don't want to get you in any trouble."

Bosch knew he could pull the San Fernando badge, but he didn't want a move like that to possibly track back to Valdez or Trevino. That would cause trouble he didn't need. Instead, he made a move to go back to the citizen's window, choosing to keep his private and public detective work separate.

"It no trouble," Flora said. "Not for you."

He ended the charade and remained at the LE window.

"Well, this one might take a while," he said. "I don't have all the information and I need to go way, way back."

"Let me try it. What you want?"

Bosch always had to guard against chopping his language the way she did. But his natural inclination was to start leaving out words when he spoke to her. He had caught himself doing it in the past and he tried to avoid it now.

He pulled out his notebook and looked at some of the dates he had written down that morning in Vance's office.

"Looking for a birth record," he said while reading. "Talking about nineteen thirty-three or thirty-four. What do you have going that far back?"

"Not on database," Flora said. "We have fish here only. No hard record any more. Let me see name."

He knew she was talking about records transferred to microfiche in the seventies and never updated to the computerized database. He turned his notebook around so she could see the name and spelling of Vibiana Abas. Bosch hoped that he would catch a break with the unusualness of it. At least it wasn't a common Latino surname like Garcia or Fernandez. There probably weren't too many Vibiana's around either.

"She old," Flora said. "You want death too?"

"I do. But I have no idea when and if she died. Last time I have her alive for sure is May nineteen fifty."

She made a frowning face.

"Ooh, I see, Harry. But we miss you here."

"Thanks, Flora. Where is Paula? She still here?"

Paula was the other clerk he remembered from his frequent forays to the basement while a detective. Locating witnesses and families of victims was a key part of cold case investigation, usually the foundation of any case. The first thing you did was alert the family that the case is back under active investigation. But murder books from old cases rarely contained updates on deaths and marriages and the migration of people. Consequently, Bosch did some of his best detective work in the halls of records and libraries.

"Paula out today," Flora said. "Just me. I write down now and you get coffee. This take time."

Flora wrote down what she needed.

"Do you want a coffee, Flora?" Bosch asked.

"No, you get," she said. "For waiting."

"Then I think I'll just stick around. I filled up this morning and I have stuff to do."

He pulled his phone out and held it up by way of explanation. Flora went back into microfiche archives to hunt. Bosch sat down on one of the plastic seats in an unused microfiche cubicle.

He was thinking about next moves. Depending on what he came up with here, his next move was to St. Vibiana's to see if he could get a look at baptismal records or the main library downtown, where they kept reverse phone directories going back decades.

Bosch pulled up his phone's search app and typed in "USC EVK" to see what might come up. It got a hit right away. The EVK was still operating on the campus and was located in the Harris Residential Hall on Thirty-fifth Street. He pulled the address up on his maps app and was soon looking at an overview of the sprawling campus just south of downtown. Vance had said Vibiana had lived only a few blocks from the EVK and walked to work. The campus ran along Figueroa Street and the Harbor Freeway corridor. This limited the number of residential streets in the area with direct access to the EVK. Bosch started writing them down along with address spans so that he could look up the names of residents in the reverse directories at the library.

It soon occurred to him that he was looking at a 2016 map of the campus and its surroundings. He realized that the Harbor Freeway may not have even existed in 1950 and that would give the neighborhood around USC and completely different makeup. He went back to the search app and pulled up the history of the freeway also known as the 1-10. He soon learned that the freeway, which slashed a eight-lane diagonal across the county from Pasadena down to the harbor, was built in sections in the 1940s and 50s. It was the dawn of the freeway era in L.A., and the 1-10 was the very first project. The section that edged the east side of the USC campus was begun in 1952 and completed two years later, both dates well after the time Whitney Vance attended the school and met Vibiana Abas.

Bosch went back to his mapping and started including streets that in 1949 and 1950 still provided walking access to the northeast corner of campus, where Harris Hall and the EVK were located. Soon he had a list of fourteen streets with three- or four-block stretches he would search in the reverse directories. He would go down the address listings in search of the name Abas.

He was leaning over his phone's small screen, checking the map for side streets he might have missed, when Flora came back from the bowels of the record center. She was carrying one spool for the microfiche machine triumphantly up in her hand and that immediately put a charge in Bosch's bloodstream. Flora had found Vibiana.

"She not born here," Flora said. "Mexico."

This confused Bosch. He stood up and headed to the counter.

"How do you know that?" he asked.

"It say on her death certificate," Flora said. "Loreto."

Flora had pronounced the name wrong but Bosch understood it. He had once traced a murder suspect to Loreto, far down the inner coast of the Baja peninsula. He guessed if he went there now he would find a St. Vibiana's cathedral or church.

"You already found her death certificate?" he asked.

"Not taking long," Flora said. "Only look to nineteen and fifty-one."

Her words sucked the air out of Bosch. Vibiana was not only dead, but dead so long. He had heard her name for the first time less than six hours ago but somehow Bosch had felt a connection to the girl who walked to work at the cafeteria and had wanted to keep her baby. He held his hand out for the microfiche reel. As Flora handed it to him she told him the record number he should look for—51-659. Bosch recognized it as a low number, even for 1951. The 659th death recorded in L.A. County that year. How far into the year could that be? A month? Two?

A fleeting thought came to him. He looked at Flora. Had she read the cause of death when she had found the document?

"She died in childbirth?" he asked.

Flora looked puzzled.

"Uh, no," she said. "But you read. Make sure."

Bosch took the spool and turned back to the machine. He quickly threaded the film through and turned on the projection light. There was an automatic feed controlled with a button. He sped through the documents, stopping every few seconds to check the record number stamped at the top corner. He was all the way into March before he got to 659th death. By then he realized it had not been a death in childbirth. The math didn't work. If she told Vance she was pregnant in May she had probably conceived in April. The following March was too long—eleven months at least—if she even carried the baby to birth.

When he found the document he found that the State of California certificate of death had not changed much over the decades. It might have been the oldest such document he had ever looked at, but he was intimately familiar with it. His eyes dropped down to the section the coroner or attending physician filled in. The cause of death was handwritten: strangulation by ligature (clothesline) due to suicide.

Bosch stared for a long time at the line without moving or breathing. Vibiana had killed herself. No details beyond what he had already read were written. There was just a signature too scribbled to decipher, followed by the printed words Deputy Coroner.

Bosch leaned back and took in air. He felt immense sadness come over him. He didn't know all the details. He had heard only Vance's view of the story—an eighteen-year-old's story filtered through the frail and guilty memory of an eighty-four-year-old. But he knew enough to know that what happened to Vibiana wasn't right. Vance had left her on the wrong side of goodbye, and what happened in May brought about what happened in March. Bosch had a gut feeling that Vibiana's life was taken from her long before she put the rope around her neck.

The death certificate offered details that Bosch wrote down, beginning with Vibiana's birthdate. She had turned seventeen two days before taking her life on March 5, 1951. Her next of kin was listed as her father, Victor Abas. His address was on Hope Street, which had been one of the streets Bosch had written down after studying the map of the USC neighborhood. The street name seemed like a sad irony now.

The lone curiosity on the document was the location of death. There was only an address on North Occidental Boulevard. Bosch knew that Occidental was west of downtown near Echo Park and not close at all to Vibiana's home neighborhood. He opened his phone and typed the address into the search app. It came back as the address of St. Helen's Home for Unwed Mothers. The search provided several websites associated with St. Helen's and a link to a 2008 story in the *Los Angeles Times* marking the one-hundredth anniversary of the facility.

Bosch quickly pulled the link up and started reading the story.

Maternity Home Marks 100th Birthday

By Keisha Russell, Staff Writer

St. Helen's Home for Unwed Mothers is marking its 100th birthday this week with a celebration that honors its evolution from a place of family secrets to a center for family life.

The three-acre complex near Echo Park will be the site of a full week of programs including a family picnic and featuring an address from a woman who more than 50 years ago was forced by family to give up her newborn for adoption at the center.

Just as social mores have changed in the last few decades, so has St. Helen's. Getting prematurely pregnant once resulted in the mother being hidden away, delivering a child in secret and then having that child immediately taken away for adoption...

Bosch stopped reading as he came to understand what had happened sixty-five years ago to Vibiana Abas.

"She had the baby," he whispered. "And they took it away from her."

WATCH IT. READ IT.

The second season of *BOSCH* based on
these bestselling novels by Michael Connelly

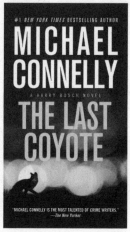